Stanislav   Dymov

Odessa's Gimmickry

Collection of stories

"Odessa's gimmickry - are the ones, which are peculiar for Odessa and which at absolutely different times caused absolutely the same reaction of administration".

(From the vocabulary of Odessa Language)

Order this book online at www.trafford.com
or email orders@trafford.com

Most Trafford titles are also available at major online book retailers.

Note for Librarians: A cataloguing record for this book is available from Library
and Archives Canada at www.collectionscanada.ca/amicus/index-e.html

Printed in Victoria, BC, Canada.

ISBN: 978-1-4269-0485-1 (Soft)

*Our mission is to efficiently provide the world's finest, most comprehensive
book publishing service, enabling every author to experience success.
To find out how to publish your book, your way, and have it available
worldwide, visit us online at www.trafford.com*

Trafford rev. 8/31/2009

 www.trafford.com

North America & international
toll-free: 1 888 232 4444 (USA & Canada)
phone: 250 383 6864 ♦ fax: 812 355 4082

Satirical stories in which with sharp humour inherent in Odessa some fragments from a life of modern Southern Palmira are described are included in the collection.Now collections of stories the " Odessa's Gimmickry-2" and "Odessa's Gimmickry-3" prepare for publish.

Contents

Introduction

Within the territory of post soviet space there is a city, known to everybody, from baby to adult. Far back in the past its fame exceeded all boundaries – both real and virtual. This is Odessa city, located on the shore of the Black Sea. Odessa is known throughout the world not only as a city with a developed infrastructure, as a city, provided familiar scientists, writers, composers and pianists, as a city, glorious by its architecture in combination with a pleasant, gentle sea air and blossoming chestnuts. Odessa is famous in the entire world as a city of intellectuals, adventurous people, workaholics, and the most important is the fact that Odessa has been always famous for cheerful, always vivid citizens with an inimitable Odessa colouring and light vein of humour. It does not have the notion of nationality, though here live Russians, Ukrainians, Jews, Bulgarians, Armenians, Greeks, Moldavians and other. Here the only national notion exists - an inhabitant of Odessa.

Hospitality and a good-natured character have always been national characteristic features of Odessa inhabitants, which allowed them "sharpening" tongues in respect of each other and outsiders, visiting the city, as well.

But evil be to him that decided to oppose this character, saying nothing of those who unceremoniously got in the city without invitation. It is almost impossible to make an Odessa inhabitant to fulfill something against his will, since a spirit of contradiction has been born before him.

For Odessa inhabitants Odessa is much greater than the motherland with all its gimmicks. Moreover, over its history, Odessa has been located one hundred twenty one years within the territory of Russia, seventy four years within the territory of Soviet Union, and already seventeen years within the territory of "independent" Ukraine. And only God knows to what shore it will be washed by the next history zigzag.

No city can boast of so many shaped songs, devoted to it, as Odessa can. And what songs!! Unfortunately, it is a shame but last years a number of Odessa songs, composed in the native city, were decreased to the utmost. As it is nowadays put in Odessa, "Odessa songs get the native town as a humanitarian aid from the USA, Germany, Israel and other countries", not included into "ESSEN GE"(CIS), sold to Odessa people by commercial organizations, working under protection of Odessa Mayor's office. Abbreviation "CHГ" (CIS) is considered to be indecent as translation into the Odessa language, since in German and Yiddish "essen" means to eat and what "ge" means - is not difficult to guess for people, who are at least a bit familiar with the Russian language.

It has always been considered that an Odessa inhabitant it is not belonging to the city, it is not even a profession, this is a diagnosis. Here people have never been classified according to nationality, education or material position. Classification was simple: you are either an Odessa inhabitant, or not.

But in the past decades a genotype of an Odessa inhabitant has changed. In good old times in Odessa there were significantly more intellectual, thinking people, valuing humor and satire. It was not possible to meet a citizen of Odessa, who did not know history of the native city, every street, every yard, who did not know its native Odessa language. And what is now?

For the most part genuine Odessa inhabitants left for remote countries, and those who remained in their native city, were lost in the crowd of newcomers. They live under the conditions of occupation. Odessa was occupied by third-raters, scandalous people and other.

Lack of culture, ignorance and manginess as an incurable disease stroke Odessa. But who is at fault? First of all people, their inner manginess progresses by reason of material bankruptcy of majority, everlasting survival, uncertainty in future. Slackitude, jealousy, malice and fear predominate in relations between people. It is also a fault of government, which officials use their position only for personal advantage without taking into consideration the city and its citizens.

Events and characters in stories are mainly fictive, but every coincidence is not accidental, since it happens in our nowadays life at every step. We have a lot of negative and unparticular to Odessa and Odessa inhabitants; part of every person, living today in our city has a significant meaning, but of course contribution of the Mayor and other officials can not be compared with contribution of an ordinary Odessa inhabitant. But when only a governor or mayor, prosecutor or head of police, taxation authority or deputy is accused of all sins - it is pure slyness. No one knows what could be if every of us took these positions. Perhaps, it would be worse?

If, having read these stories, reader will think over the sense of his life, will ponder – it is already much. Indeed, only a person, escaped from a nut hospital, can count on the fact that government will stop lying us – people, and we people will stop lying government.

It was written in the most democratic and easy for study Odessa language. It is written as spoken and spoken as desired - and what is the most important - as thought. I tried to observe the only rule of the Odessa language - an absolute absence of rules.

Encounters

It was the beginning of February at the calendar, but the nature was already breathing with spring. The sky was clear and blue. The sun was bright, and its rays were not just shining, they were also warming mildly. The air was clean and fresh. Buds in the trees seemed to be ripening in a short while, and at one beautiful moment they were going to burst open with green young leaves. Young green grass was also about coming off the ground.

This spring spirits of the nature all in itself passed over to people, who were in that fairy spring-like morning in good mood, in spite of all the loathsome life they were waging.

Nikolai Ivanovich, a pediatrician, was also in good moods. He was after his night shift in the regional hospital for sick children, he was tired after a busy night on duty, but still he decided to go to the manufactured goods market "Seventh kilometer", which was actually a flea market. He wanted to find some presents for his wife and daughter for the Women's Day – 8ᵗʰ of March.

On that Saturday morning "Seventh kilometer" was not as busy as usually, and Nikolai Ivanovich was walking leisurely along the rows of the market, switched from one container to another, examining attentively the goods displayed for sale.

There were very many goods of different kind, including lingerie and appliances, but it was mostly Turkish and Chinese stuff, similar in all the rows, and the quality was far from being satisfactory.

"At the stores the stuff is the same, quite the same. It was either the same contractors, or the goods were taken to the stores from the market

– at wholesale prices. But the prices at the stores are incompatible to those at the flea market" – Nikolai Ivanovich thought.

At one of the rows a salesperson from a container called him: "How are you, Nikolai Ivanovich."

Nikolai Ivanovich recognized the salesperson – it was one of his former fellow-students in the Medical University, Dima Morozov. After graduating from the University he had lived from hand to mouth working as a district pediatrician. He had a great family to support and he had been waiting for his scanty salary to be paid for months. So, he abandoned his job and went to work as a salesperson at the flea market.

"Hi, Dima, I am glad to see you" – Nikolai Ivanovich smiled greeting Morozov and strongly squeezed his hand. – "I am after my night shift. I just decided to come to your market to find some presents for my women for 8th of March. How are you? Missing our job? You used to be a really good specialist".

Dmitry frowned: "That is the point – I used to. Every day here starting with the early morning I am not mastering my knowledge and qualification. On the contrary, here I am gradually losing all my skills. But if you look at the financial side, it's different. My income can't be compared to yours. Though you can't imagine how hard I work here, how much humiliation I suffer, how many spongers I have to feed.

I have to give bribes to the police, to the sanitary inspectors, to the tax administration and to many others. I can't even mention all of them, but anyway, in our loathsome conditions it is income, hard as it is, but income. My family has food, clothes, and shoes to wear. I can afford buying tickets for a concert of a celebrity. And I am sure you can't afford that for yourself and your wife."

Nikolai Ivanovich shrugged his shoulders: "You, Dima, is a good boy, no doubt. Not anyone can manage that. Yes, you are just a good boy, and you look good too."

Nikolai Ivanovich did realize that Dima was constantly aware that he was not demanded as a doctor, that sales were not his vocation, that he was suffering and that made him so nervy and biting. And Dima was not the only one who had to earn his living at the market; it was full of former teachers, University educators, musicians, and scientists. Intellectuals who seldom heard a rude word, at the market had to be constantly in the atmosphere of coarse language, fear and humiliation.

"Listen, Nikolai, come over in an hour, we'll go to a cafe, stay there for half an hour, talk. My fellow worker will be here and I will have a chance to have a break." – Dima suggested. – "And I heard a rumor that tax administration guys are here again, they are so greedy. We will close our container for a while, lest we had problems."

"What kind of problems can you have? The goods should be certified, it has to have passed the customs. Do you have the necessary documentation?"

Dima grinned: "Look here, Nikolai, they are always up to something. It is either a signature missing, or they just seize the goods. After that we have to go to their office, beg and pay for our own stuff to be released." A month ago they demanded that salespersons, selling outer clothing, should have sanitary test books. It's just ridiculous! But they locked and sealed containers."

Nikolai Ivanovich was really surprised, though he himself heard more than once all kinds of incredible stories told by the parents of his patients. All the stories described the illegal actions of tax administration, interior departments and municipal officers. He promised to Dima that he should return in about forty minutes and went on around the market examining the goods and thinking of life issues. "Seventh kilometer" was a flea market that had existed for about fifteen years already. It was a great and complex structure, which included dozens of thousands of people working there, tons of goods of all different kinds, which was brought to the market, sorted, stored, sold both retail and wholesale. There one could meet buyers from all the Ukraine, Moldova, Russia and Belarus. Great amounts of money were involved there, the amounts were just crazy and to a great extend of criminal origin. Nikolai Ivanovich felt that, but he never realized how great that structure was. As a rule, such places were full of people who were ready to get something of somebody else's expense. "Seventh kilometer " was not an exception.

Near one of the containers Nikolai Ivanovich encountered face to face with another former fellow student of his, Valera Protsenko.

"It is just the day of meetings. All former fellow students meet at special parties, and we just organized one at the flea market this morning." – Nikolai Ivanovich laughed, shaking Valera's hand.

"I have just met Morozov, and now I am meeting you. Valera, let's in half an hour pick up Dima and go to a cafe. We'll have a glass of cognac or coffee, stay together for a while and talk".

"No, Kolia" – Protsenko replied sharply and moved backwards from him. – "I am at work. Maybe some other time."

It was only now that Nikolai Ivanovich had a close look at Valera.

"What, evaluating my looks?" – Protsenko smiled. – "See, cleaning up containers. I am currently working at the department of sales of seized goods. In our department I am responsible for selling seized technical equipment of farmers, different companies, who owe payments for loans to banks, as well as to tax administration and to others. I drive to different districts of the region during the weekdays, and on Saturday I assist the tax administration to seize goods at the flea market.

"Look here, Valera, this is no good." - Nikolai Ivanovich tried to object timidly. – "People are scared as they are, they are in poverty, and you still restrain them."

"We don't restrain those who are our friends." – Valera answered in a self-contented manner with a happy smile. – "We don't to against those who pay to us regularly, who gives us hints about the candidates to be restrained. We even warn them, we also give them some stuff for selling. But those who don't want to be our friends are quickly taken measures against."

Nikolai Ivanovich saw how seized men's shirts, jeans, fitness suits were packed into plastic bags from one of the containers. Two young tall men were calculating the items with the business-like looks, packed them into plastic bags, and two other loaders loaded filled bags to the carriage, which was beside them. Besides there stood a short man who made noted about the seized goods into his notebook.

"Have you taken enough plastic bags?" – Valera asked the loaders in a busy and strict manner. – "See to it that if there are no enough plastic bags, you will have to buy some yourselves." But the loaders nodded in order to assure him that there were enough plastic bags.

Nikolai Ivanovich saw a happy person in front of him, whose cherished dream had at last become real. He watched a person, who had already got all he wanted from life, who was satisfied with his fate and with himself. But watching this happy Protsenko Nikolai Ivanovich felt sad. He felt a hard feeling come over his heart. He looked at his watch, excused himself, turned away and was quickly gone. He felt disgust after the meeting with Valera. He imagined Protsenko's self-contented face with his always pink, like a young pig's, cheek. He was wearing clothes brought to the market from Turkey, sure it was some of the seized items. Beside him he imagined scared salespersons, whose goods were seized for the only reason, which was that the lease agreement for the container was at the owner of the goods possession. He imagined the faces of the people who had submitted to the unlawful actions that were taking place; the faces of people who expressed non-resistance to the evil.

Nikolai Ivanovich remembered that Valera Protsenko was the same kind of person at the University as well. And after graduating from the University he worked as a pediatrician in a district hospital for only half a year, after that he applied for the Ministry of Internal Affairs. And in a short while he was already hires as a sanitary doctor in one of the prisons in the city. There he was employed until he had the rank of a Captain, then he was laid off due to his own will. Evil tongues gossiped that Protsenko had only one choice – either to quit on his own will or to have criminal charges. Afterwards he tried a job in a company, which dealt with harvesting in the region and sales of the crops, but that time he again had to quit as he had great debts in the company. Everywhere he bluffed; he pretended to be a great friend of the police administration in one place, as a great criminal boss in other places. Nikolai Ivanovich had all this information from his friends from the Municipal Department of the Interior. In fact, Protsenko was a paid intelligencer, or, to put it simple, a sneak, even since he was a student.

All of a sudden Nikolai Ivanovich remembered a joke about a rural guy who was seeking a job in the city. Somebody asks him:

"Where are you going to have a job?"

"In the police" – he answers.

"But if they don't hire you?"

"Then at the Fire Station"

"But if they don't hire you either?"

"I will go to the tax administration"

"But if you fail there too?"

"I don't know. Anyway, I am not going to work."

This joke was exactly about Protsenko. But Nikolai Ivanovich was upset for some different reason: he thought about the impudence and idleness of the officials of any level of administration, about the ignorance and brutality of the majority of people, who had, as it seemed, good education, about poverty and dirt, both inner and outer, about hard drinking and drug addiction, about degeneracy, hypocrisy and lies...

At the same time from more than a million of inhabitants of this city there is no a single one who would cry out, express his indignation against the lawless actions of the government officials against the majority of the population. And there seemed no end to both: to the lawless actions on the one hand, and to the resignation and the silence on the other hand.

Old Aunty Dusia

During the fifty years that have passed after the war, the City has grown a lot, and even several villages were included into the municipal territory. In one of such villages on a small hill there was a plain-looking, dilapidated during the past years, small house. A lonely old woman lived there. Everyone in the village called her just old aunty Dusia. She was not just one of the oldest residents, she was also considered to be a long-liver, as she was already ninety four years of age. In spite of her venerable age, she was in her right mind, at night she would watch TV and she was aware of all current events both worldwide and in the country. She was still able to have a glass or two of wine every day; there was mush wine in the village. But her legs were a trouble. She couldn't walk and work a lot, as she used to, her legs were swollen, the legs constantly ached. Old aunty Dusia got used to the ache, she treated herself with different herbs. She never consulted a doctor due to several reasons. First of all, she didn'l have much confidence in them. Secondly, she considered the doctors in the village inexperienced and undertrained. Thirdly, old aunty Dusia had practically no money. The scanty pernsion she received was enough for buying bread, salt, sugar and some minor houseware. Old aunty Dusia has stopped growing something on her lot a long time ago, as she didn't have strength for that any more. She had no relatives. Her husband and children died during the war. Her distant relatives have already died too. Some of them, still alive, have completely forgotten old aunty Dusia.

Everyone in the village knew that old aunty Dusia was very difficult to deal with. She was short, her figure was crooked, her face was exhausted, with lots of wrinkles, her body was extremely skinny and her legs were swollen and thick. She went out very seldom, she preferred to stay home or to sit on a bench near the wicket. Boys next door usually did shopping on her request, when she received her pension. She gave some change to them for that – to but some chewing gum.

The war events took place in the village twice. Especially fierce fights on that hill were in August, 1944. It was seamen who fought intrepidly. In 1944 marine forces landed near the village, and again there were severe fighting there. The killed soldiers were buried in a great hurry right in backyards and gardens of the village.

Many decades have passed since then. The village is living a peaceful life and the people recall that severe war only on the nineth of May, on the Victory Day, when all come to the monument to the perished soldiers, situated on a small hill at the curve of the highway. People make speeches there, the music is playing, everyone have some wine for the peace of the soul of each perished soldier. After that everything comes down for one more year, people being absorbed with their routine chores and problems.

Time and nature made it so that the remnants of the perished soldiers, buried in a hurry, came out of the soil and could be seen on the surface. Especially many remnants there were at old aunty Dusia's yard and on the waste lot by her house, at which boys used to play soccer.

That early spring, after great melting of the snow and heavy spring rains, it seemed that all the remnants of the perished soldiers came out to the surface. They seemed to be asking those alive to bury them properly. Old aunty Dusia was indignant with the indifference of the residents and the administration of the village, but no one would listen to her. So, once she gathered all her strength and reached the building of the former collective farm management, later it was the building of the farmers' management, which actually consisted of the same persons. She was not allowed to enter the office of the former chairman of the collective farm, who was also the current manager by the name Dobrokhod, and she waited patiently sitting on the top stair of the entrance staircase.

In a while Dobrokhod showed up at the door.

The robber has grown still fatter! – old aunty Dusia looked at the former chairman with hatred. Dobrokhod, a tall and fat man with a red chubby face and great volume of hair on his head, noticed old aunty Dusia with displeasure. She was sitting on the staircase and he thought she was a troublemaker, she would never stop quarreling and she would not go to meet her Maker.

- She is still alive, the old hag, nothing can screw her up, she is going to be one hundred soon – he thought to himself and pronounced out loud the following:

Why don't you stay quietly at home, old aunty Dusia? It's a sowing season! Don't you understand that? Or maybe you want to work in the field? – he laughed out loud, happy with his own witness.

No, dear chairman, I am not. I have come to settle one thing which does not interfere with your sowing season problems. It is necessary to arrange military men and young people from our village and to bury the remnants of the soldiers perished during the hard times. It won't do if on the wasted lot boys are playing soccer right on human bones.

Dobrokhod interrupted her with vivid irritation,

- Look here, old woman, I am telling you not to lecture me. I am having the sowing season and I am not able to take care of the bones on your backyard.

Old aunty Dusia stood up and seized his jacket tightly,

- I won't let you go anywhere, my dear friend, until you arrange everything for solving this important problem. Otherwise you will get punishment from the God.

Dobrokhod got furious with the old witch who was telling ill prophecy.

He teared himself off her and pushed her down the stairs. She lost her balance and fell head over heals. She was badly hurt, her head ached, so did her legs. Old aunty Dusia sat at the bottom of the staircase, crying with offence. Dobrokhod got into his car and left to see the fields.

Having returned home, old aunty Dusia produces a sheet of paper out of her chest of drawers and wrote letters requesting to re-bury the remnants of the perished soldiers. She mailed the letters to the Governor and to the President. She managed to get the necessary addresses with the help of a neighbour's son who worked in security department of the municipal administration office.

To her great happiness, in two months there came the Head of the Regional Military Committee with a large group of officials. They had a talk with old aunty Dusia and thanked her for her positive social attitude on behalf of the President and the Governor. In a while their was some excavation work on the territory of the previous war military actions, and the perished soldiers were re-buried at the village cemetery in a proper ceremonial manner.

Next autumn the Governor of the region arrived at the village with a great number of assistants. On behalf of the President he presented an order to old aunty Dusia right in her house.

Old aunty Dusia could hardly move, the leg problems were becoming more severe. Following the Governor a lot journalists arrived to interview the restless old woman, awarded an order at the age of ninety four.

Old aunty Dusia spoke her mind out loud once in front of journalists:

- What the hell do I need this order for if I am hungry, staying in the dilapidated cold house, trying to sooth down my reumatism, with no one to care for me.

That was a good question! What did she need that order for? The journalists shrugged their shoulders and left the village. On their way home one of the journalists told a joke which appeared in eighties:

- A Soviet delegation comes to Sweden to take part in political discussions. At night they went to one of the Stockholm movie theatres to see the Russian movie "Shadows disappear at noon", which was in the Russian language with Swedish subtitles. The film was interrupted for commercials from time to time. In the first commercial the US President in Washington, in the White House, receives astronauts, who have just returned from the orbit. Everybody is smiling, the President thanks them and presents ten thousand dollars to each of them.

After that the movie continues. In an while it is interrupted for another commercial: The General Secretary in Moscow Kremlin receives cosmonauts, who have just returned from the orbit. Everybody smile. He thanks them and fixes the Gold Star of the Hero on the breast of each of them. After the cosmonauts leave, the General Secretary, alone in his office, draws out a drawer of his desk, produces one more Star of the Hero and fixes it on his own breast.

After the journalist told his joke, all started laughing and joking on all their way to the City. The old forgotten joke of the Soviet times was so matching the old aunty Dusia's current case.

A Cop

"A cop" or "a copper" translated from the language, spoken in Odessa, means just "a bobby". Once the term "a bobby" sounded for police officers as unpleasant as the word "a cop".

But as the time passed and the time of Perestroika came, they understood, that the word "cop" sounded much better than any other nickname. They even liked this word, as the head of the police division of one of respectable districts of the historic part of Odessa in nineties likes to say: "It's impossible to do away with mafia, it is possible only to become its leader". Another expression that he would use was "A good cop is a dead cop". Residents of Odessa still have no idea of what he meant.

The well-known TV serial "Cops" helped to push out of use such endearing and easily understood words as "fuzz" or "bobby". The place of birth of the word "copper", when used to indicate a police officer, was, of course, Odessa. As early as in nineteenth century the police officers were called in our city by the word that sounded like "mojser", which, when translated from the language, known all over the world, meant "a sneak", or "a spy". Afterwards "mojser" turned into the word with a similar pronunciation "musor", meaning "a copper".

In the twentieth century this word sweepingly extended over the territory of the former Soviet Union. It was quite understandable, as often it were people who had mentality and behavior of a pig or a bum, something reminding animal behavior at a garbage place, who went to work in the police. Not all of them were, of course, of that kind. There were also decent and selfless policemen, like Zheglov and Sharapov, personages from a well-known TV movie, but that was a minority. The same correlation of worthy and mean employees was in any government office in the past, it is the same in present too, in the future, no doubt, it will be the same.

There is no need in honest, decent and smart officers, they are outsiders in enforcement departments, the officers in ruling structures are sick of them. Are good persons in demand there? But still there are exceptions, of course; decent people are an exception, a sample of something forgotten long ago, of something not of this world.

In fact, if you have a close look at each person, you can notice, that his nickname or pseudonym reflects the inside or the outer traits of the person. For example, when you examine the traits of character of a common TV personage, you ask yourself a natural question, if the pseudonym "Moth" is meant to reflect only outward appearance, or his inner world as well? It seems to be a complex attitude. But if a person is called a moth, it should mean something.

The position of a cop is inaccessible for a resident of Odessa, though it is his home city. In Odessa they used to say: "It's easier to find a black man in " Ku-Klux-Klan", than a resident of Odessa in the police". The same situation is in the regional committee and its modern associated institutions, such as regional administration, city administration, academies of different kinds and middle level of government offices. If someone is interested where decent population is getting lost, they will explain to him that some of them have left to some far away countries, others – to some closer countries, and some of them have left to the next world. A small part, left here, is sitting in the shade of chestnuts, so dear to the heart, and wait quietly for the coming Flood, or a revolution, or a counter-revolution, as a result of which we, Jews will be done away with, and the next victims are going to be national minorities, or it could be vice versa. Is it possible that everything falls back to its place and Haim and Sarah will return to their home shore? But the chance is one to a million.

Georgiy Vartanyan had served for twenty years in the ranks of the police. It was more than once that he, "armed to the teeth" with a pen and a notebook, walked to a den to arrest a bandit, as there was no gas to fill the tank of the police car. Once, in a fit of temper, he spoke his mind to a human resources inspector from the regional department. The inspector was a short, fat Colonel with pink cheeks and a strict look. The result was that he warned Georgiy that he should be fired from the cop's position due to his ineligibility, in case he would continue to speak on the undesirable topics.

At the beginning of nineties Vartanyan, having failed to see any positive changes in the police, put his police i.d. and all the enclosures to it on the table of his supervisor and left the police to pick up the career of a private entrepreneur. He didn't owe anything to anyone. In ten years Georgiy became a real businessman, who knew the rules of the market, who was aware of the illegal actions of the government officers, who had enough means and connections to control the market and make it develop in the way profitable for them.

But he didn't get all this at once. There were years of trials, mistakes and disappointments. At the same time, those were the years of search and achievements. Vartanyan started his business with resale of pantyhoses and lingerie, then he switched to sex shop goods. When there were eliminated restrictions connected with pornography and sex issues, there seemed to be lots of persons who, having been restrained for many years, at the beginning of nineties rushed into each other's arms. Age and difference of sexual orientation did not seem to matter a lot, the main thing was to have an intercourse. It didn't matter with whom and where, the fact of having sex was of importance.

First sex shop goods attracted not only sexual giants, but all the people, including impotents. Some of them wanted just to have a look, others were curious, some needed diversity, and some thought with hope that some items could help them. Nobody could understand the sacramental thing: a man always wants, be not always can, and a woman always can, but not always wants.

Georgiy made a success at that time at the wave of sexual craze. He chose those sexual goods that had the following effect: those men, who bought an item, always could, and the women always wanted.

When curious ex-fellow-workers met him, they would ask what he did for living, and he answered in a brief manner: "Condoms and stimulants".

Have you got anything for us?

I don't sell cleansers. – Vartanyan answered, laughing.

He tried not to think about his police service. This made him feel upset. The reason was that he went to this service because he felt it was his vocation, he was a born cop. But he had no luck in this career. He had an independent attitude and he was not used to lick somebody's boots. Georgiy saw that those who were honest and devoted to the job they had been doing, who were real professionals, left the service in the police. The remaining were, as a rule, lazy crooks, scoundrels, and felons. Their mail aim was to acquire something for nothing without any effort.

Vartanyan watched how the police, which used to be meant for protection of people from criminals, gradually turned to become a bandit organization by its psychology and actions. The difference was that the police used the law as a cover. He watched the district police inspectors take bribes from beggars and hawkers. He watched old women selling cigarettes which the district police officer seized from hawkers and gave to them for resale, and the old women got some money from him for their work. He saw officers in the passport department process files deliberately slowly. They told the customers that in order to expedite the file it was necessary to grease their palm. He saw how cops spent their time in night clubs and the casino, and it was obvious that they didn't spend their regular salaries there. He saw what kinds of houses were constructed for department managers, not to mention the representatives of a higher level of administration. That was a system! He himself tried to be outside this system. Everyone in the police knew Vartanyan, his character and his connections, and they tried not to have any relations with him and his business, they let him alone.

Later Georgiy had a bigger company dealing with gas, grain, tourist business, he even had his own security department. It took him several years to unite professional businessmen, and it took him some effort, but he achieved the desirable result after all.

Lenin was right when he said that "human resources determine all", and he wasn't at all a silly man. – Vartanyan liked to say.

The chief accountant in his business was Iakov Aronovich. Vartanyan had known him as a decent and professional accountant even since he worked in the criminal investigations department. Iakov Aronovich could professionally make accounting for both legal and illegal parts of accounting at the time of his employment in the Grain Products department. Iakov Aronovich used to say to Georgiy from time to time:

"You, Armenians, like us, Jews, more than you like people of your own nationality. That is the correct way to be, as, if we are done away with, you will be the next."

Vartanyan laughed sincerely. He liked Iakov Aronovich's lambent and business-like humor, he also liked his professionalism and decency. There were very few such people left it Odessa.

Iakov Aronovich got never, at any circumstances, discouraged, he was always joking. When leaving home for work, he would say:

I am going to the office, it's time to cook lunch. I will make the dish "bashmala", this specialty of Odessa is always tasty when I cook it. I am a good cook, as my rivals say.

But once he came to work very upset. He came to Vartanyan's office and told him what had happened to his thirteen years old grandson. His son lived separately with his family in Cheremushki area, he ran his own business together with his wife. They owned a small company selling appliances. They did have some profit from their business, and it was enough to live a decent life. They had an only son, a blockhead, but he was OK, nothing to worry about. He was doing quite well at school, he had all hobbies that were available for his age, and even a little bit more. The parents found him more than once smoking weed.

To make the long story short, according to Iakov Abramovich, a policeman brought the grandson home three days ago. The policeman was in the rank of a senior lieutenant, he introduced himself as an officer of the criminal department dealing with criminals of minor age, and he produced his i.d. It turned out that in the school bag of the grandson there was found some weed, which was seized by the officer, Igor Kosorotov, according to the lawful procedure, in the presence of witnesses and with a protocol signed.

What are our actions? – he asked the astonished parents. –

Proceedings will be instituted against your son and he will have criminal charges.

The parents were scared to death. They started begging the officer to be merciful to their child.

- We will punish him ourselves, it will never happen again. - The head of the family assured the officer. – How much can it cost?

The policeman looked indignant, - How dare you?

But in a short while he changed anger for mercy:

It will cost you a lot of money, no less than five thousand bucks. Do you know how much trouble you are going to have? What do you want?

Three thousand dollars, and we just get out of it. I will tear up the protocol in your presence. But this should be the last time.

The father counted the three thousand bucks with his trembling hands and the protocol was torn in the presence of both the parents and the policeman. The latter left.

Vartanyan listened attentively and smiled, -What's of that? Are you going to surprise me, Iakov Aronovich? What kind of surprise is it? Everyone knows cops take bribes. This is not a piece of news. This is as old as this world. As early as nineteen seventeen the head of the municipal police took money from you, Jews. This is not a secret. The same situation with your people was during the Bolshevik rule. The same it is now."

- My dear young man, you are too nimble. Be patient and listen to my story up to the end. I am and old Jew and maybe I am a little bit mentally sick, but not as mush as that.

Georgiy apologized and realized that if Iakov Aronovich came to him with this problem, it should be something serious.

- You see, my dear Zhora, at night my son and myself interrogated my grandson thoroughly. He assured us with tears in his eyes that he did smoke weed, but he had never had his own stuff, he had never carried anything in his school bag. I do believe him! If there were something, he would have confessed. He is just a weak child after all.

- So, Iakov Aronovich, you are trying to tell me that the hemp was planted in your grandson's school bag? – Vartanyan sounded interested.

- That's exactly what happened. The hemp was not planted at the time of the search, I know those cops' tricks. My grandson is sure that the package was planted to him at school, and the cop was aware in which section of the school bag it was. – Iakov Aronovich finished his story enthusiastically, seeing that the boss was interested in the case.

Do you think the senior lieutenant makes money using this system?

I have no doubt. I think he has found a way of making real money.

- Somebody plants packages with weed and he checks school bags right near the school. He makes protocols of seizure of drugs and blackmails parents, getting much enough money, be sure of that. Just for my grandson he got three thousand dollars. My grandson says that he did hear rumors that some students were searched and some money was paid to stop criminal charges, but he didn't pay much attention to it, he thought it was just rumors.

Vartanyan called the manager of his security department who used to work with him in the criminal department of the police.

- Valera, here is a task for you. – He explained briefly the situation to the manager and gave him a task to organize watch on "the drug mafia fighter" with the name Kosorotov.

As soon as in a week Vartanyan had a detailed report about Kosorotov's activity. The cop appeared to have created a system of making this kind of business and money was literally pouring to his pocket.

He has a whole pioneer group of young traitors. – The manager of the security department was reporting. In three schools there are as many as twelve students who are his agents. Each of them in the past was caught for some illegal actions, such as drugs, theft, even attempted rape. He send his own young female agents who tempted young guys and Kosorotov made a protocol about rape and thus he took them by the throat. The guys were ready to fulfill any task in exchange of his silence about their disgraceful goings-on. Such young agents planted packages with weed or even with heroin to the school bags of their classmates, sons of well-to-do families. The policeman catches the children the next moment, with the stuff waiting for him. He stops a boy right near the school and tells him:

- Young man, please show me your bag. We have information that you have drugs in it.

The guy, being sure that the policeman is just mislead, opens the bag and there was a package, The guy is just shocked.

Look here, during the week that we watched him, he took care of as many as three duffers. It comes to about six or seven thousand bucks. What were the parents to do? I had a confidential talk with one of the mothers. She was telling me with tears:

- Who wants to spoil one's own child's life? And a jail at the start of the young life is just ruinous for his fate. I have never expected any trouble. I have always believed my son. And here is that thing. I thought it was my fault, as I worked many hours at the flea market, and didn't have much time to take care of my son. And the result was the court, a jail, a detention center. No, I am not going to allow that go. I am ready to pay any money to save him from jail. I will give all my money, I am ready to have great debts, but I will not allow my son to be convicted.

- So, they paid. – The manager of the security department went on with his report. – He had a system. His agents were even paid from time to time. He paid them much enough – from twenty to fifty bucks. For students this is big money. They search for a new victim themselves. They are mean guys, but they seem to be born like that.

Vartanyan took video and audiotapes compromising that super fighter against drugs mafia and called to his former fellow-worker Volodya Uvarov, who was employed in the department of Internal Security of the Police.

That night they met. Georgiy told the whole story in detail and submitted all the facts of illegal actions of the brave cop Kosorotov.

In this package there are video and audiotapes with the evidence of the actions of this business-cop. You are to decide what actions to take up against him. It is your problem. But my request is that in twenty four hours this guy is to bring three hundred dollars to the son of my chief accountant. He is to bring one more thousand for moral detriment. His apologies are also a must. If he doesn't meet my requirements, he will have great troubles, you know what I mean. As far as the rest is concerned, it's your matter. If you don't want to make a public issue, he can be just fired according to his own will. Maybe you will hire him yourself? He seems to be ready to take up service in the Department of Internal Security. – Vartanyan attacked his former fellow-worker, laughing.

Uvarov lit a cigarette, inhaled deeply and looked at Georgiy severely.

- Don't attack me, please. Both of us know what is going on. If there have been some restrictions, now there are no. What internal security we can talk about? We deal with lots of emergency situations. Like firemen. We try to put the fire down, but if we fail, we have to lay off the person to blame. We put a past date on the orders to lay off a person. We make deals with persecutor's office. In that office there are so many similar problems, that they always come to an agreement with us. They are not interested to make the cases of corruption public, because we also know much about their cases. As far as this pig is concerned, we'll see. Maybe we'll detain him. Maybe we'll fire him. The management will make the decision.

The next day Iakov Aronovich ran into Vartanyan's office, his face was shining with joy.

- Dear Georgiy, thank you so much! You are a great person. Yesterday that rotten asshole brought four thousand dollars to my son and a bunch of roses to my daughter-in-law. He apologized, bowed scraping his feet and so on.

Georgiy burst out laughing, - OK, Iakov Aronovich. I do respect you and other associates, I appreciate your work and I will avenge myself on anyone who threatens you. This is the reality. As far as the law-enforcement system is concerned, it is rotten and smells badly, and not only in Odessa. And we can't help it, my dear.

In two more weeks the manager of the security department reported to Vartanyan that Kosorotov was sorry for his behavior and asked to lay him off due to his own will. He knew what he would do for living, as he had already bought a bar near Cheremushki market and a couple of containers at "The Seventh kilometer ". The report of his illegal actions was submitted to the prosecutor's office, but there they decided to shelve it.

At night Georgiy sat in an armchair at his home looking through newspapers. He paid attention to the article in one of the papers with the astonishing headline "The Police in Odessa does not spare soap". In the article they told about the action "Clean hands" performed by the officers of the Department of the Interior in order to clear up the ranks of the police and remove the associates who break the law.

- Another campaign. – He said to himself, having read the interview with the chief of the municipal police, who said: "We are not going to conceal illegal actions of policemen. Esprit de corps is good when the hands are clean. We need great quantity of soap to clean everything up."

- The mission is impossible. All the soap and other detergents produced in Turkey are not enough to clean everything up. And the persons doing the laundry are stained up to the top as well. This dirt is for ever...

Suddenly he remembered an extract from a bestseller by Valeriy Smirnov, not really appreciated by the residents of Odessa: "The people did make great progress, in spite of the effort of the government and despite one more crisis. Everyone has a cell phone, a car of foreign make and a gold chain around the neck. A son asked his father: "Are they bandits?" The child cannot realize that those are not at all bandits, nor they are municipal deputies. He can't make the right guess. Those are just cops, whose salary has been reduced once again."

Wishes and Possibility

During the last two years at school Vera and her friend Masha thought over their plans, changed opinions and discussed their future life. They were to decide where to go to work or to study after school.

They resided in the settlement called Buyalyk in Ivanov district, Odessa region. A godforsaken place, which used to be a populated settlement, where an aviation regiment was based. The aviation regiment provided working places for the residents. There was also some entertainment in the Officer's Recreation Club for the young. For girls it was a very good time, for sure. So many potential boyfriends, young officers with an apartment, good salary and other benefits.

But those times have passed. Only alcoholics and bootlegger live in the military settlement now. All the military property was gradually stolen. The aviators stayed only in the memory of mothers and in stories told by them.

The young people in Buyalyk gradually became alcohol and drug addicted, as there was no lack of alcohol and drugs there. Many escaped from the disaster and found refuge in Odessa, which attracted with its opportunities. The same was the decision of both Vera and Masha. They decided to find some job or to study in Odessa after finishing high school.

And they did finish high school, and the time came to make a serious decision. Vera was a tall, stately girl with dark hair. She was a daughter of a Bulgarian father and a Ukrainian mother, and she was very beautiful. The reason was either the mixed blood, or she was just like this by nature. Masha was as beautiful, but her hair was blond.

They had different temper. Vera, or Verunchik, as they called her, was determined and firm. Masha was very kind-hearted, easy-going and trusting.

Before they left for Odessa both of them were scared to confront the unknown. What would their life be like?

Of course, there was great hope, inspiration and wish. They wanted to study, to work, they wanted to live. They understood the reality: no pain, no gain.

But deep in their hearts they dreamed of meeting a prince in Odessa, a rich, handsome, with good manners. They dreamed of being happy with the prince.

Like most of boys and girls right after school, Verunchik and Masha couldn't afford paying for a University course. They did realize that in order to enroll to a subsidized course it was necessary to give a bribe. Was it ever possible in Odessa to enroll to some educational institution without giving a bribe, no matter what period of history it was: the Monarchy, the Communist rule, and especially at the time of democracy. The first question has always been:

How much?

The answer: "As much you can afford" did not shock anyone.

The girls decided to enroll the cheapest faculty in the University, that was philological.

- There is no harm in trying. – Verunchik said. She liked to make use of sayings in her speech.

But the first trial was a failure. The girls passed all the exams, but they were not admitted as there was great competition. Verunchik was an optimist.

- OK, the attempt was not a success. We didn't want to study there anyway. The position of a teacher is not the best one, and the salary is small. And plenty of work to do.

But it was just talks, they felt different inside. They didn't have any place to get in, there was no use in looking for some other University to enroll, and there was no point in spending one year doing nothing. There was no point in returning to wearisome Buyalyk. While taking the exams the friends stayed at the place of Masha's remote relative. After the exams they were supposed to find some other place.

- Nowadays any acquired occupation means a job. – Vera said decidedly. She suggested that they should enroll to a school which trained cooks. The vocational school was famous in Odessa, it used to train cooks for the Black Sea steamship line. Though the Black Sea steamship line disappeared like the Atlantic continent, the demand in cooks did not become less, they were still demanded both in the sea and on the shore.

- I saw an ad. – She tried to persuade Masha. – Though we never thought of becoming a cook or a waitress, we have to do it, as we don't have any other option.

Masha was in doubt. Vera got mad, - Why can't you make the decision? You are so irresolute! You have the following options: a salesperson at the flea market or a hooker at the road called "stometrovka". But you can't just get into the business, there is also some competition there. And for that you also need money. Or we can go home, but what kind of life are we going to live? Here, at school, we will live at a dormitory. The tuition is very good and free. The level of education is equal to that in a college. You are going to get a qualification of a cook and a waitress of third or fourth category. You will get employment after graduation. Where can you find such benefits?

Under the pressure of the friend Masha surrendered. She realized that the friend was right. There didn't have any other option.

OK, I agree. When and where are we to go?

Take your documents and let's go to school.

In a week the friends enrolled in the school after medical examination and submission of documents. They had an interview. Besides, they had a test in English, which was an important subject in the curriculum, as they could get employed on a ship which traveled abroad.

Masha passed the test with the excellent mark and was supposed to study in a specialized group. Vera had just satisfactory knowledge, but she solved the problem quite easily: she paid twenty dollars to the foreman and got into the same specialized group, as Masha.

- We will study together. – Vera said to her friend. – That is safer and there is also more fun.

The enrollment was easy and free for Masha, as she was an excellent student in high school. There were no special enrollment exams, but at the interview one had to fill forms inquiring if you could sing, dance, play musical instruments, run, compose poems.

- Only decent and smart guys and girls can be our students. – The principal said before the interview, when all the applicants gathered together in the school club.

Excellent and good students passed the interview easily. As far as those with satisfactory level are concerned, they had to make some extra effort. Some bought new furniture for the school, but most of them paid some money, like Verunchik. No doubt, the enrollment did cost money for some students, and it was the parents who had to pay.

- You were supposed to study and not to go out for dancing. – The mother lectured Vera. – Masha went to high school with you, she finished school with honors, and she didn't have to pay anything for enrollment.

- Don't count your chickens before they are hatched. Wait and see which of us will graduate with honors from this school. – Vera answered, laughing.

By the first of September the friends were enrolled and they were to stay in school for a year and seven months. They were given a room in a dormitory, it was officially for free, but in order to get there one had to pay twenty dollars to the superintendent. The money was supposed to be used for renovation.

On the first of September the principal made a welcome speech. He explained some conditions of education. He warned that the rules were strict, that the students were to do their best and not to rely on parents' help, that nobody accepted any bribes at school. The students were introduced to foremen and educators, most of them appeared to have no University education. But they had long-term experience as cooks and waitresses on board the ships. The level of education was no longer important in Odessa. There are many unique persons who finish secondary police school and later become professors, Doctors of science, dealing with reforms of all possible kinds. As a result they can cook "bashmala" perfectly, and this occupation provides them a well-to-do style of life, they can afford to entertain their offsprings at the cost of the Pacific Ocean.

The first-year students were told, that every year a representative of the famous company "Kristal Marin" comes to school and conducts an interview in order to check knowledge in English and in the main subject. The result is that if you pay five hundred dollars, having the foreman as a middleman, you can ensure employment on board a ship for yourself. It was a dream of many of the students. There was a cheaper way. You could go to one of numerous employment agencies in Odessa, pay ten or twenty dollars and wait for an offer for several years. Those, who don't want to work in the sea, can continue their education in Lomonosov Academy. After finishing the school, you can be enrolled to the second year of education in the Academy.

Those who are interested neither in working in the sea, nor in continuing the education, can get an employment as a cook or as a waiter in one of the bars, cafés or restaurants of the city. This employment offer also needs some financing.

Vera and Masha liked the options, everybody liked. The friends started making plans for the future.

- I will go to the sea on board a passenger liner as a waitress, I don't want to be a cook. A snow- white ship, idle rich passengers. I will seduce one and make him marry me. He will be a German, or an American. And an African would be OK. Can you imagine me with a black guy? But not a wife in a harem. What do you think of that? – Vera spoke her dreams out loud, lying in bed in the dormitory.

Masha laughed: "It will be an old man, as young people don't go to cruises, they say, they work hard. It is senior people who travel."

- Why not? An old man, a widower with lots of money. That's a good option. I will fuck him to death in a month and all his money will be mine. It's better than the same age. Those are younger than twenty, but they are no longer fit for love because of alcohol and drugs, all they want is to have a drink or to inject themselves. And no assets, only empty bottles are all their property. – Vera spoke her mind.

The first days of school came, and the friends got disappointed. Vera, who liked freedom and didn't stand any pressure of any type, was especially upset. The principal had been working in this position for thirty years. All his concepts and actions had the style of the Soviet period. The attitude of the teachers to students was simple: you got enrolled, so you have to bear it for two years.

- You can stick your opinion into your ass. Nobody is interested in it. We don't care if you like or dislike the attitude of the teachers. You can express your protest at home, to your mother and you father, but not here. – The principal lectured them.

On the very first day of the school year the first year students cleaned all the classrooms right after the principal's instructive speech. After that they stayed unsupervised in class for a while, and then left for home. All the week was like that. As it became clear later, all first year students were used for all kinds of hard work. Like unqualified workers, they cleaned, removed, unloaded, loaded, renovated. And they always were told that their education was free.

But after all the actual studies began. As a rule, teachers came to work either after a good party with lots of drink, as a strong smell of previous night's alcohol spread all around the classroom, or there was a smell of drink, just taken in the teachers' office for freshening the nip. The teachers constantly used foul language. The girls were very much amazed as they were accustomed to obscene words in Buyalyk, but they had never heard such vulgar language as their teachers used in class, they even couldn't imagine that was possible at all.

Vera immediately changed the well-known saying "to swear like a trooper". She said during the break:

- Girls, you should say "to swear like a cook"! I am sick and tired of them all, I want crocodiles to fuck all these bitches. And they make us wear a uniform, white top and black lower part, it is still good they don't restrict the length of the skirt and don't check if there is a bra on.

Different checks really irritated. Every morning in the hostel there came foremen and started their search at the dawn. They produced bottles from night stands, cigarettes from pockets, all the stuff from under the beds. Girls, including Vera and Masha, were not virgins, they had made love with boys since the age of thirteen or fifteen, and they finished schools being women. This considered to be improper. They knew all the methods of having sex. They could teach their parents how to achieve orgasm. They were also aware of all real and unreal methods of contraception. That is why the hostel turned into a small brothel. Guys got into girls' beds and girls got into boys'. All this considered to be a violation of the school rules. Once Vera hooked a cool guy, who worked at the flea market "The Seventh kilometer", and he slept over in their room. He and Vera made love all though the night and in the morning they slept. During the check a naked Apollo was found in Vera's bed.

All the students were lined up, and the principal shamed Vera in front of everyone, called her a whore and told her to pack her belongings and go home. That morning Vera was not the only one, in a boys' room the foremen found girls from the same school, and it was clear that during the night they did something else, but not prepared their home lessons.

Verunchik went home, brought fifty dollars, and all was settled. Of course, those who were from distant places or from poor families, had to endure everything. They were afraid of being expelled and they patiently and silently tolerated all abuse and insulting. On the contrary, those, who had some protection or rich parents, did not pretend to observe the rules. They lived their own style of life, took drugs, missed classes. They were numerous, but everything was allowed to them. At the end of the course they passed all the exams successfully and got good work positions.

Once, in about two weeks after the school started, the foreman brought grants to class, as much as seventeen grivnas to each. The girls were glad, but the joy was premature. Ten grivnas were held for a present to the principal on his birthday. Five were supposed to be used for arranging the competition for the title of the best cook, and two grivnas were given for each girl.

Vera said, mimicking the principal:

- Let them stick the two grivnas into their asses, bitches. – And she left for a party in the Institute of the Ministry of Interior to Arcadiya with her new boyfriend.

Masha didn't take part in her friend's numerous adventures.

Verunchik changed her boyfriends almost every day, and she wasn't very much concerned what kind of person each of them was. The main thing to her was that he had pocket money to pay for dancings, bars and night clubs. She invited them into her bed almost every night and she made love to them paying no attention to two other girls sharing the same room with her. At the very beginning Masha and Olya tried to object, but in a while they gave up and got used to fall asleep having voluptuous moans of the lovers as a background.

Masha had a boyfriend who studied in a vocational school next door, he was going to become a constructor. Yura was born in Belyaevka, his future occupation was tiler and facing worker. Masha had long walks with him around Odessa, they talked to each other, hardly noticing other people and paying no attention to the time that passed. Yura told her about his school. It turned out that the rules there were the same as in Masha's. Numerous cases of abuse and hard slavery. Students had no right to say something to anyone or to complain. They were persuaded by their foremen that they were unable to do fulfill any work, that they were dull and helpless, that they were supposed to do everything the foremen told them to do with no objections, only in this case there was a chance to achieve something.

- You see, Mashenka, everything must be paid for. You have made an omission – you pay, pay for the thesis, pay for credit tests, pay for exams and for all other stuff. If you want to get training practice at a good group of workers, you also have to pay.

When a holiday comes, and there are so many holidays nowadays, that you are just not able to remember all them all, it doesn't mean that it is a nice time for us when we could have some rest for a day or two, it means much money will be drawn out of our pockets, and the joy disappears immediately.

It is just regular collection of money for the foreman to have a good holiday. If you don't want to pay, you will be expelled. What if I quit? I can't as I want to acquire the occupation of a constructor, I like it, especially I like tiling. And the salary of a tiler is usually good.

Masha agreed with him. She was also sick of constant threats, unfair and abnormal treatment. Many of her fellow students didn't want to bear it, they cursed the school together with its money grubbers, as they called the teachers, and together with the frozen-minded principal. They sent them to hell or somewhere even farther, took their documents and left. During the second year there were also those who left, as the conditions were still more severe. But there were very few who left, as they were losing much money already invested into that damn education, much time was lost and too much effort. Vera calculated all the expenses for the education and burst out crying. She figured out that with the money she could have been able to pay for two years of tuition in a University.

At the end of the first year there came the time of exams. The students were warned that everything would be very hard, that no bribes could be accepted, that everything would be strict. Those, who didn't study properly, could be expelled for bad results. Everyone was worried, except Vera. She inquired the foreman and knew the prices for the thesis, the credit test and for the exam. She watched her friends indulgently as they thoroughly studied the contents of the textbooks and notes at night.

- How silly you are! Go home and bring money. Don't study those textbooks, relax and call your boyfriends. Just enjoy the life.

Verunchik got accustomed to Odessa rules very quickly. For one month she had been living with her boyfriend, a barman from one of the night clubs in Arcadiya, in his apartment. She quickly came to a conclusion that free education was not at all free, and one had to pay for it anyway. They just talk about education for free and collect money just shamelessly.

- Why should I waste my time and effort if I can pay and buy a diploma which has the price as small as one hundred and fifty bucks.

Vera did pay the money to the principal, got her diploma of a cook and a waitress. In a month she was already employed as a waitress in the night club, where her smart boyfriend worked as a barman. They made good money as it was a busy season.

Masha tried to pass all her credit tests and exams honestly, having studied all the material, but she failed. She got unsatisfactory marks. As a result, she had to pay eighty bucks in order to have a chance to continue her education during the second year.

She had hard feelings. Everything around was so loathsome. During the second year they worked as waitresses at different banquets, weddings, presentation parties. They worked hard, and all the money were paid for foremen. She felt sad, she felt humiliated. It was unbearable for her to see only evil around, almost no kindness. At school they were taught to be honest, decent and kind. In real life it was quite different. She just got discouraged. The only joy for her was the love that she felt for Yura and Yura felt for her. They were making marriage plans after graduation. Yura had already finished his technical school and he was working as a tiler at construction sites of Odessa. He was employed by a private company. Part-time he did renovation of apartments. They needed money for the wedding. Yura also had to pay some money for having been employed, and the amount was as much as five hundred bucks.

Vera, having learned about her friend's intentions, came to the dormitory.

- What are you doing? Are you sick? Yes, go and get married to Yura. You will give birth to a dozen of kids, as poor as yourselves. No apartment to live, no steady income. Think twice, my dear friend.

Finish that damn school, save some money and go to the sea. Sure, you can live with Yura. But don't make silly things, remember you are not even twenty. Why should you commit yourself? And see what kind of person you are with. A young lad who is under twenty, who has no backup, only debts to pay.

Masha listened to her friend patiently and silently.

After she finished Masha answered quietly:

Everybody is different. You are looking for a prince of your childhood dreams. There is no real princes in real life. A poor girl will never marry a rich, handsome young man with nice manners. Rich men have their own girlfriends. I have found my own prince, we love each other, no matter how poor we are, no matter that we don't have an apartment to live. We will build our life together, step by step. We have the main thing, that is love. Sorry for the truth, but you have already fucked few dozens of men and you still don't know what is happiness and love. I wish you came to know this feeling once in your life, then we will be able to talk to each other and understand each other.

On her way home Vera thought:

- I will make my dream real, then I will go to the sea. Everything will become clear then. This is not my vocation. But I am still young. I am just nineteen. All the life is in store for me. What about the school? What about Masha? All losers like Masha will keep studying at schools like this, there are plenty of losers around. They are attracted by education for free, they are just dreamers. Those like me will go to the sea from the very start.

- Sure, - Verunchik sighed, - I wish I were getting training for the occupation I liked, I wish I had money. I wish our desire coincided with our possibilities.

The Spirit of Our Homeland

A representative delegation of Estonia, the head of which was the President Rъъtel, had a flight on board of two planes from Tallinn to Odessa. That was a friendly visit. The second plane carried mostly Estonian businessmen who wanted to get an idea of the market in Odessa; they also wanted to know if there was a possibility to establish business contacts.

Georgiy Ivanovich Tkachuk, a former military man, and nowadays a successful businessman, was a member of the delegation. He was tall, skinny, with a rich chevelure, his hair was just a bit gray on temples, and his old acquaintances and friends were surprised to meet him and see how little he had changed during the past thirty years.

- Look here, Zhora, you haven't changed much, as skinny and curly-haired, as you used to be when a young captain.

- Regular mode of life plus a young wife, ecologically clean Estonian atmosphere preserve the former resident of Odessa, Zhora, in his primary appearance. – He used to joke.

Sitting in the armchair on board the plane Zhorka got absorbed with his memories.

He was born and grew up in Odessa, in a small and quiet street, in Slobodka area. His mother worked a jute factory; his father was a dockworker in the seaport. He was the only child in the family. The parents wanted him to become a sailor. In fact, all residents of Odessa dreamed of becoming sailors or of their children becoming sailors. The Sea Institute was located not far from their home. But Zhora after finishing school, quite unexpectedly to everyone, enrolled in Odessa antiaircraft military school and in three years he became an officer. The parents couldn't admit the fact that the son was going to be a military man and not a sailor. But after graduation Zhora showed up at home in the uniform of a leutenant. He was hansome and tall, he looked like a real officer. The parents understood that it was their son's choice, and the choice had been done once and for ever. In a month the leutenant Tkachuk left Odessa and went to the North-Western border of the former USSR.

Zhora was used to large and busy Odessa, the small Estonian town Tapa was unusual for him. At the start he was to serve at the headquaters of an anti-aircraft subdivision. Many of his former fellow students from the military school envied him. He was really very lucky. He was assigned to Estonia, to the subdivision headquarters. Anyone could only dream of such a start. Many of his friends were assigned to serve to so-called "points", far-away garrisons in Chukot, Kola Peninsula, Pamirs, Kazakhstan, Turkmenistan. Many of them couldn't understand, why Zhorka, having no protection, no influencial parents, received such a good assignment. He was assigned to Baltic region and to the headquartes. It was just luck, Zhorka seemed to have born under a lucky star. In fact, he was born at a spring night when the sky was full of stars. Odessa taught him many lessons in his childhood and youth. The first lesson was about being independent and brave, about trimming his sails to the wind and taking his opportunity. Besides, it was Odessa, which brought him up as a decent person. He had always kept in mind that no one was supposed to count other people's money, to intrigue against one's fellow-workers. He knew that when in a team one should be a real part of it. He knew that there was no good to deal with rogues.

This was the reason, why the jolly lad from Odessa, the handsom and tall leutenant, very smart and clever enough, without any showing off, was immediately accepted by the men in the subdivision. His service went on smoothly from the start.

It was Estonia. During the first year Zhora could not get accustomed to signs on the stores that he couldn't read, to the different language, to strange rules and regulations, to Estonians, who were people of different kind. They seemed to be leading secluded life, to smile very seldom and to talk too little. And he compared all this to what he was used to in Odessa. Tapa was a small town situated between Tartu and Tallin with the population of about ten thousand people. Half of the people were Russian speaking, as there was a railway junction with all the communications where many Russian people were employed. When compared to Odessa, Zhora liked clean streets of Estonian cities and villages. Everything was neat: houses, front yards, stores, bars and restaurants, work places. The main thing was that the relations between people were also pure. Zhora couldn't get accustomed to the foreign Estonian speech, especially in the country. He went to the country to his business trips to visit anti-aircraft missile emplacement. They were scattered along the shore of the Gulf of Finland and in the Estonian swamps and woods. He had an impression that Estonian people looked at the military men with hatred and considered them to be invaders. There were many different cases, in fact, like fighting with Estonians at a dancing party in the Railway recreation club or at a restaurant. There were cases when Estonian young people cried out "Heil", when passing by an officer, and streched out the hand in the Nazi salutation. But years passed and Zhora got accustomed to Estonians, he came to understand them. He saw that they were hard working, honest and decent. Every autumn cars and buses came to Tapa to pick up those who wanted to work at digging out potatoes and picking up stones in the fields. The salary was high enough, cash was paid every night. Zhora also went to the work at the weekend. He didn't think it was something to be ashamed of, "to earn two kopecks", as he called it in the manner, common in Odessa. The stones seemed to be growing in the field. Every autumn they were removed, in spring grain seeds were sowed, and next autumn after the harvest time it was a new season of removing stones. He couldn't help wondering how Estonians managed to gather in such harvest of grane-crops per a hectare on such soil, as it was much more, than in black earth zones in Russia and the Ukraine. Zhora understood that it was the result of the combination of hard labor and high farming standards. It was also inside culture of the local population. Once he visited a meat-packing factory in the district center called Rakvere. He went there on a business trip to organize additional food supply for military men. He was just surprised by the high standards of the production, by the labor discipline, not to say anything of the cleanness and neatness of the factory itself. The quality of the produced goods was also very high. He thought of the Odessa meat-packing plant at Peresyp area. In his childhood they called it "nausea place". There was nothing common.

Gradually Zhora got accustomed to the life there.

He could talk in the Estonian language, he came to have some acquaintances, and later – some Estonian friends of different circles of the society and different occupations. The people were severe and unavailable only from the outside. If they see that you are a decent person, they easily contact you.

Zhora was surprised by the fact that in friendship and in everyday life, at recreation time Estonians didn't make much difference with whom to mix, as far as social position and occupation was concerned. Esonians liked that Zhora was interested in their household rules, life, history, that he learned the language and tried to speak it.

For many years Zhora had been single. When he got the rank of the Captain, he visited Odessa, where he spent his vacation every year. That particular vacation was an unhappy one. His father died in an accident at the port. On the third day after the father's death and the funeral his mother died quietly. He burried them both side by side at the Second Christian cemetery. His childhood friends, who by that time got high positions on the city and the regional levels. After the parents' funerals Zhora understood that he was quite alone in the whole world. Only then he came to understand that he was a fool not to pay enough attention to his mother, who worked so hard that she ruined her health at work, and to his father, whose work can't be described adequately neither in verses, nor in prose. he offered them several times to move to Estonia to his place, but they did not feel like moving.

- Oh, no, son. Are you sick? How can we leave Odessa for unknown Estonia? No, our dear son, we have lived our life here in our own den, we are going to die here as well.

After his parents' death he came to Odessa more and more seldom, usually once in two or three years. Odessa attracted him with its southern spirit, with the sea, the chestnuts, actually, with its nature and history. But as years passed, Odessa attracted him less and less, as he saw that there were less and less local residents in the city, that the city was mostly inhabited by newcomers, who were far from being the best. Actually the new people in Odessa were male and female vulgarians. He saw that Odessa was gradually degenerating from inside.

He was accustomed to the culture and traditions in Estonia. He couldn't imagine himself drinking vodka from a plain glass or a tall wine glass. He couldn't come to a restaurant without a tie. He couldn't swear or spit in the street, neither he could drop a piece of paper or garbage outside a garbage bin. He did feel that Estonian reality and their way of life influenced him positively.

He was offered good positions, opportunity to study in the Academy, but he did not accept any offer under different excuses. Tkachuk was managing the repair and technical department and he liked his position. He could do any kind of work himself, and he could make technical decisions. He fulfilled all the task of the headquartes thoroughly, he also helped a lot to enterprises and collective farms when they needed their machines to be repaired. Zhora was well known and respected in many districts of Estonia.

After the parents' death Zhora started to think of marriage seriously. He didn't wage a secluded life. During the leisure time he could have really a good relaxation. He had a lot of girlfriends of different ages and religious denominations. He was a tall and well-built, dark-haired young man from Odessa, he had a Greek-like sideview, and he was very popular among the female population. But Zhora had habbits of a resident of Odessa with many generations as a background. He managed to avoid all the nets set skillfully for him. He didn't have a relationship longer than two or three months. All the girls he dated accepted his offer and were in his bed as early as the second or the third date. Many colleagues envied him, some of them suspected him to be a shaman, that was capable of some special magic attraction gift. The main thing was that all the women he abandoned did not keep any hard feelings, they just wanted to find a way of staying at least one more night with him.

Most of all he liked Estonian girls. They were not spoiled, they didn't start planning the future at once, as Slavonian girls did, they started wondering in bed during the first intercourse, how she would look in the registar office during the marriage ceremony, if their first child would be a boy or a girl.

Once at the age of thirty three he was on a business trip in the City of Orekhovo-Zuevo near Moscow, the city of weavers, there were plenty of girls there, each of them was a beauty. Once Zhora got accidentally acquainted with Anya, a beautiful brunette with coal black eyes. He was returning home from the store and the bag was very heavy, she almost dragged it. He asked her to tell him the way to the long-distance public telephone office. She described the route in a quiet soft voice. Zhora thanked her with a smile and went away, but something made him look back. He saw her crossing the street with the heavy bag that made her bend with the weight. He caught up with her and took the bag out of her hands without saying a word. He saw her to her home.

Anya had just had her eighteenth birthday, she lived with her mother, Rayisa Alexandrovna, who had worked at one of the weaving mills as a weaver, and by that time she was retired. She was a nice woman with hospitable manners. She somehow resembled his own mother to Zhora. He found himself in the atmosphere of home comfort, genuine simplisity and sincerity. Zhora stayed in the city on a business trip for one more month. He met Anya every day, he even stayed for the night at her home. They kissed, hugged each other, they even slept in one another's arms, but Zhora had never thought of taking advantage of her, though, of course, his body wanted her, as she was a well-built girl, and just one touch drove him mad. The reason was that he fell in love with her, and he couldn't even imagine that he could hurt her with a careless word, not even a gesture.

Once she told him: - I am yours. If you want, you can do anything to me. I love you.

- No, my dear Annushka, let everything go in a regular way. Our first night will be after the wedding, let it be really the first.

In a month they got married. For the garrizon of the subdivision his wedding was like a thunderstorm. The headquarters of the subdivision by that time was located at the district centre of Rakvere, where Zhora got a one-bedroom apartment in the military camp. Everyone wondered how this plain Russian girl managed to carry away such a resident of Odessa, like Zhora.

Their married life started. Zhora couldn't imagine that they could be as happy as that. Anya enrolled in Tartu University, famous all over the world, at the faculty of journalism, she chose the correspondence form of education. She appeared to be a very talented student. In a year she spoke fluently and wrote in Estonian. In two years Estonians thought she was one of them. Anya appeared to be not only talented in sciences, she also was a very good wife. Their apartment turned to be a cosy, nice, modern home due to her effort, and she called it "our house". Everyone was surprised to see that this plain girl from Orekhovo-Zuevo had decorating skills and what was the source of this talent. She was just talented by nature. She was not at all lazy, she read a lot, she was very observant.

Everyone wondered seeing the changes that took place in Zhora's personality, who used to be an unsurpassed philanderer. He suddenly became respectable, he didn't think of adultery, he even didn't notice other women. They lived for each other, they loved each other and made each other happy. In bed they were passionate lovers. Every movement seemed to be fresh and exciting. They didn't tell that to anyone, they were happy being together, in their everyday problems and chores.

Years passed, their love was as strong, no hardships and difficulties couldn't change their attitude to each other. They had two kids. Anya's mother moved to their place, to Rakvere. Anya worked as an economist in one of the co-operative enterprises in the city. Zhora was thinking of retirement, especially after the USSR had split. Estonia declared itself an independent country.

The time was hard. The subdivision changed its locatiion for Leningrad region, Russia. It was necessary to leave. It didn't take Zhora long to make a decision. He came home and said:

- We are staying. I have been here all my life. We won't be losers here. Am I supposed to move to Odessa? Who is waiting for me there? The graves of my ancestors. Nothing else. Nobody misses us there.

Rayisa Alexandrovna tried to object: - Georgiy, let's move to Russia, to our home country, we all are Slavonian people. What are we going to do here? Look, what is going on outside. Every now and then you can here the words "Russian swines, go home" or "Enough, occupants, get out of here".

Zhora looked at her attentively,

- Dear Rayisa Alexandrovna, who is waiting for us in Russia? Is anyone waiting for us in Orekhovo-Zuevo?

- But my dear, they say, the spirit of the homeland is sweet and pleasant. The native land, familiar faces, Russian speech...

Zhora interrupted her: - Drunken faces, laziness, thefts. That's what I see when I come to Russia and to the Ukraine. No, we are not moving. We are staying here, we'll wait and see.

The family did not object. They stayed. Zhora retired from the army and started his own business. His Estonian friends helped him. They helped him to get a loan on preferential conditions and started a small conveyer of meat development at the meat packing factory. He, so to say, expanded his business and he owned already several conveyers that produced sausages and semi-processed meat products. Zhora bought equipment in Germany and opened a brewery in Tallinn. Besides, he equipped five beer bars in the capital city. All his profits he put into his business development and expansion. He spent much time with the family too. Anya by that time was employed by him. He was the owner of the concern, and she was a chief accountant there. The constructed a beautiful house at the shore of the Gulf of Finland, at a resort place called Vyzu, it was forty minutes drive from Rakvere.

They no longer lived in the military campus, they bought a luxurious two-storeyed townhouse in the centre of Rakvere. In general Estonians accepted Zhora and his family, as they spoke the Estonian language fluently and waged a decent way of life. The children had already finished school and were studying in Tartu University. The son was going to become a lawyer. The daughter took up after her mother – she was studying at the economic faculty.

The wife's mother, Rayisa Alexandrovna, was suffering all the years, she longed to return to her homeland, there was nothing dear to her in Estonia.

- Devil! I want to here the Russian speech so much, just speech with no accent, I miss it so much, I even miss the Russian dirty swearing. – She was full of indignation inside.

At last, she told to Anya and Zhora:

- Look here, my dear children. The grandchildren are grown up, they live in Tartu. You are independent. As far as I am concerned, I want to go to my homeland. Don't try to dissuade me. I know that the life is hard in Russia now, but senior people enjoy respect there. They get certain benefits. In Russia people have always been close to each other, like relatives. Anyone is ready to help any minute. I am leaving, and you don't dissuade me. I would like to live at my homeland and to die not in the foreign country.

And she did leave for Russia, it was in 1999. But a year hardly passed when Rayisa Alezandrovna understood that she had made a great mistake. Her dream was to stay at her homeland and to feel its spirit. Not only the spirit that she wanted to feel. She also wanted to experience the brotherhood of the nation. The severe reality of the Russian mess ruined all her dreams in a moment. The main rule in the society was disclosed by the abbreviation «oow», which meant «one to one is a wolf». In spite of her weak resistance, and there was some, Zhora took Anya's mother back to their place in Estonia.

All these reminscences were refreshed in the memory of Georgiy Ivanovich Tkachuk, who was on board the plane as a member of the delegation of businessmen, on his way to his native City of Odessa, the city of his childhood and youth. He was going to the Ukraine which had become independent.

The plane was descending from the see side. Zhora peered into the opening, but the clouds were very low, and he failed to see anything from the height. Of course, the heart was aching. It was his native land, his native city, the city of his childhood and youth. It was the city where his traits of character were formed, it was the city where at the Second Christian cemetery there were the remnants of his parents.

Georgiy Ivanovich planned not only to take part in the official ceremonies and meetings of the high-level delegation. He also intended to visit the grave of his parents and just to walk around the city, he had been absent for five years already from that place. He was too busy. Besides, he wanted to contact his former military service friend, Vasyl Vasylich Pekar, who after many years of hard service was assigned to Odessa. By the time he was already in the rank of a General.

Odessa met him with chilly autumn weather, though it was not raining. But it seemed to had been raining for at least a week before his arrival. On their way to the hotel Zhora felt ashamed because the Estonian members of the delegation saw the untidy streets of Odessa. When compared with neat and clean streets, parks and squares of Tallin, Odessa looked like a garbage place. There was some exceptions, such as small areas like Primorskiy Boulevard, where they were accomodated at the hotel «Londonskaia». But when Zhora looked out of his window into the yard, he understood that not everything was OK there either.

He had a free night and he tried to contact the General Pekar over the phone. The latter appeared to be available, to Zhora's delight.

- Hello, Vasyl Vasylich. Do you recognize me?

- Hello. I am sorry. I feel something familiar in the voice, but I don't recognize you.

Zhora couldn't help laughing.

- I will not play puzzles with you any longer, it's me, a retired Deputy Colonel Tkachuk, Georgiy Ivanovich.

- Zhora, is that you? – He heard Pekar's delighted voice. – Where are you?

- I am here, in Odessa, I have just arrived. Have you heard about the visit of the Estonian President Rьъtel to Odessa? I am a member of the delegation that has arrived.

- Where do you stay? I am coming to your place, my dear, so many years have passed.

- I am in «Londonskaia». I hope you know where it is. My room is two hundred and one. OK, Vasylich, I am waiting for you. – Zhora hang up. Then he called to the restaurant and placed an order to be delivered to the room. After that he made several more calls to his childhood friends and arranged a meeting with them in a day at the cemetery.

Exactly in half an hour Pekar Vasyl Vasylich was entering his room. He was of a medium height, skinny, nice-looking General.

Hello, Zhora!

- Hello, dear General! – They hugged and kissed each other . – Let me have a look at you in the General uniform. – Zhora pushed Pekar aside and gave an attentive look from top to toe.

- You look really cool, as we say in Odessa. You have a more respectable look than you used to have when you were a deputy colonel.

- And you, Zhora, also look very well. You don't change at all. Some get older, become decrepit and bold, have big bellies, but you are in your best shape. How can you manage that?

You know why, if you haven't forgotten.

Vasyl Vasylich burst out laughing: "I do remember: Healthy way of living, a young wife and ecologically clean spirit of Estonia preserve the ex-resident of Odessa Zhorka in his perfect shape." – He cited the famous Zhorka's expression.

Both burst out laughing, both were enjoying the meeting. The memories came up in their minds quite unexpectedly.

- Let's drink a glass of cognac to our meeting, Vasyl Vasylich. – We are still great friends, ours is old, real, officers' friendship. – Zhora said, filling the glasses with the cognac.

They tasted the drink and burst out laughing again. This is a kind of Estonian way, I am not used to it. – Vasyl Vasylich said. – We don't taste a drink here, we are supposed to drink everything at once. They say, if you don't drink the whole glass, you are either sick or a scoundrel.

He stopped laughing and said sadly: - To tell the truth, Zhora, of all my memories the memory of my service in Estonia is the most pleasant. The positive spirit of the nature and the people, especially of the people, their neatness and decency, the communication culture make the difference. We lack all this here. Here, on the contrary...

He changed the subject: - I am not going to tell you all the sad things. Let's go to my place. Galya is expecting us and she is cooking the dinner. I live nearby, at Bazarnaya.

- At Bazarnaya? Oh, yes, I remember the street. During the Soviet rule it was Kirova Street, as far as I know.

Exactly. Are you coming?

Sure.

In a few minutes they were driving in the General's car to his place.

On their way Pekar told briefly about his hardships during the latest ten years. First he served in the Russian Army, before he managed to get a transfer to the native Ukraine. He had been in the Ukrainian Army for seven years already.

The General resided on the second floor of a four-storeyd building, the street was quiet, so was the area around the building. Zhora was astonished at the sight of messy front sides of the building with peeling paint. There was garbage in the streets, the back of the building was also unclean. Their was a strong smell of urine at the staircase on the ground floor. It was obvious, that the code lock at the entrance door did not prevent the tramps from coming inside. Zhora, being a tactful person, did not say a word. At the entrance of the apartment they were met by the hostess, Zhora presented a large bunch of roses to her. He had bought the roses on their way to the place at a flower market.

Hello, dear Galochka. – He hugged her and kissed.

In a while, having briefly exchanged opinions, as it always happens when old friends meet, they called to Estonia to Anya. The latter was very glad to know that Zhora met their old friend who had served in the army with her husband. Later they sat to table. They drank to their meeting, to friendship, to their children, to Zhora's late parents.

- So, how are you going there? It's just horrible what we hear in the news. They keep reporting about the cases of persecution of Russian speaking people in Baltic republics. – Galya asked.

Zhora grinned: - First of all, my family is not Russian speaking, it is multi-language. All of us are fluent in Russian, Estonian and English. If you want I can tell you about the life non-Estonians, so-called Russian-speaking people, live in Estonia. I will tell you everything as it is, with no exaggeration, and I will also tell you my opinion.

So, I will start with the description of residential and property management issues. I have approached your place. Garbage, walls with peeled paint, ugly buildings, broken roads, broken sidewalks, messy backyards, staircases with urine smell – that's what I found here. Is it the fault of the authorities? Sure it is. But it is also the fault of the people who are accustomed to live in the pigsty. I have a video with me. On this tape you can see the modern life in Rakvere, Tallinn and on the sea shore. Let's watch it a little bit later. You can compare. There is nothing in common. One of my colleagues in brewery business retired and is currently employed by a superintendant in Tallinn. The building is old. The tenants are people with rather low income, just ordinary residents of Tallinn. But the front is renovated, the entrances and the staircases are also renovated, the roof is covered with beautiful tiles. The building has its own Internet site, its own bank account. Payments for rent, parking and other services are processed over cell phones. I am not mentioning heat, gas, electricity, cold and hot water supply. What do you have? It is a cold autumn outside. You have to heat the apartment with electric heaters. There hasn't been hot water in the tap since early spring. Galya says they often cut off electric power in winter. Can one live such a life? You tell me it has always been like this. Everyone got accustomed to the difficulties. All got used to this brutal way of live.

Zhora made a pause, thought for a while, and then started to talk again.

- Look here, I have just remembered my childhood and youth in Odessa. If there had been anything like this at that time, the Odessa residents would have strongly lobbied the authorities. Nowadays it is quite different, as I can see. You can praise your Estonia to the skies, but we are used to a different life style. We can go to visit other people without any invitation. If I have run out of salt, pepper, onions or potatoes I can go to the neighbor and borrow some. You don't do this there. It's boring. No one to communicate with. – Galya objected.

Zhora laughed out loud: - You are kidding! To tell the truth, there is some longing for the motherland in my heart. There are moments when I feel anxious inside. I can't just come whenever I want to visit the cemetery, my parents' graves. I need to apply for a visa, to cross the border, to pass other procedures. What else do you have?

How can you fail to understand that you are not meant to live and successfully overcome all the household problems. Today the electricity is cut off. Tomorrow there is no running water. The day after tomorrow the heat and gas will be cut off. The list can be continued endlessly. I am not mentioning the ugly messy staircases and yards, destroyed streets.

Some people say that the Baltic republics bribed Russian speaking people, that's why they were not willing to move away. It is so. But they didn't give us tasty fresh sausages of all kinds as a bribe. They attracted us with smart way of arranging the life, with clean streets, yards and well equipped parks. We don't have any household management problems. You have so much dirt here. Not only you, it is the same in Russia. Calculate the quantity of dirt per a square meter. But the most dangerous is not the outside dirt, which can be cleaned up. The most dangerous is the dirt inside people that can't be removed. The relations between people are based on hypocricy, lies, fraud, it concerns both the authorities and the people. You do cheat each other and tell lies to each other constantly.

When I visit Odessa, I come to "Privoz" market. It is just horrible there. Dirty swearing, spoiled food, dirty salesmen. In Estonia fresh meat is the meat of a warm young pig on the counter. The customer just says what part of it he would like to buy. If the meat is not sold out the same day, the next day it is three times as cheap. Here the meat is being sold for weeks, it goes dark, but the price stays the same. We have just dropped in a store. All the food is packed in vacuum packages. Why so? We have only coffee beans packed like this in order to preserve the smell.

How you and those in Russia can't understand that we, Russian speaking people in Estonia, how we are called in mass media today, are not the same Russians and Ukrainians, that live in Russia and the Ukraine. We are a different nation. We have different household rules, we have different family life style, we have quite a different life. What is common between us and you is only the past and the language. You think we live differently. And you seem savages to us, sorry about that. Speak too loudly in public places, everywhere there is dirty swearing, you visit each other just because you need to chat with somebody, because you don't have anything else to do. You, Galya, have mentioned that you go to each other to borrow salt and matches. And the way you kiss when you meet somebody – it's a long kiss, and it's terrible. Have you ever tried to have a look at yourself from the outside?

During the recent years a new generation if Russian people have grown up, and they can't be pulled to their home country even with a rope. If you ask my children if they wanted to live permanently in Estonia, it will take them a while to give the answer. If they are asked about moving to Russia or to the Ukraine, to Odessa, they will answer negatively immediately.

My son had practical training at the University of Narva. He is telling with laughter about the home sickness of the residents of Narva. Once they feel home sick, they go across the bridge to Ivangorod, which is a Russian city, they see the reality there, compare the quality of life and in fifteen or twenty minutes they go back. No traces of homesickness any more.

Another example is prices for apartments and houses in Russia, the Ukraine, in Odessa in particular, that can't be compared to those in Estonia, Latvia and Lithuania. There is nothing to compare at all. You live in poverty, but your prices are astronomic. Have you ever think why your prices for food and consumer goods are so high, the quality and the service level being quite unsatisfactory?

Soon we will be accepted to European Union, then the admittance to different European countries will be free. You or Russian citizens have to suffer lots of humiliation in order to get a visitor visa.

Not everything is so smooth in our life either. There is homesickness as well. I do miss Odessa, it's my native country, I dream about it rather often. No doubt, we would like to go to the theatres to good plays, to musicals. We don't have such theatres, just guest actors perform in our city. But we have quiet and balanced life. Of course, there are cases of discrimination on national grounds, especially they were frequent on the first stage, that is at the beginning of nineties. Now the cases are seldom, but still there are some.

There is one more thing I'd like to tell you: there are no poor senior people in our country. The pension allowance is enough to pay for rent, for utilities and for food. Your senior persons live in poverty, they have only one opportunity, that is the cemetery. This is scaring. I watch your life at a distance and see that only officials live well, some businessmen too, maybe those, close to the authorities.

- Look here, Zhora, - Vasyl Vasylych interrupted Tkachuk. – I do understand all that. There is a saying that fish looks for deeper water, and a man looks for a better environment. The result is that the best place is the place where we are absent from.

- Let well alone – this is my answer. I will give my mother's-in-law example. You know her very well. In nineties she just insisted that she wanted to return home to Russia. There was no choice for us. She still had an apartment in the weaving mill dormitory. It could hardly be called an apartment, though. But is doesn't matter. She moved to Orekhovo-Zuevo as an emergency settler. She took only the necessary belongings with her, as she didn't want to have a complicated customs and immigration procedures. Rayisa Alexandrovna was happy, it was her home country, her friends, her childhood friends, not to say anything of her native speech with some dirty swearing.

- I don't need any help, I will have my pension here. – She said decidedly.

- I thought she can have a trial for a year, how to survive for a pension allowance. Then you will have to ask us to take her back. She was a participant of the Great Patriotic War, she was a participant of a partisan detachment as a girl. She was given in nineteen ninety upon arrival to Russia as much as six hundred rubles, that is about twenty dollars, and it was five times as less than she received in Estonia.

If in Estonia the money was enough for paying for rent and utilities, as well as for food, in Orekhovo-Zuevo everything, including utilities, was much more expensive. The same is here, at Bazarnaya street in Odessa. My mother-in-law called to us and asked what she was supposed to spend the money for. The staircases were dirty, with no light, the garbage stayed unremoved for a long time, no hot water, there were also much more inconveniences. You know all this. And she stopped paying. She told that she knew in Rakvere for what she was paying. The staircases were clean, the garbage bins washed with detengents, cleanness everywhere, the light is as bright as the daytime, there is always running water, gas, heat and so on. In Orekhovo-Zuevo, on the contrary, the gas heater didn't work and the technical support persons never showed up.

According to the Russian regulations, the emergency settlers were eligible for apartment renovation for free. But Rayisa Alexandrovna did never have such renovation. She thought the seniors were as respected in Russia as they used to be in the USSR, but she couldn't get an appointment with a doctor before the gave a bribe.

To make the long story short, she watched the life in Orekhovo-Zuevo and then called to me: "Georgiy, do you know who is ruling in Russia? There is violation of the law everywhere here. I tried to get an appointment with the municipal officials as a participant of the war, but I was refused."

I answered her that scoundrels were ruling in Russia, who were originally from the common people, all of them were born is a regular way. She got offended, but she didn't give up. She went to Moscow to the Governor Boris Gromov. You know him, he is a former military man, a General, he withdrew the troops from Afghanistan. She wanted to share her thoughts with him about the much better life of Russian seniors in the Baltik countries, when compared with the life in Russia. She also intended to tell about illegal actions in Orekhovo-Zuevo. It turned out, however, that nobody cared for her problems there. In Estonia she could easily go to the office of the Mayor of the City of Rakvere, she could have an appointment with the Ambassador of Russia in Estonia, or with a Minister. In Moscow she coulnd't even get registered in a line for the Governor. Gromov doesn't care for people's needs, he plays his own game.

Rayisa Alexandrovna made her own conclusions that the spirit of the homelands was poisonous and stinking and in a year of hardships she returned back to our place. Now she is remembering her trip to her native land as a nightmare, which she never wants to experience again.

Having listented to Zhora's story, everyone was silent for a while. Galya was the first to break the silence. She signed:

- You are right, Zhora, I still remember my young years in Estonia as the best of my life. It was not due to our youth. It did matter, of course. We lived in a civilized society, even it was still a Soviet Baltic republic.

To my mind, no matter what kind of political system is settled, the inner culture, decency, honesty and neatness will stay.

- And hard work, Galochka, don't forget about that. Estonian people are very hard working, not like Russians and Ukrainians. – Zhora said, smiling.

- That's right. We came to the Ukraine, to our native land after having lived in military campuses outside the Ukraine, but the motherland accepted us as outsiders. My husband could pronounce only the word "lard" in Ukrainian, for this he was almost dismissed from the army. Now the situation is better. Now he speaks like the President, mixing Russian and Ukrainian languages. We are still alive. We received an apartment. How could we get it? You know, that Vasyl Vasylich is a bootlicker, it's his nature. It is me who is the real resident of Odessa. He flatters before the management. "Would you like this? Or that?" He flatters them day and nignt. Isn't it disgusting, Zhora? He doesn't lick his ass, all the rest he does. But gets nothing for it. I am telling they like dollars – he doesn't know where to get them. I am telling him to steal. Everyone around steals. He says he can't and won't steal. The Commander and the manager of the headquaters are construction great cottages and the seashore, even businessmen envy them. My fool can't even buy a small bungalo at the sea shore. His salary is less than two hundren dollars. Tell me, Zhora, if one can survive in Odessa for two hundred dollars? He is just an asshole general, sorry about that. He has his pants with the stripes on the sides, but there is nothing in the pants, nor in the pockets. No accounts, no cash, no pleasure.

Zhora burst out laughing: - Oh, you are so eloquent! You temper never changes, Galyna, it is regular Odessa temper.

He looked at the General. Vasyl Vasylich smiled silently, looking at his excited wife, he was accustomed to it during the latest twenty five years and of life together, and he paid no attention to her.

She will talk her mind and get quiet. – He thought.

Why don't you retire from the Army? – Zhora asked.

He grinned: - What will happen next to my retirement? I am a General now, a Deputy Commander. I am not a civil senior, there are dozens of thousands of them in Odessa. Where am I to go? Am I going to be a security officer? Or a salesperson at a flea market? I can't do anything for living.

Galya said: - That is correct. You didn't get any other occupation during your service, that licking somebody's ass.

- You got completely spoiled at you "Seventh kilometer". You swear like a flea market saleswoman. – Vasyl Vasylich got mad.

She burst out laughing: - I am a flea market saleswoman, I do sell on the flea market. I am not alone with a University education there, there are also people with a Master degree. It's OK for them too to drink one hundren grams of vodka when it is very cold outside, they also use dirty words, and your ears can't stand that language, as you are too intelligent and soft-hearted. You don't have anything hard about you – neither your character, nor something else.

Zhora changed the subject, and they started to exchange their memories about Estonia. They also watched the video about Estonia. He told them about the purpose of his visit, about its duration and they settled that they were going to see each other again before he leaves. Late at night after the tea Zhora thanked the Pekar family for their hospitality. He decided to walk to the hotel in Odessa streets. Vasyl Vasylich offered a drive to him, he wanted to call his car, but Zhora insisted that he would walk.

- I want to walk in my native city at night, I want to breath Odessa air in.

He walked till Pushkinskaya street swearing, the pavement was all broken, he street was not lighted at all. Pushkinskaya street was also dark, but the pavement was not broken, it was mostly tiled. Zhora sighed with relief, though he was not at all a coward, he didn't feel safe in dark Odessa at night.

He thought about drug addicted persons who could meet him and strip him and hurt him.

He gradually calmed down and he went slowly towards Primorskiy Boulevard. He thought about the life of his former fellow-officers who were now serving in Odessa. Vasyl Vasylich was very well known to Zhora. He cringed to the supervisors, he flattered, he showed his readiness to serve them day and night. He also played the role of a caring and smart manager to the subordinate. All was hypocrisy and nothing else. He lived his life in hypocrisy and donations. He got a piece of meat at one place, some vegetables at another and thus he supported his family. He also extracted some means for renovation of his apartment from the subordinate detachements. Now that he, the General, got two hundred dollars, he just had to steal. That was the reality. In Estonia the pigsty like this can hardly be found. Nowhere. In Estonia at night every street and every house are lighted. Here it is different. The Odessa residents are doomed for surviving in the conditions with no elementary conveniences.

Zhora was shocked by a story about his collegue, also a General, who received a new apartment in a new building in Arcadiya area on the tenth floor. The building had already been inhabited, but there was no electricity, no cable, no elevators working. There was no running water, the tenants were taking water from the next building in buckets. There was no gas connected.

Zhora shrugged his shoulders at the thought of the life like this.

- No, I will never return here, even if I am promised greatest benefits. Now I do realize why the flood of emigrants is no less, it has even become greater.

Having returned to the hotel in such moods, Zhora fell asleep at once.

The next day was full of appointments. As a member of the delegation he visited the Odessa Port and several industrial enterprises. They met Odessa businessmen at the Governor's office. Several mutually beneficial contracts were signed. So, the business part of the visit was a success.

On the third day of the visit, before the flight, Zhora visited the graves of his parents. His childhood friends also came there. They arranged the graves, drank to the memory of Zhora's parents. The graves were not neat, it struck Zhora, but he didn't say anything. He have one hundred dollars to one of the cemetery's workers and asked to take care of the graves at least once a month.

On board the plane, looking at Odessa from the opening, Zhora thought:

- Oh, no, my native land, you are neither cosy, nor friendly. Nothing attractive here. Rayisa Alexandrovna was right. The spirit of the motherland is no longer pleasant. It is the spirit of devastated cities and villages, it is the atmosphere of stagnation in relations between people.

The Disguised

Once this word was applied to people who changed their European names and got Slavonic ones in their birth certificates. This was a method of easier enrolling to educational institutions during the Soviet rule. It was also good for employment purposes and it helped to make a good career

Many contemporary variety stage stars, leaders in economics, political leaders, not to mention such a minor sphere as science, started their career with the last names which had the ending "man" or "vas", and now they have the endings "v", "va" and "ok". Nowadays they would like to switch back to their original names, but it could negatively influence their careers. They used to call themselves leaders, now they call themselves elite strata of the society.

On the other side, for sick people, European names, like European type renovation, have quite a different meaning in Odessa, when compared to other parts of our former vast territory of our Motherland. It was not at all related to Europe.

Those good Soviet times passed away long ago. But there still watchful "people's avengers", who, like ban dogs, are still search and eavesdrop if there is a disguised somewhere. There came great changes, but the main thing is there came a real opportunity to move overseas without being disguised. Old residents of Odessa took the opportunity at once, they didn't want to wait till they are eliminated completely by a "mister-know-all", who were multiple in the city. They were heads of different organizations, parties, foundations and other offices. It was the result of long-term process of drainaging the sewers in the sea of life, while the main collector is out of order, and it means a long-term people's brain problem.

Those "misters-know-all" during their leisure time try to master the art of diving, but they fail, in spite of experienced trainers and a load hanged up. It turns out that their heads are in water and the body is outside and would not go down, no matter how hard they try, as the rule "shit never drowns" can't be changed.

The fashion changes, and at the end of the twentieth century both so-to-say Russian and Ukrainian persons started to change the "ov" and "ok" endings to European first and last names. But it was much more expensive and painful to become a Fridman or some other "man" or "Izya".

But with all the changes of "flora" and "fauna" in Odessa, that took place at the time when two ages met, there were a great deal of great patriots of the Soviet country that were not going to change the names due to technical reasons. They changed the fashion of their shirt and the shoulder strap. During the Soviet times in Odessa there were many different party members with the post-revolutionary experience, many educators and scientific workers who had the presentation of their thesis for Master or Doctor of Science degrees on the topic of Marxism and Leninism not in the pub "At Two Karls", but in the Higher Party School. After August, 1991 they didn't know what step to take. And they, loyal members of the Communist Party, grown up not at Peresyp and Moldavanka, not even in Lenposyolok, but in rural komsomol and party centers, boldly took up three ways, or routes, as Lenin had taught them.

Some of them changed neither their last and first names, nor their nicknames and party denomination, party member book with the registration enclosure, their orders and honorable badges and all other stuff of the epoch of socialism. They just put the stuff into boxes and put them away in case they would need them some time in the future and rushed into the authorities structures, grabbing the property, stocks and cash, no matter what the origin of the money was: party, economic money or illegal cash, it didn't matter for them, they main thing was the money itself.

Afterwards they became governors, mayors, people's deputies. Some of them became bank owners, some owned plants and factories. The owner! It didn't matter that they had been members of the communist party for a long time. When they apply for a position in the government, as well as to a position of a judge in the court, they make the period of their employment before 1991 very modest: they were born, had some education, worked somewhere. But after 1991 they give a very thorough description of their biography, including cases of feeding a senior or a homeless child and taking care of them.

It turns out that during thirty, fifty or even sixty years of their life during the Soviet rule they lived a very modest life. On the contrary, during the latest ten years the "servants of the people" make heroic deeds every day. They improve social life of the people, they help to overcome the difficulties of the bad heritage, both economical and social, that was got from the Soviet period of life. It should be mentioned, although, that they didn't fail to fill their own pockets and improve their own lives.

Could it be different? No, it couldn't. They transformed from losers to well-to-do bosses who supervised everything that was going on in the city. But they didn't quite understand themselves what process they were supervising.

They supervised weddings and births, beaches and schools openings, organization of concerts and presentations for the title of "Mr." or "Miss". The only thing they seem not to supervise is conception and related matters.

So, the category of the "great patriots", so to say, acquired all the main positions and opportunities, starting with presidential and government departments levels and extending to all the ruling positions in villages, settlements and small towns. They know how, they know whom, they know what for. If they don't know the above-mentioned items, they just know for whom, and they are never mistaken. It's all for themselves, actually...

They don't care a shit for us, nor do we for them. They used to say that they were communists, now they say that they are pragmatics. Good for them, they are not gays, thanks God. And thanks to them they were not involving us anywhere, as they used to, otherwise they could take us to a dead end... God save us!

The first category of the great patriots disguised very quietly, without any noise and pomp. They didn't swear the past. They were thankful deep inside to the policy of Lenin, Stalin and all the rest, because due to this policy they in 1991 at the right place and at the right time turned out to be at the ruling positions, and not in a shaft, not in the field, not in any other not attractive place. As a result, they used to be party leaders with personal benefits and summer cottages, and they became elite of a different kind with personal accounts. As far as the benefits are concerned, they ensured fantastic benefits for themselves, they ensured their lives for the period of more than one hundred years after their deaths. So, go ahead, guys!

Another part of the "great patriots" of the Soviet country taught Marxism and Leninism in the terms of the course of "Brief History..." alongside with the contents of the three-volume edition of "The Minor Land", "The Revival" and "The Virgin Lands" in Universities, Institutes, military and police schools. There in their enthusiastic lectures they furiously stigmatized everything self-made and of national origin. They were internationalists, real successors of those who had established the cast-iron discipline in the forties of the last century in Western regions. They were Marxists of a minor significance when compared with those of the first category, due to their height, size, and mainly due to the weight of the gray cells in their brains, if any at all. First this group of loyal "communists" praised real and false accomplishments and achievements of bolshevism. After August, 1991 the same loyal subjects with the same energy and with inimitable spite started to throw mud at Marxism and Leninism, together with the Soviet regime and the life in general.

They became members of RUH (organization which worked for separation of the Ukraine from Russia and for creation of an independent state) and other parties of different trend, which at that time were appearing as quickly as mushrooms after the rain. In Odessa they used to say: "Abram, you always get into something: either a party, or some shit". This category of newly disguised always join some party, always having something else under the double bottom. And that "something" was in great quantities. At the beginning of the nineties they used ideologists of reforms and independence in their own purposes. Those disguised with the habits of mongrels threw mud on the stuff, which during the Soviet rule was the source of their own living. At that time they turned for a certain period of time into leaders and connoisseurs. And nowadays they are nothing more that used condoms, good for nothing. But they contributed to persuading some people that civilization had started not in Atlantic continent, but from Zaporozhye Sech, that Odessa was built by Cossacks from the Black Sea region, and that it was the monument for their horse that is in Kirov Park, twenty four hours being guarded by a double police detachment, lest it should run away to Tavriysk steppe or lest gypsies take it away to Moldova.

In this group of the disguised there are individuals much more impudent, than Ostap Bender, who had pronounced the phrase well known all over the world: "Maybe I need to give you the key to the apartment where I keep the money?"

Those individuals Quit CPSU in 1991 and managed to create the CPU and become its leaders.

Dear Sirs, CPU is not a bullpen and not a GPU (special security service, later called KGB), it is the Communist Party of the Ukraine. Its leaders have never studied the books by Lenin, to say nothing of Marx and Engels, don't know their theory, they just use quotations from the newspaper "Pravda" issued as late as in nineteen eighty five for their successful struggle for social benefits for the people. They never forget about their own benefits either. All is for themselves! That's the main thing. It is Lenin's style. Lenin also led the Worker's Socialist Democratic Party of Russia, being in Switzerland, even from a hut in Razliv. The first Secretary of Odessa Regional Committee of the party got not bad at all "hut" with a few hundreds square meters in the most respectable area of Kyiv. He got that apartment for putting an indecipherable signature when distributing budget funds into other officials' pockets. He successfully leads the party in Kyiv, he sends "letters from far away", to the party newspaper, which has the name "The Truth of" and publishes lies. The lies published are of such cheap quality.

So, many of the leaders and connoisseurs at the beginning of the twenty first century moved to Kyiv, where they work as Ukrainians and constantly apply for getting Soviet awards, such as the medal "For Liberation of Odessa".

At last, there is the third category of the disguised. This kind of folk got with the help of Marxism and Leninism Ph. D. degrees and positions of professors, deans, senior educators, in the Higher Party School, in Universities and Institutes. To the same category there belong those, who joined them in 1991. Those were officers of the Communist Party of the medium level of importance, who were at that time jobless. They were not able to do anything, but wash somebody's brains.

It was this very category that was very well and exactly described in one of historic document in Odessa:

"The assistant professor Shkalik instead of criticizing imperialism and bourgeois Ukrainian nationalism, he tells students about Moscow Bolsheviks' outrage upon The Mother Ukraine with the same enthusiasm as other former Soviet and Party officers. His fellow-worker Vist, who had taught Historical Materialism, started lecturing on basics of management. He had a very vague idea of this subject, as well as other than Scientific Communism. Besides, these educators swear inside the newly introduced borders, which are on their way when they smuggle icons and pictures, as they used to do before, now this business has so many difficulties due to these new circumstances."

Before August, 1991 in such a quiet, cozy and beautiful place in Odessa, like Arkadia, there was one of the most respectable and highly valued educational institutions of that time – Higher Party School, which trained and upgraded the communist party officials. That was not just Lomonosov University or Plekhanov Institute, not just Mikki Mouse Odessa State University named after Mechanical, not even part-time University of Marxism and Leninism, it was something much more significant.

There was also The Academy of Public Sciences, but it trained higher officers for the General Committee of the Party, for the Central Committee and its branches.

At the beginning of the nineties due to the effort of the chief ideologist there was a reorganization of the Higher Party School, which was renamed into Ukrainian Academy of Management under the supervision of the President of the Ukraine. Many people wonder why it was Ukrainian Academy under the supervision of the President of the Ukraine, if there could be a Ukrainian Academy under the supervision of the President of Russia or Honduras. Or maybe there is a Russian of Honduras Academies under the supervision of the President of the Ukraine? It's like saying salt is salty. But it sounds good! It doesn't sound like Higher Party School under the supervision of the CPSU.

Petro Ivanovich Gnilodushka taught Marxist and Leninist philosophy in Odessa Artillery School during the old, good Soviet period, and he was very proud of it. Everyone remembers the importance of artillerymen whom Stalin himself gave orders to, whom the Motherland called for heroic deeds, who were as numerous as hundreds of thousands detachments and of whom they sang songs.

Oops... In 1991 Petro Ivanovich is already jobless, with a military school and part-time University of Marxism and Leninism as a background. He also had a three-volume edition of Lenin's books, a large family consisting of a wife, four kids, a mother-in-law and a father-in-law. Moreover, he was a lazy-bones, he liked to sleep a lot and eat a lot.

His own former party fellow, also a deputy colonel, like himself, whose name was Stepan Zakopailo, who also taught Marxism and Leninism, borrowed some cash with no interest from his father-in-law. His father-in-law was employed as a meat cutter in the Food Store #1. He bought a small gas station and diluted gas with urine and other stuff. Thus he made money. When he stopped the business, he used the money he had made for obtaining the position of the manager of all the parking lots in Odessa. Now he is already a big boss.

Petro Ivanovich couldn't do the same things due to two reasons. First, his father-in-law was not a meat cutter, not even a farmer who could produce greens with the pictures of US presidents. He didn't have such amounts of money, he didn't earn dollars, to say nothing if rubles.

The second reason was that he was used to stay in his office and wait for a student to bring him a present for a credit or for passing an exam, at least a pot of cream.

But still his father-in-law did help him. The former worked as an instructor of the regional party committee. It was the very committee, where the future leader of the Higher Party School worked. Then he made his career and became one of the first assistants of their President, the leader of the Ukrainian Academy of State Management at the Central Committee, oh, no, sorry, at the office of the President of the Ukraine.

After some bureaucracy procedures Petro Ivanovich got the position of the junior scientific worker at the faculty of state management and legislation. He was anxious about the work he was going to perform, as he didn't have any idea of the management issues, nor he had any idea of legislation, except one thing: "The right person is the one who has more rights".

But in a short while he got accustomed and realized that there was nothing difficult there. He spoke his native language, he threw mud at everything he used to praise not so long ago. This was enough to get a candidate of science degree. As quickly as in a year Petro Ivanovich took part in writing the greatest book on the history of The Mother Ukraine, about its leading part in crushing Napoleon and Hitler, not to say anything about Swedes at Poltava, about the ruinous influence of Russian population on the genetic resources of the nation; also about stealing of Ukrainian oil and gas condensate alongside with the gold reserve from oil, gas, gold and other cables by tyrants from the Kremlin.

The Head of the Academy constantly reminded at the meetings of the academic council the following:

- The main thing was never stolen from us – this main thing is the human resources,

it's the elite and the leaders, who have always constituted our welfare. In no country in the world there is no such politicians, businessmen and outstanding women, not to mention stars of the show business and beauty competitions winners, also winners of other competitions, which involve nudity, scientists included to this group too. As far as stealing is concerned, it is Russians who have been stealing for ages, here it is different, here we call it corruption, like in all the civilized world. One has always his own stuff in his pocket. Here they don't steal, they are just corrupted, or, putting this in plain words, they put somebody's stuff into his own pocket. One never gives his own stuff and shows it to nobody, except maybe in bed, and not to everyone.

While listening these smart speeches from the great heralds of reforms and something else, Petro Ivanovich thought that he needed to learn more of the methods of pronouncing such smart speeches, so that he were also able to present smartly such nasty words as stealing and bribe-taking.

- And I really don't need this. Officers from district administration bring from time to time bribes for marking the presence at the lessons, for credits, for term papers and for other services, and they bring more than some sour cream in a pot, as it was with the students of the military school and his parents. Now they bring green colored bills, which we call dollars, they don't bring much, but they do it regularly. And that's good, thanks to the president with its Academies and strategies. The main thing is that they don't change their policy, so that he could get accustomed to it.

In the Academy of Management, as they call it now, and at the Higher Party School, as they used to call it, there are students, young and inexperienced, who are aware of the cash available from the parents, who wanted their child to be trained for the position of a mayor, a governor, a president, or at least a people's deputy.

Besides the younger generation in this exclusive educational institution there study people of older age, that is stiff-minded officers from district, municipal, regional and even state levels. Most of them have education, which can't be applied to their practical activity. But here, amidst the exclusive Ukrainian philosophers they obtain the volume of the necessary knowledge, such as state human resources policy, leaders and leadership, management of serfdom individuals, that is people, as well as psychology together with ergonomics. The main thing is that they learn how to scientifically prove the appropriateness, necessity and inevitability of taking bribes and of using budget funds in their own purposes under the motto: "Our business is right. It is getting greens and no obstacles on our way." It means that we have always taken bribes, we will take them; we have always taken budget money and put it into our pockets, and we always will. Don't try to be concerned, it will take away years of your life, and you'll be able to see a real life only if you become an officer in a state office.

The most important and crucial task set before all the professors of Marxism and Management was as follows: to make all the three types of the disguised look scientific, to give a civilized European looks to all the crooks in the authorities and the politics. They did manage to fulfill the task successfully by creating the book "Human resources, elite and leadership", where they called this kind of people elite, the word not common in Odessa, they called certain chieftains as leaders and they called stealing as corruption.

For all this they were awarded high titles and rewards, they were allowed to give everyone who wished the scientific titles of Bachelors of different sciences, as well as candidates of science and Ph. D. degrees – for a certain amount of bucks or euro. Thus, Petro Ivanovich Gnilodushka became at one and the same day Ph. D. in Law and a Professor. The Academy continues to train human resources. The lecturers are still the same disguised educators of Marxism and Leninism, with the rector as the leader, sometimes they are joined by disguised First Secretary of the Regional Party Committee, the First Secretary of the Regional Young Communist League Committee, some other secretaries... Watching all this you really come to a conclusion that the saying in Odessa "A brothel is not an institution, and a mess is a system". The main thing is that if you make the sign "Chastity" on a brothel, it won't change the essence of the main prostitute lady and her employees.

Shall We Send a Courier?

At the airport of Odessa Georgiy Pavlovskiy was met by his University friends Yasha Naumov and Kostya Chebrikov. He hadn't met them for four years, since the time he had to leave for Moscow. It happened at the period of political opposition in Odessa at the end of nineties.

Gosha, as his close friends called him, was one of the most talented correspondents of the local television. He was responsible for the economic program, he used a plain language understandable by everyone, he analyzed figures and facts, and he also gave his direct business-like suggestions. Few people knew that Gosha was an economist by his first education. He had graduated with honors from the Institute of People's Economy. In two years he graduated, again with honors, the literature faculty of the Odessa State University and devoted himself to journalism.

Being employed as a journalist at the television studio, he at the same time had many offers to take part or to develop himself a business plan for this or that company. Gosha had very many offers, and he had never experienced lack of money. But he did experience lack of time. He considered his economic part of work as a passion, or, a hobby, as they said at that time. In spite of his comparatively young age, he had already seen a lot in the Ukraine, in Russia and all over the world. He profoundly studied history, literature, there he tried to find roots of the problems, which people inhabiting one sixth of the planet can experience. He tried to explain the thoughts and actions of people. He knew Russian and Ukrainian languages very well, he easily communicated in English and German.

But he was just shocked and it grated on him when he heard conversation at official receptions between persons of high position who used modern Russian and Ukrainian slang, especially when it was used together with English jargon. The expressions like "people devour", "filter your speech", "let's go and have pleasure during the weekend", "let's lay down the table at the lawn" and so on. Once he heard such or similar expressions from a person, he immediately lost interest in him.

Four years ago Gosha had to leave Odessa as the team came to the rule which he didn't accept, as well as they didn't accept him. Gosha was immediately suggested to find some other environment for his creative activity. The time will show if he was right or wrong. The time will put everything in its place. But he was sure and said over TV more than once, that the ex-party official, who was for a long time a leader of the city, created absolutely nothing during the last twenty years. He said that at the new time he was not able to do any useful thing for the city either. He could do only spoil the things. And he provided arguments to his statements.

Since then four years had passed, and Gosha longed with all his heart and sole to come his native city. It was not that he didn't have money or time. He just still felt hurt in his heart because of those events, four years old. It was a dirty commotion, public struggle of two dishonest groups. He couldn't call them otherwise. In this struggle almost all the population of Odessa was involved. Two strange guest actors, as Gosha called them, who had nothing to do in Odessa, practically turned the city into Waterloo.

But thanks God, all was over. Remembering those days, Gosha felt upset not because one was the winner and the other was the loser. In any case Odessa and the inhabitants were losers. Then and nowadays he thought about Odessa and felt upset because in such a city, once a historic, cultural, industrial and trade center in the South of the State, there could not be found a decent candidate for the position of the mayor.

When in Moscow, where his acquaintances very quickly helped him to get a good position at Moscow TV studio, where he was responsible for the creative program "Business", Gosha was attentively following the events in Odessa. He regularly received local newspapers, sent to him by train, he had long talks over the phone with his friends. He was ashamed to notice how quickly the style of publications was changing, the contents of which no longer reflected the real events. The newspapers turned to be hypocritical and cynical praising of the "heroic deeds" of the current mayor.

That year in spring the next elections to the position of the mayor and the municipal council had already taken place. As before, there was no choice. Again there were to candidates to chose from, they were just exchanging roles: one was ex-mayor, the other was the current mayor. Those were calm elections. Odessa with its inhabitants started its routine life again, dull and petty, till the next election campaign.

So, Gosha decided to visit his native city at last. It was the anniversary of Odessa. The friends that came to meet him were in the bar in the waiting area of the airport. Yasha Naumov was a tall redheaded guy with a constant ironical smile on his face. After graduating from the faculty of journalist of Odessa State University, he worked in "Vecherka", as they called the newspaper "Odessa at Night". He was a good journalist, and a good career of a journalist was in store for him, but his sharp irony in words and actions were on the way of his career. His sharp way of wording stopped his career, but he didn't grudge. He worked as a regular journalist in the newspaper, he wrote satirical short stories and he was published in many satirical magazines. His stories were a success. His friends and acquaintances teased him because of his red hair, he was called a redhead during his student years. In nineties he got the nickname "floater" due to the privatization events that took place at that time. He had always been asked as a joke: "Can a Jew be red-headed?" Yasha had always answered: "He can, if he lives in Odessa".

Kostya Chebrikov was a complete opposite to Yasha. He was short, fat and bold, with a kind smile, he was softhearted and calm. His friends said of him with love:

"He is not good-looking, but he is strong in love!" They hinted at Kostya's great popularity among women. Almost every week he introduced a new gal to the public. Nobody could explain the secret of his popularity with women. Women, when asked, would smile meaningfully and say that that phenomenon couldn't be explained, it needed to be experienced.

Kostya put it in simple wording: "Friends, women need to be loved! In this case there are no hearts closed in front of you!"

He was a deep-rooted bachelor. Chebrikov also graduated from Odessa University, but the faculty of Economy. After graduating from the University he was employed as an officer at one and the same place, that was the Municipal Council. Ruling people changed, so did the ideas, but it turned out that talented economists were always in demand in the financial department of the Municipal Council. Kostya was appreciated not only as a professional economist, but also as a clerk who knew its own place and was not too eloquent – that was a very important characteristic in the contemporary life of officials in Odessa. Outside his working place he was free to talk on any topics except his work. His friends and acquaintances had stopped inquiring him about the situation in the mayor's office long ago. They didn't ask him about the outlook of economic development of Odessa either.

Kostya and Yasha lived in one and the same city, but they seldom met during the past years. Usually it happened when Yasha wanted to have a really good rest that was to have an entertainment with young girls, though it was not so easy. His wife worked as a reader in the same "Vecherka". But what really united Kostya and Yasha was their great friendly attachment to Gosha Pavlovskiy. They respected him as a friend, as a man, who was able to an action, who had his own point of view, and it was proven and well reasoned.

The envied Gosha in a friendly way, they envied his inner talent, his intelligence, and his attitude. They secretly wanted to look like him, but they failed due to the lack of strong will. At that moment at the airport they were anxiously waiting for Gosha's arrival.

On the eve he unexpectedly called to his friends and said that he was coming alone for three days. He wanted to breath in Odessa air, he wanted to enjoy Odessa specific life, wanted to see the celebration of the Day of the City, just to see Odessa with his own eyes. He missed the city he was born in, which had always been in his sole and heart. Yasha and Kostya planned every minute of the three days. The plan included a trip around Odessa, walks in the old historic part of Odessa, a visit to aqua park, the night club "Cosmo", which Pavlovskiy used to like. A private program was also created, that included a party in one of private hotels on the ninth station of the Great Fountain with the participation of young talented students of the faculty of journalism of Odessa State University. Of course, favorite fishing time on the Dnestr was also on the agenda.

But the central element of the program was Dasha Arabadzhi, Gosha's student love, a tall slim beautiful blonde with green eyes. She broke more that one male heart in Odessa. Her marriage to a Egyptian businessman was a mistake. Now she was working in Odessa branch of "Komsomolskaya Pravda". After the divorce she was well to do, but she continued working, as mixing with people and colleagues made up for her inner loneliness. She asked Yasha confidentially to set up her meeting with Gosha.

Please, don't think I am planning something about him, - she said, - I am just missing a strong man, not only nice-looking, but also nice from the inside. This type is rare now. Now there are more weak men or mean men. I think Gosha will be glad to meet me.

The arranged it so that on the first day of Pavlovskiy's stay in Odessa they would meet.

At last the plane got landed. After passing the checking at the airport Gosha came out and met his friends. Gosha threw his travel luggage to the bench and gave a hug and a kiss to Yasha and Kostya in turn.

Ok, welcome to the native land, my dear, - Yasha said. – Let's drop to the bar and have fifty grams to our meeting. We will have a drink and you will get acquainted with the program of your visit. Then we'll go to the hotel.

Everyone laughed. – OK. Yasha, you are always like this. OK, let's go. – Gosha answered laughing. They went to the bar and had a shot of cognac to the meeting, then a cup of coffee, they also discussed the plan of their actions.

I am at your disposal, my friends. I just want to relax. I am tired desperately. To tell the truth, I am tired not so much of being busy, but of the real life itself. Besides having a rest I would like to clear out some questions about your situation in Odessa.

He immediately corrected his mistake as he saw the reproachful glances of his friends: Sorry, with our situation in Odessa. I would like to know if it has become better or worse here in Odessa, or it is as everywhere, or Odessa is in front in spite of all the hardships.

Gosha didn't have any close relatives left in Odessa. He didn't want to visit his remote relatives. He didn't want to disturb his friends. So, he asked over the phone to reserve a room in a hotel for him. The friends knew the stubbornness of Gosha and didn't object, they reserved a room in the hotel "Odessa" at the sea terminal, where they headed from the airport.

Out of the car window Pavlovskiy was looking with interest at the Odessa sites, so familiar to him. He noticed the abundance of signs in the streets, but he also noticed the shabbiness of Odessa streets, he was shocked with pot-holes on the roads, absence of marking signs on the pavement, dirty traffic lights, lawns which were not taken care of, bent down trees, shabby fronts of buildings. He did remember that Odessa had never been a very clean city. He got excited at the sight of renovated front and a cultivated lawn near the cognac producing plant.

- Have a look, my friends, here there is an owner. The one who respects himself and his company. – Gosha said in approval voice. – It's just an oasis, an island of well being in this steppe and desert. Look at the trees, grapes, lawns, flower beds they have done! – He continued admiring. – I should say that even in Moscow there are companies and firms that have millions at their disposal, but their offices from the outside ate dirty and untrimmed, so that you even don't want to approach them. I have seen lots of them all over Russia. Those are just god-forsaken places, untidy both from inside and outside.

It was pleasant for the friends that Gosha saw not only negative things, but also good things in the appearance of Odessa. They were patriots of their own city, which was rare in Odessa. There were many of those who spoke of patriotism, who created the false public image, but there were very few left who really cared for Odessa.

Many changed had taken place during the past four years. Gosha was pleasantly surprised to see the grand look of the territory and new buildings at the sea terminal. He liked the new hotel very much. It was a tall building which matched the surrounding sites. Outside it was the early fall, and the weather was warm and sunny. The eyes enjoyed the combination of white and blue colored building of the hotel and the blue and calm sea.

- Let's go for a walk, - Gosha suggested. They dropped to the hotel room, left the luggage there and went to the sea. During the next hour Gosha and his friends went to a sea club, where there yachts and boats were exhibited and sold, visited a church near the sea line, at a picture gallery and at a concert and exhibition center of the sea terminal.

Gosha was excited because of his friends' presence and mainly because the native Odessa air was just making him drunk. He enjoyed the sight of the familiar sea harbor with the lighthouse. He was in Odessa! His friends went up to his room on the seventh floor. It was a one-bedroom luxury apartment, beautiful and comfortable. Gosha was delighted.

- At last in Odessa there is a real hotel where it is not shameful to reserve a room for any guests. – He was sharing his impressions with his friends. – To tell the truth, "Arcadia", "Passage" and "Central" are not the updated level at all.

Yasha smiled. – You, my dear, haven't seen the hotel "Mozart" near the Opera house yet. Now there are a lot of small private hotels with all the conveniences and services, including girls. There is any kind of services, even for sexual minorities.

Gosha smiled: - I didn't become a gay in Moscow. Though there are lots of them there. As far as sex is concerned, my dear guys, everything is postponed for tomorrow, as has been agreed before. You will be more furious. Tomorrow night we'll have some fun. Today I would like to talk to you, to share thoughts, impressions, reminiscences, I would like to listen to you.

Pavlovskiy took a shower, changed his clothes. His friends were making some follow-up calls. After that they exchanged their impressions about Gosha.

- One of the classic writers noticed very exactly: the sprit of the homeland is very sweet and nice to us. – Kostya Chebrikov said, looking out into the window at the sea port, at rushing people, at the machines working.

- Good or bad is the life, one is always attracted to his native land.

- It's not always like this. – Yasha answered quickly, while sitting cozily in an armchair and enjoying cold beer, which he drank from the bottle. – Not long ago I met one of the founders of our comic magazine. He is a retired military man, he was born in Russia, and after the Soviet Union split he happened to stay in Odessa for the service and stayed here for ever. This year he visited his native place near Belgorod. He said he was sick and tired of his native air in one week. Drinking, drugs in the country and in the city, laziness, neglect and dissipation. And the main thing is the despair in the appearance and behavior of people. As if it was the end of the world. He communicated with people of his age, with his childhood friends, and friends of his youth, with retired military men. He was ashamed to admit that his life was OK, that he was a well-to-do middle-class businessman, who provided living for his family and developed his business, could afford having dinner at a restaurant, go to a far away country for vacation, etc. He says in Odessa the life is quite different, the situation is quite different, everything is active here. It is not to the desirable extend, but still there is some progress, some steps forward. He brought his mother here. Try to tell him to go to his native land. Motherland, native places are good things. But a person is a creature who wants to live there where he feels comfortable, where he feels a human being. Of course, this applies to people who respect themselves. What about Gosha? Gosha is a stormy petrel, I hope I don't sound not in too high-flown manner. Pride, being in demand. He is never going to do a job he doesn't like.

- God save us from both doing a job we don't like and living with a person we don't love. God save us! – Gosha declaimed, coming out of the washroom. – What's going on, as they say in Odessa?

- I think they say the same not only in Odessa, but also in Moscow. Or is it different with Russians? – Kostya answered.

They laughed out loud. It was pleasant for them to communicate with each other. In half an hour the friends went up to the nineteenth floor and places an order at the restaurant, after that they went out to the outlook balcony. Gosha was impressed with the sight of the sea landscape in front of him.

- Here is the place for painters of sea scapes to paint. There is the sea, the harbor entrance, the port, the coast here – everything makes you enjoy.

- It is not at all Moscow – Kostya made a joke.

- Look here, Moscow also has its own great stuff and peculiarity. Sorry that a human being can not only create, - Gosha disagreed.

- Beware of the hungry and also beware of the satisfied. – Yasha interfered, - mind that, old man. But those who rule the world forget this sacramental postulate, maybe they have never knew it. It's a pity! There should be the happy medium. Look at America. What else do they lack? They live in great economic and social conditions. Outside and inside comfort. But to my mind they are now a real menace for the mankind.

- Do you mean they are too well off?

- They are. Not only the president and his environment, but also the people, which is more dangerous. Even the September 11 events didn't give them a lesson. The world is very fragile nowadays, more that it ever has been. On one side there is poverty of Asia, Africa, on the other there is richness and glow of the States. – Yasha said seriously. - The world is in real danger. Europe, as usual, is a buffer, it will be the place of the main events. One of my favorite movie actors used to say: "We are on the eve of great commotion!"- he said, joking, at the end of his speech.

Gosha looked at the sea landscape, thinking. He said: - You, Yasha, noticed that correctly. I would like to tell you that pragmatism that has captured the minds of people won't lead to anything good. I am not an altruist, but this is what we lack today. Now Odessa viewed from the nineteenth floor is green and full of trees, in spite of all. Who did it like this? First of all, it was Ribas, Richelieu, and Lonzheron. These were the first mayors of the deserted steppe coast, where in summer there was nothing but burnt grass. Where there was lack of drinking water, they created an oasis. By the way, they didn't use somebody's labor, they did all the work themselves. The were not pragmatics, in the contemporary sense of the word, they loved people, they loved the world which surrounded them, they were patriots, they were honest persons who served their country. They didn't surround their own villas with a fence three meters high, they didn't have trained security staff, as it is common with contemporary mayors. Ribas is the sample...

Kostya interrupted him. – Sorry, guy, let's move towards the table and continue the conversation. I am so hungry.

Gosha laughed out loud. – You, fat guy, can't live without bread.

- Why just bread? I also like meat, much meat, some good siding, vegetables and spices. – Kostya corrected him with a laughter.

The friends sat down to table with a lot of noise. The table had already been laid down.

- Let's drink to our friendship, to us. It's good we have preserved those traits of character that allow us to look into each other's eyes honestly. – Gosha pronounces taking up his glass with cognac. Yasha and Kostya had their drinks and started eating the salads with great appetite.

- There should be a very short period between the first and the second shots. – Kostya said, filling the glasses. At this very moment Gosha noticed a familiar female face from the side view at the doorway.

- Dasha! – He exclaimed, hardly believing his eyes. He wanted to see her, wanted to inquire about her, but he felt awkward about asking his friends about her. Dasha waved her hand to the friends and in a nice manner came up to the table. Gosha felt at a loss for a moment. Then he stood up, embraced her and kissed.

- Dashutka! Hi! You just can't imagine how glad I am.

He turned to his friends, - Thank you, guys, I have understood everything.

Dasha was also glad to see him. She looked a real beauty. Her beautiful jeans suit showed her body, her long blonde hair was loose on her shoulders.

- You haven't changed at all, you are just more mature. – She said, looking at Gosha, her eyes scanning him.

In a short while, having exchanged short greetings, the four friends were celebrating the meeting. Inadvertently they switched again to the conversation about the contemporary Odessa and its people. Dasha had just returned from a briefing in the municipal council, where they discussed the restoration of the Spaso-Preobrazhenski Cathedral.

- Look here, Gosha, the mayor and his men present the construction of the cathedral on the place of the destroyed one as the restoration of spirituality in the city. Let Kostya who is present here apologize me, but the mayor with his chicken brains can't realize that the faith and the church is not the same. One can't start building a cathedral with one hand and use the other one for taking budget and other money to one's own pocket. This is disgusting and this can't be called restoration of spirituality.

Her cheeks started blushing with excitement and she was again recollecting the situation at the briefing.

- Is it moral to say that when preparing to the winter season the heating in the buildings and hot water would be turned on as soon as the temperature outside becomes eight degrees. Please tell me, Kostya, the officer from the mayor's office, is hot water provided just for heating and not for some other needs? Is he not cynical? What kind of restoration of spirituality is he speaking about?

Gosha gave her some cognac. – Dashenka, let's have a drink, my girl, your are smart, honest and irresistible as you used to be. You are to dance at the podium, not to stay at a briefing. – He tenderly kissed her in her lips. She felt longing to him and desire and leaned closely against him, having completely forgotten about all her troubles.

Kostya clapped his hands. – That's much better. – And they all laughed out loud. They had some more food and drinks, spoke about the beautiful view from the window, but then they again switched to the same topic.

- Kostya interrupted me at the terrace, when he said he was hungry. – Gosha started. – I was saying that Odessa was a green city, and we are to thank its first mayors for that.

If we talk about restoration of spirituality, the mayor is to start with himself. What did he personally do for Odessa, how much of his own means did he contribute to the construction of that very cathedral? To my pity, there are very few who knows the history. The brothers De Ribas founded our contemporary city garden. The first trees were brought from Uman, from the count Pototskiy's gardens.

Yasha supported Gosha's words: - You are quite right. To tell you more, those brothers and later the duke Richelieu . de Valan and Lonzheron arranged the sites of Odessa using their own money. All of them were great patrons of art. They did a lot with their own hand and were not afraid of hard labor.

Dasha added: - And the current mayor is not a patron of art. He is just a patron. Here and there reports can be heard that the patron was supervising this or that event. This all is done to laundry the money and to gain cheap popularity. No, they are not able to do good. I didn't like the previous mayor, but I agree with him that the current one is a real disaster for the city.

- By the way, my dear friends, mind that the brothers Ribas were not Russian citizens, they were just employed in Russia, including the founder of Odessa the Admiral de Ribas. They were citizens of Neapolitan Kingdom.

Kostya listened and eating, mainly the meat.

- The cat Vaska listens eating, - he said, finishing one more portion of barbeque meat. – I would like to remind you, that the neglected and practically having no plants Dokovskiy part used to be a luxurious cottage of the Duke de Richelieu, full of plants, with no fence and security guards. It's important to mention that the second founder of Odessa supervised and contributed his own labor into the construction of the cottage, he himself planted the trees and flowers. By the way, at the lot there was spring water. It is also interesting to mention that it was his concern that near every house there were trees. If he saw that a tree was neglected by the owner of the house, he watered it himself.

Gosha was thoughtful. – Yes, my friends, really, the brothers de Ribas were Spanish, the Duke de Richelieu and Lonzheron were French, de Volan was a Dutch engineer. Even the Russian Tsar Alexander the First said that Richelieu was an outstanding person, with clear and pure mind, extreme innocence of his sole and besides, he was a genius who served the country. Lonzheron was of the same kind, porto-franko was established due to him and this was good for the city.

– Can we just compare these outstanding persons with those petty, greedy and worthless men who changed one another at the end of the twentieth and the beginning of the twenty first centuries. – Yasha said sadly.

Dasha stood up from the table and said: – I think they don't change any more, I think they keep electing one the same person. Let's leave them alone. Let's have a dance, Gosha.

– With great pleasure. – Gosha got up quickly from the table and they, embracing each other, started to dance.

– How are you, Dashenka? How is your life?

Dasha smiled: – Nothing is happening. I live with my work, with communicating with people. Nowadays it is hard to find somebody decent, but there are some. I should tell you there still remain in Odessa smart, intelligent people, specialists in different branched, in business included. Not everything is bad. In politics there are decent persons. But to tell the truth I am sick and tired of all here. I am divorced, he has his own life, and I have my own. But in fact I don't have any private life. There are some boyfriends from time to time. Maybe with you I will be able to relax during the coming days. – She looked at Gosha's eyes with a question in hers.

He embraced her tighter. – I was dreaming of it on my way here. I thought my dreams could not be realized. But here we are – not dreaming!

She moved away from him. – Please don't think I have some serious intentions. Nothing is going to happen. I am an independent and free woman. I don't be committed to anyone. But today I want to be with you. You are a strong man and I want to feel weak, I want to feel like a woman.

They stopped dancing in about twenty minutes. When they came up to the table, they saw that Yasha and Kostya were quite drunk.

71

- Sorry, guys, but Yasha and me are leaving. – Kostya said. – We still have something to prepare for tomorrow.

Dasha laughed out loud, - I know your tomorrow's plans. Your are like an insatiable male dog, again you are going to spoil young students till dawn.

Yasha raised his hand and said: - Be quiet, Dashenka! Please take care of our friend and in the morning we are going to meet again. As far as young students are concerned, we are not spoiling them, we are going to learn the science of love, and the process itself is long and multi-sided.

The friends stood up and went away quickly, waiving their hands at the doorway.

Gosha and Dasha spent about two hours at the restaurant, had some Champaign and ice-cream, danced, talked on easy topics. Gosha told her about his achievements at the Russian TV, about his interesting projects, which he was working on. At the end of the conversation they started to talk about Odessa again.

- Do you want to return to Odessa? – Dasha asked, looking at him with hope.

- No, I don't. I understand that the situation is calm right now. But inside there is so much dirt, it can easily be seen. Sorry, but there is so much dirt everywhere around, but here...

Dasha thought for a few minutes and then expressed her opinion,

- I think one of my girl-friends described the situation in the city very precisely. She said: "I am so sorry for our mayor. For four years all the local mass media has been telling us about the heroic deeds of the head of the city. He gets money for the city from different departments, he gets gas, electricity, in spite of the bad situation left for him from the previous mayor. The mass media didn't mention bad situation left for the current mayor by the Soviet regime and the monarchy. Everything bad, according to them, that is mud, broken roads, demolished houses, absence of heat, hot water, electricity, salary payments and other disasters have had one and the same reason for the past four years. The reason was the bad heritage from the previous mayor and his team. And the mayor is shown on TV as cutting the ribbon at grand opening of well-rooms, a complex of houses or a part of a road after renovation – he was just a specialist in cutting ribbons, he had cones because of scissors.

Why he should be praised for that? It is his job and he is being paid for it. It is his direct duty to clean up the city. Street cleaners, plumbers and electricians are not telling anyone about there heroic deeds. Street cleaners don't cut ribbons in the presence of mass media on the occasion of starting to use a new brush. They just do their work and get salary. But unlike the mayor, they get it quite irregularly.

For more years have passed. I wonder who is going to be a scapegoat this time? If again they start again to say that it is the bad heritage of the previous mayor, it would be possible to say that the ex-mayor was really a Titanic.

For the inhabitants of Odessa it makes no difference at all if the mayor is Jewish, Ukrainian, Moldavian or Russian. It doesn't matter what he is busy with at his leisure time: playing tennis, writing books, sleeping with girls. It is his private life. But let him and his officers who are more numerous than garbage cans in Odessa, not prevent the inhabitants of Odessa from living, working, trading, treating patients, studying, publishing newspapers, having a rest at the beach or at home. Let him become invisible and noiseless, but let heat, electricity, water be in every building, let the roads be repaired and the yards cleaned, let all the other things done. Let the street cleaners get their salary in time, and let their brooms not be broken in the bushes.

If the mayor needs to make heroic deeds and break his health in order to keep everything running, the inhabitants of Odessa don't need this kind of sacrifice. One don't need to become a higher officer in the authorities and become disabled at this work. Let him better have a rest.

Gosha listened to her attentively, without interrupting. When she finished, he kissed her hands and pulled her tenderly towards himself,

- You are a patriot, and not a single one here. I thought, that with out departure, there is no one left here. Sorry for being rude, but I thought everyone has become the mayor's puppet.

- It doesn't matter, Gosha, new or old, all of them are hypocrites and crooks. Enough for today, let's have a good drink and dance.

They had a drink and danced, standing tightly one against the other. Then they went to the terrace and kissed, like young students. They remembered their young, careless years. Long after the midnight they when down to Gosha's room, embracing each other. They took off their clothes, saying nothing, and embraced each other. The didn't sleep till dawn. Dasha was a skillful lover. He was of the same kind. They were devoured by great passion, as deep inside they had longed to each other for so long.

Only when it got light, they fell into a careless sleep, still leaning tightly one against the other.

Gosha woke up at about eleven and to his deep disappointment found that he was alone. Dasha was not in the room. He took a bath and freshened up himself. On the mirror he found a note made with a lipstick. "I kiss you and love, you are incomparable. See you at night. D."

- It isn't a dream. We did make love all the night though with Dasha, - Gosha smiled with a happy smile.

At the same time Dasha was going to the office and thought. In spite of the alcohol taken yesterday and the stormy sleepless night Dasha felt great. Her moods were high, he wanted to sing and shout that she was happy.

- Is it much that women want? A tender look, tender hands, love words and passion.

She looked in the mirror. She was satisfied,- A satisfied woman is a great woman.

Behind the car windows the having awakened city was full of life. It was the day when the city was celebrating its anniversary. The Day of the City!

Who celebrates it? The authority of the city is making another show for themselves and their environment. Young people will come, having taken lots of beer before the night, or even blunted with drugs. For the most of the people in the city it is a regular day. - Everything is getting routine and dull, and this is dangerous, - Dasha thought. – How can one be indifferent to holidays, elections, and actions of the authorities, to the world around, to one's own fate as well.

Having arrived to the office, Dasha asked the secretary to prepare some coffee and started thinking again.

- Half a year ago there was the election to the municipal council. Like before, two main candidates were opposing each other. Again it was two dull persons, having no intelligence, no experience, and, which is the most important, no conscience and no shame. Dasha was ashamed for the inhabitants of Odessa and for the city. Every election campaign the situation was the same. How can it be that in the city with a million population there can be found no candidate who wanted to become a leader not for satisfaction of his political ambitions, not for creating his private business on the cost of budget money and bribes from people, not for cutting ribbons and making presentations, but for running the city economy, which means to put to order and maintain the residential buildings, roads, parks, running water and draining, so that there is heat, electricity, gas, hot water, so that the inhabitants of the city felt comfortable. It is necessary to tidy the trees, the lawns, and the plants. It is necessary to change the old trees with young ones. The main thing is that they didn't interfere with the matters of business, culture, sport, trade and others.

Dasha couldn't help wondering why they needed so many officers in the mayor's office. Just impossible to imagine! The trade is practically concentrated in private companies, there is a trade department. Dasha couldn't understand why there were created the youth department, the sports department, the culture department, and the parking lots department. And many other departments. Why they needed the municipal council at all? Just for nothing. All the decisions are made by the mayor and his team, good or bad. It doesn't matter if someone likes or dislikes the decision made, all the same it will be ratified by the session of the municipal council. The deputies would be brainwashed or bribed. Who needs this show?

Coffee was served. Dasha said thanks for the coffee and lit a cigarette. She was thinking again. To her mind, the election didn't mean anything to the people, just expenses. No matter what the results of the elections will be, the life of people is not going to change for better.

She remembered the inscription of one of self-made slogans at the time of the election. It ran: "No matter if you vote or not, all the same you'll suck". She smiled.

Vulgar, rude, but precise expression.

She was aware that during the election campaign budget money was used for the election purposes. Chairmen of election commissions are appointed from obedient and familiar surrounding. They come with all their stamps and seals to the headquarters of the current mayor and prepare all the necessary for the victory quantity of voting papers on the eve of the elections. The main thing they should provide is the attendance of the people, they were needed to come and vote. Shadow expenses of some of the candidates to the position of people's deputies were almost a million and a half dollars. Hundreds of buses with people headed to the necessary ballot districts and voted. So much money is wasted during the election.

- What would happen if one is elected once and for the life period? Nothing is changed in the legislation system and the judges are appointed for the life time. The same could apply for deputies and mayors. Less trouble, less expenses. People would just benefit of it.

Dasha laughed out loud as she liked the idea. She was satisfied.

- I am satisfied, my body is satisfied and my brain works OK. The thoughts are plain. It's easy to breath and work. It is not just sex and physical satisfaction, it is sex with a person you have feelings for, which is different. No matter what happens in the future. So many years have passed and we are still attracted to each other. It's complete harmony in bed, - thought Dasha and smiled. – I haven't had that for a long while.

Suddenly it occurred to her that she could postpone everything for the day – the work, the city with its mayor and the problems. There was Gosha in the hotel. And there was herself. She stood up out of the desk, told her secretary that she was leaving for the day and she could be reached at her cell phone in case of emergency. She got into the car and drove to the sea terminal.

Gosha was going down in order to have a walk at the seaside, and he met Dasha near the elevator.

- You! – He embraced her. Their lips met in a passionate kiss. They didn't say anything, went to the elevator and went up to the room. There existed nothing around them. Just them. Again the wild passion captured them.

When their passion was satisfied, they came back to reality and remembered about Yasha and Gosha.

- They even didn't call. I think they are having fun. – Gosha said as a suggestion.

Dasha laughed out loud, kissing Gosha tenderly in his lips. – You are so stupid! They understand that we are not discussing some problems, and they don't want to interfere. Where are they, what do you think?

Gosha shrugged his shoulders.

- I am sure they are here in the bar waiting for us to invite them. – Dasha said, smiling. – I am going to the shower. After that we'll join them. Let's go to the city. We'll show it to you. You do want to see it, don't you?

- Sure, my sun. But I have one condition: at night you again stay with me.

Dasha answered from the shower: - What about the girls, the students, they have prepared a whole harem for you.

- I don't want anyone, but you in Odessa. I think they won't come up to your level of temperament and making love experience. – Gosha answered.

- OK, agreed, - Dasha said. – But this time we'll go to my place. – And she turned on the water.

Later they met Yasha and Kostya who were real friends and had been waiting for Gosha for two hours in the bar, drank beer with crabs.

- Love is OK, it comes and goes, but we always need to eat. – Kostya exclaimed.

- Kostya, you are cynical. – Dasha said to him smiling.

- You are like a couple of birds in love. I wish you could see yourselves in the mirror. – Yasha said. – A good couple! Maybe we will marry you?

- No, my dear "Floater". – Dasha said joking, - You won't be able to do that. As early as being a student I realized that Gosha and myself are great lovers, like-minded persons, but nothing more. Let's it be as it is. Otherwise, you'll spoil everything, it won't work. Everyday life, household routine will quickly end everything we would like to keep. At least I would like.

Gosha clapped his hands. – Bravo! Good answer!

In an hour they were having lunch in the restaurant "Kumanets". Gosha praising the Ukrainian cuisine. – You see, my friends, there are Ukrainian cuisine restaurants in Moscow. The cooks are Ukrainian, the waiters, the food are also said to be Ukrainian, but the result is different. It's so great here.

Yasha laughed: - Everything in Odessa seems great to you. It is Odessa.

After the lunch they drove all over the city. They visited Moldavanka, Peresyp, walked along Deribasovskaia and Primorskiy Boulevard. Gosha had a lot of impressions. He was delighted with new stores, casino, nightclubs, and movie theaters. But he was upset by the sight of mud and garbage, neglected yards, broken roads, loutishness everywhere and the expression of people's faces far from being happy. Privoz surprised him most of all: the market was just stinking.

- How can one buy food here? Sorry, but I feel like vomiting here. – He didn't want to continue the trip and asked the friends to stop it.

He made one conclusion, that business in Odessa was developing more rapidly, than anywhere else. It was due to the fact that Odessa was a port with its traditions and peculiarity, which can't be eliminated, no matter how much one could try. He made another conclusion, that in four years there happened no changes in Odessa. The authorities were living in their own virtual world. They raise the level of their own welfare, playing the game of show and presentations. The people live in the real life of today, just surviving. The authorities takes care of everything: politics, business, even beauty contests, but it never takes care and it does not take want to take care of its direct duties. There are many reasons for that. The main reason is the absence of decency, purity and responsibility in the blood of the fathers of the city. To put it in plain words, no brains, no honor, no conscience.

The night was spent at the nightclub "Cosmo". They drank a lot, but didn't become drunk. They had a lot of fun. Kostya and Yasha had already found themselves in the company of young beautiful creatures.

- My dear friends, I am grateful for you for the warm reception and for today's trip over the city. I know you would like to know my opinion. I am going to share my unprejudiced opinion. Odessa has always been, it is existing and it will be. To my mind, nothing can take it away: neither tyranny, nor democracy; neither a Jew, nor a Moldavian; neither earthquake, nor a typhoon. It is so because Odessa is not just a lot and a part of the sea. It is its people, its soul, its heart and it's a lifestyle. Believe me, we are parts of Odessa, scattered all over the world, due to bad luck. Every time we come to Odessa and step on our land with trepidation. We are glad to see everything positive that appears here. We feel bitter when we watch all the negative stuff which is now spread all over Odessa. We have never divided people on national grounds, all of us were the same. We have always been correct and polite. The humor used to be kind and real. Now the main menace is poverty of minds and hearts. It can be seen in Odessa everywhere now. A driver and a pedestrian gave way to each other, nodded to each other and smiled. Now it is different. Everyone is rude to each other. Rudeness, impatience to each other, trivial jokes and funny stories, even among people dressed well enough. A friend of mine in Moscow likes to say: "The way we are dressed is not important, the main thing is that we are well mannered". To my mind, it is true. We need to try to be better: our soul, our dresses, our intentions as well as our actions. Maybe, the situation will change here? I think it can. You can take my words as a joke or seriously, but I suggest that there should be gathered a people's council for the inhabitants of Odessa. It should write a letter not to the Turkish sultan, but to the president of France, Spain or of Holland. Let them send to us for work new, modern specialists like de Ribas, Richelieu, de Volans and Lonzherons. It was at their presence that Odessa was developing and flourishing, it was a real South Palmyra. Later there was stealing, embezzlement of public funds, hypocrisy and falsehood. It is not a coincidence that the monument to Alexander Sergeevich Pushkin which was built with the money of the people, is turning its back to the municipal council. Even at that time not responsible people, not patriots of Odessa were employed there, to say nothing of the contemporary situation. So, the inhabitants of Odessa are supposed to send a courier to fetch a decent mayor.

Everyone at table was listening to him attentively. When he finished, they applauded.

- Shall we send a courier? Let's drink to it. – Yasha exclaimed.

They were having fun for a long time. They drank, danced, and discussed problems. After the midnight Gosha wished a good nights for the friends and left together with Dasha to her country cottage, where in a cozy and intimate place they started to do the things a man and a woman are supposed to do when they are attracted to each other. In their love and passion they forgot about that mad, dirty and petty world, which was outside the house. They were in the kingdom of love and passion.

Ten Hundred Moneys

In Odessa they count money in hundreds of moneys. Ten hundred moneys is a thousand of US dollars. This shows what they consider in Odessa to be money and what is just conditional currency.

Yura Granovskiy who failed to graduate from the Institute of People's Economy, started his own business at the golden nineties, like all the Soviet people. The business was buying and selling something or stealing and selling something.

He was of medium height, with a plump figure, with chubby cheeks and a bold head, thought he was still young. His head was constantly full of crazy ideas of getting rich. Yura had an active lifestyle. By the age of twenty five he had already experienced three marriages and he was about getting married for the fourth time. One wife didn't suit him, another didn't suit his mother, the third cleared the things herself and left him, the fourth was ready to marry him.

Yura's activity could be observed not only in his love affairs, but also in so-called business. He was a middleman when selling sugar, flour, bananas and other foreign products, as well as home-made. He had a phenomenal capability of a crook to make an impression of a responsible person to other people. Nobody knows if it was a born or acquired capability. He was born if a far away god-forsaken village in Kirovograd region. His childhood and youth he spent near school number seventy five in Odessa in Sadovaya street, where his mother was transferred to the position of a teacher as early as in the beginning of the seventies. They got an apartment with shared kitchen and bathroom close to the notorious school where retarded children studies. Actually, it was a branch of an asylum, and its influence seemed to have passed over to young Granovskiy's mind.

At least this influence contributed to development of great ability for cheating and deceit.

Usually Yura came in the morning to one of the numerous markets in the city and slowly walked along the rows in the halls of the market, inquiring in details where the stuff was coming from, what was the price and examined the quality very attentively. Many trades persons did their best trying to prove that their goods are the most popular, of the best quality and the cheapest. They saw a potential buyer in Granovskiy and tried to persuade him that their stuff was just the best. He had a respectable appearance, wore a tie and a shirt, with a case and a very serious expression with a shade of thoughtfulness and a light sadness, he made an impression of respectability and trustfulness.

Nobody could think that this man had just one thought in his head, that is to get some cream from some shit. That could mean in Odessa language only one thing: Granovskiy wanted to get money from any unpopular stuff, preferably on selling the air and get the greatest profits from that. With his ability to persuade people Yura could sell a TV set to a blind, some sugar to a diabetic, a bicycle to a person without legs. Actually, he could sell to anyone the stuffy air from the catacombs or fresh sea waves, to say nothing of some foam or a lot at the cemetery, which, according to him, was opening soon in Shevchenko park under the supervision of the limited liability company "Chernomorets".

Walking along the rows of Privoz, Yura paid attention to the activity of the limited liability company "Kolos", which, as he found out, was under the patronage of the deputy manager of the market. Yura made some thinking and then made a decision.

- They are not going to investigate!

He came up to a salesperson of the enterprise, a nice-looking blonde with dirty hands and with the expression of constant desire in her eyes.

- Hello, my dear girl, my name is Yuri Mikhailovich, I am trading sugar and citrus fruits wholesale. I can offer two or three tons of sugar to a trial at the lowest price. Please ask your boss to give me a call to my cell phone.

He gave her the phone number of his acquaintance, disconnected for non-payment. The next day he went to the office of the manager of the company "Kolos".

- Hello. Are my prices for the sugar suitable for you? If not, I will give the sugar to other companies who want to get the sugar. As they say in Odessa, see you in the morning.

The manager with the last name Penkov agreed, as the salesperson was offering home-made sugar at the price which is sixty dollars cheaper than current wholesale prices for a ton. Seeing a very respectable-looking person in front of him, Penkov didn't think much before he paid ten thousand grivnas cash with no receipt on condition that the sugar would be delivered by the night. Yura, having got the money, was not going to deliver any sugar.

The next day he was walking along the rows of the market "Yuzhnuy" where he used the same method of influencing the manager and the expert on merchandise of the association "Odessaplodovoshch", where he offered bananas at a very cheap price.

- They are not registered, they have no documents, for cash. You are going to pick up the stuff yourselves.

The potato bosses thought they could both get some good and quick money on that and they agreed. The next day in the morning they met at the Tamozhennaia square at the entrance of the sea port. In the car Yura got a package with a hundred thousand grivnas and while the unlucky customers were registering for obtaining the passes to the port, he just disappeared.

Yura was triumphant. In two days he deceived two nincompoops and made one hundred thousand bucks on the spot. The amount was in grivnas, but still it was OK. He thought he could go to the Crimea while the commotion was still on in the city. But his appetite was already growing. The same day Yura made a deal with the manager of the firm "Pivden". The deal was about wholesale of sugar in the amount of ten tons stored in the basement of the Food store Gastronom number one. The firm "Pivden" was selling at the new market different stuff like food – sugar, flour, citrus fruits and sunflower oil. His last name was Moldavan, but he always said he was a Jew. His name matched, it was Sema.

Sema, with his six years of education and thirty years of market experience out of his thirty six, thought that he could make quick money if he took sugar and sell it wholesale at once. He went his cashier to pick up the sugar together with Granovskiy to the Gastronom number one and gave him twenty thousand grivnas cash. Granovskiy took the cashier to the basement of Gastronom, took the money and went to the next room to get the sugar. From there, using another door, he successfully escaped.

Yura didn't challenge the fate, he left for the Crimea by train the same night. There he had a rest with cheap Russian and Ukrainian prostitutes as a rich man, but he didn't spend much money. Yura was a greedy man by his nature and lifestyle. He loved money but he didn't like to waste it.

Having returned to Odessa, Yura stayed home for a while. The family had a small private house in Slobodka. But once he decided to take a risk and relax. He went to the nightclub "Kosmo" where there was a Jew with a Gypsy face and with the last name Moldavan. He recognized the crook and rushed in him immediately, shouting:

- Where is the money and the sugar? – He started to hit Granovskiy, he even managed to hit him in the stomach with a folk. But Yura's stomach was so thick that the strike didn't have any consequences for his health.

The police arrived, having been called by the security of the club, and Yura was detained. It turned out that all the deceived firms had reported to the police, though they had paid cash. They reported that they were cheated by a crook who resembled the deputy mayor, according to the created computer image. It was quickly figured out that the officer of that level couldn't be that crook, as he was deceiving businessmen every day at his own office, and he didn't collect the money, he was delivered money to his office. They were looking for a crook who was not a government employee, but there was a chance the crook worked in some enforcement offices.

Granovskiy, as well as his mother, who had abandoned her teaching practice long ago, as it was ineffective, couldn't imagine that the case would be taken up by the sixth department of the police, where not just sneaks and just cops were employed, but individuals who seemed to have never had either a mother or a father.

The same night Granovskiy was transferred from the district department to the sixth department. There he was severely beaten up by three doctors, as they called themselves. He was beaten skillfully, so that there were no bruises. Then he was hanged up to a tube on his leg for an hour. In the morning he was brought to the office of the investigator.

- Where is the money? If you pay two hundred bucks to us, we'll stop the investigation and you will be released. – The Investigator was persuading him. It was a short man with a face that resembled fox's muzzle.

Yura was not stupid and he understood that they were extracting money from him.

- You suck, you are not getting any money – He thought. And he said out loud: - I didn't take any money from anyone. They are just mistaken or misleading. I am asking for a lawyer. I am going to talk only to my lawyer. And call a doctor to confirm the beating.

The investigator grinned.

- Yes, you will have a lawyer and a judge and also a long-term sentence. I do promise this to you.

In two hours Yura was transferred to the detention centre. At that very moment the sixth department was busy extracting information from Yura's mother. She used to be a nimble teacher, nowadays she was working as a beggar in a public place, in the hotel "Passage" area. She didn't recognize himself in disguise, but that was a real and profitable kind of business. She usually went to the place in the afternoon and she didn't overwork. Besides, she was a casher at home and, as Yura said, she was the keeper of their savings. When the police came at night with the search order, aunt Faya was calm.

- Look for anything you want. But what do you want to find? We are poor people. – She started grumbling, then she became silent.

They turned upside down everything in the house, they even dig some areas in the vegetable garden. After making a report of taking fifty grivnas the guards of the order left.

- Police spies! – Aunt Faya grinned, when she was left alone. Could the cops have thought that the smart aunt Faya had a belt made of broadcloth, in which she kept her precious stuff, including dollars and Ukrainian grivnas. During the day she kept it in the basement in a place that even Yura couldn't find. At night she puts it on. And she used to be a teacher at school number seventy five.

- You suck, - She was saying gloatingly, looking at the leaving cops.

The time was going on, the investigation was over. The court proceedings started. Yura and his mother realized that the court had no serious evidence against him. They had only the applications and their words. They were sure that Yura would be found not guilty and he would be released from the hearing room. They didn't even hire a lawyer. It turned out to be a mistake. They say in Odessa that greed can kill a guy.

During the court procedure Yura said that the force structures should be interested not in his activity, but in the activity of the regional prosecutor, who had built a luxurious villa which cost several hundreds thousands bucks, and in the activity of other officers of the force structures, who behaved in the same way as the prosecutor, when acquired the best lots in Odessa.

His mother Faya visited the judge, whose last name was Gomnyuk, who was in charge of her son's case, and he said to her frankly:

- Dear lady, if you want to see your son released, pay a thousand of moneys.

- A thousand of grivnas? – Aunt Faya asked with hope.

The judge laughed out loud: - Dear lady, I have clearly said that it is a thousand of moneys.

Aunt Faya thought and decided not to give bribes to anyone. First it was the prosecutor who asked for a thousand of moneys, now it was the judge. She shook her head.

- So many expenses! – Though she hadn't pay anything to anyone so far.

A lawyer in the court was appointed by the state, and he did his duties OK, according to the criminal code and according to the amount he received from the defendant. It was an elderly person, who had been in retirement age as many years as the defendant was old, but he did remember the rule: "You get as you pay". As no one paid to him, he was not doing anything extra for the guy.

Before the final trial day old Khaim, led by his warm feelings to the defendant, met him and explained the situation for him.

- My dear friend, don't give a headache to your mother and to yourself for the rest of your life. You can get ten years of imprisonment and expropriation together with great charges. Do you really need this? Write a note to your mother, I will give it to her, let her find some money, one thousand moneys is all you need to get. And you are going to be released. What do you think? Are you sick? Don't think that a jail will cure you.

- You are an old man, but I see that you were sent to me by the judge, - Yura said, smiling. – I am innocent, there is no evidence against me. Don't try to get money from me.

Khaim looked at Granovskiy as if he were mad.

- You are really mentally sick.

His meeting with the mother was also of no result.

- OK, go ahead. – Old Khaim was really upset and mad with them. He was not upset because of the conviction pending, but because of a small amount of money he was not getting.

The next day Granovskiy was convicted in stealing of great amount of government and co-operative money. It happened in one of the dark and stuffy hearing rooms of the regional court.

The defendant refused to plead guilty and testified that he hadn't stolen and extracted the money from the companies mentioned at the trial, he said that the witnesses were slandering on him.

But the representative of the trial board announced that the guilt of Granovskiy was proven by the testimony of the witnesses and, which was of major importance, by the material evidence, that was two elastic rings which were usually used for packing money. They were found in the house where Granovskiy lived, and they were recognized by the witnesses. It turned out that the elastic rings were those which were used for packing the money taken by Granovskiy at the Tamozhennaya square.

The lawyer examined the elastic rings in his hands, thought that they didn't differ from millions of other elastic rings of the same kind, used for packing money, but he didn't express his opinion. Nobody cared about that.

So, the trial board of the most humane and just courts in the world, that is of Odessa regional court, took into account the character and social damage of the crime, as well as the personal individuality of the defendant, all the extenuating circumstances and aggravations, including the fact that he started his sexual life very early, and sentenced him to eleven years of imprisonment, expropriation and payment of the amount of one hundred and thirty thousand grivnas by Granovskiy to the victims.

The only material evidence, that is two elastic rings were supposed to be kept in the file. At that moment Yura thought that he could have been convicted of rape of a virgin who had never existed in Odessa. In that case the material evidence would be a condom found somewhere in the streets of the city.

But it was too late to do anything. Already in the jail, after a few days had passed, Yura thought:

- This is the fate. One thousand moneys would have solved all the problems. There is a conclusion drawn for the future: don't be stupid. If one says to you to pay a thousand moneys, you should not interpret it as you would like to. They were speaking about one thousand dollars, not about any other kinds of money.

Years passed. Eleven years Granovskiy got for his not-European behaviour, in spite of his European last name. Eight of those eleven years he spent not very far away, he spent them almost in the centre of Odessa.

During those years his mother became a permanent beggar, she gave a policeman some tips and the latter allowed her to work right in Deribasovskaya Street. She was quietly making her money. After his release Yura tried to get into the business circles, but it was already the time of nineties. Odessa businessmen looked at him and said: "It is not the same thing – to drink vodka and to brainwash somebody. He is no brainwasher. He needs some sheep's brains, then he could resemble a human being at least."

But Yura was energetic, and in a couple of months he got beautiful identification documents of a taxation office worker, as well as of a health officer, a fire inspection officer, a special inspection officer, and he used them successfully for getting his everyday money from private entrepreneurs. He was thinking of getting an i.d. of a representative of the President and of a People's deputy assistant. He was not afraid of consequences. He was afraid of violence. As far as the law was concerned, he could solve his problems with the help of one thousand moneys. It was kept in a secret place in the garden and was waiting for the time it would be needed, if some force major circumstances occurred. He didn't know that in the twenty first century one thousand moneys was no longer able to solve that kind of problems. It was different time, and the prices were also different.

Presidents' Dreams

It's difficult to say if it happened in real life, or it was presidents' dreams, if presidents have any dreams at all. But there are some rumours in Odessa. And here is on of them.

Once in spring, on the eve of another commotion connected with the next leader candidate, that is on the eve of election campaign, when people's deputies, or the parliament, and the mayor were supposed to be elected, three presidents arrived to the South Palmyra at one and the same time. They didn't arrive at a random March day. They arrived on the Forgiving Sunday. If they had some sin in their soles, the meeting on such a day gave them a chance to forgive all the previous troubles and not to start new ones.

To Odessa there arrived Presidents of the neighbouring countries: Russia, the Ukraine, as well as Moldova. Each of them had his own escort, not a small one, different persons included. There were assistants and great bosses, fortune tellers and crooks, financial specialists and swindlers. With the help of those people the presidents discussed the questions not harmful for anyone, such, for example, as attaching Moldova to the electrical system of the Ukraine and consequently, to that of Russia.

This attachment is not happening for the first time. Some still remember the energy system "Mir". In general, this way of transfer of Russian electrical power to Europe gives big opportunities for crooks from the escort of the president of the Ukraine and the president of Moldova. It was not the only item on the agenda. The president of the Ukraine told his news of preparation to the election campaign to the Superior Rada. Numerous Russian specialists in the questions of elections promotional campaign (not to be confused with the word "feast", though there is no much difference between the elections promotional campaign and the feast during the plague), gave a piece of advice to their Ukrainian colleagues how to brainwash the people and get their candidates through and make money on the election campaign. Election is a very profitable business. It is easy to get seven digits amounts of cash money with no effort, with no signatures and receipts. It's a pity this kind of business was periodical, and happens not very often. Thus, one of the main election adviser of the Russian president was completely against having elections of the parliament and the president at one and the same time, the same concerning the elections of mayors. Watching those crooks it occurs to you that Nikolai the Second had a more easy life, so did Russia in general. He had only one advisor – Grigoriy Rasputin, and not they are as numerous as flies in a certain place on a hot day.

On the talks of the three presidents the main topic seemed to be that of Dnestr region. But at the press conference everything became clear when the presidents of Russia and the Ukraine said that the president of Moldova would clarify the question to the journalists. The president of Moldova was at a loss when he heard that he was supposed to make the speech.

- What kind of speech is this supposed to be? Greeting?

When he was explained, that he was to announce the results of the negotiations, the only thing he could say was as follows:

- We have settled everything.

The residents of Odessa understood at once that on this press conference there were no deep questions discussed and revealed, just brainwash with the help of TV. They knew that the residents of Odessa would experience no changes whatever the results of the transfer of energy talks were. They used to make supplies of flashlights and candles for the winter season, then were going to do it in the future. The elections come again and again. Presidents arrive and leave. In Odessa there used to be partial blackouts in wintertime and there would be. It was the way the regional energy department could make some extra money for themselves, the disliked mayor including. The same mayor was going to be re-elected during democratic election campaign.

The residents of Odessa knew that no matter how they voted, as the mayor would be elected the very candidate whom the president supported. It was much better to relax and enjoy life. The Dnestr region was of no interest to Odessa residents, they just didn't care for it with its horse stealers and neighbouring budget money stealers.

The presidents discussed the problems and made a conclusion that there was no point solving all of them at once. Then there would be no point of meeting again. They just went to sightseeing.

The humour specific for Odessa was demonstrated during the visit as well. A week before the presidents arrived the mass media showed speeches of the mayor and the governor in which they asked the residents of Odessa to restrain from visiting public places and driving private cars in the centre of the city, actually hinting that it would be preferable if the residents of Odessa just left the city for a while. Along the whole route the city and the country leaders put out specially trained people for watching and greeting, very numerous nowadays. They overdid while fulfilling the task and they removed all the benches from Primorskiy Boulevard, they didn't remove only the monuments to Pushkin and Richelieu and the famous platan trees. It is surprising they didn't remove them, just incredible!

The ass lickers also did their best when the president of the Ukraine proudly brought his colleagues to a group of his supporters. The latter were carrying slogans with greeting words in his address and suddenly started to greet the Russian president.

After the trip over the city there was a dinner in honour of the great guests in a quiet, cosy house in Sanatornyi Street. The presidents had a reasonably modest dinner and went to sleep. The escort members stayed to discuss the current problems and continued the feast according to their interests and branches of activity.

The night was clear and there were stars in the sky, a breeze was blowing from the sea and several military ships were there, being alert and protecting the dreams of the presidents from attacks of aggressive swimmers or Chechen soldiers, or from suicide bombers of Yulia Timoshenko's team, or from underwater swimmers sent by Dnestr region leaders, or by Ben Laden. It didn't actually matter from whom they protected, the enemy could be easily invented.

The Russian president couldn't fall asleep for a long time. It was unusual for him. Usually he fell asleep at once, no matter where he was: in Moscow or somewhere else. The last two years he travelled a lot. Even in the air he slept well and didn't see any dreams. It was different in Odessa. When he finally fell asleep, he had a nightmare.

He was woken up: - Comrade Dzerzhinskiy is calling you.

- But...

- Later. You will explain everything in the office. Get dressed.

It was only at that moment that the president saw that in the room there were three men in riding breeches, long shoes and leather jackets. They had belts on and there were big guns on the belts. The president got dressed and silently went to the exit, escorted by the three government security officers. At the entrance there was a black Willis. There were no servants and security.

- Where are they? Why do I keep them and for what do I pay for them? – President thought nervously. – The president of Russia is taken out of his warm bed at night and nobody cares. If these people are sent by Ben Laden or Maskhadov, which is still worse, what happens then? Or if Berezovskiy sent his men from London? – The president sweated.

- They can take me to a washroom and murder me there. Or they can make me run and swallow the dust. Or they can cut my penis, like Muslims do. And who am I: a Christian or a Catholic? If they ask me, I will answer like they do in Odessa: "Which is preferable?"

At the time the president thought his vague thoughts the car arrived to Lubyanka square and the monument to Dzerzhinskiy was in its place.

- Thanks God, Yuri Mikhailovich managed to put the monument back in its place. Thanks.

He had a hope that in the building of the Federal Security Bureau he would be met by his men. But there was the sign The All-Russia Emergency Committee. Inside there were officers of that time who were looking unfriendly at the president, and that sign was not a good one.

In the reception they waited for a minute, then Dzerzhinskiy called the president.

Felix Edmundovich was sitting at the rear wall of the office, at a big desk, in an official looking military uniform, green in colour, Menzhinskiy was beside him and Lacis was farther, near the window.

-The council of the three! This is fatal! They are going to kill me. – The president thought, his throat dry and his legs weak.

- Good night. – Dzerzhinskiy greeted him. Come in, take a seat, please.

The president came to the desk and sat on the edge of the chair, his legs weak, like made of cotton with fear. Silence set. Only a table lamp was lit in the office. The light of it was directed to the president. His was watched and examined by the government security department officers. As far as Dzerzhinskiy was concerned, he was reading documents laid in front of him. At last he put them away.

- Look here, comrade. I have studied your personal file very attentively. There seem to be no point of being concerned about you. We laid a very important task on you. Comrade Lenin himself gave references to you. He, in his turn, listened to the references of German friends who characterized you very well and appreciated you highly. And you? What have you done?

The president was at a loss. – What is going on?

Dzerzhinskiy looked at the president with his piercing eyes and the latter shrinked.

- We planted you into the contemporary leading structures of Russia to save it. Vladimir Ilyich said: "The motherland is in danger!" Decisive measures needed to be taken. You were planted there like... How do they call it now? – He looked at Menzhinskiy.

-"Like a mole" they say, Felix Edmundovich. – He answered.

- That's it! Like a mole! And you, my dear, may I ask, what have you done?

The president conquered his excitement and started reporting. He had a lot of things to report. He also had some persons he would like to give information about.

- Felix Edmundovich, I received a very bad heritage from those who were doing out work earlier than me. I will submit a list of their names. The state foundation, the system of control, economy and financial system were destroyed.

- What about yourself? Have you stolen a lot? – Lacis interrupted him.

The president started sweating again.

- Everyone knows everything. You can conceal nothing.

He tried to smile, but the smile was miserable.

- As for me, I didn't steal myself. If there was something, that something came to my pocket itself. But I will contribute that to our mutual fund.

- Go on reporting and stick to the point. – Dzerzhinskiy demanded.

- I restored the state foundation, I returned the hymn of Russia to the country, I strengthened the structure of the power, I am conducting a reasonable foreign policy, I am driving the life inside the country to order.

- These are general phrases. You can use them when talking to other countries' leaders and mass media. You are in the Emergency situations committee, my dear. – Dzerzhinskiy said, getting up. – You are supposed to explain why there is decline in economy, what are the reasons, who are the persons in charge, what measures have been taken by you. Some individuals, beside you and your favourite guy from London, transferred abroad two hundred billion dollars, stolen from the people. By the way, what is your relationship with the family?

- No relationship, I broke all the relations with them. If it is necessary, I will kill them all. – The president reported hurriedly.

Dzerzhinskiy grinned: - OK, kill them. Remember, what we had to do with the Tsar's family in the hard years of the civil war. It is either they will celebrate the victory over us, or it is vice versa.

- I do understand you. – The president got up to his feet and clicked his heels together.

- As far as economy is concerned, all the natural resources monopolies are to be taken by the government. All the heads of the monopolies are to be summoned to the Kremlin. In twenty four hours they are to transfer all their funds to the government. Let them get the minimum payment of a oil production worker, give them one developed oilfield and let them earn their minimum payment all together. If they survive, it would mean they are real bosses. If not – thanks God!

There is a person with the name Pal Palych, who enjoys your support and protection. You are to take everything away from him, just leave one suit, a shirt and a pair of shoes, give a minimum teacher's salary to him. The money you get from him you are to use for building contemporary nursing homes for orphans, where they will be taken care of and educated. They will go there with pleasure, I know that, I worked on that in twenties. Pal Palych for his love for children is to get the position of a janitor in one of the children's homes. Let him be busy. Otherwise, he will start covering roofs with gold again. Is this clear to you?

- Yes, it is, Felix Edmundovich.

- Don't forget about your friend known in Russian criminal circles under the nickname "Red", or "Voucher", who tries to acquire Lenin's plan of electrification of Russia. He is not trying to be acknowledged as an author of the idea, he is trying to make it his property. Give him the minimum salary for an electrician and let him install polls in tundra to pull electrical wires to the Far North territories. Right now he is trying to push the last nail to the cover of the coffin of communism. Let him install polls into the frozen soil, then he may come to understand that there is no way of burying the theory, acknowledged by the whole world. If he doesn't understand that, he will do a useful thing anyway – he will install electricity in the Far North. – Menzhinskiy added.

Lacis, who had kept the silence, bent down to the president and said meaningfully:

- All the leaders of the party and all the Supreme council deputies are to be sent to help the electrician. Let them have a salary of a helper and think of the meaning of the life and the price of a word. Don't forget about the Communist Party of the Russian Federation leaders. You yourself are to create the All-Russian Communist Party, but not the one like "The Unity", otherwise you will have a helper's position as well.

The president saw that he was still enjoying trust. He was encouraged.
– I will do everything, but I would like to have someone to help me. There is no one I could trust, all around there are only horses stealers and budget money stealers.

Dzerzhinskiy smiled. - You will have some help. Do you remember, what a real government security officer must have?

- Yes, I do, Felix Edmundovich. It is a cold mind, a hot heart and clean hands. – The president was solemn and pronounced the words like an oath.

Dzerzhinsliy pressed the button of the ring which was at the side of the desk.

- Good boy! Now our comrades will cool your head and clean up your hands a little bit. Sorry, but we don't have any modern shampoos and cleaning stuff, other than rods and ramrods. But they know their job. Nobody has ever complained about the quality of refreshing and cleaning. You asked for some help. You will get it. – Dzerzhinskiy said at the end without any smile, looking piercingly into the president's eyes.

Three security officers in leather jackets entered the office. The president stood up and went out, followed by them.

-You have one week to fulfil the task. – The president heard the voice of the Iron Felix on his way out.

At this very moment the president woke up. He was wet all over.

- Oh, my God! What kind of dream have I had? Was it a dream? – He looked around and understood that it was a nightmare.

- Oh, thanks God. It was a dream. What a nightmare. – The president became quiet and turned over on the other side. In a while he was asleep again.

But again he is dreaming. He is in Stalin's office. The latter is shouting angrily and hits the desk.

- Why the Chechens are still not being removed from the Northern Caucasus? A train should be immediately sent there. All the Chechens both from the refugee camps and from Chechnya should be loaded into the trains. You have twenty four hours for this. The budget money stealers – the current leaders of Chechnya should be there too. The supervisor should be that very guy who has experience in waging negotiations and who has now the position of the Ambassador in the Ukraine. His manner of speaking is very much similar to that of Chechens. They will understand him very quickly. Don't send them all to Kazakhstan. Send them to Chukotka, to your own friend in the party and in business. Let them work together. Let peasants and former governors cultivate the soil in Chechnya. According to your information, the crops are good there. Let the governors walk on minefields, not on fields covered with dollars. You have twenty four hours for all this. Otherwise, you will go to Lavrentiy Pavlovich for a cup of tea.

The president knew that the word combination "To Beriya for a cup of tea" meant the end of everything. At this very moment he woke up again.

- That's it! I am not going to sleep any more, otherwise Gulag and cutting the penis will be in the next nightmare. – The president of Russia decided. And he stayed awake till morning.

The president of the Ukraine after the dinner fell asleep at the very moment his head touched the pillow. He didn't bother himself with thinking, as in the morning everything is much more clear that at night. Lately his whole life has become a nightmare, not only his dreams. No trust in anyone, everyone betrayed anyone. If you bought something, you are blamed for that, if you sell something you are blamed as well. He was blamed not only for selling Ukrainian oil, gas and electricity. If he had a secret deal in the Middle East and sold missiles there, Washington knew about it immediately. The notorious "Kolchuga" was sold with the help of three middlemen and the whole scheme was reported to Washington. He couldn't make a step. He persecuted by the opposition, by a proposition, by an oil boss, by miners. At least it was good he was greeted in Odessa as if he was a tsar, as there were his own men everywhere. Otherwise, he would have no place to go.

He often dreams about Gongadze, who is calling him. Lazarenko also pulls him by the hand into his cell. Most of all he dreams about the three opposition guys. He was used to those dreams, he paid no attention to them. But in Odessa his nightmare was just terrible.

He was in the office of Stalin. Beside the leader of the peoples there were Molotov, Kaganovich and Beriya in his office. Stalin was walking to and fro along the long table. His colleagues were sitting at the table. He was keeping his famous pipe in his hand. He was speaking quietly, but distinctly.

- The fact that you, comrade president, are helping our friends from Iraq with armaments and military machines is good. You are doing the right thing. We are to oppose American imperialism with our consolidation. You are also doing the right thing when you help to arm the Balkan countries and our African friends.

But why the money received from trading the armaments is spent not for the benefit of the people and for making the country stronger? Why does the money go to your accounts?

Stalin stopped opposite the president and looked at him with his sharp look directly into his eyes. The president looked down, it was impossible to look into the leader's eyes.

- I thought it was safe, comrade Stalin. From the government accounts the money could be stolen, and I can keep it. – He pronounced, frightened. He invented the answer on the spot, like a drowning man who is trying to catch a straw.

Stalin came up to the end of the table. In a while he broke the silence.

Ok. Today transfer all the money to the account of our party. And you…-

He went to a big map on the wall and looked at it attentively.

He went on:

- Where will you send him, Lavrentiy Pavlovich?

The president felt frozen all over inside. Beriya, looking at him from over his glasses, answered loudly:

- To the brigade that is digging trenches of one of the detention camps, which is building the canal Odessa – Brody.

Stalin grinned. – Right you are, comrade Beriya. Let him work hard and make his plans true: oil loaded ships will go from Iraq directly to the centre of Europe.

- But we have built an oil pipe line, comrade Stalin. – The president tried to report.

Kaganovich interfered: - What kind of oil pipe line? You just dig some iron into the earth. The money spent for it could be used for construction of a pipe around the Earth.

The president felt pain in his heart. He thought:

- Still the construction site is better than being shot.

- You'll go to an advanced brigade to the site where your previous president is already working. He works trying to remember, in what off-shore regions he had hidden three hundred ships of the Black Sea fleet. – Beriya said meaningfully, while standing up. – May I take him to my department for a talk, comrade Stalin?

- Sure, you can, Lavrentiy. – Stalin waved his hand with the pipe wearily. At that moment he paid attention to the president's hands. The latter kept his hands together in front of him.

- What is going on with you? Why do you keep your hands on your balls, like Hitler? Do you imagine yourself a Nazi leader? Lavrentiy…

The president felt his legs bend. At this moment he woke up.

- Oh, my God! I am in Odessa, in my own bedroom. Thanks God! I am not going to sleep any more. Such dreams are a bed sign.

The president of Moldova didn't understand the meaning and the purpose of the meeting. After the meal he went to bed. He wanted to escape stealthily across the Dnestr region to Kishinev. The people were Bolshevik-minded there, you could expect anything. Everyone knew that the Dnestr region problem was being discussed at the meeting. They really spoke more about wine and Odessa. The Dnestr region was mentioned only at the press conference.

The president was deep asleep. But before morning he saw a dream. He was dreaming about his vehicles being captured by horsed brigade of Grigoriy Ivanovich Kotovskiy. Three strong horsemen pulled the president out of the car and took him to a narrow, shallow gully, where there was Kotovskiy's headquarters.

Grigoriy Ivanovich had just had lunch. He sat on a big stump, covered with a felt cloak, attentively and with interest examining the man they brought to him.

- Who are you? – He asked at last in a hoarse voice.

The president looked at the horsemen that surrounded him in the uniform of the Red army and said gladly:

- You are ours! Oh, my friends, I thought you were Smirnov's kazaks.

- You, good guy, didn't answer the question. Who are you? Who are Smirnov's kazaks? We have heard nothing of them. – Kotovskiy asked again with a grin.

- I am the president of Moldova, that is Moldavia. I am a member of the Communist party.

- Do you have the party i.d.? Submit it.

The president smiled, he was at a loss.

- Sorry, Grigoriy Ivanovich, but I don't have it with me, I keep it in the safety box in the office.

- What kind of communist are you? You are a bourgeois spy, not a communist. Communists always carry their party i.d. with them. Who are Smirnov's men?

- The Dnestr region wants to separate from Moldova. They declared independence there and created their own army. Hell with him, this Smirnov, he is the leader of the Dnestr region. He wants to be independent.

Kotovskiy looked at him, screwing up his eyes.

- What do you want? It was you and your predecessors, false communists, who ruined Moldavian resources. It was you who put everything upside down. In textbooks they say that everything is having the beginning in Romania and Moldavian territories are historically Romanian. What flags did you hang in the cities? You are saying you are a communist. We are going to support the Dnestr region.

The horsemen, who closely surrounded them, started talking quietly in approval.

- Shoot him! – said Kotovskiy abruptly and stood up. He went to his fighting horse, ready for the rider.

- Grigoriy Ivanovich! – The president begged.

At this very moment he woke up.

In the morning at breakfast the presidents were thoughtful and silent. They were still impressed by the nightmares. After breakfast they accepted with great pleasure the invitation of the metropolit to visit the bell tower of the Spaso-Preobrazhenskiy Cathedral which was being restored. They were going to pray for forgiving of all sins, major and minor. In the church they did pray hard silently asking the God to forgive them.

The president of Russia thought while praying:

- After I return I will supervise economy very thoroughly. I will cut the opportunities of the industrial bosses. I will take care of Chechens.

The president of the Ukraine thought:

- Really, why there is an oil running pipe, but no oil is running there? Is it because the oil is stolen before it gets to the pipe? Or is it because the pipes are laid only in Odessa and Brody, and there is no pipe line between them? I need to check that.

The president of Moldova had already decided that he would go to Kishinev by air, he was not going to tempt the fate.

- I need to warn the Ukrainian colleague to cut off the electricity for the time of my flight on their air-raid complex missiles.

Leaving Odessa the presidents of Russia and Moldova promised to themselves to restrain from paying official visits to this city, as it had negative influence on their minds.

The life was going on. The elections ended with the victory of those who were supposed to win. The results of the elections were announced on the Humour Day, on the first of April. Additional electrical power was not connected by that day. The Dnestr region is living its own separate life. No benches were returned to Primorskiy Boulevard. The main performing persons and their assistants looked smart to some extent, as they say in Odessa. But not smart enough to be admired.

A Call-in Guy

After graduating from the military college Max was sent for work to a military unit stationed not far from Odessa. The first two months everything went on smoothly. Max got a room in the hostel, a good position of an engineer; he was welcomed by the people in the regiment with understanding. He had heard a lot of negative things, but in real life everything seemed to be vice versa. Quite close there was Odessa, just in thirty minutes' drive. It was a city of which Max had heard a lot. But it was his first visit to it right before the military service. He was born in a small village near Chernigov. Max was single. But there were lots of girls around during his school years and during the military training in the college. He looked very handsome, he was tall, he had blonde hair and he was well-built. His face was also very handsome.

The first trips to Odessa with his friends, also lieutenants like himself, excited Max. He was impressed by great disco clubs, night clubs, casino, bars, and restaurants. He liked available, beautiful and sun-tanned girls, who were extremely energetic and didn't have any negative complexes. Almost every Saturday he went out to Odessa to relax. There he enjoyed good time with young girls. Though, it turned out that all this entertainment trips required money in big amounts. There was nothing cheap in Odessa. For free you could get nothing but a glass of vinegar to drink at the market or you could strike a telegraph pole – that was also for free. This occurred to Max in two months, when the money, sent by his parents for his settlement at the new place, was gone.

He didn't turn for help to his parents, as he didn't feel comfortable about that. The parents had saved the money for many years, they had scare wages in the village, and he squandered it in two months. The payments in the army were not paid in time, and they were warned that it was not likely that they would get any payments before the New Year Season. Many of the officers had to go for night shifts as a security officer or as a loader (depending where they could find a vacancy) to support their families.

Max also had to find some additional job, but he didn't want to work hard. He left his village and enrolled in the military college for the reason that he had hated physical work since his childhood. First he was taken to the position of a security officer in the machines area in the casino in the centre of Odessa. He had to work at night, but during the daytime he had some time to sleep. As soon as in a month of his military service he came to the conclusion that he was to stick to the policy of the majority of the officers up to the higher ranks. They pretended to work hard and to care about the work, but in reality they minded their own business and didn't ask unnecessary questions. "Yes, Sir. Right you are, Sir. No, Sir" – were all the words they needed to use. The only thing they were to mind is to look devotedly into the boss's eyes, praise him and agree with everything he was saying.

Max got one hundred bucks for his security job. So, he had some money, but it was enough just to make both ends meet, no more. And he wanted to continue his entertainment trips to Odessa, but he couldn't afford even limited entertainment program with this money.

But he was lucky, as he was noticed by one of the owners of the casino and soon, before the New Year eve he was promoted to the position of the security officer in the main areas of the casino. There he got much more money, but he also had more responsibility there. And still there were much more temptations there…Max watched people who won and lost crazy amounts of money there in just a moment. He saw girls there who made him stop breathing. He could hardly manage his temper when seeing the real beauties that seemed to have come there from all over the world. Max was given a nice suit to wear at work. He was a tall and handsome blonde man, and many women winked at him, said something nice to him and gave plain hints. Sometimes they openly tempted him. Max did understand that during the business hours there was no chance to have a drink or to flirt with somebody. He had been warned about it very strictly. His inside feelings and wishes were supposed to be left outside the casino.

But Max had a new wish, which was an unreal dream. He wanted to earn much money, or to grab it from somewhere at a quick moment, and then to have a rest and to relax, as rich people in the casino did.

He had many thoughts in his head. He thought of finding a treasure with jewelry, or some hidden money. He also thought of robbing a drunken client of the casino. But those were just the thoughts. He couldn't realize anything, as he was a coward by nature.

Gradually he acquired some acquaintances in Odessa. One of the constant clients of the casino, the owner of several cafes, Ashot even asked him several times to drive him home after having drunk too much and being unable to drive himself. After his shift Max drove Ashot to his suburb cottage. Once he was bold enough to ask Ashot to lend him one thousand dollars for three months. Ashot didn't say anything; he just produced his wallet and gave Max the necessary amount.

Keep the money, my dear. I like you. You have a woman-like face and your

bum is attractive... - He laughed and looked at Max with his drunk and bawdy eyes. The latter felt embarrassed because of that look, but he didn't have any choice, he needed the money.

One thousand bucks he wasted in three days. He visited a few night clubs with two first year students from the Medical University. Once in the morning he woke up and looked in the mirror. He was critical and saw a face with traces of kisses and with blue circles under the eyes.

That's it. Have had a good time... Where am I supposed to get the money now?

He was deep in thought. He was supposed to get a part of his salary in the regiment, but it was nothing. The amount was less than one hundred bucks. He couldn't steal anything at work, as he was an engineer and there was nothing to steal except secret information, which was of no interest to anyone, as it had already been sold in Kyiv. Max didn't have access to any material stuff and food that could be sold.

The time ran quickly, and there came the moment when he was supposed to return the debt to Ashot. He had no money. By that time Max had also a debt to the security department manager in the casino.

How are the things, nice looking guy? Where is the money? – Ashot asked, striking Max gently on his cheek. Ashot came to the casino with his friends to have a good time.

Sorry, Ashot. My friend, I can't return the debt now. I will return it, believe me. – Max begged.

- No, my dear. If you can't return the debt in time I will make you pay or you can render certain natural services to me. – Ashot grinned and slapped Max on his bum with his hard hand.

The latter went pale. – What do you mean, Ashot?

I mean what I am telling you. If you don't give me the money by morning we will fuck you. We will make you a girl. You won't be Max any longer, you will be Maxiutka. Is it clear to you?

Ashot's friends laughed out loud. They entered the casino and spoke their own language. There was nowhere to get the money from. There was no sense escaping.

- They will find me anyway. – Max thought. Ashot will get drunk and will forget about everything for today. Tomorrow I will think of some way out.

But Ashot did get drunk with his friends, but forgot nothing. He lost and was mad. When he saw Max at the exit he ordered:

Get into the car.

He was pushed inside the car and driven to a cottage out of the city. Max did not remember clearly what happened next. He was beaten up, he was given lots of whisky and they made him drink so that he was almost unconscious. Then they stripped him and abused him all the five of them in turn.

When he came to his consciousness his first thought was to hang himself. In a few minutes he thought the better of it. It occurred to him that he could pay back all his debts and make some money for a careless life by making money as a gay. He had heard before that there was a kind of gathering of such men at the bar of the Russian theatre. It was a kind of a gay club. He decided to go there. Ashot promised to kill him if he says something to anyone about turning him to a girl. And he was supposed to return the debt in a month.

Max went to the gay club and offered his services. He was introduced to certain persons; he was tested for venereal diseases and aids. They hired him at once, as he was handsome and well built.

Max had to quit from the casino, but he didn't regret of that. He didn't regret of what had happened to him in Ashot's company. As quickly as in a few months he was residing in a separate apartment in the center of Odessa. It was a quiet and nice area. The company paid for the apartment. He had to work hard. As a young gay with the body as Max had, he was in demand with the clients, most of which were men. Max was working as a call-in boy. First he had to get some training. Max appeared to be a talented student. He didn't regret the fact that he had to make money by using his body. The privacy was fully guaranteed. Clients paid fifty to two hundred bucks per hour. Though Max received just thirty per cent of the money, Max didn't regret that either. The clothes and the apartment were the company's expenses. He did bring good money for the company, that was four to six hundred and it was big money. He himself had one hundred bucks as a minimum daily. In a year Max had a foreign made car of his own. He could afford visiting and night clubs and he had paid all his debts.

When the Russian theatre was closed for renovation, Max took the advantage of this and quitted the company. He started to work for himself. He accepted calls over the phones at a certain time. He had his own business cards and he said the cards were for girlfriends.

He couldn't make money otherwise, nor did he want to. He knew he was good for nothing else.

He hated making sex to men, but there was nothing doing. He was extremely popular with the men of non traditional sexual orientation and there was a bunch of clients, many of them well established. Max could afford choosing. He had enough permanent clients among bankers, high-rank officers and there was even a prosecutor and a judge. He sometimes joked that a lawyer was missing in the company.

He didn't quit the military service, but it didn't interfere with his life. "Let it be, just in case". – He thought.

But he had no plans of staying in the army for the whole of his life. He was not planning to be a call-in boy for a long time either. Though in the gay club there was a call-in boy of about fifty.

No private life at all. I will work for myself for a couple of years and they I will quit. – Max thought.

He constantly had a risk of catching some disease; he was humiliated, sometimes beaten up. He got acquainted with a girl and the relationship was developing well. But soon she understood who she was dealing with and she dumped him.

Beside men he also received orders from women. Max liked it. Usually it was the calls from middle-aged well-to-do women. There were also women who were unsatisfied by their impotent husbands. Businessmen's wives were his clients as well. Most of the businessmen usually changed their old women for younger ones as soon as they had some money in the pocket. But the age, great constant stresses, alcohol influenced their potency. Young wives, yesterday's young girls, wanted passion and diversity above money, which they got at the meetings with Max.

And he did enjoy the time with them! He could allow to do anything with them, and that what exactly what they wanted.

- Bitches! In bed they are exactly like beasts, they growl and moan and want more and more and more...

Those women differed from men in their generosity. But there was one problem: if you rendered services only to them, you would not earn anything, as almost all the clients were men.

In a year Max retired from the military service. He got married to a rich Jewish woman who was immigrating to Germany. She was almost twice as old as him. He abandoned his filthy occupation and left with her. In a while in one of the cities of Germany Max opened a gay-club of his own. And again he was in his habitual business. As they say, a pederast is everywhere a pederast, even in Africa.

A woman's Fore-Part

This autumn not far from Odessa there happened something that was noticed by many entrepreneurs dealing with laundry detergents. There was a grand opening of a small plant producing detergents, such as soap, shampoo, laundry detergents, dishwashing liquids and other stuff of the kind. The grand opening was really grand, with the presence of the Governor. There were also representatives of the country administration there, some other officials, as they say. There were also representatives of the Turkish investors and representatives of the Embassy of Turkey in the Ukraine. The orchestra played some music, the ribbon was cut and, no doubt, there was a reception.

Sonya Fisher was lying in her sofa in the living room, watching indifferently the events on the TV screen.

- So much ado and aplomb about all this. What is the use of this plant? It can produce as much detergents per week as three containers of the products from Turkey. I own a company which monthly receives twenty containers of goods from Turkey only. There can be no competition here. And the prices of the local products can't compete with the cost of the imported goods. No doubt, they are much higher. They did create about two hundred working places. But that is all they did. And they keep making so much ado about it all over the world.

Sonya switched off the TV and went to the washroom. For an hour she was relaxing in Jacuzzi and thought of nothing. She just gave herself a good rest after the busy week. She stood up in the bathtub and rubbed herself dry with a towel. She looked in the mirror and examined her body. She felt satisfied with her appearance. She was tall, with a good

107

figure, dark thick long hair, Greek profile and blue eyes. She smiled with her charming smile which drove many men crazy, no matter what nationality and religious denomination they were. – That's great! No one could tell my age, and I am twenty eight. My breasts pop up so nicely. What about my bum? It's just great.

Suddenly she was captured with a great desire to find herself in the hands of a passionate, strong man and to make love with him, forgetting about the whole world. But in a minute she conquered her desire and went straight to the bedroom.

- I need to rest. Tomorrow I will have a hard day. I need to think over and consider everything. What, actually, she was to consider? Her business needs to be expanded. Sonya was born in a family of a Soviet office worker; she abbreviated it as "sovofworker" when she was inquired about her childhood. She didn't like to remember that period. Actually, there was nothing to remember. Who was her father? It was difficult to determine that. He mother graduated from the pedagogical institute and was working as an instructor in the district committee of Komsomol. At that time she was a beautiful girl with a languishing look which almost directly gave a message to the male population:

- What's wrong with you? Can't you see that the girl wants?

For the first time Mother Vera surrendered as early as in the ninth grade to the fitness and training teacher. It happened in the school gym on a floor mat. And then it went on. She had sex with almost all the men in her school, including her classmates.

Before the time she was finishing the school she was noticed by a secretary of the Komsomol committee of the pedagogical institute, they called it "pedin" in Odessa. Right after school she enrolled in "pedin". She didn't want to study. She didn't need it either. Having a sexy appearance, she had sex with everyone available in the institute, and she had no problems with her studies. She was married four times. The marriages didn't last long, as in a few months the husbands became aware that the wife was having sex with anyone who was wearing pants.

The years went on, and she had three kids already. It didn't matter to her if they were by her husbands or not. Actually, she didn't know that herself. Till the age of forty she lived easily and lightly, as she was close to the ruling class representatives. First she worked in Komsomol offices, and then she was hired as an office assistant to the second secretary of the

Ilyichev district committee of the Communist party. Then she moved to the office of the first secretary... So, anyone was taking advantage of her. Party bosses had sex with her when they wanted, where they wanted and as much as they wanted. They said she had a weak fore-part, meaning that she was always willing to have sex with a man, no matter how old he was, what was his appearance; the place and the time didn't matter either. He bosses often used her for pleasing the heads of different commissions. And the bosses had those commissions rather often. At every parties and entertainments she was in the center of the event. She liked this kind of life. She was even given a luxurious three bedroom apartment in a very good apartment building constructed during Stalin rule, located in Gorky street. In the apartment she had beautiful and expensive furniture, refrigerators full of tasty food and drinks. She was wearing expensive and beautiful clothes. She always had money. She was always updated about all the political events, as well as the changes done by the human recourses development departments. Vera helped all her acquaintances to solve their problems. She was not so very kind-hearted, she just felt pleased at the thought that she could solve any problem. The evil tongues used to tell:

- See, how Vera, a real hook, managed to get everything in her life. The fore-part is the tool to earn her well-being and luxurious life.

- It's not for ever, as the fore-part will get old and shabby and we'll see what happens to her then. She won't be as prosperous, for sure. – The neighbors discussed her gloatingly. – Maybe she will implant a silicon fore-part then?

Vera didn't pay any attention to that. She was well known in Kyiv and Moscow. She got upset for one reason only. She said to her girl friends lighting when discussing intimate things with them: - You see, girls, I had sex with the second secretary, but never with the first! But I hope everything is still in store for me, I am still young. It's a pity there is no leaders in the International, as I would like to have sex with international leaders too. - It was not like this in real life, as in Odessa there were many delegations of foreign communist parties, and she always found herself the bedroom of the head of the delegation.

The years passed and they left their traces. Constant parties, drinking, night orgies did their work too. Vera never restricted herself in taking alcohol; she usually drank till she was unconscious. Then she had sex with anyone who wanted to, as many times as they wanted, in any place, in different positions. Everything has its own limit. By forty she looked different than she used to. No masks, no make up could help, but she couldn't quit the show, as she called her life. In 1991 the communist party stopped to exist, and Vera found herself overboard. She couldn't't and didn't't want to work. No one hired her as an office assistant. A new generation came to the world, eighteen years old geishas with long legs and good looks. They were youth and health themselves. Vera couldn't compete with them. With the help of her former acquaintances she was hired by human resources department of the regional committee, where she got small salary, enough just to make both ends meet.

The children were already grown-up. The elder daughter and the son lived separately. Verka lived with her younger daughter who was in school. She came home after work and drank till she was unconscious; she remembered her past joyful, well-to-do and easy life. She gradually became addicted to alcohol. In rare sober minutes she dressed up and went to her ex-boyfriends from the party leaders begging them for help.

- Bustards! No one of them is overboard. One is a plant manager, the other is the bank manager, the third is the rector of the institute, the fourth is the mayor, and the fifth is a deputy. – Verka was indignant. – Everyone is having a good position and money. I don't interest them any more. When I was young they fucked me so hard that the neighborhood was aware, and now they don't want to know me. I come into a reception, where there sits a twenty years old kid and she doesn't let me in. - But Vera was not very much upset to see the young lionesses at the entrance of the high-rank leaders. She boldly went in and demanded just one thing – money. Some of them paid to her so that they could get rid of her, some of them sent her to hell.

She hated her children. The younger one was the exception. She adored her, as she conceived her by the man she loved. The daughter did remind her of that love, which occurred when she was no longer young. She reminded her of those sweet days when she was satisfied not only physically, but also spiritually.

The elder daughter, Sonya, was a girl with a great body and a beautiful face. Vera wanted her to wage the same life she herself used to.

- Nowadays you can't sleep with a party secretary, as the party no longer exists. But with your appearance you can find some position in the mayor's office, or the Governor's office, they need officers there. Now they are ruling and they also have money. Don't be silly. Otherwise you can get into a bad company and become a regular hook, with a woman-boss. A hook is a hook everywhere, even in Africa. And to be a mistress of a higher-rank leader is a real occupation.

Sonya listened to this madness till she finished school. After she got the certificate from school she said to her mother directly:
- You used to sleep with communists all you life, but you don't know what Lenin said. When his elder brother was executed, he said to his mother that they would take a different way. So will I, my dear mother, I will take a different way. I have my own head on my shoulders.
It was at the beginning of the nineties. Sonya finished computer courses right after school. It didn't take her long to get a position of an office assistant in one of the companies which was in cosmetics business. The manager of the company, Ashot, Armenian by nationality, was told directly that she was not going to sleep with him.
I am a serious girl, I am going to enroll in a University, and I am waiting for my fiancée to be released from a jail and whom I madly love.
Ashot knew that the fiancée could be release and take revenge on him. But on the very first day he put her right on the desk and tried to take advantage of her with all his Armenian hatred, and she didn't fight with him, she just said quietly that if he did that, she would write a note to the prosecutor and jump out of the window of the office form the seventh floor.
It was hard to say what influenced Ashot more, but he had no wish to have sex with the secretary, though his heart was beating quicker when she entered his office, and he was tense all over. He didn't change the office assistant. Sonya fulfilled her functions well, and she was attracting clients with her beauty, soft voice, friendly and attractive smile, and all that worked better that the efforts of the most experienced manager. The business partners also tried to drop to the office to Ashot more often, even without any reason for that.
- They are attracted as bees to the honey, - Ashot smiled. It suited him, and he even raised Sonya's salary.

As for Sonya, she gradually went to her goal. In the company she was considered to be a touch-me-not person, who was waiting for her bandit from jail. At that very time Sonya had been having sex, as they call it in Odessa, for a long time. She did like it; she was frantic in getting sexual pleasure. One man couldn't satisfy her, and she got satisfaction, making love to three to four guys per day. She also had her boyfriends in the medical institute, where she visited the gym. There she hardly worked out, she rather made love. In order not to get pregnant or not to catch a disease, she always had a complete set of condoms.

As for her goal, it was to seduce a rich guy, to drive him to the condition when he was ready to make absurd steps and then to marry him. Then she was going to take control over his business, or at least to get her interest at divorce.

I will be rich and independent. – This was her decision.

- I need to gain the position in the society and money with the help of the fore-part. Money is the priority, then the position will be of a higher level and not as low as being a hook for communist bosses, like her dearest mother.

There was one more condition that Sonya set for herself – that was not to fall in love and to restrain feelings at the very beginning, right at the start. She had a strong will-power, most likely by her father, whom she didn't know and never saw. It was that sense of proportion and will-power that helped her to conquer her feelings without any effort.

At last the time came when she met her victim. Ashot signed a contract with a new business partner for organizing regular deliveries and wholesales of detergents from Turkey and Greece. The new business partner was Misha Fisher, a nice looking Jewish guy, at the age of thirty. He had already made a success in business and was a rich resident of Odessa. To tell the truth, he was belonged to Odessa due to his background and his childhood, spent in Odessa. Since the age of twenty he had been residing in Tel-Aviv and was a legal citizen of Israel. He started his business with the financial help of his aunt, who also shared some business managing ideas with him. Misha was a charming person with an analytical type of mind and a business-like character. He easily found the necessary business information and knew where to invest. In a short while he got great profit from those investments. He had an acute feeling for a profitable deal.

It seemed to be natural for him to get the right approach to any person. By the middle of nineties he was a rich man and owned a part of stocks of oil producing companies. He also developed his own independent scheme of delivery of detergents and cosmetics to the Ukraine and to Russia. He was not a greedy person, but almost all his money was invested in the business. He worked with enthusiasm and he liked it. The only weak point he had was love for pretty women. All through his life he tried not to miss a single skirt passing by. That was the point when he didn't spare time and money. In case he couldn't get the sympathies with the help of his own charming personality, he used such means as expensive presents, overseas trips and great quantities of flowers.

The successful businessman took notice of Sonya at his very first visit to Ashot's office. But his initial flirting and his unambiguous hints did not have any effect on Sonya. She just didn't't notice Fisher. That irritated and excited him.

- Ashot, look here, tell me the truth, if you have already fucked your secretary. Or are you having regular sex with her? Give her to me, be a friend to me. – He once said frankly to his partner.

The latter laughed out loud and said: - I am not sure you will be a success. I can tell you that as far as I know many men tried to gain her by ruse, flirting, force, but nothing worked. She is a woman made of stone. She says she is waiting for her boyfriend to be released from a jail, where he is serving his sentence, he is a bandit. Many men, having this information, just don't want to deal with her. But she is an attractive creature. I do use her nice appearance to develop my business. As far as girls for pleasure are concerned, there are lots of them willing to make love with me. So, my advice is that you shouldn't spend your time and money.

But Fisher was not a person who gave up. Since then he almost every day dropped to Ashot's office. But he paid his visits not to the latter, but to Sonya. He came with flowers, stayed in the reception for a long time, made Sonya laugh at his jokes and funny stories of his own life.

She accepted the flowers with great pleasure and listened to him, but all his invitations for lunch or dinner were definitely refused. He started chasing her in the street. He waited for her at the entrance to her apartment building in the morning and at night. Furthermore, he established good contact with her mother. She actually didn't want much, just a few bottles of good cognac and some snack were enough for her. Now she received expensive presents every day.

But Sonya, as they say in Odessa, showed off, she just behaved independently and decently, no matter what the circumstances were. She did like Misha and she did want to check if his sexual abilities were corresponding to the rumors about him. But she suppressed her desire and satisfied herself in the company of guys from the gym. She was a real connoisseur in sex. All the tricks in love she got from a post-graduate student from the Chair of the Sports Medicine, who was of ordinary appearance, but in bed he was an unsurpassed lover. But to tell the truth, all the plain furniture in the post-graduate students' room was their bed. Fisher was patiently waiting for Sonya near the medical institute, in his car or in the bar. He thought that she cared a lot about her body, as she went in for aerobics, and she at that time satisfied her sexual demands in a group sex on gym mats.

She was tall, with beautiful well-shaped legs, strong breasts coming out of the sun-dress. As she was coming like that out of the educational building of the Institute, easily descending the stares, smiling charmingly, Fisher was going crazy and gritted his teeth.

You will be mine, no matter what it costs to me. I will gain you.

She just ran by, nodding to him: - Good night, Mikhail. Would you like to join some of the clubs? Or are you waiting for someone? If you are waiting for me, I am sorry, as I have some personal matters to take care of.

After that she gave her beautiful and promising smile to Misha and disappeared behind the corner. Misha dreamed about her. He saw himself undressing her, he saw them making love. She constantly was in front of his eyes. He dreamed of her. He lost his appetite, he was not as smart at work any more, he was not satisfied making love with other women, he lost his peace.

Sonya was aware of all that and she let Fisher closer to her. They were having lunch and even dinner together. She let him see her off to home, they often went out to theatre, concerts, night clubs. Sonya received his presents with pleasure. But she didn't allow Mikhail even to kiss her. Once he hugged her in the car and tried to take advantage of her by force. But she made him retreat saying: - We are not going to meet each other any more.

Misha Fisher was in love, it was a real love, like the one a youth experiences for the first time in his life. He told Sonya about his love on his knees, on an autumn night, near her home, when it was raining, in wet and cold weather.

I propose to you, Sonya, my love, marry me. – Fisher begged in despair.

I must consider how serious you are. Everyone is talking about you as a light-minded person, who changes women every now and then. I am not a pair of gloves, which can be easily changed, remember that, my dear Jew. I am an expensive girl, you need to value me.

She felt pity for him, wet and miserable, and invited him inside, where she treated him to coffee and cognac. Then she put him to her own bed, she went to sleep separately. At night he crawled inside her blanket, hot with excitement, she almost surrendered, but the common sense prevailed.

No. We'll do it only after the registration of our marriage, my dear. – She put apart his arms.

Fisher couldn't wait any longer. The next day their marriage was registered, and in a week they had a reception. His parents and all his relatives were strongly against that marriage. There were several reasons for that. First of all, Sonya was not of Jewish origin. Secondly, she was a daughter of the most notorious "communist party bitch", as his aunt said.

- Once you marry this bitch, you'll find a headache for all your life. – His father said to him over the phone.

The relatives didn't come to the wedding and didn't send their greetings. – That didn't upset either Sonya, or Misha. He bought a three-storeyed detached house in Tzarskoye Selo, and it was his wedding gift to her. There were security and housekeeping services in the house. Besides, he presented her a luxurious car. As she was not driving, he hired a young but experienced driver for her.

Both were really happy. Misha was happy because he at last obtained Sonya, he was crazy about her. As a mistress she was very skillful in bed, it was her natural gift or experience, but no one could compare with her. They went to America, to Miami for the honey moon. Sonya was just struck by the splendor and richness of America. There she declared to Misha, changing the text of the most famous of Pushkin's tales, that she didn't want to be a sea queen, but she wanted to obtain American citizenship.

There was nothing he didn't want to do for his beloved woman. And Misha promised that he would solve the problem. After their return to Odessa, following his young wife's instructions, he changed Sonya's background and she became a Jew by her father. After that she applied for permanent residence in USA.

Sonya got into the business very quickly. Misha was surprised how quickly she got acquainted with all the problems. In a while he understood Ashot who didn't like the idea that Sonya was not going to work for him any longer. She persuaded Misha to make her his partner, and he did so. He was glad to have her as a partner. Her beauty, her charming appearance made all the doors open for him. At his first visit to Istanbul together with Sonya the Turkish partners in less than two hours accepted all the conditions set for them by Misha. Before that he had been insisting on those conditions for a whole year with no results. The first year of their married life was like a moment for him. By the end of the year he appointed Sonya as a manager of all the business links in detergents and cosmetics branches. He concentrated on oil. Besides, he was working at a project of a big supermarket and an entertainment centre in one of Odessa districts.

- You do all the negotiations with Turkish and Greek partners much better than me. – He said to Sonya. – Make all the decisions yourself.

That was what she wanted. In Turkey she could easily solve any problem. In her first business trip to Istanbul she took advantage of the chairman of the council of managers of a company producing detergents. He was just crazy about the sex appealing beauty from Odessa. In future as soon as he wanted to have her in his bed he started to delay deliveries. If somebody else went there, there was no result. There were thousands of reasons, important and real, for the delays. But once Sonya went to Istanbul, all the gates were opened, all the deliveries occurred as scheduled with no delays. She solved the problems with deliveries, prices, customs and others. Those were questions that usually required the effort of a whole department. Sonya laughed to herself: I have just one part of my body that can solve all the questions quickly and with high quality – that is my fore part, which is just irresistible.

Soon she had an idea of signing contracts with French companies, famous all over the world. Though Misha tried to persuade her not to do that, as it was not their level, but much higher, he understood that he could not change her mind. She left for Paris and spent a whole month there. And the trip was a success, she signed a few profitable contracts. French partners gave money for arranging a constant exhibition of French cosmetics and perfumes. It wasn't easy for her to get all that, as it was hard to overcome the refined-looking French women, who were also sex appealing in bed. She did overcome everyone with her charm, irresistible modest appearance and inner absence of restrain.

When she was back, Misha examined the contracts and was struck. He couldn't restrain himself and said bitterly: - You couldn't have done that without sex.

She smiled to him and answered abruptly: - If I need that for the business, I will sleep with all the men in Paris. Your advice and remarks are not needed here. Maybe you thought that in Turkey I also modestly stayed in line in reception rooms waiting for the contracts to be signed? Don't be hypocritical, you little cunning Jew. You knew where you sent me. What kind of details do you want to know now?

She burst out: - But for me, your business would have choked long ago at the start. I restored it from the ground and you are reprimanding me for that. I did bring the money to the company – by means of my fore-part or of my brains. And you spend this money in casino or for bitches. Don't approach me until you submit me a medical certificate.

The security officers had already told her about the orgies which her husband arranged during her absence. Misha had no idea that her beloved wife had sex with a security officer on the fifth day of their marriage, at the tiled floor of the bathroom, while he was out. Since then all the security officers, and there were three of them, tried to get a shift when the husband was out. It was them who reported to her about all Misha's steps. And, no doubt, they didn't do that for free.

Misha did realize that his beloved Sonya was not as innocent. And it was the first quarrel that happened between them, He got mad and went to a night club. There he got drunk and was telling his friends all about all his troubles.

She is beautiful and sexy. She fucks not only with me, I can feel that. Once I catch her, I will tear her up, as toilet paper.

At that very moment Sonya was having sex with one of the security officers in her bedroom. Earlier, before marriage, she had to keep her attraction to males in secret. Now she didn't restrict herself, she had sex with anyone who attracted her. The only thing that could stop her was the untidy looks of the partner. Lately she was mostly attracted by young boys who had just finished school. They were so energetic and passionate, they had no restriction and were really hot. They couldn't be compared with businessmen and officers of her surrounding, who had irregular life style and experiences frequent stresses. Sometimes when Misha couldn't know, she visited youth disco clubs where young guys were entertaining themselves. They were eager to get a bitch with no restrictions. And she fucked with them with great pleasure in apartment buildings and in the bushes, once even in a men's washroom.

It's for diversity. – She used to say to herself. – I have everything in my life!

I have a position in the society, I have really big money, I have a husband, no matter how hot he is, still I have one. There are lots of willing men everywhere. I wonder if there will come the time when I will be satisfied. Now I need more and more. I always want sex. I would like to live in a man's arms and in ecstasy.

She did realize that her marriage with Misha would not last long. Furthermore, his parents had already found another woman for him, she was a young Jewish girl, who had just finished school and enrolled in Law Academy.

Misha would not listen to his parents. He would be glad to dump Sonya, but there were three reasons for not doing that. First of all, due to Sonya's effort the company activity expanded every month. Secondly, according to the prenuptial agreement, signed in USA due to her being very insistent, half of his real estate, money and stocks belonged to her in case of divorce. And there was the third reason – that was the fact that he still loved her passionately and couldn't imagine a life without her.

Sonya was sick and tired of the Jewish style and she decided to file for divorce herself. She needed grounds for divorce, and she invented one. She met her girl friends from the medical institute and paid them big amount of money. They were supposed to attract her husband in the night club "Kosmo".

Everything went on according to the scenario. Misha thought that Sonya had left for Istanbul. He was drunk in "Kosmo" and he agreed to spend the night with two beautiful blond women with no restrictions.

He relaxed with them in the club and then took them home to Tzarskoye Selo. There the three of them had sex till morning. Before the dawn the light in the bedroom went on and Fisher saw infuriated Sonya.

The same morning she filed for divorce. She would not accept any reasons and would not compromise. They got a divorce within a week with the help of former enemies, who appeared to be helpful in the situation with the divorce, those were the parents and the numerous relatives of Fisher. According to the prenuptial agreement she owned two houses. One was in Odessa in Tzarskoye Selo; the other was in USA, in Miami. Fisher's company lost the branch which dealt with detergents, cosmetics and perfumes, now it belonged to Sonya. She spend three months in business trips to France, Greece and Turkey, she received additional shares for goods, she went to Kyiv and with the help of influential persons in the parliament settled the problems with the customs and sea ports, she also got financing in one of the banks. She didn't just keep the business alive, she expanded it so, that she was considering taking part in banking business.

She seemed to have born under a lucky star, as any business she started was flourishing and brought great profits. Many businessmen considered it to be a privilege to have business with Sonya. She was even called Sonya – golden hand, as she was bringing luck. As for her, she smiled to herself and told just to herself that she had a golden fore-part, and it was golden due to her wits.

She didn't have girl friends. She had known since childhood that girl friends were envious and cunning. It was much better to have men as friends, as it was better for her sole, and body and business.

Fisher started drinking a lot after the divorce. His relatives even had to turn to doctors for help. They hired the best specialists in alcohol addiction treatment. In a year in Israel he recovered, married a Jewish girl, found by his parents. The wedding was grand, the marriage ceremony took place in Tel-Aviv. Misha lived with his young wife in Haifa, but he often visited Odessa. His wife continued her education and Misha came on business trips, as he did open a supermarket and an entertainment centre. From time to time he met Sonya. Their friends invited them for different picnics and parties where Fisher and his wife always were given seats at one and the same table with Sonya, opposite her. It was the way the friends had fun. She didn't pay much attention to that, she treated him favorably, but the young wife went mad. Fisher also felt uncomfortable, as he couldn't remove that woman out of his heart. He still loved her. In a year after the divorce she became still more beautiful. She was just flourishing. Many men were attracted by her, she was a beautiful woman with the position in the society and with big money.

She was generally satisfied with her life, but still she was lacking something. She had a permanent boyfriend, which was not her lifestyle. He was a student of the medical institute, a modest, smart and decent guy from Nikolayev. She told him a lie that the house in Tzarskoye Selo and the business was received by her from her parents who were residing in America, she bought some clothes for him and introduced him to the society. More and more often Sonya visited theatres, concerts and night clubs with a tall nice looking man with good manners. They had eight years of age difference, but she told nothing to him about it. He thought they were the same age. He lived in a student hostel, but more and more often he slept over at her place.

Once Dima went to her parents for two weeks, and she understood with fear that she had deeply fallen in love with that guy. She was suffering for a week, and then she couldn't suffer any more. She went to Nikolayev to meet the beloved man for just an hour. She spent a night with him in a hotel and left for Odessa. She had a choice. Dima wanted to introduce her to his parents and get married. Sonya realized that she was supposed to quit business and change all her lifestyle. Otherwise Dima would make out and realize, who she really was, in a month.

After long thinking she made her decision and bought an airplane ticket for Antalia. There during two weeks she spent time with rich idle men from Russia and she forgot all her feelings and love to Dima. The great sea air and great sea water, sex with no obligations, just minutes of passion, influenced well upon her. She made a final decision.

Love is just nonsense. I am not alone, I am in demand in the society and among men. While I have all this, I am not going to change anything. There would come the time when the fore-part will be breaking from time to time, I will be over forty and the first wrinkles will appear, then I will think of somebody to share my loneliness.

Sonya Fisher returned to Odessa in two weeks. She was sunburned and full of energy. She was intended to continue her courtesan lifestyle which gave her physiological satisfaction and also completed her businesswoman's set of necessary things.

Transit

The retired colonel Ivanov, Alexander Sergeevich, had not been to his native city, in the old Russian city of Pskov, or as he liked to call it, "Sunny Shacklemakerstan". There were different reasons for that.

He didn't feel any special nostalgia. Actually, there was nothing special that attracted him to his native place, to Russia.

He was seventeen when he left his native home. He studied in military college and in military academies in Russia, all the other time his military service was outside the country. Ivanov changed the location of his military service every two or three years. He got adapted to a new place quickly. Being a sociable person, he quickly got acquainted with people, even different from him in judgments and social position. He had many friends in different parts of the former Soviet Union and overseas. At every new place he found its own good point and something familiar in nature, in people, in household style.

For many people changing location is an event in their lives, connected with some emotional experience. As for Ivanov, moving was a regular thing for him. That was the reason why the feeling of nostalgia was unknown and strange for him. But deep inside he was proud of his roots, his native place, where he was born and grew up.

He was proud of the fact that Peter the First himself stressed that the in Pskov there were very skilled shackle makers, as they produced very good shackles for ships. That was why the residents of Pskov were called shackle makers. He was proud of the fact that Pskov was an ancient city with a thousand years' history, rich with events. He was proud that Alexander Sergeevich Pushkin lived at Pskov region and created his poems there; that Pushkin was his namesake and his remnants were resting in Pushkin hills. His native place was connected with the life and professional activity of the mathematician Bradis and the composer Mussorgsky. The Red Army was created on the Pskov land. In the ancient times Alexander Nevskiy smashed Teutonic knights on that land.

At the same time he remembered for ever some negative sides of the life and household style of the shackle makers. That was ancient and wild ignorance, which was very conspicuous and which was reflected first of all in hard drinking, hoarse language and rudeness. Every time he came to his native place he was very much upset with the fact that the ignorance of his fellow countrymen was not any less, and on the contrary, it was progressing with every year, with every decade, and especially it was obvious at the end of the twentieth century. It was as many as ten years ago that the Soviet Union split, and Ivanov retired from the armed forces. Many things had changed since then, both visible and invisible, Ivanov's life had also changed. He didn't have any nostalgia for his former life in the soviet society. But being a military man, he liked order in everything, he liked being organized and he liked fairness in everything. All those things were missing at the territory of the former soviet republics. Ivanov waged a life of an ordinary resident of Odessa, which was a city constantly unquiet and overcrowded, as it was a port, a big trading and business city. Ivanov had been living in Odessa for almost twenty years and he came to like the city for its unique atmosphere and peculiarity. It was the sea, the chestnuts in the streets of Odessa and of course, its residents, who were always optimistic, witty and resilient, who had their own specific humor. That was something one couldn't help liking and being proud of.

But nowadays it was no longer that Odessa. The streets, the chestnuts and the sea seemed to be the same, but the city was different. During the latest decades it was abandoned by the best intellectual residents, smart and enterprising persons, who had left Odessa and were residing mostly overseas, as they had foreseen the future unlawful style of governing by rude officials. But no good place can stay vacant. Residents of Odessa used to say about that phenomenon: "What do they call the sacred land? Jerusalem! They are supposed to think. Odessa is a real sacred land. The moment Jews left this place, Arabs came here".

Every time Ivanov passed by the mosque, constructed right in the centre of Odessa at the end of the twentieth century, those words came to his mind. They called it the Arab Cultural Centre.

Odessa became full of people who came from villages around Odessa and from former soviet republics in order to find some easy way of making money. Odessa was filled with ignorant people. In Odessa they were called "Jlobs". At first the word was not insulting, it was a derivative of the English word "Job", and it meant "a hard working person". Only the phrase "Jlob with a wood-cut face" was insulting. Later the word "Jlob" became a synonym of the words and word combinations "a country bumpkin", "a cad" and "a person who didn't have an elementary idea of good manners". That was why the former Odessa residents who visited their native city from time to time, usually said:

- You can spit anywhere and you will hit a jlob with jlob females and jlob kids.

Ivanov was aware of that and he was very much concerned. By the end of the week he was usually tired of constant communication with jlobs and he wanted to go outside of Odessa so that he could relax and get some distraction of all those Odessa relationships. He also did realize that relations of the same kind were spread all over the Ukraine and all over the former soviet territories.

During the summer Ivanov with his wife usually left for Zatoka to the seaside for the weekend. There one of his friends owned a cottage place. The atmosphere there was quiet and friendly, the beach was nice, the sand was clean, and the sea water was also clean. The positive aura was in everything, and they had a rest from all the loathsomeness of the contemporary life in Odessa.

In spite of all the turns of the destiny and total ignorance and mean relations between people, in Odessa there was successfully developing big and small business. Many enterprises were working. Retail and wholesale trading business was busy. So, one could make some money in Odessa and there were also places in the city where he could spend his money. Just keep going. In Odessa everyone was busy. It was a regular thing that a lazy person didn't stay long in Odessa; he didn't fit there, even if he was an officer. Even at an official position one had to move, as he was to consider everything he got in a day, in a week, in a month and to distribute the stuff accordingly. Something was to be kept by him; something was to be shared with the boss. That was the rule.

Ivanov was busy with his own life, he had his own problems, but there was something that he felt as a load in his heart. At Pskov region his mother and aunt were buried, and there was no one to take care of the graves. He hadn't been there for eight years. He was going to travel there every year, but every time the trip was delayed due to one reason or another.

He felt ashamed for that, he felt reproach on the side of his wife, his children, his grandchildren and the God.

He very much regretted that he was not able to pay more attention to his mother and the aunt, who was babysitting with him in his childhood, while they were alive. He felt ashamed that after their death he failed to take care of the graves. According to human rules and to his own understanding of morality and decency he was supposed to do that. There were no excuses, no reasons and problems could be taken into consideration.

It was the beginning of June, when the Ivanovs decided to use available seven days for the trip to Pskov, to the graves of his relatives. They decided to drive there. They wanted to combine business and pleasure, they wanted to enjoy the natural sites, to see other cities and villages, to get acquainted with the life and household style in different parts of the Ukraine, Belarus and Russia, which were situated along the road from Odessa to St. Petersburg. It was about one thousand and five hundred kilometers' drive to the destination point.

During his trip Ivanov decided to visit the city of Opochka, where more than thirty years ago he graduated from a military college. Besides, he wanted to visit Pushkin Hills and to show the beauty of Pushkin-related places to his wife. The latter had never been there. It was the time when the poet's birthday was celebrated.

Ivanov heard a many contradictory opinions about the contemporary life in Russia, Belarus and the Ukraine. TV was showing one thing, newspapers were writing of something contrary, people were telling something else. What was the truth? Ivanov wanted to see the life with his own eyes. He had always wanted to drive along the roads of the former Soviet Union, to see how people lived in the former republics, nowadays in separate countries. He wanted to talk to people, to get inside their problems, which were not allowing them to live richly, peacefully and happily on the land, which had greatest natural conditions in the world.

There seemed to be everything for that kind of life there. Ivanov deep in his heart understood that people themselves were to blame, as they had all the old drawbacks, such as laziness, ignorance, addiction to alcohol and envy. He wanted to find proof to his thoughts. In all the periods of time people in Russia were asking the same questions: "What are we to do?" and "Who is to blame?" Ivanov knew the answers to those questions, but he wanted his conclusions to be proven by what he was going to see with his own eyes.

Of course, he hoped to see many good things as well, at least some positive things in the life of people.

They started off early in the morning at dawn and in half an hour they were on the highway from Odessa to Kyiv. The road was not busy, and Ivanov kept the speed of one hundred and twenty to one hundred and thirty kilometers per hour. In Odessa and all over the Ukraine it had been raining for two weeks. Before that the weather was dry and sunny. There were talks that the crops could have been burnt and now all the fields were flooded with water. Ivanov could see from the road that in the fields the wheat crops were even, almost ripe. So were other grain-crops.

- Look, they said the crops were damaged. The rains did well for the crops. The wheat is really good. – He said to Lena.

The latter nodded. She looked at the fields, plants, villages along the road with interest, as they passed by. She liked traveling; she enjoyed going by a car and seeing beautiful nature and nice looking villages.

Before the turn to Ivanovka, which was about seventy kilometers from the starting point, the road was comparatively good. It had two lanes in both directions; one direction lanes were separated from two other lanes with a green lane covered with grass. Beyond that point the road was narrow, it required reconstruction, at some parts there were multiple pot-holes. They had to drive at a lower speed. Metal fencing at the sides had untidy looks, the paint was peeling, and the metal was rusted. The road from Odessa to Kyiv didn't cause any positive emotions.

Ivanov was angry.

Just imagine, this road is used by people's deputies almost every week, they drive on Friday home to Odessa, and on Monday they go back to work to Kyiv. There work, although, can hardly be called work. They are shoveling money to their pockets, but they are unable to make the road decent. They don't have to spend their own savings; they could use the government money.

Lena agreed with him:

Sure, the road is considered to be one belonging to the government, and the president must be using it too. All the trade export and import deals are conducted through the port in Odessa. And there is no communication with the port except the railway and this very road.

They were indignant, and they were not alone in their indignation. Practically everyone who had to use the road more or less often was unsatisfied. Everyone expressed the indignation. But the authorities were indifferent to that indignation, as no one of the state officials expressed it.

None of the state officials would join the ordinary people. Before buying a position in Rada, they were profiteers, empty bottles collectors, shoplifters. Some of them were respectable persons like a salesperson in a second-hand store or foreign currency dealers. One of them was as waging wholesale and retail trading of fake Nescafe goods and in two years made money enough for buying a deputy position. – Ivanov was telling on of Odessa rumors.

In Kyiv region they were surprised by the abundance of rusty fence along the road, as well as abundance of persons selling sugar right at the side of the road. The Ivanovs found it funny that at the side there were white bags with sugar, and right beside them there were self-made signs "Crawfish". It turned out that they sold both, sugar and fresh crawfish.

- I do understand that they are selling crawfish from the ponds and rivers around. But where is all this sugar from? – Ivanov was asking himself. – It is obvious that the sugar comes from the sugar producing plant in Belaya Tzerkov. Are they being paid with natural products there? – He was puzzled.

- It more seems like they are stealing sugar from the plant. – He came to the conclusion in a while. – Everybody in the country, from a peasant to the president are stealing something, the difference is just in forms and methods of stealing, and, of course, in the quantity of stolen stuff. The purpose of stealing is also different, as a worker and all the plain folks steal to survive, and the authorities steal for the purpose of acquiring more property.

They decided to take the express route that passed Kyiv, though Ivanov did want to see how changed the capital of the Ukraine was during the so-called years of reforms. He hadn't been to Kyiv for the past ten years. He was a person that was supposed to be using and usable, as he was used by practically anyone. But in reality, according to the absence of stamps in his passport and according to his lifestyle, he didn't use the opportunity to be using anything, including traveling.

The traffic became much heavier in Kyiv region. There were two crowded lanes in both directions. Along the left lane black Mercedes cars were passing by at a great speed with their lights on.

- Those are government officers rushing. – Ivanov said. – Those "servants of their people" are hurrying to their offices to collect money. Some of them are hurrying to the airport to go somewhere to spend that money.

But the moment they Ivanovs passed Brovary, the traffic became much less busy, and in Chernigov region a car coming from the opposite direction was rare. It was pleasant to drive, as there was no rain, it was warm and sunny, the sun didn't blind the eyes, the road was dry.

In about two hours Ivanovs drove up to the borderline between the Ukraine and Belarus. The place was called Novye Yarilovichi. Though Ivanov didn't have anything wrong in his trunk, he felt ill at ease at the border.

He had heard the stories about abusing behavior of frontier guards and customs officers on all check-points at automobile roads. Ivanov hated officers who humiliated people and so he was preparing himself for the situation of that kind, he persuaded himself that he was supposed to be controlling himself and not to get mad.

There were no posters with the customs rules and payments at the customs office, thought Ivanov would have liked to see them and study. Two active young officers learned that he was going to Belarus, to Gomel, and they told him that if he had some benefits, he was to pay less. If not, then he was just not lucky...

I have benefits. – Ivanov said.

Then you are to pay sixty hryvnias here and six hryvnias to the cashier. It is the payment for the sticker on your car proving that the car is registered in the Ukraine. That's it. That young man will fix the sticker on your car.

Ivanov didn't go into details, he just wanted the procedure to be over as soon as possible. He paid, and they fixed the sticker with the letters "UA" on his trunk. He drove further to the frontier check-point, but he was still wondering what the payment was for. It would be later that he would understand that he was just cheated as a fool, but it would happen later. It served him right!

At the border check-point there were three cars and a bus. Just one officer was checking passports of the bus passengers; it took him half an hour. No one approached the cars. Two other officers were playing backgammon. They paid no attention to the cars that kept coming and to the line which was long enough by that time.

Ivanov persuaded himself not to get mad and not to interfere in any quarrels. Inside, though, he was furious.

Lazy bones, there is no order, all the official departments need to be cleaned up, starting with Kyiv, they are good only for taking bribes. Sons of a bitch!

After all the delays due to the laziness and indifference of the independent frontier guards to common people, the Ivanovs, at last, crossed the border of Belarus. The check-point at Belarus side was much more comfortable and substantial than the one on the Ukrainian side. Solid modern buildings with a mini-market and a café, nice-looking uniform, polite and ready-to-serve customs officers and the frontier guards. All the procedure took twenty minutes. The Ivanovs filled the customs declarations, paid the insurance payment of twenty dollars and entered the territory of Belarus.

It was clear that the order and readiness to serve was due to the supervision system set there. At all the places there were posters with the telephone numbers in Gomel and Minsk, one could dial the number right from the check-point and complain of any abuse on behalf of an officer. All in all it took them two hours to cross the border, and the car line was not at all long. It was just the careless attitude of the officers at the Ukrainian side that caused the delay.

They must have had too much lard. – Ivanov was kidding.

In one more hour they were in Gomel. They easily found the street and the apartment building where Lena's friend's sister was living. They decided to stay at her place till the next morning. Gomel surprised them with its neat and clean streets, which were well paved, the traffic lights were clean, and all of them were in order. The lawns and flower beds were well taken care of, there were lots of trees and flowers everywhere around. When compared with dirty and untidy Odessa with its broken roads, the cozy Gomel was producing a strange feeling.

The hostess was also Lena; she lived with her two kids and her mother. The husband was in Odessa, he earned good money there at construction of summer cottages. The Ivanovs were surprised with the clean entrance and the staircases, which had been newly and properly renovated. The apartment building was constructed during the years of Khrushchev; it was typical for that time, with small apartments and tiny kitchens, where two persons could hardly fit. The hostess said that it was the municipal services of the district which did the renovation and maintained the building and the front yard. For the Ivanovs it was surprising, as in Odessa all the municipal services didn't maintain anything, they just put the money into their pockets, and their business was still prospering.

At night the Ivanovs were shown around the city. It was their first visit to the Gomel. First they took a trolley-bus to get to the centre of the city. Then they walked slowly to the recreation park. It was the feeling that the city did have a caring landlord, as there was order everywhere. The municipal traffic was regular, the trolley-buses and streetcars were painted, and they were clean both from the outside and the inside.

Ivanov was greatly surprised when he saw two police officers in the rank of lieutenant colonels that were having their working paper cases and were taking a trolley-bus at a bus-stop.

Look, Lena, - He laughed out loud, as if he saw aliens. - I would like to see a police officer in the rank of a captain, who would take a municipal bus in a uniform.

They paid attention to the fact that people were smiling more and were friendlier there. Ivanov couldn't stop being surprised everywhere they went. He was surprised that in the centre of the city there were steam houses working, the prices were reasonable, and they were clean. The parks were with clean alleys, people didn't throw garbage on the payment, ponds had clean water, with white swans on the surface. When compared with Odessa, it was very surprising. He compared the prices for goods and services. The prices for food were almost the same as in Odessa, but the consumer goods were much cheaper and of a better quality. The consumer goods were produced in the country, it was not the low quality stuff brought from Turkey and China. The services were much cheaper than in Odessa.

Ivanov asked about the attitude of people to their president. The opinions were different. But all of them were united in one: due to his efforts Belarus preserved its potential and the state property and the money, which could have been stolen, as it happened in the neighboring republics. All the enterprises were working, workers got their wages, which was enough to support themselves.

See, everything is in order in the city. Everything is working. The municipal authorities don't make any extra effort for that, they just fulfill their functions. It is different with our mayor, who, according to his own words and the articles in newspapers controlled by him, is making heroic deeds in extremely difficult conditions. And as a result, the city is still in mud. – Ivanov made the conclusion. – But the mayor's face does not show that he had ever known hard life. He had been on the top no matter who ruled, and he had always had white bread with butter and caviar for his meals.

The impressions of Gomel were the best, and in the morning the Ivanovs thanked the hostess for her hospitality and left the city in the direction of Russia. The road was empty, almost no traffic at all, but still there were more vehicles than in the Ukraine. The road was well paved, and it was just pleasant to drive. Behind the car windows there was a forest on both sides, the landscape was beautiful, and their moods were high. The Ivanovs liked the neat nice looking Belarus villages, order was in everything around; there were no signs of carelessness, at least along the road. They passed by neat houses, neat fences, nice-looking, ornamented with carved wood draw-wells. There were surprisingly many car pools along the road, the ramps were comfortable, so were the parking lots. Right in the forest, on lawns, there were wooden tables and benches, neatly painted in a color matching the landscape.

The Ivanovs passed Mogilev, Orsha, Vitebsk. Everywhere they were surprised with the neatness of the cities, their cleanness and order, which was not common for the Ukraine, not to say anything of Odessa. They were pleasantly surprised that in the villages people were working in the fields, they were busy cutting grass for hay.

About noon they approached the check-point on the road at the Russian border line. Belarus officers checked their documents without any delays, wished them a safe trip and let them enter Russia. Russian customs office surprised Ivanov with its being so uncomfortable and neglected. The customs house occupied railway carriages with squeaking stairs. Ivanov went up the stairs and felt disgust when he had to touch the dirty door knob.

- Oh, is it Russia? Is it so hard to clean the knob? – He thought. When he entered inside, he had no more question. The wall paper inside was dirty, with traces of flies, the curtains were dirty, as if someone used them to wipe dirty hands, the customs officers looked untidy, their shirts were unclean and not ironed, no shoulder straps on the shirts, the ties were just black with dirt in the neck area, the board with the documents was also with traces of flies all over.

As they say in Odessa, you are just to make shit and stop living. Bustards!

How can they live like this? They represent the government, but it is not the face of the state, it is just its bum. What kind of state it is supposed to be! – Ivanov thought, frustrated. But he didn't pronounce a single word. His documents were thoroughly examined, he was inquired about his route and the purpose of his visit to Russia.

Ivanov lost his temper,

- I was born in Pskov, you know. I am going to visit the graves, can't you understand that?

Be quiet, you are not in Odessa, you are a Ukrainian citizen, and you seek entrance to Russia. – The officer was lecturing him. His mouth smelled of traces of vodka or home-brew mixed with onions. Ivanov felt nausea. – How much do I need to pay so that I could continue my trip as quickly as possible? – He asked, as he understood what all the inquiries were about.

At last he paid twenty dollars to them, took his documents from the frontier guards, who were also in dirty untidy uniforms, spit on the ground and sat into his car.

That's it, Lenochka, we are entering the native miserable unclean Russia, let it be OK.

You were mad about the customs services in the Ukraine. Were they any better in your Russia? The same abuse, two hours' time lost, twenty bucks gone for nothing, dirt everywhere. Oh, my God! – Lena lectured him, laughing.

The great difference between the order and neatness in Belarus and the dirt, trash and disorder in Russia could be seen with naked eyes. When leaving the check-point they were just horrified to see the village with tall weeds all over everything, with ramshackle black houses, fallen fences and dirty untidy human beings. The grass right outside the village was as tall as a human being's height, but there were no signs of preparing to cut it for hay.

Russia has always been untidy, ugly-looking, inhospitable, uncomfortable, with lazy drunk people. And it is still the same. – Ivanov made his first judgment. – As they say, "only the coffin can fix the hunch".

The road was not wide, but Ivanov still drove at high speed, as the cars from the opposite direction were very rare. They were driving and admired the landscape. The Russian landscape was really very beautiful. The forests coming close to the road, the rivers, the lawns, the lakes. Numerous lakes, surrounded with green forests in Nevelskiy district of Pskov region was just like from a fairy tale. On the background of the natural beauty and the richness of the landscape the ugly looks of the villages they were passing was just disappointing. The site was monotonous. Squeaking houses, matching fences, everything covered with tall weeds. The same were the peasants, unfriendly and in untidy clothes.

Ivanov was just mad,

They live in very beautiful surrounding, in such natural surrounding people should also be beautiful. And what they do is pollute the nature, turn it into shit and live in the shit for ages. Is it so hard to fix the house and the fence, to cut the tall weeds? Is it so hard to wash the clothes and to iron them, as you are walking in those clothes?I don't understand the Russian people, although I am Russian too. – Ivanov shared his thoughts with Lena with bitterness.

On the sides of the road they started to see signs of the Pushkin reserve. In order to be able to read the text one had to stop and get out of the car. The signs were done unprofessionally, the letters on it were tiny. But the signs with the words "As a citizen I vote for V.V.Putin" were very numerous and they were conspicuous from the distance and well colored. More than a year passed after the election to the Supreme Council of Russia, but the signs were still there, maybe till the next electoral campaign.

- Bootlickers! They are just waiting for licking something belonging to bosses. Bootlicking is in the blood of the Russian people. – Ivanov thought. His moods grew low because of his encounter with Russia, it became still worse with every other minute of his stay on the native land.

He had had plans of applying for the Russian citizenship, as he was a real Russian man, but his citizenship was Ukrainian. He even had an appointment in the Russian consulate. But after his first hours of the visit to Russia he began to hesitate.

At two o'clock in the afternoon they arrived at Pushkin Hills. Ivanov drove directly to the Saint Uspenskiy Svyatogorskiy Monastery. At the territory of the Monastery the remnants to Alexander Sergeevich and his forefathers were buried. It was the first time Lena was at the place, and everything there interested her. He was curious too. He hadn't visited the place for more than thirty years, but he had always remembered the beautiful landscapes of Pushkin Hills area, especially he liked the country estate in the village of Mikhailovskoye, its alleys, its peaceful atmosphere, the house of Pushkin, the one of his babysitter, Arina Rodionovna. The alley named after Kern often came to Ivanov's mind. In that alley Pushkin made a declaration of love to Anna Kern, and later he composed his wonderful poems.

They parked the car at the entrance of the Monastery and entered its territory. Ivanov was surprised when he saw numerous shopping booths which sold souvenirs and church related things. It was not like this before. Svyatogorskiy Monastery was a quiet and cozy place. The Ivanovs went up the stairs to the chapel where the burial service over the poet was read. They came up to the grave of Alexander Sergeevich and saw the plain grave obelisk behind the fence. They stood silent for a while thinking their own thoughts. They were realizing the grand nature of the Russian poet, which became no less with the ages. Then they came up to the graves of Pushkin's ancestors and went inside the chapel.

Everything inside was shabby and required renovation. Ivanov thought that three years ago they had celebrated the two hundredth birthday of the poet. Couldn't they fix everything by that time? Pushkin and persons like him are unique in Russia. As usual, there was much ado about the event, but nothing was done for the chapel, the money went to somebody's pockets. It's still good they didn't rob the chapel stuff and didn't sell it. Though nobody knows, maybe something was gone.

Sixth of June is Pushkin's birthday. Usually Pushkin memorial days were organized there and they lasted for a week. Famous scientists, studying Pushkin's works, poets, writers, and bibliographers made speeches there. The Ivanovs came to Pushkin Hills on the eighth of June. It was a quiet Saturday, no very many tourists were there, local residents mostly stayed home. After visiting the Monastery the Ivanovs went to Pushkin's country estate in the village of Mikhailovskoye. They parked the car at the entrance and walked through the forest. It was a warm summer day, it was a great pleasure to walk in the forest, the air was fresh, the birds were singing with their different voices, the plants were green and smelt nice. All this made a great influence on Ivanov's moods. The nature relaxed him.

Not far from the country estate there were recently built one-storeyed motel cottages. Ivanov went on with his wife passed the cottages along the alleys towards the estate, to the house where the poet used to live. He was surprised not to see those great trees with the branchy crowns which used to grow there thirty years ago. They alleys were not so picturesque any more. In the house they met a guide who showed them and some more tourists around.

She skillfully and enthusiastically told about the life of Alexander Sergeevich in Mikhailovskoye. The following remark of the young female guide struck:

- That is the window out of which Alexander Sergeevich looked at the neighboring small villages. Almost two centuries have passed since then, but not many changes took place.

She pronounced those words, overlooking far away at the river Sorot out of the window, with sadness in her voice.

Ivanov remembered the situation, and inside he was grateful to the delicate girl for that exact and short sentence she pronounced, which characterized the Russian village in general, all the lifestyle in Russia. Two centuries passed after Pushkin's life there, but almost nothing changed in the life of the Russian people. Ignorance, poverty, laziness, alcohol addiction, thefts, lies, deceit, meanness were the same. That was something permanent in Russia.

Pushkin memorial places impressed Lena greatly. She was also impressed by the unusual beauty of the landscape. Ivanov mostly was impressed by the visit to the estate of Pushkin.

He had experience and careful attitude to everything, and he couldn't help paying attention to the fact that they could afford constructing cottages right on the territory of the country estate for recreation of rich people, but they couldn't afford planting young trees in the alleys and maintaining the alleys properly. He thought of that and sighed. It was not decent care and it was not humane.

In an hour and a half they were approaching his native city Pskov. Ivanov tried to keep calm, but the heart was beating hard in his chest. It was his native land, where he hadn't been for eight years, where every bush and every path was familiar. That was the forest where his mother used to take him to pick up berries and mushrooms. To that place he used to come to cut some birch twigs for the steam house. That was the river Mnoga, a confluent of the river Velikaya, there he used to go fishing in his childhood.

They entered Pskov. Ivanov was surprised at once by several things. At the suburbs of Pskov in a picturesque forest at the bank of the river there appeared a whole village of country cottages of "new Russians". Later he found out those were mostly government officers from Pskov and St. Petersburg, who were prospering with the government money and bribes. Those were magnificent villas. And they became a must for all the Russian cities.

On the contrary, at the entrance to the city Ivanov was struck by the ugly and dull look of old houses which badly needed renovation. The fences were falling, the roads were broken, there were piles of garbage everywhere.

- Look, Lena, this is the place where the well-known Pskov landing force division is located. – He pointed to the military settlement in Cherekh, the southern suburb of Pskov. Look, they are constructing a monument to the landing force company which was destroyed in Chechnya two years ago. – He said, pointing to a great concrete parachute canopy, already erected by sculptors at the entrance to the military zone.

Passing by the native streets where he spent his childhood, by the streets in the centre of the city, he couldn't help surprising with the carelessness of the authorities, as the pavement was broken all over, the buildings were shabby, the lawns were trampled down, garbage, piles of garbage were everywhere. He was astonished not only with the careless attitude and stealing on behalf of the authorities. He also wondered why his fellow countrymen, the shackle makers were so ignorant and careless.

The Ivanovs decided to visit the cemetery first, to the mother's grave. They wanted to buy some flowers and they dropped to a private houses area in the settlement of Korytovo, where the local people were complaining about the weather. The weather was hot and dry. Every plant in the garden needed water. They also complained about the prices which were far from being reasonable and small pension payment and wages.

Both of them knew the place where the grave was, but it took some time for them to find it. No one had taken care of it for many years, and it was hidden in tall weeds and dog-rose twigs. The first thing they did was removing the tall weeds and the dog-roses with their roots, as they were covering the entire grave and the monument with the mother's picture. It became much lighter at the grave. It even seemed that the mother was smiling from the picture, contented that the son came at last to visit her. The Ivanovs placed the flowers on the grave and stood silent for a while, thinking their own thoughts.

Ivanov was asking his mother to forgive him for his eight years long absence. There were some obstacles that prevented him from coming there. He hadn't been there for eight years! He stood thinking that the world around them was cruel, that there was neither mercy nor compassion in the world. He thought that he himself would never become merciless and indifferent. He had never been like that, he was not like that and he was never going to become like that.

Ivanov paid attention to the church which had been built at the cemetery. He was satisfied to learn that at the Orletzovskoye cemetery there was settled a new lot where mostly young people perished in Chechnya were buried. It was something terrible to see the cemetery where mostly kids were buried. There was no excuse for that.

In an hour the Ivanovs went to the hotel "Rizhskaya". At Zavelichiye area almost nothing had changed for the past eight years. The only difference was the new casino at the side where there used to be a restaurant. The Ivanovs filled the forms for checking in quickly, but there was a problem. They had cash in US currency, and there was no currency exchange in the hotel. It turned out to be a problem to exchange currency in the city. It could be exchanged only in banks, and the banks were closed for the weekend. Only currency exchange dealers could help, as they were working twenty four hours. The other place to try was the casino.

But the dealers can just cheat us. – Ivanov protested.

But the hotel manager just shook her shoulders. Lena laughed out loud.

That is you "Sunny Shacklemakerstan", the centre of the civilization, the hub of the Universe. – She imitated Ivanov. –Four borderlines nearby, and not service at all. Ivanov didn't say anything and went to the casino. There he was refused either. He walked to the bank, but there was no luck there. The dealers seemed to be watching the world championship in soccer or drinking. It was hard to say.

When he was back to the hotel, the manager took pity of him and called the doorman. She asked the tall huge guy:

Vova, please exchange dollars for the guests from Odessa, they just don't have a place to go now.

Vova seemed to be working full time as an undercover for all the departments of Russia, that was the security agency, the police, all the criminal structures, both legal and illegal.

He looked at the Ivanovs all over with his professional eyes and said that he could exchange no less than a hundred bucks.

Ivanov was glad to make a deal, though the rate of twenty five rubles for a dollar was exorbitant, but he had no choice.

As soon as in half an hour the Ivanovs parked the car at the parking lot of the hotel, had dinner, took a shower and went to bed. They were tired after the trip and full of impressions. But they didn't feel like sleeping. They were exchanging opinions, they had many recent events to discuss. In Pskov at that time was the period of light nights. It was midnight, but outside the window it was as light as during the daytime. For Lena it was unusual, it was her first experience, though she had heard a lot about the light nights before. She was curious about that.

Ivanov didn't sleep well. It was stuffy, mosquitoes bothered and he had some nightmares. But early in the morning he was up. He took a shower, freshened himself up and went to the parking lot to check the car. He pulled the car up to the entrance.

They had breakfast and went to the municipal market to buy perennial flowers to plant them on the grave.

Ivanov didn't enjoy driving along his native city and seeing it untidy. He passed the centre of the city, but he didn't come across a single traffic light that was not out of order. There were also no visible marking on the roads. The city was dull. He passed by the movie theatre "Octyabr", where he used to go as a boy. Its shabby appearance upset him, as once it used to be one of the best movie theatres of the city. Everything became clear to him when on his way to the market he saw the Drama theatre named after Pushkin, which required a major renovation. He understood that the city, as well as the whole country, was ruled by persons who never cared about the country, they cared just about their own stomachs and well-being.

Near the theatre he didn't notice the sign which restricted entrance to the street. There was nothing to be surprised of, as the sign was covered by poplar twigs. In spite of that police officers from the local district department of transportation were there at nine o'clock in the morning and they stopped Ivanov.

Let's go to the police car. – They said to Ivanov.

He thought that it was documents check and followed them. When he was inside the old, broken small "Zhiguli", he understood that those were corrupted Russian cops who were collecting money for freshening the nip. Those were not the cops from the well-known TV show with the same name. Those were cops who worked for the police, but were ready to sell their own mother for a bottle of vodka. For ten bucks they were able to sell the president with its understanding of the state, with his chauvinism, the Kremlin and its gold reserves.

In the car there were three cops in dirty creased uniforms, which looked like someone had chewed them, there was a strong smell of alcohol. Ivanov thought that in Odessa bums looked better.

- Are you from the Ukraine?
- I am.

So, you violated the restriction of the sign. We are going to keep your document. Tomorrow, on Monday you are supposed to come to the office and they will investigate the case and return the license to you. – The one who was supposed to be the supervisor, said to Ivanov, looking at him through the back mirror.

-Easy, guys! I am a shackle maker too! I have come home, to the grave of my mother. Tomorrow morning I am going back. That won't do. Let's solve the problem somehow. The sign can't be seen at all.

It can be seen by somebody, but somebody else can fail to see it.

Ivanov understood that there would be no results if he insisted any further.

- How much?

Two hundred rubles is fine. We'll let you go.

Ivanov silently produced two hundred rubles and gave the money to the cops. He took back his documents and got into his car. He drove to the market. His moods were completely spoiled. The city itself looked like a refuse pit. The inside world of its shackle makers was no better.

The Ivanovs were surprised that it was nine o'clock in the morning, but there were hardly any people in empty streets. They were still more surprised that on Sunday at that time of the day almost every booth was closed. The salespersons were just coming to open the booths.

- Lazybones! They are utterly lazy. – Ivanov expressed his indignation. – At our Privoz by this time of the day many of the salespersons have already all their goods sold out! It's just horrible. Look, Lena, there is garbage covering the ground almost up to the countertop. It is past nine and they haven't even started to clean. That's no good. I considered Odessa to have no order, but I seem to have mistaken. Now I see I have been wrong. I want back to Odessa.

Lena laughed out in content.

That's what I was telling you. Listen to what I am telling you. There is no place better than Odessa nowadays.

Ivanov didn't say anything, but he thought:

But still there must be at least something good here, in my native city.

It was mostly people from the Caucasus region that sold at the market. They didn't sell Oriental sweet or exotic fruits. They sold local food that was meat, eggs, soft cheese, sour cream, strawberries, dried mushrooms and fish.

- Look here, Lena, some Russian Vanya and Manya protest against the people from the Caucasus region, the so-called black-bums, who are too numerous at the market. They say that they are also at other trading places, like bars and restaurants. Do you have an idea, why?

Those Russian drinking lazy persons should be glad to have those people working hard, while the former heat their bodies near the furnaces. They trade, they buy, they construct bars, restaurants, stores. But for them, everything here would go rotten and would perish with low quality self-made alcohol.

Lena was silent and she agreed with him. She saw that Ivanov was excited and tried to calm him down. At last they bought the plants outside the market and drove to the cemetery. For two hours they were tidying the grave of Ivanovs' mother and the place around the grave, they planted the flowers and watered them.

Not far away from them, near a grave of a soldier perished in Afghanistan, there stood a gray-haired old woman with her granddaughter. They had already watered the flowers and were just sitting silently. The Ivanovs borrowed a shovel and a bucket from them. They started talking. Valentina Ivanovna buried her son in nineteen eighty seven, he was killed in Afghanistan.

First I almost lived here, especially in summer. I used to sit on the bench near the grave and thought that I was not alone, that there are other mothers whose sons were killed. I thought I would go mad. But it was my granddaughter who saved me. She gives courage to me, moral and physical strength. – The old woman hugged the sixteen years old granddaughter in gratitude.

You know what is going on now. – She continued. – There appeared a whole cemetery "Orletzy - 2", where only young people are buried, those who were killed in Chechen wars. There are lots of mothers and widows who spend much time there. One can really go mad. But believe my experience, it's better to come to the cemetery. I am sitting near my son, I am talking to him, and this makes me feel better. Here, at the cemetery the atmosphere is better, it's different from that of the city, everything is cleaner here: the air, the moods and the relations.

The Ivanovs told her about themselves. Valentina Ivanovna appeared to have relatives in Odessa too.

Don't worry, I will take care of the grave of your mother. It is quite close to my son's. It's easy for me. I promise that there would be no tall weeds any more. I will water the flowers and in spring I will plant some more. – She promised to the Ivanovs. He tried to give some money to her, but she got offended and refused.

Don't give the money. I just have to do this sacred thing.

Ivanov was grateful to that skinny plain Russian woman, who was honest, decent and respectable. Later he often thought:

Where are the bustards appear from? They are so numerous around!

Soon the Ivanovs left the cemetery. Before that they bought a metal cross for the grave of Ivanov's aunt, who was buried two hundred kilometers away from Pskov in the direction to St. Petersburg. Before leaving the city Ivanov decided to go to the technical service station which he saw not far from the hotel. He wanted to change the front tires. The technical service station was seen from the distance, a large sign was colored with all the rainbow colors. There were also lots of flags fixed there. The technical service station was a branch of a Russian, Swedish and German joint enterprise. Ivanov thought that the service should be expensive there, but the quality, the attitude and the warranty should be OK. That was not a mighty-mouse garage, it was a big company.

He was greatly mistaken. When he drove closer to the entrance, he was surprised to see the sign which restricted the speed at the territory of the technical service station at five kilometers. Between the poles there hang some dirty horse reins which were supposed to restrict the entrance. The territory of the technical service station was polluted, tall weeds were as high as a human being. The weeds came as close as the parts store, belonging to the technical service station. Ivanov found a foreman and explained to him what was to be done.

- It would be OK, as we have the necessary tires in the store. Drive to the garage department. It will take thirty minutes.

Ivanov was glad to drive to the garage department, but there seemed to be a problem. There was a metal beam of about twenty centimeters high, which blocked the entrance.

How do I drive in?

Like everyone does, just go straight. – The foreman said calmly.

Ivanov shrugged his shoulders and drove slowly inside. He thought:

Couldn't they make a ramp? Otherwise, the rims are damaged.

He stopped asking questions when he came into the store and saw the shop windows stained with flies. The documents were also dirty. The prices turned out to be exorbitant, but he had no choice.

Could you please make a cup of coffee for me? – He asked the manager of the technical service station. She smiled at him.

No coffee here. You can go across the road to the beer bar and ask if they have any coffee there.

Ivanov and Lena looked at each other and laughed out loud.

Unobtrusive Purely Russian service, mixed with some Swedish and German.

Everything is so retarded.

Ivanov just didn't know how to react to all that. They crossed the road and entered the bar. From the entrance they felt a strong smell of cheap sour beer mixed with the smell of stagnant urine.

In an hour they were driving along the road from Pskov to St. Petersburg. They enjoyed the nice landscape behind the car windows. Bright green color of the trees contrasted with gray villages and multicolored big signs with eternal citations, like "As a citizen, I vote for "Yedinstvo".

I have noticed that the more an officer is licking his boss's boots, the more money he puts to his pocket. – Ivanov said, laughing. He mocked at the transit police officers who were hiding in the bushes and went out after they spot a car driving at a higher speed. They rush to the road, waving their sticks and experiencing great difficulty, as their big stomachs made the running hard. They ate too much and had too much alcohol.

In two hours they arrived at the village of Pogorelovo, where nine years ago his aunt died in a nursing home. Eight years ago they visited the grave and installed a wooden cross there. It appeared that the nursing home didn't exist any more. In the same building there was a medical facility for addicted persons. It could be felt in the village, as it was full of drunk bustards in shabby dirty rugs, as they couldn't be called clothes. The villages they passed caused the feeling of pity and disappointment, as people lived that kind of life. In one of the villages, where the Ivanovs bought flowers, they noticed that it was not sickly old people who lived in those shabby houses. They were inhabited by lazy persons of their own age and even younger.

The cemetery was neglected, covered with high grass and tall weeds, there were no visible graves, just low burial hills, which could be hardly distinguished in the high grass and tall weeds. It was hard and horrible to see the scene. People were not buried according to Christian order, they were just put in the ground. The place was beautiful, at the side of the village, on a high bank of the river Plyussa.

No one could tell, whose grave that was, the cemetery graves had no names, no care, no registration. Barbarian-like negligence. Ivanov and Lena found the aunt's grave with difficulty. There were no traces of the cross on it.

Why is everything like this? – Ivanov was indignant. – Is it so hard to take care of the graves? They could have installed crosses, there is lots of wood in ten meters from the fence. The beautiful nature is contrasting to these two-legged shallow bustards.

He went to a house and in one of them he borrowed a shovel. Lena and himself started to put the grave in order. They trimmed the border line from all the sides, put some turf all around, installed the cross that they had brought and put the flowers.

I am sorry, aunt, but that's all I can do for you. – Ivanov mumbled, looking at the grave.

At the same time in the village somebody was watching a soccer game over TV, somebody was drinking home-brew or alcohol wash. The grass was high, it was June, the weather was sunny. It was the time of making hay. But people didn't seem to care.

Russia is lazy all over. It's also drunk, ignorant and dirty from both inside and outside. That smog has been covering it for ages, and there have been no attempts to get rid of it. The conclusion is sad, but truthful.

On the road at the entrance to Pskov he was stopped by the road police. He was driving at the speed of seventy, which was forbidden inside the city.

Ivanov got mad:

It is not the city, it is the road with the forest on both sides.

But they wouldn't agree.

It is in the Ukraine that you don't have order at all. – A policeman said to him, meaning that in the Ukraine there was a rule not to fine anyone right on the road.

We have the order. If you violate the rules you pay to the government and not to the pocket of the police officer on the road. – Lena interfered.

The police officers became angry because of her remark. The Ivanovs didn't know that a similar regulation was to be introduced in Russian legislation in a month. The cops were mad because they knew that.

In Pskov they went to the Cathedral of Alexander Nevskiy in the centre of the city, lit the candles for the peace of the souls of the mother and the aunt, asked to read a prayer. At that place Ivanov also saw that everything was dull and shabby. About twenty years ago there was a major restoration, but it was all destroyed with the time.

Before the night they drove to the area where Ivanov's childhood passed. They went inside the apartment building where he used to live. Everything drove him mad. So many years had passed, but there were no any changes. It just became still worse. The streets were neglected, everywhere around there was garbage and dirt. People were unfriendly. The Ivanovs were leaving the city the next day, so they visited the mother's grave once again. Ivanov felt sad in Pskov. It was the first time during the past several years that he entered the city with joy and was leaving it in sadness. It was a hard burden on his soul, he felt ashamed for his fellow countrymen, for the native city, for Russia.

They drove to the river Velikaya. The banks were polluted, everywhere there were piles of garbage, some junk came out of the water. And so many bums were wandering there.

At the checking desk in the hotel Ivanov couldn't help asking:

What did you turn the city into? – Ivanov was indignant. – About twenty years ago it was a beautiful provincial city, blooming and cozy, and it was pleasant to visit it.

A Latvian man kept up the conversation:

- Right you are. I haven't been here for ten years. And my first impression is that it's a different city, not Pskov. The impression is just horrible. How can people live like this? And it is on the eve of the one thousand, one hundred and tenth anniversary, which the authorities are going to celebrate.

Ivanov laughed out loud.

- They can make a party and drink vodka, shackle makers are really experienced in that.

At night they went to a café for dinner. They ordered pork chops and the chops were disgusting, as if someone had already chewed them.

Lena, I want home, to Odessa. – Ivanov moaned. – It's the limit. I want back to Odessa, which seems to be the best city on the Commonwealth of Independent States territory.

Lena laughed, as she was glad Ivanov came to that conclusion.

- By the way, do you know, how they translate "Commonwealth of Independent States" into Odessa language?

No, I don't. – Ivanov seemed to be interested.

"Essen", which is the first letter in Russian abbreviation, means "to eat" in the Jewish language. And second letter stands for the word "shit". So, you understand the meaning, and residents of Odessa think that good stuff can't be named with indecent wording.

Both laughed out loud. But Ivanov's mood was really bad. He realized that all Russia's drawbacks were as old as the world itself. Those were laziness, alcohol addiction, ignorance and absence of education. There was no remedy for that, as it was in its people's genes, its blood. It was for ever.

Rich Russians call their own people a cattle, and they are right, as there is no other name for them. – Ivanov said thoughtfully while they were having a walk near the hotel before going to bed. The light nights were set in the dark city, full of ignorance and dirt, which was both inside and outside its people. It was the city Ivanov used to be proud of, and not only him.

The next day they were driving early in the morning in the direction to Odessa along the road St. Petersburg – Odessa. On their way they dropped to the district centre Opochka, where about thirty years ago Ivanov graduated from the military college. Opochka didn't surprise them with its dirty untidy look, as there was nothing better to be expected after they had seen the regional centre. The same kind of broken roads, shabby buildings, dull faces. He was surprised to see the buildings of the college and its lot. The well built dwellings had their windows boarded up. Tall weeds were coming up to the second storey. A female security came out to meet them and explained that for five years the district executive committee was fighting against maintaining the place, and the whole complex was coming to the shabby condition, as there were no more military support there.

It's a great complex to start a children's asylum here, or a nursing home for seniors and disabled persons. They could also start an enterprise here. It is going to be destroyed! – Ivanov was indignant. – No, there is no a real caring governor in Pskov region. The same situation is in all Russia. Look, Lena, in the region they can start seeding and harvesting long-fibred flax, they can just arrange its processing, they can develop weaving and sewing industry here. Linen is in demand all over the world. No, they can't do that, all is wasted in Russia.

He was leaving his native land with a heavy feeling in his soul. No, he was not going to seek Russian citizenship. Never in the future. As there is no light at the end of the tunnel. There was eternal darkness for people, all their life was dark. They got accustomed to that kind of life, they are not seeking a better one. They don't want to. Maybe they do want, but they would like all the good stuff to appear on the spot, like in fairy tales, on the magic carpet, with the magic of the golden fish or Aladdin's magic lamp, while they would lie on their backs doing nothing. Just by the wave of the wand, according to their will!

Ivanov wanted to go away from that Russian unpleasant reality. By the night they already crossed the two borders and arrived to Chernigov. They stayed there for the night in a hotel, and the next day by noon they were at home in Odessa, which seemed to be a paradise when comparing with all the negative impressions experienced by Ivanov during the trip.

Grudging Ten Hryvnias?

Roman Ivanovich was in high spirits. For five years, after retiring from the army, he has been teaching military science in one of Lyceums of the city. He tried his best, teaching and educating the students of the Lyceum, as he had enough experience gained in the army during his more than thirty years of service as a political educator. As far as knowledge was concerned, he constantly kept it updated.

Roman Ivanovich did not like to fulfill any work with carelessness. If he took up something, he did his work with all his strength and energy. This attitude always returned hundredfold to him. On that very day on an official meeting in the office of the Principal of the Lyceum he was thanked for his work, he was set as an example for other teachers, he was given a bonus. It was just fifty hryvnias, but for him it was big money. It was not actually the matter of the amount, though he did need money, the main thing for Roman Ivanovich was the good and warm words he was addressed with. At the age over sixty a warm word and a caring look meant a lot.

Roman Ivanovich, in excellent moods, was driving his fifth model of the car "Zhiguli", that was "VAZ 2105", which he pampered as a fiancée and took care of. It looked new, thought it was ten years old. He was driving along Karl Marks Street, which was renamed into Ekaterininskaya, but he called the streets by their old names, it was a habit.

As a real political educator, he had read somewhere, that the classic theoretical workers with different "ism" endings used to say that Russia would turn to a giant with its legs cut off, should it be deprived of St.

Petersburg and Odessa. Maybe due to this and maybe to the habit of covering everything, somebody started to paint with black color the signs with new names of the streets on the buildings. It happened as soon as the street was given a new name, which it used to bare long ago. They tried to explain to people, that the street was named after Ekaterina the Second, and not Ekaterina Vorontsova. But in Odessa they still liked Karl Marks and didn't want Russia to become crippled without Odessa.

Roman Ivanovich wanted to buy some cosmetics for his wife, and he directed towards closer to Deribassovskaya and visit the stores of the Passage, where he intended to chose and, maybe, to buy something decent, which, of course, he could afford, for his wife. They have been living with his wife for forty years in perfect harmony.

From Karl Marks street Roman Ivanovich turned to the left to Lastochkin Street, and right behind the corner he was stopped by two nice-looking blondes in the uniform of the road police.

- Good afternoon. - One of them said, – Please give us your documents for inspection.

Roman Ivanovich produced his driver's license, the ownership and the checking card from his wallet.

One of the blondes, in the uniform of a senior lieutenant, looked through the documents quickly, smiled cunningly and said:

- Is that all?

- What else do you want? – Roman Ivanovich asked perplexedly.

- You violated the traffic rules; you didn't yield to a pedestrian...

- Which pedestrian? What are you talking about? There was no one on the road. I am certain that on the road there was nobody.

The girls laughed out loud. One of them brought an old woman of more than seventy to Roman Ivanovich.

- Here she is. Old lady, please tell this driver how he didn't yield to you.

The old woman became anxious and sniffed:

- There are many careless drivers, one can't cross the road because of them, he almost hit me, please write this down in the report.

Roman Ivanovich was just in a shock, it seemed to him that it was a nightmare that didn't concern him at all. He had seen clearly that at the time he was passing the crossing there was nobody there. Furthermore, there was a car of foreign make in front of him, but nobody stopped it for some reason. There was something wrong with the whole situation.

- I object! I didn't violate any rules. I was driving to the green light, for pedestrians it was red, on the road there were no pedestrians.

The senior traffic police officer came up closer to him. – Are you drunk by any chance, old man? To make the long story short, pay ten hryvnias and get lost.

Roman Ivanovich was indignant.

- You can't talk to me like this. I am a colonel in reserve. You could be my granddaughter according to your age. You are not polite and you are making a show here.

She just put his documents into her bag and returned the ownership document to him.

- We are making a report; you are free not to sign it. You refuse to pay the fine on the spot. You will be called to the traffic police office. There you will be instructed, you will pay the fine and then you'll get back your driver's license.

She made up a report, which he refused to sign, and he left the place. He parked the car at the parking lot at Gavannaya Street and walked slowly to Passage. His moods were low; he was just shivering because of the abusive behavior of the traffic police officers.

- Suckers! They have just broken out of the eggs and started to be rude at the spot. They were rude to me, a colonel, who had served in the army for thirty three years. It would have been different if I had violated the rules. I would have paid those ten hryvnias. But I do clearly remember that I didn't violate anything. And who was that old woman on the pavement? I will be insistent and I will make an appointment with the head of the municipal traffic police office. That's a pity, as the day had such a good start. Where does such kind of people appear from?

Being upset, he didn't choose any present for the wife and drove home deep in thought. He didn't tell anything to his wife as he didn't want to upset her.

The next day Roman Ivanovich was sitting in the reception of the head of the municipal traffic police office. The secretary had told the boss about the visitor. He had been sitting for two hours, but nobody called him in. Traffic police officers went to and fro, entered and exited the office, carrying some document folders. It was a regular business atmosphere of an office. He also saw those blond officers, who went out of the boss's office. They saw Roman Ivanovich, laughed out loud and went away along the corridor, leaving the smell of French perfume behind them. At last he was called in.

When he entered the office, Roman Ivanovich saw a deputy colonel with pink cheeks in front of him. The latter had a big chevelure and cunning eyes. He looked unfriendly at the visitor.

- Come in and take your seat. – He said. After Roman Ivanovich took his seat, he continued without giving the former an opportunity to start speaking.

- So, Roman Ivanovich, you violate the rules, don't you? And you grudge ten hryvnias? How come, that you, as you say, a colonel in reserve, offend helpless girls? You were supposed to encourage them. As they say in Odessa, you could have unzip your pocket and pay the girls. That would be the end of the story. Otherwise, it is going to cost you more.

- But I... - Roman Ivanovich tried to interrupt him.

But the head of the traffic police office didn't give him a chance to speak.

- You can tell to a psychiatrist the story of how you didn't violate the rules of crossing the traffic lights. But not to me. Oh, man, he grudges ten hryvnias!

At that moment an officer in the rank of a major came in.

- Please take the documents of this colonel. Let him take a driving test. Let him learn the traffic rules, pass the exam and then you'll return the documents to him. But it will happen only if he passes he exam. But I have a feeling that it would be really hard for him.

He looked at Roman Ivanovich.

- Good luck. Go and study. Pass the exam and drive your small Zhiguli again. But don't violate any rules.

Roman Ivanovich left the office with the major, he felt like in a dream under anesthetic.

- Look here, major, why do they treat me like that?

The major shrugged his shoulders. - It is not a question to me. On Saturday please come to the traffic inspection office by nine o'clock for the test.

Roman Ivanovich left the building feeling in deep shit. He had never been humiliated like that. He parked the car and on his way home he dropped to a small bar where he drank with a random guy to get some relief from the insulting attitude of the officers with shoulder straps. He spent all the fifty hryvnias he had got as a bonus. When he was drunk, he felt a little bit better. The fellows at the table were telling stories and jokes related to traffic police office.

- A driver, who was not fastened with his safety belt, was stopped by a traffic police officer.

- Why do you violate the rules? Pay ten hryvnias.

He was driving on, with his belt fastened. Again he was stopped by a traffic police officer, who checked his belt.

- It is not properly tightened. Pay ten hryvnias.

He paid and fixed the belt properly, tightening it as much as he could. He was driving on. Again he was stopped by a traffic police officer.

- See, what kind of people we have, they are ready to get strangled by the belt, but not pay ten hryvnias.

They laughed out loud. On of the boon companions was drinking less and was listening. At last he said,

- It's all useless. You are not going to get any results. The head of the traffic police office was right when he said that it would cost you more. You will remember his words more than once. Now to get your driver's license back you will have to pay at least one hundred bucks, as the rate for passing the exam nowadays is fifty to two hundred bucks. As far as the traffic police officers are concerned, they get a certain task at the beginning of every shift. The task is not to make a certain quantity of reports, but the task to get a certain amount of money. They are given cars which have no gas in the tank. You have your police stick and use it for making money for the gas. They have to stop cars, extract money or vouchers for gas. Sometimes they even make drivers give gas to them.

Besides, in order to become a traffic police officer in our nice city it is necessary to pay the enrollment fee of two or more thousand bucks. That was the payment for the right to stand with a police stick at the road side. There was that was the money they wanted to get back, besides they had to pay daily to the boss, that is to their division manager, their department manager and other managers. As a result every week to Kyiv there go couriers packed with green stuff.

That process hasn't appeared today, it did not appear yesterday, it has just become more perfect and smooth.

Besides, a traffic police officer after all the payments has to keep something for himself too. The areas and spots on the roads are distributed between them, they make money there. They stop drunken persons and make them pay as much as one to two hundred bucks. They check speed and make those drivers also pay, but a little bit less. The volume of speeding fines is much greater. They also do tricks like they did with you. They hire an old woman or a bum, pay them five hryvnias and that person walks to and fro across the road at the traffic lights. Traffic police officers stop drivers like you and collect ten hryvnias from each, and by the end of the day they have a rather big amount of money.

So, my advice to you is that you get ready with a hundred bucks, go to the traffic police office or to the head department to the same major and beg them to return the driver's license to you, otherwise it will cost you more.

In the morning Roman Ivanovich woke up with a headache,

- I was a fool to get drunk. – He thought with bitterness, looking at his worn out face in the mirror. He freshened himself up and went to the Lyceum. He had eight hours of classes that day.

After the working day Roman Ivanovich went to his old friends, with whom he served in the army together, who had positions at the regional administrative office that was the Governor's office. They listened to his story and advised that he should call to the reception of the chief of the Head office of the traffic police in Kyiv; they also gave him the necessary telephone numbers. But Roman Ivanovich decided not to call before he tried to pass the test on Saturday. He thought he would pass the test, as he had driving experience of more than several dozens of years. He knew the traffic rules well enough.

But on Saturday after he answered five questions in the computer class, he was stopped and told that he was to go and study more. He could come again next Saturday. He appeared to have made three mistakes. Roman Ivanovich started to argue, as he knew there were no mistakes in his answers. But the senior lieutenant, with a red-skinned face and a belly like of a pregnant woman, would not listen to him and just pointed to the door.

Roman Ivanovich understood that they were carrying on the instruction to make the disobedient colonel in reserve to come to his senses and stop being picky.

But Roman Ivanovich decided to prove that he was not dump. He called to the office of the chief of the traffic police to the number given to him by his friends. In a polite manner the secretary explained to him that he could settle the problem in his own city, he could go to the office of the head of the regional traffic police department.

- What do you think I have to discuss with the chief in Odessa? – Roman Ivanovich got furious. – Your protégé here have already acquired an entertainment centre on the seaside, with a hotel, a restaurant, bars and dancing halls. Where did he take money for all that? That is the money he collected on the road from us. I am not going to him.

- Get quiet, don't shout at me. By the way, if you want to talk to our boss, you will have a chance in a month. He will visit one of the traffic police divisions on the road to Odessa. Call me in about twenty minutes, and I will tell you the exact time and date. – The secretary told him.

- I am not going to wait for a month. I do ask you to write down what is my complain about. – He asked and then dictated her all his complains.

In a week he went to the exam again. Again he was sent home, with no results, as he failed the exam again. He understood that the process was continuous. In a few days he received a letter from Kyiv, in which he read that according to the results of the inquiries in the office, Roman Ivanovich had violated the traffic rules and was supposed to take a computer test. The letter was signed by the chief of the Department of the traffic police. In the letter they also mentioned that there were cases of bribing among the officers of the traffic police, but the administration was taking effort to stop that and that year thirty eight associated were fired for the bribes. At the end of the letter they wished health and success to Roman Ivanovich.

He spit and threw away the letter.

- They are all of the same kind, as all of them get the money collected on the roads.

Roman Ivanovich was unaware that the general had already called to Odessa and said:

- Why is there a fuss about ten hryvnias all over the country? Make the witty colonel understand that one couldn't violate rules and avoid fines. Grudging ten bucks in Odessa, that's surprising...

Roman Ivanovich had a meeting with a general who served in Odessa and with who he used to be together in the army in the rank of lieutenants. He told him all his story related to the traffic police and asked advice from him.

- Tell me, Petrovich, what am I to do?

The general laughed out loud.

- Roman Ivanovich, you do look smart, but you can't be as smart as that! Do you think traffic police have started to take bribes today? It was the same during your own Soviet rule too. I served in the army in Zaporozhyie about twenty years ago. They have a police checking spot at the exit to the road to Simferopol. At that time one had to pay one thousand rubles in order to get a position at that checking spot. Now it is still harder to get there. Everyone wants to eat, you know. The new administration of the traffic police boasted to me that they followed the advice of the European Council and the head office of the traffic police was renamed to the Department, and is now called The Department of Traffic Police of the Ministry of Interior. It sounds European-like. But they used to collect money in Asian way and continue to do so. My dear friend, we have a system of taking bribes and stealing money, no matter who is ruling.

How can I help you? I will call to the head of the traffic police right now and I will ask to take care of you. But I can tell you for sure that you will have to take the test, you will have to pay. But for you I can arrange a low price, which is one hundred bucks. I can't make it less than that, sorry.

Roman Ivanovich agreed after some thinking. He had no choice. The general called on the spot to the traffic police, they promised not to persecute him any more, as he did realize the situation, there was not point of torturing him, as he was already seeing the things clearly.

On his way home Roman Ivanovich was thinking.

- There seems to be no officer in traffic police, who does not take bribes. If there were one, he would be kicked out of there in a flash. All of them take bribes, and they don't take only when they are given, they also extort money, they demand boldly as they know that the experience of any driver depends on them. If one takes driving school as an example, there they collect fifty dollars for passing road tests. Part of the money goes to the administration of the school; the other part is paid as a bribe to the inspectors who conduct the test. Those who don't pay, have to take exams till doomsday. The same is the situation at technical tests. On the roads the inspectors with the sticks behave as real robbers, the difference is that they wear uniforms. The life is a bitch, really.

The next Saturday Roman Ivanovich came to the traffic police office to take the computer test. Before entering the computer class he was called to the office of the boss and he paid one hundred bucks there. In half an hour he passed his test and got back his driver's license.

In a week Roman Ivanovich was watching Ukrainian news review. He was interested in the briefing of the Minister of the Interior. The general was furiously speaking about corruption, about their struggle for purifying the staff of the police, about bad financing of the police and about bad support on behalf of the government. It turned out that uniform shoes were given to every twentieth policeman.

Roman Ivanovich laughed out loud.

- Can you imagine that nineteen cops were walking barefooted, and just one, which is the twentieth, is in shoes? I need to send twenty hryvnias of my pension to the minister for his shoes. Maybe somebody else will follow my example. If we are to believe the police general, all police officers are poor.

May be we need to advise that he should organize courses to upgrade the bribing skills? It's a big question where is the multi-storied mansion in the luxurious district of Kyiv received from. The family of the general resided there. It was in all the papers, it was discussed in the Supreme Council.

Roman Ivanovich tried to persuade himself that it was just for bonus money.

In about a month he was passing by the same ill-fated crossing and again he was stopped by inspectors. They were in shoes; their faces were pink and looked healthy, according to their faces and the size of their bellies they didn't starve.

-You have violated the rule of crossing the traffic lights. – One of them started.

Roman Ivanovich interrupted him.

- How much?

The other grinned: - Ten hryvnias.

Roman Ivanovich gave him ten hryvnias and they returned his documents to him. They wished him safe driving.

I am Naming You a Carp

The general Pryadko, Sergey Ivanovich was born and grew up in Odessa, at Bugaevka area. After graduating from the military college located at the fifth station of Bolshoy Fontan, Sergey Ivanovich started his service to his country at different garrisons far from his native land and came to Odessa just for vacation.

At the time the Soviet Union split he was in the city of Chita at the rank of a general and on the position of a corps commander. After great trouble, nervous situations and humiliation he managed to get a transfer to the Ukraine at the beginning of nineties. There he swore to be loyal to his people and was hired by the Ministry of Defense till nineteen ninety nine. After that he was transferred to conduct scientific research work in the Institute of strategic research. It was hard to explain briefly what they kind of research they did there, but the salary and bonuses were good. The minister of Defense often interrupted Pryadko's work in the Institute and took him for inspection business trips to garrisons, using his experience.

Sergey Ivanovich's family was united, it consisted of the wife Marina and their two grown up sons. One of them was serving in the army in the rank of a captain, he took after his father, and the other graduated from Kharkiv Law Academy and was employed as a legal adviser in one of law firms in Kyiv. But five years ago he wife got seriously ill, she was diagnosed with breast cancer, and she had already had many surgeries. Her health condition went worse and better at different periods.

During the Soviet period Pryadko was an atheist, he believed in great future communist ideas, survived all the hardships of military

157

service with courage and considered that to be necessary for the security of his country and for achieving a better life standard for his people. But the years passed, and the life standard of his people became still lower. Pryadko saw the discrepancy between the theory of the communist party and real life of communist party professional members. By the end of eighties he, as well as the majority of soviet people, he didn't believe in the hell and the devil, neither he believed in the great future of the whole mankind. He hated professional party leaders with their marked Gorbachev with all his men. He used to say a popular rhyme of those days about a carriage of three: Mishka, Rayka and Perestroika, which raced all over Russia, meaning Gorbachev and his wife.

In nineties he gradually started to become religious. He started to read books related to religion, to go to church, first out of curiosity, later he went there due to his own will. He didn't have deep belief in God so far, but he tried to understand and learn about the appearance and the essence of Christianity. He started to observe religious traditions after his wife became sick.

He seriously conceived the words by Jesus Christ: "Therefore I say unto you, be not anxious for your life, what ye shall eat, or what ye shall drink; nor yet for your body, what ye shall put on. Is not the life more than the food, and the body than the raiment? ... But seek ye first his kingdom, and his righteousness; and all these things shall be added unto you".

Sergey Ivanovich was already a regular visitor to the church, he went there on Sundays, but he didn't stay there long. He came in and quietly stood looking at faces of Saints and silently communicated with the God. He asked to forgive him for his foolish behavior earlier in his life, he asked for health to him and his relatives, he asked advice. He just stood silent. When he was leaving the church, he felt more confident.

At home Pryadko made a religious corner, which had the icons of the God, the Holy Mother and the Saint Nicholas. He learned the "Our Father" prayer by heart and early in the morning prayed. He tried to be alone at that time, so that no one interfered with the prayer. He considered belief in God, prayers and communication with the God to be a private issue of every human being.

He was deeply indignant every time he saw former professional communist party leaders, former ideologists and communist party secretaries of the central and regional committees, yesterday's ardent atheists, standing in churches in the first rows, with candles in his hands, trying to get in the view of video and TV cameras, so that the moment was recorded. He considered it to be the highest degree of blasphemy, of abuse of the faith. He couldn't understand why the church was so patient to those people, who took part in different actions in the church.

Among his friends, sitting at a glass of vodka, he used to say frankly:

We always rush from one extreme to another. Our nation seems to have no happy medium. First we created an extremely centralized soviet economy, now we get rid of all moral norms and give way to market relations, if this messy bazaar could be called a market. The first enterprise finished with the national tragedy, the second one produced many unsolved moral and economic problems and will finish, to my mind, with a national catastrophe.

All the leaders are talking of reforms. What kind of reforms can we talk about, if the economy and the people are spoilt morally? If there is no conscious, no honest, no real care for people, no constant sticking to moral rules by everyone, starting with the president, ending with every simple farmer, they can't be any economic achievements. If there are any, they will be short-term gains and everything will have a crush and exile at the end for some people and losses, poverty and despair for others. You are sure to remember me and my words.

To my mind, we are at the eve of a moral catastrophe. To avoid it we need to get fundamental measures on behalf of the leaders of the country. We are all to be involved in it. All of us watch movies over TV, which contain violence and adult entertainment. We don't stop silly showmen of different kind, who spoil our children. We continue buying products of the companies who advertise in slut programs. We, as taxpayers, don't demand that the government stop giving tax benefits for publishers, shops, theatres and TV channels with contents of dubious moral level. Have you ever seen a drunken man with abusive behavior to be stopped in the street? Does anyone try to stop a drug addicted person or a hooligan? The list could be continued. We don't do anything to stop all that. We don't protest against immoral behavior, we just state the fact and go on living alongside with immorality and sometimes we look like that kind of people too.

Many questions that he asked himself, had no answers. He also couldn't understand everything in the church. He came to a conclusion that the church and the faith were different things, sometimes even opposite.

Studying history, he saw that in the church there had always being struggle for the power, it was for ages, like in any state. The struggle was really desperate. It was no good if the faith is imposed by force. Everyone was supposed to understand that there was one God. One was to respect any religion, no matter what it was, Christian, Orthodox or Catholic, Muslim or some other.

To his regret, Pryadko could state that for many ages there had always been a struggle between creeds. The same was the contemporary situation between Moscow Patriarchate and Kyiv, between Moscow Patriarchate and Vatican. He saw that the reason for all the contradictions was not some theoretical arguments, but money. How could one and the same person serve the church and hypocritically call laity for something completely different from he is doing in his real life. Sergey Ivanovich couldn't understand how the church could call upon people to wage a healthy life style, at the same time applies for the government for benefits to import alcohol and tobacco goods and fill stores, bars and restaurants with that stuff. It was unpleasant for him to realize that the church cares more for transfer of pre-revolutionary property back to it, than it cares for the morality of the state. He read in one of N. Karamzin's books that as early as in the seventeenth century the church in Russia owned innumerable riches, as well as lots of fertile land where peasants were mercilessly exploited, where there ruled deceit, robbery, bribery. Pryadko had known since childhood that the fish started to go bad from the head. If the authorities were immoral and had no consciousness and honor, there was no point expecting people to observe moral rules, as everything was connected. The people were immoral and the authorities were the same. The ruling classes have no conscious, and the people take after them. Usually ordinary people said one and the same thing in that case, that was the advice to push one's honesty deep into one's ass.

Praydko was not a Decembrist, neither he was a revolutionary, he was, as everyone around him, a part of the plain grey crowd, a small piece in the world, which could mean nothing. He was an ordinary man in the street. He didn't try to become outstanding, when he was taking part in the inspection business trips, he took part in parties, didn't refuse presents and bribes in envelopes. Deep in his soul there was some weak protest, but he suppressed it, so that to be like everyone around.

Once during the Lent he had to go to his native city together with the minister to inspect the Southern troops. They had a great reception, they were accommodated in a modern hotel at the seaside, and at night they were invited for a party. The reason for the reception was their arrival and the twenty third of February, the holiday, which used to be widely celebrated all over the country. The tables were catered in a great banquet hall in a very cozy place with the outlook to the sea. The guests and the banquet were the administration of the city and the region, of military department, of the police, as well as some businessmen and clergymen. At the beginning of the party they were shown a short concert performed by the actors of the philharmonic society. They lived in the independent Ukraine and had their own day to celebrate the anniversary of the Military Forces, but they gathered together on that day due to the old tradition. It was just a reason for a party.

The tables were full of food and drinks; there were lots of different kinds of treats. Cognacs, vodka, different kinds of wine, including local Shustov and French, as well as any kind of beer. The hors d'oeuvres were really diverse, there were meat and fish snacks, red caviar, shrimps, crawfish, even crabs and lobsters.

Sergey Ivanovich was observing the Lent. It was not his first fasting, and he didn't find in difficult. Pryadko didn't say he was fasting, but when he was treated to some food, he firmly refused to eat it. It had become fashionable to fast, some fasted due to religion, some wanted to get slim, some was just curious. Most of the people never fasted. Sergey Ivanovich knew for sure that religious people of different creeds didn't always fast. He remembered that in Egypt where he as a lieutenant executed his international mission, Egyptian officers came to his blindage and had a drink with him, sometimes it was even spirits, ate lard as a snack, though it was fasting time. He laughed and asked them:
- What about Allah?

They would answer: - Allah doesn't see that.

The same was in Odessa. At the banquet table he saw how the representatives of ruling classes drank during the Lent, had substantial meat snacks, had good deserts, and looked longingly at big breasted long-legged serving girls. In the eyes of the girls there was clearly seen the expectation of the coming orgy. Everything was paid for.

The minister was respected in those circles, they were also rather afraid of him, as everyone knew his close relations with the president. That was the reason why every official, who considered himself to have some influence, tried to wish something pleasant to the minister, to express his gratitude for everything the minister was doing for the prosperity of the Mother Ukraine together with its loyal troops.

Sergey Ivanovich was seated at the table together with a clergyman. The parson, who sat on the right of the general, was having his shots in big quantities, he drank only the vodka Shustov. He had big pieces of meat as a snack, with spicy ketchup and every time he expressed his satisfaction, saying: - That was a good shot. Really good...

The parson's eyes longingly looked at the breasts of the girl who served the next table. The breasts were just peeping out of the snow-white blouse.

- That's a good girl, - He said, when he stroked her on her nice bum, while she was serving him his next shot. The girl giggled and pretended to be embarrassed.

Sergey Ivanovich got acquainted with the parson, his name was Vladimir. Pryadko told him about all his doubts, told him that he was trying to observe religious rules and the God's law, that he was fasting.

- What about you, Father? It is the Lent, and you are drinking and eat meat snacks. – He asked with interest.

The parson laughed out loud and continued to strike the nice bum of the girl.

- What if I have desire? Dear general, I consecrate every shot and every snack before I take it. I am looking at a good piece of meat and cross it and say: "I am naming you a carp", and that's it, you can easily eat it. I am not taking meat, I am eating fish.

Sergey Ivanovich was struck how witty the clergyman was. But he was not interested in him any longer. He was used to see the parties, where officials of different levels drank and made orgies. It was the same in Kyiv and in the most remote parts of the country, as the representatives of the authorities didn't have shame and conscious, to tell the truth, shame and conscious of the officials at that part of the world had always been lacking. He saw hypocrites, as they were called in Odessa, bootlickers, but he had never seen clergymen among them. He did realize that the restored and newly constructed churches in the Ukraine were not of the same kind. Some of them were small and quiet, some, especially in the capital and in big cities were grand and greatly expensive. He saw the process of making or laundrying money on that construction. It was quite possible, for example, to cast bells in the Ukraine, where the founding industry was developed, or in Russia. They placed orders for dozens of million dollars in Greece, made a show out of it, demonstrating starting of churches construction. It seemed to him that shame and conscious were lost not only by the authorities, but by the church too. They supported each other, both were lacking spirit, morality, they didn't observe any moral rules.

- Really, the faith and the church are different things in our life. – Sergey Ivanovich confirmed his conclusion.

When he left the banquet hall and went to the fresh air, the general met the reverend Vladimir sitting in an armchair with the blond waitress. They were making love in a pervert form.

When Sergey Ivanovich went outside, he spit. – I do agree that one could lose shame, but not to such a degree! "I am naming you a carp" – He imitated the priest.

I Wish You Health!

Zhora and his wife Tatiana were a united family. He loved her and he received the same kind of love and warmth from his wife. The years passed smoothly, the children were grown up, and each had a family of their own. After they exchanged their apartment with the children Zhora and Tatiana moved to a small and cozy well-built apartment in a building constructed during the Stalin rule at Dvoryanskaya Street. They were not rich at that uneasy period of time, they were not even well-to-do, but they were not poor either. Zhora was employed as a cook in a restaurant, and Tatiana was a private entrepreneur, she sold consumer goods at the markets of the city, those goods she bought wholesale at the market "The Seventh Kilometer". They said good bye to each other early in the morning and met late at night. Weekends they spent relaxing, in summer they went to the sea and in winter they went to the theatre, to his friends' place, but mostly they sat on the sofa watching TV. During all their life they hardly had a single serious quarrel.

During the latest years Zhora started to grumble his dissatisfaction with some things at home. Something was in the wrong place. The light was not switched off. Sometimes he commented out loud the news he had heard over TV. Most of all Zhora was expressing his dissatisfaction while driving. He himself could notice that he was grumbling every now and then, sometimes without any reason, he tried to control himself; he gave promises both to Tatiana and himself. But he couldn't help grumbling.

He went out of his apartment, went down the stairs and saw garbage of the stairs, some cigarette ends and traces of spitting. – Bustards, how can they live like that, is it pleasant to live among garbage?

When he went out of the building he saw that the front yard was not cleaned by the janitor. – Why is the supervisor doing nothing? Why is it necessary to tell the janitor of the supervisor that the cleaning should be done?

Then he noticed that the entrance gate was wide open, one of the tenants left the territory and was lazy enough to close the gate, or maybe he was in a hurry.

– Scoundrels! Lazy-bones! Is it so hard to close the gate? It was the decision of all! – Zhora started to express all his indignation to Tatiana. When he was driving he was grumbling protest against anything his sharp eye could catch.

– Where are you driving? Where? – He became mad when someone cut his way or drove on the red or yellow light at a crossing. He was indignant because of the great carelessness of drivers. He was right, as during the past ten years the quantity of vehicles in the city increased, the drivers became more careless, as even if you mixed drinking and driving, even if you did not obey a sign, you won't have any trouble if you have money. That was why many young men and young ladies were driving expensive foreign made cars, bought for them by their mothers and fathers. The money those cars were bought with were honestly earned by someone and stolen and bribed by others. Their kids were speeding all over the city, without observing any rules, the situation on the road and paying no attention to traffic police officers who became wet in their pants at the sight of a twenty dollars bill.

Zhorka was always mad with pedestrians, crossing the street anywhere they liked.

– Where are you going? Are you tired of life? A car can't be stopped as easily as a man; can't you understand this, lady? And you? Where are you rushing with the kid? In twenty meters there is a pedestrian crossing. Our motherland gave birth to so many heroes!

In Odessa the roads had not been repaired for about two or three decades. There were lots of holes on every square meter. There was change of ruling systems, of officials on different levels, but no one was going to take care of the roads.

- Utter fools! Not leaders, but bustards! – Zhora got mad when his wheel got into one more whole hole on the road. – In a regular country you can go to court for that and you will be paid for damage and spiritual injury. And here? I can apply to the court, but it is going to be a headache, they will charge lots of money, and there will be no result. They need to be killed; those officials need to be used for filling the holes in the asphalt. Robbers!

Tatiana sat nearby listening. She agreed with her husband in some points, in some she disagreed. She knew that Zhora will speak his mind and become quiet.

- You reproach the current authorities. Was it any better when your communists ruled? Were the roads broken in just ten years? – She pinpricked him when he went seriously furious.

- You don't judge by the communists who ruled in eighties. Those were mainly crooks. In nineties they disguised into democrats. What was the current mayor at that time? He was the first secretary of the municipal committee of the communist party. Communist ideas are sacred. But to our regret, they are Utopia in out society. We have always been known and we are still known for bad roads and fools, as Nikolai Vasilievich Gogol said.

When he drove to the parking lot of "Privoz", he saw young people with blue noses and badges "Parking services".

- See, the authorities are collecting money. One of two hryvnias from each car, it's big money made in a day, in a week and in a month. Where do they spend that money, those millions of hryvnias? Not for repairing of roads. It would be good if they made at least a single European-style parking lot in the city. There should be good pavement, marking, all the necessary signs, the machine for payments and receipts, security and all that stuff. As far as those with blue noses are concerned, they share half of the collected money with their bosses. The other half of the money goes to the pocket of the officials. They just collect the money on the broken pavement.

Zhora didn't pay for parking on principle. – I would rather give this money to a begging old woman, than to you. – He said directly to the parking service men. – Just do something wrong to my car, and I will kill you.

Even when Zhora was walking along his favorite street Deribasovskaya, he was mad because the pedestrians were using coarse language, which was really very dirty and diverse. He couldn't just pass by a group of young people who at the sight of a beautiful girl said: "See, what a gill! Maybe she will go with us? Let's fuck this bike all together!"

He was mad when he saw a young man walking together with his girl, who spat on the pavement in front of him, and she was nibbling sunflower seeds and trash the shells under her feet. Zhora was rebuking them: - Shame on you, young guys!

They usually look at him as if he were an alien: - What's wrong, old man? Do we disturb you? Pas by, otherwise you'll get your nose hit."

Zhora became mad on the spot, blood flushing to his face, and in his imagination he hit that young lout right in the bridge of his nose. But he controlled himself as he understood that he would break the law and still he would be helpless in his confrontation with the evil.

- If I kill this bustard in the spot, he will die as my blow had training in sailors' fights. And it's impossible to fight with everyone, if every other of them is morally retarded. It's a sick nation. I could have my arms stained with blood till the elbows, but they won't be cured, nothing will be changed.

At that very moment a decently dressed man blew his nose right on the pavement in front of him.

- That's a bustard, how many heroes like this did the Motherland produce? – Inside Zhorka was swearing bitterly, and at that very moment young girls, obviously, school students, passed by him swearing in such a coarse language, that he turned back and went away from Deribasovskaya, thinking: "It's good that grandchildren don't swear like this!" But he understood that it was a lifestyle that every day and every hour the same things were happening in the squares and streets, in offices and stores, in houses and apartments, everywhere...

On the stairs of the pedestrian subway across Preobrazhenskaya Street there sat a female bum with a child and was begging for some money. Close to her there was strong stinking, not far from her there were three young guys with an empty bottle of vodka and three syringes. One of the guys was strumming the guitar, all of them were doping. Father on a torn dirty mattress two bums were lying, beside them they sold books from a hawker's stand and a karaoke cafe was open. In the subway there was a real smell of a garbage can.

- Drug addicts, damn them, they are everywhere nowadays. – Zhora thought bitterly. – Sons of a bitch, they made people drunkard, now they are making them drug addicted.

Not far from the restaurant where he was employed there was a high school. He often watched school girls and school boys smoke during the break and had pricks of drugs at the gate way of the restaurant's backyard, not far from the service entrance. He pushed them away several times, but it was useless.

He saw very well that "Privoz", which he used to like, had become a sales market for drug dealers; one could buy any dope any time of the day or night. The police were well aware of that, so were the authorities, but no measures were taken. Once in three months the police chained the market, filled buses with drug dealers and their clients, in two or three days all of them were released for twenty or fifty dollars. Everyone was satisfied, both the police and the drug dealers. Everyone was satisfied, except regular, psychologically healthy individuals, but the latter became less and less in quantity, according to Zhora's opinion. Zhorka understood, that drug mafia was different from gypsies and petty drug sellers in "Palermo" and at other markets. They were not some unknown persons, they were persons among authorities, those who were ruling. While the things were like that, there was no hope for changes for the best. He remembered that not long ago they showed over TV the president of Russia who had a summit where he ordered to organize a committee or a department in the Ministry of Interior for fighting drug mafia. At the same time in the interview with the minister of health there was a question: - Why nothing has been said about fighting alcohol addiction? In Russia, and it is well known, everyone from the most remote village and the Kremlin become alcohol addicted.

The minister of health answered the following: - The president has a gradual program which right now is concentrated on the struggle with drug addiction, and later it will come the turn of alcohol addiction.

Zhorka was furious. – How can it be? How those two thongs could be separated from each other? It was hypocrisy and just a campaign which leads to no results. In Korea they caught a drug courier and he was sentenced to be shot. The same rules should be here. That would scare those who acquire great amounts of money selling drugs. The authorities doing small steps, which was populism, would be scared too. The president of Russia says that caravans of drugs cross the border with

Kazakhstan, he says nothing of the fact that in Russia there are lots of poppy and hemp plantations as well.

– It looks like one needs to escape to an uninhabited island. There is nothing pure left in this world. – Zhorka was full of sad thoughts. – If one turns on TV, there are commercials, cheap movies containing violence, pornography and blood. Explosions, shooting, criminal stuff mixed up with hypocrisy and lies of all the levels of authorities and mass media as well. In this life everyone tries to grab or steal something, to cheat on somebody. People seem to live their last day, nothing exists, but today only.

Zhorka once bought a great bunch of roses for Tatiana in the flower market in the center of the city. The saleswoman persuaded him that the roses would last long in a vase with water. The petals began to drop in an hour after he brought the flowers home.

- What am I supposed to do with that saleswoman? A scarecrow! You are in Odessa, can't you understand that tomorrow I will come to you again? What kind of shameless person she is? – Zhorka was mad. In the morning he went to a Gayevskiy drug mart to buy smekta, but he was told that the medicine was sold in a bulk of three packs only.

- Why? What if I need just one or two?

- No, it's sold only in a bulk of three packs.

Zhora laughed out loud. – Maybe you attached condoms to that bulk or remedy for diarrhea? On his way home he thought: - No, we are never going to have normal happy life here, as they live like gypsies – always ready to cheat, steal, spoil something and make damage.

Zhora thought with bitterness that neither apartments and cottages, nor garages and cars were protected against robbery. Earlier, about twenty or thirty years ago houses and apartments were kept unlocked, there was no necessity for that. Nobody used grates or iron doors. Now it was impossible to leave a car unsupervised, and it would be deprived of windshield wipers, the door would be broken, the tape recorder would be stolen. He remembered a story told by the manager of the restaurant, who left his Mercedes at a trading center for five minutes. On a conspicuous place he had left his sunshades which cost one hundred and fifty dollars and in the glove department there were sunglasses thirty hryvnias, but they had a golden frame. The super modern alarm system didn't stop them. They opened the car and stole the glasses that cost thirty hryvnias, the expensive ones they didn't take. The door lock was pulled out completely.

The wife told him: - Zhora, you'd better take away the windshield wipers and the radio for the night.

He burst out shouting: - Maybe I am supposed to take off the wheel rims or the wheels themselves? What kind of world do we live in? It's horrible. We need to escape from all that. There has never been and will never be anything good. There are some places where it is better. But it has always been like this, mud outside, filth inside. Our parents lived like this, we live like this and our children and grandchildren will live like this. Aura is negative here!

Tatiana went mad too: - Is it possible to bear your grumbling?

Starting with autumn till late in winter they constantly disconnected power in the city. It was so-called sheaf effect. It happened regularly and constantly, in one areas it was between four and six at night, in other areas it was between six and eight, that they disconnected power. It was a pitch darkness, no enterprises worked, there were accidents due to the traffic lights being out of order, people got run over by cars on dark roads, the situation in hospitals, schools and apartments was just desperate. People had to use candles.

Zhora was indignant because in the twenty first century Odessa residents had to live using candles. At the same time different regional power committees sold power to Moldova, Romania, Hungary and Poland. He was mad at the fact that Polish villages were well lighted like Kreshchatik, and his native city was in pitch darkness.

In summer, when they went to the seaside, their recreation was always spoilt by something. They stopped using Odessa beaches long ago, though during the past years they had been put into order. The sand was sifted, modern folding chairs were brought, waiters were rushing to and fro, there also were some other conveniences. But the sea water was polluted. In Odessa they hadn't upgraded the sewer system for ages. It had leading out pipe which ended in the sea within the city borders. Besides, after it rained, all the street dirt from squares and parks got into the sea. Furthermore, almost in the center of the city they constructed an oil harbor, where oil was pumped from tankers to reservoirs. Along the coast they installed breakwater constructions which not only broke waves, but also prevented fresh sea water from coming to the area. During the past ten years there appeared countless quantity of cafes, bars, restaurants, which also polluted the sea with their waste. Those who were having a rest also didn't care for the environment, there was garbage which contained everything starting with empty bottles and condoms and ending with shit. It was before afternoon that about fifty meters of water near the shore was covered with some kind of slime. A normal person with common sense found swimming in such water disgusting and dangerous. But most of Odessa residents and visitors, who came to the sea side for recreation, did swim in that slush, contributing to the further pollution of the sea. Only in the morning the water was comparatively clean.

Zhorka and Tatiana went to the sea to Zatoka, which was seventy kilometers away from Odessa. There was clean blue sea and nice fine sand. They liked one well equipped beach with tiled paths. Part of the beach was beautifully fenced, inside that area there were comfortable plastic coaches with mattresses. It was the owners of the recreation home who took care of the beach, kept it clean and well equipped. Zhorka and Tatiana were once pleasantly surprised to see the owners of the recreation home cleaning the water from the sea weeds, brought by the storm, together with the cleaners.

But there was no escape from our super well-mannered people. Especially numerous were Moldavian visitors with money and young geishas. Those were big guys with big wallets. Their wits seemed to be inversely proportional. After they consumed their first bottles they started to use coarse language, and it was conspicuous, that they spoke Moldavian and scolded in Russian. It was just hard to hear, they were having fun, but their fun was beastly-like. When they went to the water they were not laughing, they were just hee-hawing, expressing their bull-like excitement, mixing that with foul Russian abuse language. Of course, they left garbage everywhere, if they were reprimanded, they became mad.

Zhora's mood became low for the whole day after the communication with them. He sighed with relief when he didn't see Moldavians on the beach, but it was very rare. But young buffalos from Odessa didn't differ much from the pig-like Moldavians at the beach of Zatoka. The young guys who were under eighteen came there to have fun with minor hookers. They had heavy gold chains with heavy crosses, cell phones and big amounts of cash in dollars. They were relaxing and having fun to a great extent, and only the security of the recreation home could

171

calm them down. But to be fare, it should be mentioned that after they came to their senses they started to apologize for the inconvenience before others.

In those cases Zhora always thought of the rules that existed among American people, which was "Live the life you want, but don't interfere with other people's lives!" He remembered it when in the apartment building his neighbors made orgies with drinking in the middle of the night and didn't care about other people's rest. He also thought of it when crowds of drunk young blockheads walked along the city, screaming and exploding petards, and it happened after a party which was organized by the head of the city.

- That is a perfect rule, but it can't be used here. – Zhora thought, when the people around just didn't give him a chance to rest, actually, even to live normally. – We will never have any order, as the law is written on the paper, but it doesn't work, everyone is used to break it, starting with the officials, ending with their servants. Everyone knows they won't get any punishment for that. Ordinary people break the law hoping to escape punishment, and they often do!

At the same time Zhora and Tatiana became sure that many things depend on the first official. They proverb says that the fish starts being spoilt from its head. On their way home from Zatoka they often dropped to a small cozy city of Ilichevsk, which was near Odessa. Then they excitedly shared their impressions with friends and acquaintances.

- When you enter the city, you have an impression that you reach an oasis in our desert. You are surrounded with nice, calm aura. You drive and you are happy, as the city is full of trees and flowers, everything is taken care of properly. There is no a single hole in the pavement, everywhere in the city the asphalt is new, even the roads in the yards are renovated. The marking on the roads is bright, newly done, the traffic lights are clean, all of them are in order. The parking lots are equipped, no one collects money for parking there, as if they have a different kind of financing. They have a different kind of mayor, that's it! They don't steal.

Tatiana added: - In cafes and restaurants the prices are very low when compared with those in Odessa. We always have lunch in Ilichevsk. And they have great service there. It is just pleasant to go and stay there. They serve quickly and in a friendly manner, the quality of food is good, lick off your fingers, so tasty are the dishes.

Their friends opposed to them: - The mayor there got permission for unified taxation.

- Can't we do the same here? In Ilichevsk due to the unified taxation system there are public washrooms in parks, which look like beauty salons, smelling with deodorants, clean, with flowers and European-style renovation. What do we have here in Kirov Park? The washroom smells with shit for the whole park, it is situated near the monument to some Kazaks, it's just a shit house.

Zhorka made a conclusion.

- You can say anything, but in Ilichevsk there is a caring landlord, that is the mayor. Every day he and his men do something useful for the city. Ours just make a show of any petty thing they do. Presentation, cutting ribbons is all the fathers of the city of Odessa can perform.

In Ilichevsk due to the work of the authorities the atmosphere is different, there is certain order and their own style of life. People work, have rest, speak to each other in different manner. In Odessa, in the country it can be the same on condition that the ruling people would be of the same kind as in Ilichevsk. But there are just one or two cities of this kind, as we lack decent and talented men. - That was Zhora's philosophical conclusion.

When he drove from Ilichevsk to Odessa, Zhora's mood became low. He saw crowds of homeless dogs, and nobody had time to take care of them. He saw falling trees, untidy flower beds and parks, thought the landscaping enterprise was prospering in the city. He saw dark streets at night in the city, where the Regional Power Committee was also prospering, as well as its officers. Besides, there were rows of bribe-takers and those who spent budget money from heating committee, from sewer department and others. The horde of lazybones, spending budget money, who had small salary of three hundred hryvnias, were able to buy cars of foreign made, which cost several dozens of thousands of dollars. They bought country villas for several hundred thousand dollars, they lived luxurious life and cared for nothing but themselves. There was hypocrisy and deceit everywhere, not only in relations between officers and people, but between the people and the ruling classes as well. Between the ordinary people there was unfriendliness, deceit and plain envy.

- It will not do. - Zhora was mad. - I bought a new sweater, put it on, and the chief accountant at work asked him right away: - A new sweater! It must be expensive. Where do you take money from, Georgy Ivanovich?

- Shame on the nation! A neighbor wishes a fire or a flood to another neighbor. One can't sleep well if his neighbor is doing well.

Zhorka more and more often came to a conclusion that he was to move away from there, as there was nothing decent left there, there had never been anything decent and would never be. He often spoke about emigration. Tatiana became mad.

- Do you have money for that? Where can you get money from? You can't go there with empty pockets. Where are you going? Do you know that? Who is waiting for us there? Is anyone going to care of us there?

Zhora insisted: -OK, Do anyone care of us here?

She agreed: - No, No one cares for us here either, but there we would not have any one to communicate with, here we still have somebody to visit, to talk, to speak our minds to. Many people go away but many of them return because of nostalgia.

Zhorka went mad again: - What damn nostalgia you are talking about, am I to have nostalgia for this shit, for these bustards? We can come on a visit once a year for a week or for ten days, we will be deep again in this zoo and we'll hurry away again, full of impressions for the coming year. Your niece has been living in London just for three years. She came here for a month, but she could hardly believe everything she saw: - How can you live here?

Zhora was irritated with everything in that country, in that city, in the people. Tatiana used to say to him: - Try to notice good things, and you see only negative sides.

Zhora tried to ignore all the negative things and to notice all the positive things. But he failed, as shit was so much there, that everything good was stained with it. He started to notice that he and his close friends were becoming the same as the others. He could spit on the pavement, he did it stealthily, but he did. He could swear using coarse language in front of other people, it happened seldom, but it happened, he also could do some other similar things. It drove him mad. The environment influenced him, no matter he wanted that or not. He didn't want that and he fought against it.

He used to treat the previous mayor with indignation, the latter said "this people" and "this city", and then Zhora started to use the same combinations. He didn't oppose himself to the others, he just saw the deep rotten roots of the society, its decay and ignorance, which had a long history.

But most of all Zhora was exasperated when the president visited Odessa. During the recent years he had visited the North Palmyra rather often. It was true that the retinue made the king. A few hours before the visit the highest officials of the city and surroundings, ready to serve, warn the residents of Odessa thorough mass media that they were to restrict driving their private cars in the streets of the city and walking in the center. So, the residents of Odessa, kindly disappear from the city for the period of the president's visit, and we will take care of the visit. There will be decorations, even rows of demonstrators, greeting the guarantor of nobody knew what. There also would be those, serving the people of local and Kyiv levels, all mixed together.

The police seemed to be more numerous that the population of Odessa. Only the phrase "No entrance, closed here" were heard. If one calculated losses connected with the delay of trains, of people being late for work, to the railway station and to somewhere else. It was great inconvenience and multiple losses. There were expenses for the meeting reception, accommodation, maintaining of the whole visit, which was the same as chaos, called an official visit, including all the crowd of officials following the guarantor. If one made up all the calculations of the expenses related to the visit and published the results, the amount would not seem small. After such visits in Odessa there appear more and more people who hated the president and the authorities. The people didn't care that the president was not responsible for the preparation and ensuring his visit. The people just swore and scolded the president, the authorities and everyone who appeared to be on their way at the moment. A traffic police officer who had a task at a certain place was not to blame for that. But in reality it was not the guarantor, not the governor, not the mayor and not even police officials of higher levels who were scolded. All the swearing and indignation was experienced by regular cops.

Zhora remembered an old Odessa joke during the recent visit. "Once on Sunday a gun, which stood as a relic at Dunskaya square, shot unexpectedly. Aunty Sara pushed the window shutters open on the second floor of Primorskiy Boulevard and asked the pedestrians:

- What is it? Have they brought meat?
- No, it is the president who has come.

- Oh, that's it... - She sounded disappointed and shut the window.

In a whole the gun shot again. Aunty Sara opened the shutters.

- What is it? Have they brought meat?"

- No, it is the president who has come.

- Did they miss the first time?"

It was an old joke, but still of current value.

But to crown it all Zhora, who had hardly was in time to his work, at night couldn't get home for a long time. In philharmonic society there was a concert of the symphonic orchestra directed by the famous conductor Hobart Erl, and the president, the governor, the mayor and their men were in the concert hall. All the streets in the area were closed, besides, they just insulted the actors. It was impossible for them to perform in an empty hall. Or was it OK? Zhora was just furious because it was shameful to threat the actors, the residents of Odessa and Odessa like that.

- Bustards! They could have invited retired people to the concert, the latter would be grateful till their death for the charity concert. – Zhorka said to the owner of the restaurant. – Or did the president pay for the concert?

They both laughed out loud at the thought and the owner told that during the visits like that he hardly could get home, he got home only with the help of the police officers of the higher level, as he lived at Frantsuzskiy boulevard, and that was also the residence of the royalty.

- If you want to live like royalty, you have to suffer, - Zhora answered to him.

When he returned home at last, it was dark, no lights were on in the yard, there was no one to change the burnt bulbs. When Zhora came up to his apartment, he found out that there was no running water and there would be no water till morning, as the municipal water system was under planned renovation. Zhora became mad and started to shout, he used coarse language and accused the authorities in all the troubles, as well as the people, the fate, even Tatiana.

She listened to him for about ten minutes, then she hit the table with her fist.

- Enough! How much negative energy can you pour out? Why do you always pour it out on me? You energy is transferred automatically on me. I become like you, I notice everything bad and start grumbling.

What can it change? Look, the weather is fine, the nature is great, and that's good. We are healthy today – that's also good. Don't destroy yourself, don't torture yourself, you are also destroying and torturing me. I wish you health! – She was mad at him.

Zhora was astonished with the emotional explosion on behalf of Tatiana. He was embarrassed and became silent.

Before going to bed he came up to Tatiana, hugged her tightly, kissed and said with a smile: - I don't know what you mean, but we need to move!

Let the Salary be Your Only Income!

In modern Odessa there are many companies, small and big, which deal with grain business. Some of them buy grain wholesale from the producers, that is from farms, and separate farmers, and sell it on the spot to other bigger companies or sell it to flour producing companies to flour grounding plants or private mills. Other bigger companies buy grain wholesale in the port, make up cargo for ships and sell it for foreign currency to overseas companies. Some of the companies buy grain for making flour and then baking bread.

During the soviet period it was the government which did all that, and there were hardly any persons who did it as a private business. At that time they were called profiteers, second-hand dealers, shady business dealer, workshop dealer, and so on. But those were smart persons, cunning entrepreneurs, energetic, waging honest business with each other and with the government. They bought grain from collective farmers who got the grain as bonus, besides, they grew grain at their backyards and stole some from collective farm threshing-floor. Grain also was bought from collective farms chairmen for cash, who were always ready to sell excessive grain, and not excessive as well. There many ways to profit. That grain was delivered by energetic persons to bakeries using false invoices, received flour instead, packed that flour and then sold wholesale to farm markets and stores. Besides, they got bran and grain waste products from bakeries and sold all that in villages as cattle food. The schemes for wholesale buying and selling were numerous. Every enterprise had its own profit, so did the authorities and the police. Everyone was contented. But at that time there were only selected persons who were admitted to the business, and everyone appreciated every coin that dropped into their pockets.

But at the end of eighties when the co-operative business developed, and especially in nineties in Odessa and the suburbs, and all over the country private bakeries started to appear like mushrooms in the forest after the rain. Private mills appeared, the existing plants became parts of private companies dealing with grain and bakery business, and the government money was also used. Besides, there appeared very many companies and private enterprises, dealing with buying and selling grain. At the end of nineties companies dealing with oil and fuel products joined them. Yes, it was like that. Only a lazybones did not deal with grain during the harvest time. There were officials from the administration, officers of different force departments, taxation officers, health officers and others in grain business. Many farms sold the grain at the time it was just sowed. Some of them were paid by plant food, some by fuel, some credited it for interest for loans, some force department officers took the crops just for free from those who had no influence. There were no traces of decent relationship that used to be between those in grain business before the middle of the eighties. In that business the rules of wolf-like animosity reigned, the business became tough and dangerous. Lawlessness that reigned in the country couldn't help covering even such profitable business as bakery.

In that business there were very few businessmen of the previous years with their qualities left. Some of them moved overseas, some of them switched to a different business, some of them passed away. Leva, or Lev Nikolayevich Stas was the one of the Mohicans, as he liked to call himself. He stayed in the business due to his connections and mainly due to his money and his not being greedy. He used to say that he had something to eat himself and he gave the opportunity to eat to others. It was also due to his great ability to do his own business and not to interfere with others'. He had almost no enemies, everyone respected him and even turned to him for advice.

Leva had a company of his own; five persons were in the staff. He and his childhood friend Lenya Kupperman, who did the accounting, were managing the company. Besides, there was a shift manager Tanya, Kupperman's daughter and two drivers with their own "Kamaz" trucks for grain transportation. Since the beginning of the nineties they rented a small room for office at a bakery. The manager of the bakery was the godfather of Leva's child, so there were no problems with the rent, as well as with receiving and storing grain, with getting flour or bran. Many other problems were easily solved for Leva's company, as the godfather of Leva's kid had his own share. Lately the company had a conspicuous name "Hudgibey". Following the advice of some friends from the department of economic crimes, Leva closed one company and opened another one once in two years, and sometimes he had license for two companies at one and the same time. One of the companies did all the purchases of grain, and the other dealt with wheat processing and selling of flour, bran and grain waste. He had to share his profits with so many persons that if you started counting them on your fingers, there would more than ten. So, witty Leva decided to pay only to some of them, but those were well known persons in Odessa, and everyone was cautious with them. All the rest didn't demand any payments, they just wanted to be safe.

But everything was not constant in life. Leva did understand it well enough. The black period came all of a sudden and pushed him out of his regular everyday life. First it was the godfather of his kid who was laid off. The new manager didn't persecute Leva, but the latter didn't have the liberty he was used to. But Leva quickly found a way out. He hired to his company the manager of the laboratory of the bakery. It was on her that the quality of the grain coming to the bakery was determined, as well as the output of the flour. He also took care of the manager of the mill complex and the head of the sales department. He paid a hundred bucks to them each month, and they were satisfied. That was much enough! They had salary of about one hundred and fifty or two hundred hryvnias, which was paid with delays. In a couple of months Leva had the same situation as was with the laid off relative, as he didn't have to share profits with him any more.

But at the same plant there appeared a few more big companies, with big money and big supervisors. One of the companies was managed by the daughter of one of the first regional officials, who was influential enough in Odessa. She was just having that position, but the father made up a strong team there, who were professional, young and ambitious. But Leva respected people like that. "Businessmen!" – He used to say with respect. But that company could buy more grain than his own, as they had more money at their disposal, including government money.

They also had access to grain which was stored by the government as reserve.

Another company, which had a cooperation agreement with the plant, started to monopolize the sales of flour, mostly to the municipal bakeries of the city, to the confectionary plant and to big private bakeries. The owner of the company was one of the biggest banks, it was the bank "Ukraine". The company had loans free of interest, and it was hard for Leva to compete with them in prices.

But Leva Stas was a reasonable and strong person. - I had survived hunger and I am going to survive competition. – he used to say to his partners.

- Everyone will find his own place. The main thing is to have good crops. All those large-toothed persons will break their teeth pretty soon. Ambitions and pushing is good if you have some protection, no doubt. But one should remember that envy is playing an important part here, no one would allow monopolizing anything in the grain business. No one, and first of all the government and its state agricultural committee "Ukrainian Bread".

Very few people could figure out, what kind of enterprise was the state joint stock company "Ukrainian Bread". According to Leva's opinion it was just a commercial enterprise in the structure of the agricultural department, which had circulation of more dozens of millions of government money, most of which stayed on private accounts of the officials in different banks. That department owned the most of grain elevators and bread dispatching warehouses in the country. Most of the grain processing plants, or mills owned by the state agricultural committee, which was waiting for the time it could undergo privatization, gradually worked for destroying the elevators and plants so that to declare bankruptcy in the future and then to buy all the plants for cheap price.

Leva was sharing his thoughts with Kupperman, he grinned and said: - This entire stealing mob at the government would never allow any company or corporation to try to dominate at the bread and grain market. On the top there is a desperate fight for the grain market between that joint stock company and the management of the state reserve, it does not prevent the ruling top to push down those who start being too active at the bottom.

Leva was sure, that soon in the future such companies as "Yug-zerno" and "Grandy" will come down, the time would put everything in its places. He enjoyed watching the Mickey-mouse fight for the plant.

– The fools don't understand that even if they make the plant private and don't have their own established ways to sell flour, it will lead to bankruptcy and fall. The production itself is not enough, it needs bakeries. Only in cooperation with bakeries, big or small, the plant could have some significance.

Not many people understood that. Leva Stas came to know that many years ago. He was waiting for his time, he was sure it would come. One on one of the parties that took place in one of ancient restaurants in the hotel "Krasnaya" he was introduced to a businessman from Kyiv Ilya Zaltsman. They were of approximately the same age, in their early forties. Ilya Izraelevich was witty and jolly in the company, he was popular among women, he looked really handsome in his age, he was of medium height, with black thick hair and beautiful large blue eyes. He looked more like Italian, than Jewish. In Kyiv he had several businesses, he managed a small commercial bank, he owned a number of gas stations in the capital city, and he also had control packet of shares in a confectionary plant near Kyiv. Besides, he exported Western Karpaty mineral water to the USA. He had been an Israel citizen for ten years, there he had a detached house, and his family lived there.

Leva felt, that beside being respectable and well-to-do, that person was kind and decent, which was rare among people who ran business. Watching the way Ilya was relaxing at the party, Leva understood that the man followed the principle "Relax when you are relaxing and work when you are working".

In a while he visited Zaltsman in Kyiv, it was just a courtesy visit. The office was in one of the central streets, close to Kreshchatik. Leva was surprised that there were so many associates in the office. The furniture was expensive, so was the equipment. He saw that everyone was working there. Every associate had his own task and he was to come to some definite result daily.

He paid attention to extremely democratic relations between Saltsman and his associates. He saw it was the combination of democratic relations and strict order and great responsibility for the work done on this or that area. When he shared his impressions with Ilya, the latter laughed out loud and then said in a serious voice:

- One is supposed to live beautifully, to work beautifully and then everything would be in his life, success and money.

During two days Zaltsman told Stas about his enterprise, the details of his work, all points and specifications of his business. At night they relaxed in pubs in the suburbs, surrounded by many young beautiful ladies. They soon became friends. Leva signed with Ilyusha, as he started to call Zaltsman, an agreement of cooperation. They registered a company what was supposed to deal with buying and selling grain, and the main thing was processing of grain and selling flour to the baking plants of Odessa and other regions.

- Leva, it's time for you to go up to the country level, it's high time to conquer the world grain market too. I have money, there will be no problems with loans, and your part is professional dealing with the problems. There no so many people as experienced in grain business as you. They say, the breeze and the waves always work for skillful sailors. So, good luck and start working.

And the wheel started to roll. The newly registered company was called "Arkadiya". Zaltsman used his connections in the government, in the administration of the region and in the mayor's office to get shares for delivering flour to baking plants in Odessa. They also solved the problem of delivering of flour to Eastern Karpaty and Eastern regions of the country.

- You are supposed to understand, Leva, that when we are on the level like this, we need to work with everyone. In any city the question is settled easily with the help of the manager of the baking plant or of the administration of the city or the region. They should be paid for that. You need to profit from the volume. Take into account the prime cost of flour, add transportation expenses, plus eight to ten per cent of profitability. That all makes up the price. Add ten hryvnias on each ton for the manager, and he will accept your flour with pleasure, refusing local traders. Your quality is not the best, but he will prove that it is. And so on. Of course, it is desirable to have a higher profitability, but we are not Russian Gasprom, which has profitability of sixty per cent. It is harder, actually, it is practically unreal to get business in those bakery plants that have already become private and have their owner. That is useless even to try that. They have their own delivery companies, and there is nothing to talk about.

Leva understood that. He watched the events at the grain plant attentively. The managers were changed there very often, almost every half a year, the level of discipline and the quality of production was gradually getting lower. Stealing was everywhere at the plant, as well as in the whole branch and in the whole country. Everybody was stealing everything. But if workers stole flour by packages, sometimes by sacks, the management stole it by trucks. Many reprimands were due to the low quality of flour, as the management of the plant bought cheap grain of low quality. It was fodder grain that was mixed with regular and then milled all together. Many bakeries refused to get flour from the plant.

But, in spite of all that, the company "Arkadiya" signed an agreement with the plant for graining wheat and started to deliver flour to bakeries according to the agreement. One of officials from the mayor's office and one from the department of agriculture of the regional administration were hired by the company, as well as one or two officials from every bakery. Gradually, with difficulties the business started to develop and in spite of great expenses it had big profits. And at that moment the previous manager was laid off and a new one was appointed, he was Tkach, Fedor Petrovich from the province.

He started changes at once, on the very first day he laid off the head of the security department with all the staff and the next day introduced a check-in system to the administration building. In a week the chief accountant was laid off, as well as the chief engineer and the manager of the sales department. New associates were hired. Leva approved of the changes, he didn't like disorder since childhood, especially when it was disorder in industry. Where there is no discipline, there will never be profitable production business, no matter how much money you invest in it.

In a week Leva paid a visit to the new manager. He noticed at once that there was a new secretary, a young bright blonde with a beautiful body, a beautiful face and a friendly smile.

- Is she a model from the podium? – Leva thought. He said out loud:

- It's pleasant to visit the manager. Let me introduce myself. I am the manager of the company "Arkadiya", Lev Nikolayevich Stas. – He introduced himself to the secretary. – Earlier when I came into the reception I got an unfriendly look, no good attitude, to say nothing of a cup of coffee. They looked so that you would think twice before you come to the reception.

He saw that the secretary was pleased, the manager who entered the reception was pleased too.

- Good afternoon, Lev Nikolayevich! I have heard a lot of you. Come in, please, let's get acquainted. There are some topics for conversation. I would like to hear your opinion, as you are a person who knows the situation at the plant in detail. I would like to get your advice how we should put everything in order and raise the quality of the products.

Leva was just astonished with such an attitude. He saw the manager for the first time. He was a tall strong man of about two meters tall, with friendly face, but a cunning smile.

- He knows what he is worth. He is cunning, firm, extremely bold and ambitious. – Leva made his first conclusions. They entered the office and the secretary served coffee, they started the conversation.

The manager, Fedor Petrovich, was a lawyer by education, but he had almost no experience till the middle of the nineties. During the soviet rule he was a professional komsomol worker, a full-time secretary of the komsomol committee at cement works, then he tried to start a business, but he failed. He was employed later as a legal consultant to a district administration, where the managers of the joint-stock company "Ukrainian Bread" noticed him.

During the conversation Leva understood the nature of the person. He was quite inexperienced in industry, he had never managed even a small industrial enterprise, but he had an extreme desire to be the first. He was extremely ambitious, he was ready to sweep away anyone on his way, no matter what method he used.

- I had a choice to accept the position of the manager of the plant or to be appointed as a judge in the district court. I have already passed the interview in the department of justice. I was waiting for the invitation for the Supreme council of justice, but at the very moment I received this offer. I didn't think long and decided to take the position. – Fedor Petrovich told to Leva.

- You'd better become a judge, it can be clearly seen that you could become a good judge, matching today's requirements. He would become better than others. – Leva thought, but he said out loud: - Graining industry is a delicate branch, here you need a skilled team of highly professional associates. There are some here, by the way. It's a pity you kicked off the chief engineer, he knew the production and he was respected by the workers…

- I will be sincere with you. He was a rival for me and he was on my way. I got rid of him and I am not going to discuss this. – The manager interrupted Stas.

- Lout! – Leva thought and shrugged his shoulders.

- It's up to you. You are to manage it all. I am interested in one thing, that is the quality of the flour produced by the plant. I would like stealing of grain and flour from the producers to be stopped. I care for my grain and my flour. In order to achieve that and so that the production was steady, it is necessary to set a strict discipline and get money for renovation and maintenance. The wages should be paid in time for everyone. There should be no unpaid wages left. Then the workers will trust you and will support you. People would like to be put in order, to normal regular work. And the work should be paid for.

- Could you please tell me about the plant as you see it. – Fedor Petrovich asked him.

Leva tried to be brief. He told about the plant, the details of receiving and storing wheat, about the work of the graining complex, about making up milled packages, about the work of the warehouses at distribution of flour.

- Everyone is stealing. The first reason for that is the wages which are not paid in time, no matter how small they are. This is the reason they all steal. This is the reason the grain of low quality is registered as high quality grain. The reason is that the laboratory workers are paid by those who deliver wheat for registering grain as of high quality, according to the instructions they receive. The chain goes on, and it's necessary to break it and put everything in order.

They discussed the conditions of the agreement about grain processing. Leva had some benefits; he paid twenty hryvnias less than others for each ton of processed grain. Ten hryvnias of that twenty he paid to previous managers. He offered five hryvnias to Tkach. But he refused to accept the offer: - I do respect your business, but you, Lev Nikolayevich, will pay for processing the same price as others. I don't want anything, and this way it will be better for the plant.

- OK, but till the end of the year I will work according to the current agreement, no one has cancelled it yet. – Leva grinned. The meeting was not a success. The new manager appeared to be an arrogant person. Lev Nikolayevich said good-bye and drove to the country where in his cottage there waited Ilyusha.

- You see, he is completely unprofessional, as a manager he is zero, but his arrogance and ambition are so big. It's OK, we'll manage him, and we used to get the better of more tough people. I see his point, he wants to switch gradually to his own independent processing of grain, and he doesn't want any bribes. To tell the truth, he is right. But he will need much money for that. All he has now is a great debt of the plant in the amount of about fifteen millions. Where is he to take the money from? He would better cooperate with our company, gradually upgrade the production process, pay all the debts and then start thinking of independence.

Ilyusha lay in the armchair imposingly and thought,

– It is not as simple as that. – He started speaking in a while. – Nobody knows, he was appointed by Kyiv, and they will be able to find the money. The so-called great amount of fifteen million is not a problem for them. Let's have a closer look at your judge. Only we and "Grif", as you say, are still in business among big grain processing companies. That's it. If we don't pay to him, how can he survive? On his own salary? – He laughed out loud. – It's an evil with in here in Odessa: "Let your salary be your only income!"

Leva grinned. – Ilyusha, I have already told you that you are to pronounce the word Odessa with a mild "e". For his salary only he will not survive one month, taking into account his position, where he has so many expenses. You are right, we need to wait. And beside money the plant owes much flour to the partners. It's a crazy amount of about six hundred tons. He owes a lot, really. We need to watch him as they can start doing the same stuff with the quality and mixing grain forage.

- Does it matter to you? What quality flour should they produce? They will do what they are expected to do, and it is not your business what they mix there. OK, - He hugged Leva. – Let's relax in sauna; girls are waiting for us there. Nice stuff, you'll see. We'll continue our conversation after I return from Israel.

They went to the basement and saw real beauties waiting for them there.

Two months passed since then. The new manager had some drawbacks, but he did put everything in the plant in order. There seized to be almost any stealing, the production process became regular. The crops were good that year too. Leva was contented, as bakeries bought big quantities of flour from him and didn't say anything about low quality.

But he knew by that time that Tkach had met the head of the city, managers of bakeries, he promised everything to them, and asked to work without middlemen, he just wanted to acquire all the volume of production from "Arkadiya". He asked officials from Kyiv to help him in that matter. But he failed. There were two reasons for that. The first was that Ilyusha and Leva paid real money to officials in the capital and to local officials too. The second reason was that Tkach couldn't get a loan. They did not trust him, as they understood that he was saying one thing and was doing something different.

At last Leva was bored with the game behind the scene and he together with Ilyusha went to the manager. They spoke on different topics and invited him to the country cottage for dinner. After some hesitation Fedor Petrovich accepted the invitation.

He had a weak point, he liked something for nothing. Besides, it turned out that he liked hookers, as he called all women with no strict behavior rules. That night he had them more than enough.

At dinner when there were three of them, Ilyusha asked him directly:
- Do you want to make much money doing almost nothing? Just don't interfere with our business.

Tkach was surprised: - How can it be?

- It's easy. You just sign a new agreement with us containing the old conditions, that is we will pay less for grain processing. You will get ten hryvnias from each processed ton of wheat. Don't interfere in delivery business, don't deal with small and big bakeries. You won't be admitted there anyway. We pay them all. And you? Where are you going to get cash? - He looked at Tkach, who was silent. – That's it. Look here, is it that bad to have three or four thousand bucks every month? What is you salary? About five hundred hryvnias? It is less than one hundred bucks. And we offer you four thousand. Even if you steal some flour and sell it you will get two thousand hryvnias, it's nothing. And you need to think to whom you are to sell the flour, so that you get paid. There is nothing much to discuss.

The plant manager was relaxing in the country cottage for twenty four hours more. Leva left Ilyusha to take care of him and left for office. His business needed care too. Beside flour production he had two more main directions of activity, that was export of wheat and bran, he had already established business links with companies which bought grain and bran for export, the price was good. He also was conducting preliminary talks with an Egyptian company and he was preparing a contract for direct delivery of forage. He understood that sooner or later grain processing would stop being profitable, as bread producing industry would soon be private, and the owners would not be interested in middlemen. A smart owner would make a cycle, the wheat would come from farmers to his mill, and his flour would go to his own bakery. He would also deliver flour, cattle food, bread, fuel, plant food and equipment to the farm.

But there was still profit from grain processing at that time and in those conditions. It was a profitable business. The time passed by, business was going on, everything was fine, Leva and Ilyusha were satisfied. The plant manager was also satisfied. At the beginning of each month Leva brought to Tkach's office an envelope containing four thousand dollars. He opened it without any embarrassment in the presence of Leva and touching the newly printed one hundred bills, said with a smile: - That's good. Bucks are bucks everywhere.

After that he didn't show up at the plant for forty eight hours, he allowed himself to relax.

But as they say in Odessa, greed killed the dandy. Tkach together with the chief accountant decided to pay all the debts in flour delivery. They bought low quality wheat to the plant at a very low price. They started mixing that stuff to the wheat of the company "Arkadiya". The chief accountant called the managers of the companies to whom they owed and put his conditions,

- Do you want to get the flour we owe to you? We agree to pay the debt, but just half of it. For example, if we owe you one hundred tons, we will give you fifty, but the invoice will be done for one hundred. Otherwise, you are not going to get anything at all.

The managers accepted the conditions, as they understood that otherwise the plant with its multimillion debts would be paying nothing to them.

The plan of the manager and the chief accountant worked, and they decided to mix low quality grain to their own products and then sell them at a price lower than at the market. The quality of the products became low. And there came the time when the thunderstorm burst out. Bakeries refused to accept flour delivered from the plant.

- We have big companies to deliver flour to us, enough is enough. We accept no arguments. We break the contract with you. – That was a unanimous answer of all the managers of bakeries.

Leva understood well enough for the rivals it was a victory. He called to Ilyusha who was in Kyiv at that time and explained the situation. They decided to concentrate mostly on exporting grain overseas.

- What can I say? An idiot he is. He thought four thousand bucks per month not enough for him. He is a fool. Now he is going to suck his own thumb. – Zaltsman said in the conclusion.

Leva came to the plant, entered the reception and said hi to the secretary,

- Is you boss in?

- He is, I will tell him you are here.
- No, you needn't. Is he alone?
- Yes, he is...

Leva understood everything, he pushed the door open and saw Tkach in his armchair with a bottle of vodka and a glass in front of him.

- That's it! – Leva said, closing the door tightly. – Are you celebrating your foolishness?

Tkach was silent, and Leva went on: - You are a fool! You destroyed a perfect scheme! What else did you want? More money? Now you stay where you are, no more of our bucks. How are you going to survive? There is no point talking to you, silly pig. You'd better had become a judge. Let your salary be your only income for all your life!

Leva spit, turned away and left the office, slamming the door. He rushed past the embarrassed secretary without saying a word.

In the car he cooled down. – Bustard! He let us down, not only himself. The plant workers started to work regularly, had all their wages paid, people became more enthusiastic. They considered our company to be a guarantor of their stability. And it turned upside down! The manager did a trick! What is going to happen next? In a few months the plant will work occasionally, the specialists will go away, the equipment will become neglected. Where did they find such an idiot? – Leva became mad again. - Really, let your salary be your only income! – This was addressed to the manager.

The Businessman Monya

The hotel Odessa was fitting beautifully into the outline of the city, when it if viewed from the sea. It was also a nice view if you look from Primorsky Boulevard, from the monument to Richelieu, to the sea terminal. You will see a beautiful landscape with the sea, the beautiful harbor, the port, the modern beautiful sea terminal and the beautiful tall white and blue building of the hotel constructed of concrete and glass.

Aleksandre Sergeevich Ofonarenko was a well-to-do businessman from Kazan. He was having lunch in the cozy restaurant on the nineteenth level of the hotel "Odessa". On the same level there was an observation area, where on could see a great sea panorama. The sea was calm, the weather was sunny and cloudless, the visibility was perfectly clear, as aviators would say. In the harbor some small quick moving towboats were going to and fro; far away at the road stead there were several dry cargo ships and a tanker.

Alexander Sergeevich couldn't help admiring the bird's-eye view. He was not having lunch alone. Opposite him there say Zaltsman, Ilya Israelevich, a businessman from Kyiv. They met and became friends during the Ukrainian and Russian business forum, which had just been over.

Ofonarenko was born in the Ukraine, in Poltava, and he grew up there. After finishing school he went to conquer Moscow, where he graduated from the Mining Institute and bound his life with oil for ever. He knew all the details of the work of the entrails of the earth explorer, he holed oil wells in Siberia, but in five years of his experience after the

Institute Alexander Sergeevich switched to the work in the communist party as an instructor of the regional committee in Kazan. But he felt the smell and taste of oil at that time, as he would often say.

At the beginning of nineties Ofonarenko trashed the party membership card as useless. Together with some of his friends from the Ministry of oil and gas industry they organized an oil and gas concern, the son of the minister of those times helped them. The same person helped to get loans. Following the advice of the minister, they started to buy vouchers, or privatization cheques, as they were called, for a very cheap price. They were extremely grateful for that to the godfather of privatization and to the government of Russia of that time. They bought vouchers in sacks, sometimes paying a bottle of vodka for that, sometimes it cost them ten rubles, so it was almost for free. At the beginning of the privatization process they acquired almost for free, for the meaningless bills issued by Chubais, about a dozen of running, profitable oil wells and an oil processing plant.

- Those were golden months and years. – Ofonarenko closed his eyes dreamingly, remembering his life. – A few frights with oil were enough to make you are a millionaire! Money was pouring in sacks, like from a cornucopia. We had many things to spend the money for. Later, in a few years everything came to order gradually. Former partners quarreled and split, everyone established his own business, his own enterprises, and his own life.

- It was good they didn't shoot each other; they were smart enough not to do that. – Alexander Sergeevich often thought.

He, unlike the majority of new Russians, understood that the acquired assets need to be multiplied and spare reasonably. Poor people also should be taken care of. He remembered the sentence pronounced by an American businessman "Easy money is bed money" for ever.

Ofonarenko read a lot, he liked history, literature; he strived to become an advanced person in different branches. He saw that the way of thinking and the psychology of rich people at the end of the nineteenth and the beginning of the twentieth centuries differed a lot from those of contemporary rich people of Russia. In the past the rich supported many hospitals, nursery homes, museums; they built churches, schools, hospitals, libraries; much money was left to poor people according to their will testimonies. The contemporary rich people were just skinflints.

He didn't consider himself either of them. But he did realize that nothing is changed in the life of people, there could come another revolution, like in the nineteen seventeenth. He also realized that those problems, especially social ones, were to be solved by the government. And the government officials were busy filling their pockets. He knew lots of officials of the higher level who were in the government and in business; they were expanding their business rapidly, filling their pockets with government money. He knew many millionaires and even multi-millionaires from the officials, who had never worked in business. He didn't like them, he hated them, they were just spongers, who took much money from people, himself including.

Those were the reasons, as well as some others, why Ofonarenko was searching regions outside Russia where he could invest money. Odessa was interesting him as he could deliver oil there. He had wanted to have his own business there, at the South of the Ukraine long ago. That was why he accepted the invitation to take part in the forum.

Zaltsman, Ilya Israelevich had been conducting business in the Ukraine for a long time, though he had the citizenship of Israel. He had different directions of his business, but the main and core branch was sales of oil products.

That business drew them together at the forum. But they became close more due to their mutual necessity, which they felt. Zaltsman was tired of being alone. There was no one to share thoughts with, to communicate of different topics, as he was surrounded mostly by persons who thought only of how to steal and cheat and to remain unpunished. He was surrounded with people who didn't like arts and sport. He had many officials of the highest level from the government, as well as big businessmen, with whom he was on friendly terms. But only some of them attended concerts of a symphonic orchestra, because they loved classic music; only some of them went to the theatre because he liked Chekhov. Most of rich people and officials went to the first nights just because it was fashionable, not because they liked arts.

In Alexander Sergeevich he felt a subtle nature, well acquainted with history, literature, visual arts. Moreover, that person had knowledge in economy, and he acquired that knowledge not at flee markets and parties. Shortly after the first meeting they started to long to each other, they met every night after the economic forum business hours were over. They relaxed in entertainment centers of Odessa, talked, argued and made plans.

That day, on the eve of the departure, they met in that cozy pub. Zaltsman looked at Alexander Sergeevich, who was deep in thought, and suddenly he laughed out loud. It was his thoughts that made him laugh.

- What is it, Ilya? – Ofonarenko asked smiling, as he didn't understand what made him laugh.

Ilya couldn't stop laughing and asked: - Sorry, Sasha, but I suddenly thought that you might have thought of changing your last name. I understand that you have parents, your dynasty and so on, but you are a businessman and you have such a funny last name – Ofonarenko!

Alexander Sergeevich laughed out loud too. – The question is OK, don't worry. For the start I will tell you a real story, not a made up one. In the middle of nineties I was in Moscow, my concern had some business to settle with the government. My friends invited me to a party to Arkhangelskoye; the reason for the party was nomination of some new ranks to some higher officers in the army and the police. It was the deputy manager of the Kremlin administration Ivan Vasilievich Chuprina who invited me.

- You will mix with the highest officials; even EBN will be present there. I will try to introduce you to him. It will do you good in the future.

I thought and decided to stay, as I didn't have a constant opportunity to mix with all the political, economic and military leaders of the country. At the same time I thought that I didn't need all that, I was supposed to be more inconspicuous. The prime minister was watching our oil wells and our profits closely, as we split in business with his son.

- Sorry, Sasha, but who is EBN? – Zaltsman interrupted his story.

Ofonarenko burst out laughing. – I didn't understand that on the spot too. You see, they called Eltsyn, Boris Nikolayevich as EBN between themselves. So, I attended the party which lasted till morning. I had time to get acquainted with a couple of dozens of different generals with innumerous number of stars on their uniforms, with ministers, deputies, actors and so on. There were so many famous people there, but all of them relaxed and drank like coachmen and janitors from classic novels. At the high point of the party EBN showed up. He was without his wife, followed by a security officer in the rank of a general. I saw him so closely for the first time. He came already drunk and drank more at the party.

- Ilya, his face was not touched with traces of intellect as it was, but there it was still more horrible… His face was swollen, his nose and cheeks were red, and eyes were narrow, red with blood. There I came to understanding that an alcohol addicted person was ruling Russia. When he pronounced a toast, he looked as if he was going to say something great and significant.

"I think that… we need to drink… to… to what? To reforms…" - His voice was hoarse, coarse, it was interrupting as if he was suffocating.

After he left Ivan Vasilievich said to me laughing: - Look here, Sasha, let's change your last name to Eltsyn and you last name will match him.

I saw that they were just sick and tired of him with his constant drinking and his drunken ideas.

As far as my last name is concerned, I never thought seriously about it. It is not a problem to change the name, especially nowadays. But will it change anything? I don't think so. In Russia and here in the Ukraine it has always been fashionable to change uniform straps, nationality, parties, opinions, last names. It is only the sex that is not fashionable to change so far. In Russia there appeared to be so many Jews nowadays. They buy documents in archives, in registrar offices and almost half of Russian population seems to be victims of holocaust. The same situation is with the prisoners of Gulag. This all is so ugly…

Zaltsman was listening attentively, and then added thoughtfully: - You are right. If we analyze the history, it was almost always that schizophrenics, fools and ignorant persons who ruled in Russia. I am just surprised, how can this country, rich with natural resources and with such beautiful nature, be so lacking of talented, honest and hard working people.

- Oh, Ilyusha, don't punch my sensitive chord! It's hard for such persons to live now in Russia. There such persons there, but they are very few. You are right, as usually. Deprived of talent and generosity persons on the top are applauded to by their loyal servants, who want to grab a piece off the master's table? There are also millions of frightened, silent, poor and lazy persons there. – Ofonarenko continued the talk.

At that moment they were serve the dessert and they asked the waiter to take everything to patio and moved there. They looked at the sea harbor and shared their impressions of the recent economic forum. They had bad impression of it. It was not the organization of the forum, the reception and Odessa itself, which they did not like. No, it was not that. They had a really royal reception. They were accommodated in the best hotels of the city, the meetings were well organized, the work of the sections, the sightseeing tours, and the business trips were perfect. The recreation program contained saunas, night clubs, casino, Odessa girls with Southern sunburn skin and endless energy – everything was just great.

- The Odessa residents don't know that all the forum expenses are on their cost, they would not feel so comfortable here otherwise. – Alexander Sergeevich said.

- I think they don't care if we drink on our or on their cost. Like in your Russia, in Odessa everyone lives today and mind just his own shit, like a cockroach. – Zaltsman answered to him. I visit this city more often than you. Indifference, absence of will, striving to grab and steal is the same as in Kyiv here and in other places.

But to tell the truth, when compared with other regions, in Odessa people seem to do something, to make at least some money. This makes them different. As far as all the rest is concerned, they are the same.

Alexander Sergeevich got up and started walking to and fro along the terrace, his pace was slow.

- You see, I have seen lots of leaders in the world of different level and different importance. I watched the mayor and his men and I have an impression that they lived in a virtual world, as he says such things that don't make any sense. He is like Khrushchev who wanted to build communism in twenty years. He wants to make Odessa the best city, but what is he going to make it from? Out of curiosity I dropped to yards in Deribassovskaya area. My hair stood on end. It's like Harlem. Destruction, garbage, broken doors of the buildings, collapsing fronts...

- Stop it, Sasha! Don't concentrate on that. I am not a resident of Odessa, but to tell the truth, Kyiv, your St. Petersburg and Moscow in the suburbs area are in the same condition too. It's the same people everywhere, it's the same shit. And you are right when you say that the mayor, who is supposed to clean up the shit together with his men, is busy with nothing but not cleaning. He is cutting ribbons, making presentations, meetings, forums, round table meetings and conducting some business. It is not like this only in Odessa. Here the situation is clear. The mayor has been in the ruling circles for thirty years already. He was a komsomol secretary, a communist party secretary, not the first, but the second, first in the municipal committee, then in the regional committee. That is the system. He was brought up in the atmosphere of hypocrisy and lies, he can't be changed. And there are many others like him.

- OK, do you think the conscious and moral principles of future leaders are formed in different environment? What kind of leaders are they going to be?

- You are right, it's hard to imagine.

They were silent for a while, watching the vast sea, but they had thoughts of the same kind, they both thought of relationship between business and the authorities. What should it be like? The same question was discussed at the forum. It's funny, what kind of relationship should it be? There should be no relationship. The state and the government is one independent thing. Business is another one. The government is supposed to determine the taxation policy, and the rules of the game should be determined by the market. That's it! Don't interfere in business! Businessmen work depending on the situation on the market, paying taxes in time. Their relationship can be related only with taxation.

But both in Russia and here in the Ukraine, and in Odessa in particular, the authorities, and namely the officials of the president's administration, the government, governors, mayors, taxation and customs officers, force structures officers and so on, want to take part in business. They want to take part in distribution of profits, to have their interest, which is big and constantly coming.

- In the Ukraine about ten years ago there were about three hundred thousand officials. Now there are more than a million. In this city the mayor has several thousands officials in his disposal, and the residents of the city are about a million. In the USA cities with the population of ten millions are governed by ten or fifteen persons all in all. – Zaltsman said.

- You see, the phenomenon hasn't recently appeared, it had been for ages like this. Officials have no limit. I had a conversation with the management of an oil processing plant. I asked him about the authorities. They told me that during one year the mayor's office managed to get a loan of many millions and spent all the money in two months. During the election campaign the mayor was asked about the money. The authorities answered that the money was spent to renovation of the elevators system. With dozens of millions of dollars they could fix new elevators everywhere. Now the authorities start talking that they need to find resources for renovation of the system of elevators in the city. The process never stops. Money is spent by the authorities instantly and nobody knows for what.

- I would agree to donate some money for social needs, but I should know where it goes. The officials won't accept that system, as they won't be able to steal then.

And the forum has no positive results as far as the question of promotion of business is concerned. The development of mutually profitable relations between us is hard due to the lawless actions of officials in Russia, as well as here. I just can't find the word to determine the phenomenon. No one wants to invest here and no one will. It is not due to political opposition of Kyiv. There seems to be nowhere in the world that hypocrisy, theft, robbery and cheating would grow to such extend. One of my American partners said to me that we needed to profit while the law is not working properly. The first capital in the USA was built in the same conditions. I agree with him that it was like that, but the scale was different! The water is so deep that you can't see the bottom. It's high time they stopped, but they won't!

- Sasha, you present everything in dark colors. But not everything is so bad. You are right to some extend. I was surprised that here, like everywhere, every enterprise is private, I mean industry. If it is not private, it is supervised by a certain ministry or a department. But still there are departments of economy in the mayor's administration where officials have nothing to do.

They would better take brooms and sweep the yards. – They both laughed out loud. They imagined just for a minute officials from the mayor's office with brooms.

- I also wanted to mention something else. We, two of us, met and settled everything. I know that other businessmen also did, for example, good agricultural contracts were planned to be signed. This is the positive result of the forum.

Alexander Sergeevich went on walking to and fro, like a pendulum.

For a minute he stopped and looking at Zaltsman directly, said, growling: - My dear Ilyusha, this is an opportunity which can result in nothing. As soon as the Russian officials know about the contract on oil delivery, that we are going to sign, they will lobby the issue.

- How can they?
- Ilyusha, you surprise me. There many ways for that. The easiest for them is to raise the customs duties for oil, that's it. We won't find it profitable any longer. You will have to raise the price of oil. – Alexander Sergeevich stopped talking and called the waiter. He ordered some food to the room. – Ilya, let's go down to my room and have a shot of cognac, have some coffee, I am a little bit bored here.

In a while they went down to the room of Alexander Sergeevich. The waiter had already catered the table.

- We need lobsters and Monya. – Ilya laughed.
Ofonarenko agreed with him. – You are right. What we need is the presence of the businessman Monya. The persons at the forum are so outstanding, you know. One of the organizers from the Russian part was a patient of a mental hospital in Odessa about a couple of years ago, and now he was making decisions on the government level. The evil tongues say, another one several decades ago hardly managed to escape from Odessa where he was charged for rape of minor girls, whose parents could have torn him apart. Now he is a muscovite with Odessa background. There is one smarter lad from Odessa, who managed some fund in Moscow.

Both of them, and not only them, were struck with the abundance of officials and other parasites, close to business circles. It was unpleasant for them to hear their illiterate speech and cynicism of most of the politicians, making their way into business. But they were unable to think and to express their thoughts.

- I made notes of the speech of my former vis-à-vis, Ilya, you just listen how deep his thoughts and sayings are.
Ofonarenko took his notebook, found the note he looked for and read: "One of the orators at the forum said that he was helping to one

company which is rising and falling now and then. Let them not go to him. If something doesn't rise, it won't ever rise again. With me it is always like that: wherever I go they always pull me by something."

There is one more quote: "I was leaned against the wall long ago: "Why are there the problems?" It happens often, wherever I show up: why and why? I ask him: "Does the Ukraine have problems with Honduras?" He looks at me. "With Elephant Coast?" He looks at me again. I am giving my own answer: In Russia we don't have any. And you don't have any. But who knows…"

Ilya and Alexander Sergeevich laughed. Ofonarenko filled the glasses with cognac. – Let's drink to that "thinking giant"; we are laughing with tears on our faces. Who is on the top?

- Sasha, but Monya praised him so much in his speech: "It is a person whom I respect. He is a charming person! He is the wisest man!"

- So, he is like Socrates. The cuckoo praises the rooster because the latter praises the cuckoo. But being so primitive, he managed to become one of the richest persons, making no business at all. He just skimmed the cream, changing the rules of the game every now and then. Now he must be busy with establishing normal international relationship. He must promote export and import transactions by accepting reasonable taxation and estimation regulations. He is to solve the problem of opening the borders, like in Europe. What is he doing? Do you know that there were more officials from Rostov, than businessmen? They spoke about free trading zone, but it was just talks.

Zaltsman sighed. – You are right. How much do they want? By the way, I heard a new joke:

"Moesha meets Isaac. The latter is old and walks slowly. Moesha says to him: - Look here, Isaac, you are an experienced official, you worked even at the time of Khrushchev. You must be aware of all the new ideas in the mayor's office. Do you know that for those officials who is going to pass away the mayor's office ordered new coffins?

- No, I don't. Is it so?
- Those coffins have pockets at the sides.
- What for?
- To pack bucks in piles there.
- What do you need bucks there, Moesha, you are kidding!
- They say, they opened currency exchange booths there too…"

The friends laughed from their heart, though they understood that they were laughing at themselves too, as they were parts of that silly, greedy and mostly ignorant society.

They were not aware that at the same time Monya was lying on his sofa and was also thinking. He was not in a hotel, he was in his own luxurious great house at the seaside in Arkadiya. Monya didn't consider himself to be a businessman. He always was aware of what was going on around and tried to be present everywhere where there was a good pie which was supposed to be sliced and distributed soon.

Earlier, during the old time, he used to be beside his namesake Monya in Odessa, who was working at a big project, connected with construction and teaching of young talented people.

He went to Moscow to bite some of their splendid pie and he didn't forget to remind in Odessa of himself. He liked glory and money, it was his weak point. He suffered a lot if he was not noticed or ignored. He went to that place again and made them notice him and let him in. They waved him away, like a bothering fly: - We are sick and tired of him, give him what he wants!" That was what he was after. By nature Monya was not greedy. He was just ill-mannered. But he got what he wanted: he was recognized, he was invited to parties by different politicians and businessmen. He even became an honorable resident of Odessa, but many residents of Odessa didn't understand, what were his contributions to the development of Odessa, that were honored so high? But he didn't care. He had a house in Arkadiya, which was not small at all. He didn't care what party was ruling: communists or democrats, radicals or liberals. He knew one thing: no matter, it was Stalin or Brezhnev, or someone else, he always would be near the pie, and he would always have at least some crumbles to get from it.

At that moment he was dreaming: - I would lie like this, doing nothing, and the crumbles would gather for me somewhere. It is my dream, to have something gathering for me, less or more, and I would guess, why today it is more, and tomorrow it will be less? I failed to become a real businessman, but I have my crumbles, but they are so scares, I would like to have more...

The system we live now is just great, it is really great. It is self-regulated. It is self-built. There are officials, who must create rules of the game. But they want to take part in the game themselves. That's why they play, constantly changing the rules of the game.

One of the businessmen at the forum, I think it was Ofonarenko from Kazan, said that the rules should be determined by the market. The money goes where it is supposed to go. He is really funny, like his last name. Who will allow that? Where all the officials supposed to go? No, my dear. The way it is not is the best way, and the money will go to the accounts of the officials. And I will have my crumbles. Those are crumbles, but I have them regularly. Changes can take place only with the change of the political system. And that change, thanks God, will take place after I pass away.

Monya remembered, how one of Russian big bosses instructed him:
- Davos is recreation first of all. Make it a real resort, and everyone will come to you. And they will negotiate there…

That was why Monya was responsible for the recreation program. He rented the ship "Pallada", which had lobsters in the menu, according to their instructions, and the second day of the forum took place on the ship, which moved along the shore of Odessa.

It would be great to wake up tomorrow at all, as after the forum instead of crumbles I started to get small pieces of the big pie. Money, money, money…

Monya fell asleep with those pleasant dreams.

The next day all the participants of the forum left. In a week Russia increased customs duties for oil, and in the Ukraine the price for gas went quickly up. As for Monya, he thought of some new ideas of organizing the economic forum next year in Odessa.

Art inside You, or Your Position in Art

Once at night Yakov Naumovich was having a walk in the area of the city hall. He had been working as a chairman of the district executive committee and he had been retired for about ten years. Near the conservatoire he met the old friend Yura Dudkin, with whom he used to play chess. The hugged each other tightly and kissed.

- How long haven't we met. Yuri Mikhailovich? It is almost a year. Are you in a hurry? Let's have a walk. Let's go to Soborka and play a game? – Yakov Naumovich suggested.

- No problem! Let's drop to a bar on our way and have a shot of cognac to our meeting. I want to have something to relief stress; it has become so hard, even unbearable to work in the conservatoire. – Dikunin sighed sadly.

Yuri Mikhailovich Dikunin used to be a rather famous violinist. At that time he was an educator, a professor of Odessa conservatoire, and he had been in low moods lately. Twenty minutes ago a meeting of the conservatoire council was over. At the meeting they discussed the question of changing the Odessa conservatoire to a musical academy. The initiator of the issue was someone from the top, from the Department of culture and arts of the Ukraine and it was willingly supported by the current president.

Less than three years ago the entire president's council of the conservatoire voted unanimously against renaming the conservatoire to academy. At that time the president was Ukrainian People's Artist academy member Nikolai Ogrenich, now deceased, and the current president, at that time vice president, also voted against renaming.

- Why are you so sad, Yuri Mikhailovich? – Yakov Naumovich interrupted Dikunin's thoughts.

- Let's go to the bar, have a shot, then I will tell you. – Dikunin answered.

In a while they were sitting at a table in a cozy bar at Sadovaya Street, drank cognac, had some snacks and had a conversation without any rush. Dikunin told Yakov Naumovich about the current situation in the conservatoire.

At the meeting of the council of the conservatoire in the report of the president was clearly expressed that only at the status of academy they could raise the level of the musical art in the Ukraine to great extend, and to surpass the European school. In his conclusion he also mentioned the following:

- It was serious opponents that three years ago refused to consider the idea of a musical academy; it was when our institution got the fourth category. They deliberately decreased the opportunities and financing of our higher educational institution.

Many council members, present at the meeting, grinned at hearing those words. A year ago the same orator was at the side of the opponents, but no one was bold enough to tell him that.

The next report was that of the Arts studies PhD Lyudmila Petrovna Fomina. She was known all over the conservatoire for being always unanimous with the opinion of the president of the conservatoire, no matter what the question was, what the time was. It all was going on for more that twenty years: she supported the president's opinion with extreme energy and unbreakable confidence.

- I assure you, dear sirs, that our conservatoire will get the status of musical academy, and it will help to show its real level in the row of European conservatoires. Everyone is to understand that the conservatoire epoch of Emil Gilels, David Oistrakh and others did not reflect the real level of Odessa when compared with European conservatoires. In musical academy we will open new departments and we will see high scientific potential achieved. It will ensure a decent level in Europe.

At that moment Dikunin stopped controlling himself and interrupted the speech of Fomina,

205

- My dear, you are well informed that the fundamental ground for musical education has always been creative and practical activity of composers, musicians, singers, who were trained by experienced specialists of high level. It was the most expensive individual classes of teaching of arts. And you, supporting the new idea, want to transform traditional essence of conservatoire education of skillful musicians into the process of multiplying master degree holders and Ph. Ds.

Professor Protsenko, a small grey haired old man, who looked good-natured, supported him greatly,

- My dear Lyudmila Petrovna, you are my associate and a very professional person. You are a professional educator of Arts theory, but you find yourself at the side of those who came to study arts theory not because of their vocation, but because they were good for nothing in performing art, just failures.

An argument started, everyone was excited, but they expressed their opinions and supported them with their own reasons. In a while the pianist Oleg Ivanovich Slabyi took his turn.

- Dear colleagues, It's hard for me to hear what has been said today by the president and moreover, by Mrs. Fomina. You know, the role and the level of a musical higher educational institution is determined not by the quantity of students, not by its equipment, not by the quantity and volume of scientific essays, and not by the quantity of academics and Ph. Ds.

Everyone is aware that Moscow conservatoire is the leading educational institution in the world. What is it famous for and why is it unique? Creative work first of all. It is the first not because of its status, but due to the artistic achievements, due to the honor in musical art. Our conservatoire is also honorable so far. We are well known all over the world. Can Oistrakh, Gilels, whose names were mentioned today, as well as Tchaikovsky, Rakhmaninov, Repin, Kramskoy, Shalyapin and Stanislavskiy be compared in significance to some degrees or nominations? Are Tchaikovsky and Oistrakh known for their Cambridge Ph. D. degrees? No, they enrich Cambridge with their creative work, not with some a scientific thesis.

Then deputy president responsible for scientific work, Alexander Alexandrovich Protsenko made his speech,

- We all know the experiments of the Ukrainian Higher Certifying Commission with giving scientific titles to artistic persons. Those experiments led to the situation when a number of creative workers of art higher educational institutions take all the effort to get a master degree or an honorable nomination at any cost, instead of creating. We know the price of those nominations and degrees, we should admit that. It is several thousands dollars, for some it is less, for some it is more. Where do they take the money from? They collect bribes from students.

It does only harm, no use of that system. Today in our sphere there are so many candidates for a master degree who don't have initial knowledge of scientific research work. They don't have enough experience for that, and the sphere of activity is quite unknown for them.

In their attempt to get a scientific degree they can be compared with a person who tries to get the nomination of an honorable artist without skills in singing or playing a musical instrument. They say, we can come across those too. It's just surprising! The difference is that you can't have protection on the stage, but you can hide behind the back of your scientific supervisor. This gives birth to false scientific research of singers, bandura or other instruments specialists. Their articles are published in editions registered by the Higher Certifying Commission, but in those read by none of us.

We are extremely sorry for our science. Its quality level dropped during the past ten years. The more new master degrees and Ph. Ds. appear in all the branches, including politics, economy, art, the lower is the level of science. The independent Ukraine in ten years gave birth to more new scientists than in all the years of soviet rule!

And you, dear president, want the epoch of academy not of music, but of talks and essays about music to come. It would be the epoch of textbooks, conferences, symposiums for the poor relatives of arts, that is for performers, it will distract them from their main sphere of activity, that is performing and teaching. Do you want the motto "Play and sing as I told you!" to be the main here? The late Ogrenich must have turned in his coffin more than once. He did warn that this kind of reorganization would cause decline of performing art. It is just silly to turn to chairs of the conservatoire - that is of theory and history of music – to turn to separate universities. First of all they are supposed to teach performers general musical subjects, such as harmony, analysis of musical works, that is they are supposed to teach the main bulk of students, that is ninety per cent of students, future performers.

Universities and academies are very nice names. According to European standards they are nothing more that courses lasting two to twenty four months. It's sinful to play with names, if you don't see the essence of the problem. In Europe they estimate first of all the creative work achievements.

Hot argument was going on for about three hours. But they did not come to a unanimous conclusion. Most of the council members agreed deep inside with the opinion of the opponents of the president. But they were not bold enough to speak their minds, as they were afraid of persecution. They were afraid of losing their current positions, the professional morality was weaker than the position of a common small resident of Odessa.

Dikunin was irritated with cautious behavior of the council members, as well as of the most part of professors and educators of the conservatoire.

- You see, Yasha, during the soviet rule they all were in the front rows rushing to party meetings. They searched a position in the central committee of the communist party using all means. At the beginning of nineties they started to demonstrate their disgust to everything communistic or soviet. They did it so that their bosses noticed that. They didn't have their own opinion or judgment. – Dikunin was upset and spoke his mind to Yakov Naumovich.

- It's a pity, it's a real pity, that Nikolai Ogrenich passed away so early. – Dikunin filled the glasses.

- Let's drink to the memory of Nikolai, let him stay peacefully in the Heaven.

They drank silently, without touching the glasses and shortly after that they said good bye to each other and settled to meet the next day and play several games of chess.

On his way home Yakov Naumovich thought:

- Why can't the conservatoire, not the academy, get an all-national status and the highest level of estimation, so that it could be called in future "Odessa National Conservatoire named after A.V. Nezhdanova"? What is the professor supposed to be: the one who has a scientific title or the one who can play musical instruments, sing, and teach music? The following saying sounds true: Love art inside you, but not your position in art!"

Passing by a conservatoire, Yakov Naumovich stopped near the memorial plate with the bas-relief of Nikolai Ogrenich. The stand for flowers under the bas-relief was empty.

- No, you can't often see flowers here. Is it so hard to bring some? Where is the civic conscious, where is the honor? Where is the elementary cultural level of those who serve to Arts?

Yakov Naumovich spit angrily. He looked at the familiar face on the bas-relief.

- Sorry, Kolya! – He turned away abruptly and hurried home.

Bosses with a Millimeter Long Brains

In Odessa folklore the word "boss" sounds like "meter" and means "ignoramus". If in other languages the word has no any negative meaning and means something decent, in Odessa language it has a negative meaning due to its double implication.

Few Odessa born and bred residents comment on the situation, when in the Russian theatre they perform a play for one ambassador, or in philharmonic society they give a concert for one spectator, saying:
- "Bosses? Meters? In arts they are not meters, not decimeters, not centimeters and your governor is not even a millimeter".

Fima, also known as Efim Leonidovich Gofman, was having a walk along Primorsky Boulevard with his tiny dog named Pin. He was not in a rush, the weather was warm; the day was clear and sunny. The weather that autumn was changeable: warm, clear and sunny days came in turn with rains, slush and cold. In spite of the assurance and all the "heroic deeds" on behalf of municipal maintenance service together with the head of the city, who was a hero of the last soviet five-year-plans, the heating season was not likely to start before Christmas. Neither for Fima and his wife Sofa, nor for other residents of Odessa that was not news; they were used to the situation like that.

- It's OK, just about a month is left, maybe two months are left for us to endure cold, and then he was moving to Australia. But it's time to stop watching those heroic intentions together with foolishness, acquired as early as in higher communist party schools, of the crippled authorities, able for nothing except robbing everybody around and telling us their bullshit.

All his friends and close acquaintances had left Odessa long ago. He and just a few Odessa born and bred residents stayed in the city; they helped Odessa to preserve its peculiarity. The city was inhabited with new residents, and Fima could admit that they lived in Odessa, but they were not contributing to the peculiarity of Odessa by any means.

He remembered the words of one of the Odessa born and bred guy, who lived in Moscow. The latter, when he visited to Odessa due to some circumstances, commented: "It is unpleasant to come to Odessa. The streets, the buildings seem to be the same, but still everything around has become different. Odessa at the time of our childhood and youth was a port of a great country. Today the port has shrinked. Now Odessa is a slow city at the sea shore, where there is no murder, no departures, poor and dull life. So, Odessa is not longer a lively city!"

Fima slowly went along the alley to the monument of the academician Glushko, a well-known jet constructor.

- God knows how many outstanding persons this land gave birth to! It's a city where so many geniuses created their works, among them there are Pirogov, Mechnikov, Glushko, Paster, Paustovsky, Korolenko, Utesov and many others. Every street reminds of a great event, every building reminds of a great person.

Earlier in old good times when Odessa was inhabited with people born in the city, a tourist could ask his way to some place, and he was told all the history of Odessa with its jokes and funny stories. Now it was different. What stories could be told with the new-comers and their kids? Who in Odessa could say at least a few words about Grygoriy Marazli or the academician Glushko? Just a few persons could.

They used to call those who lived in Odessa, but not born there, new-comers. Fima was sure that since the time when in fifties the collective farmers were issued passports, the village population started to move to Odessa, gradually and quickly, much quicker than German and Romanian troops in nineteen forty one. In a while Odessa residents realized that the newcomers became the bosses of Odessa. They allowed to born and bred Odessa residents to work hard anywhere and no matter how many hours, but they didn't allow them to take ruling positions. The only exception was the guard position number one at the monument of the unknown seaman.

Fima's friends told him more than once: - Don't you, Fima, see and feel they you are just a tenant in this big house named Odessa? You are allowed to the front entrance, but not father.

Fima did see and understand that. And he watched the newcomers who in a short while became real Odessa residents. The peculiarity of Odessa was that a real Odessa resident you could become, no matter where you were born. The only condition for that was to understand and to love the unique city, to absorb all its peculiarities inside, to know all its numerous and diverse traditions, so that the city became a part of your soul.

But Fima saw different kind of newcomers, who had primitive brains, whose level of education was the lowest, but they shamelessly climbed to the top of the society and grabbed different positions in the administration, distributing orders and other nominations to each other. They were a success. They lowered the cultural level of the city to the great extend. Thus they proved that in Odessa you don't need to love the city in order to get great benefits and to make a successful career.

Behind the monument to the academician Glushko there was a great view to the architect complex "Vorontsov Palace", built according to the order of the governor of the Novorossiysk region the count Mikhail Semenovich Vorontsov in eighteen twenty six. The architect and the author of the project was Franz Boffo, the famous creator of Potemkin Stairs. Beside the palace inself the complex contained stables, rebuilt in the twentieth century to a choreographic arts center. The classic roofed colonnade containing twenty columns, which was one of the architect symbols of Odessa, was also a part of the complex.

During the years of the soviet rule the palace was given to children. The first in Odessa and the second in the USSR Pioneer's Palace was located there. More than one hundred hobby groups and studios for children worked there, every year about two thousand children came there to study. Fima, his generation and the generation of his parents, to say nothing of their kids, grew up and were educated in the palace. The palace was situated close to his building, and his wife worked there as one of the teachers in the choreographic studio.

Now, looking at the Palace, which had a different name, that was "The palace for children and young students, named after Yasha Gordienko", Fima laughed out loud:

- Was the name given by a Turk? Who invented that name? Where are young boys and girls who are not student supposed to go? – Fima looked at the building and got upset. The paint on the front was peeling, the columns were also peeling with big pieces of stucco, the posters with the words "Do not enter, dangerous, danger of falling!" were everywhere.

The latest restoration of the palace was approximately at the end of sixties, and for forty years neither constructors nor restorers touched a single wall of it. When Fima approached the colonnade, he got still more upset. He knew that the situation was bad, his wife had told him about it, but he didn't know it was as bad as that.

The colonnade was also almost destroyed, and Fima was struck that all the columns were covered with felt-tip pen and paints writing like "Vasya was here", "Vanya plus Manya", "Bodik sucks" and others. It looked like the surrendered Reichstag or Brandenburg Gate in May nineteen forty five as shown in the movies. Used syringes and condoms, to say nothing of the piles of bottles, were everywhere on the ground.

- Youth is having fun. – Fima asid, looking at all the stuff disapprovingly.

He looked sadly at the "Mother-in-law's bridge" and thought of the regional communist party committee secretary Sinitsa, who contributed to the history of Odessa by constructing a personal bridge for his mother-in-law.

- Nowadays it is the same. Yesterday's collective farmers construct villas for themselves and their relatives, villas worth several hundred thousand dollars using government money. And they don't have money to restore the palace for children, it's shame! – Fima spit angrily and thought of a recent speech of the governor. He made an initiative to use the complex as the residence of the president of the Ukraine. His words just struck the old Odessa resident Fima:

- I consider the whole architectural complex is supposed to be used according to its initial purpose, as an official residence for reception of great visitors and conducting international meetings. Now the complex needs major reconstruction, but for the renovation of the Centre of children's creative work neither Supreme Rada, nor the Cabinet of Ministers will give any money. But Supreme Rada can give money for the South state residence, as this complex will be included to the architectural reserve "Ancient Odessa", and every year the budget will

213

allow to spend some money for the restoration of the reserve. – The governor expressed his opinion.

- But it doesn't make sense! – Fima thought. – If children are using the palace, it is not included into the reserve "Ancient Odessa". If it belongs to the president, to that old bustard, as my Sofa calls him, it is included to the reserve automatically. That's nice! This speech of the governor with his komsomol and collective farm background can be compared only to the speeches of Shura Balaganov from the famous novel "A Golden Bull-calf".

A couple of days before Fima met the governor's assistant who used to be Gofman's neighbor in the apartment building. They were no longer neighbors, as an official of that level could afford living in a newly built luxurious penthouse in Arkadiya with a personal winter garden and other "inconveniences", but they were still greeting each other and talking a little.

Fima asked him: - How come? How many bedrooms and different residences, do you think, the president needs?

The official burst out laughing: - What are you talking about, Fima? I can tell you one secret, that is such things are arranged by a whole Department of management of the president's proceedings. Have you heard of a person with the name Pal Palych in Russia? He did everything for children, he even created a family type children's home. Later he was accused in stealing and laundrying money.

We have our own Pal Palych with a Chechen last name, as we can't appoint a topknot Ukrainian to this position. The department is called "Dusia", and it takes care of many items of president's luxurious life. Just in the Crimea they have the Crimea reserve, Yusupov Palace, Gorbachev's palace in Foros, the most Southern point of the Crimea, and a dozen of the best resorts of the Crimea. Besides, there are talks about transferring to "Dusia" of the famous Crimea palaces, like Livadiya, Alupka and Massandra.

- Look here, - Fima interrupted him. - Is your president suffering with palace mania? Is he mentally sick? Or is he struck with megalomania? Let him look into a regular mirror and he will see the inscription "Struck with rachitis".

Both burst out laughing.

- You, Fima, can be right from Odessa-minded person's point of view. But they can't and won't live otherwise. Do you think that the Kyiv department takes care of the palaces only? No, it is not. They have at least a dozen of liquer plants, which run not for supplying the president and his men with vodka. They make money like this. If I talk about their demands, I should say that they steal and steal and nothing is enough for them. The renovation of one level in the president's administration building consumed about forty million hryvnias.

- That money would be more than enough to renovate the palace in Odessa and that would be a great gift for children.

- Fima, don't waste your effort, as everything will be done according to the decision of the authorities.

- Your bosses, and it is clear, were not studying history properly, or they missed it utterly. Can't they understand that soon the people will come out with the slogans: "Peace to huts, war to palaces!"

He hugged the official by his shoulders. – Maybe your governor is intending to move to Kyiv? They say, the ex-manager of the railway constructed the Western residence of the president on the shore of the artificial lake in Karpaty and was immediately appointed to the position of the minister, now he is already aiming to the position of the prime minister or the president's successor.

The official pushed himself aside and looked at Gofman attentively. He seemed not to understand if Gofman was joking or he was serious.

- Maybe, Fima, but is it your business? You are planning to move to Australia, so move, don't think too much.

Fima thought and laughed out loud:

- Really, do I need it?

But again he thought of it, looking at Primorsky Boulevard.

- How much do they need? At Gagarin Plateau behind seven fences and locks there is a house for receptions held by the municipal executive council. In Sanatorny Lane there is a house for receptions held by the regional executive council. There are lots of luxurious hotels in Odessa. There lots of conference halls in the city. Is that not enough? What else do they want?

The governor had already constructed a detached house in the weather station area, near a nice small wood, which looked like a miniature Opera house. It fit for reception of kings and sheikhs, not just a president. But he goes on making bullshit on every corner, as they say in Odessa, - Children should have comfortable facilities with change rooms, showers, dance classes rooms, auditoriums and workshops. It won't do. Is it OK if the best dancing ensembles are based in a stable?

- He is talking bullshit. – Fima thought. – Why didn't you say the same bullshit when you were a komsomol leader during the years of stagnation? The aim of the speeches is clear: to lick the boot of the president once in a while will do only good. If he started the restoration, he could make much money and gain some popularity for himself, no matter how cheap it is. About thirty years ago this kind of shallow man, who puts on airs to much, would have been pushed away as far as to the City of Ignorant Fools, now it is different...

When he came home, he found his wife Sofa in tears with laughing, she was holding the newspaper "Odessa Messenger".

- What interesting have you found in that paper, always full of lies?

Gofman had recently started calling the newspaper a liar.

- No, my dear, it is not in your favorite liar, it is if "Komsomolka", that the whole page is devoted to our governor.

- What happened to him? He received a position in Kyiv? Or was he undergo circumcision?

- You didn't guess, Fima, he is not our kind of people even by half. Don't continue, just listen.

And she started to read: - The headline: "The governor of Odessa became a sex symbol". In the region there was conducted an inquiry in order to determine the sex symbol of the region. The top lines were given to the chief of the police, of the traffic police department and some other important persons from the official circles.

- Are they posing for "Playboy" or are they working as call-in boys?

- No, they just say that the governor likes KVN show on TV, goes in for sports and he is just a handsome man.

Fima laughed out loud: - Here we are: having a governor as handsome as a model. Now it's clear what he needs Vorontsov Palace for. He wants to open a brothel there. I wonder if it is going to be a gay club or a brothel for prostitute women? Maybe it is going to be a sex shop, with the sex symbol in the shop window, so that anyone could see what kind of scoundrel he is.

He thought for a minute and then made the conclusion: - We can say for sure that for the governor it's the most successful nomination and title, but not his most exact characteristics. It's a shame! The governor is estimated by his appearance and not by his activity. As there is no activity, he was chosen to be the symbol.

At night Yasha Keifman from Moscow called to him. They were applying together for permanent residence in Australia.

- Hi, Fima! I have settled all my questions here and I have already bought airline tickets. In two weeks we are leaving. What about you?

- Hi, Yasha, say hi to Klara too, we are OK, but we haven't purchased the tickets yet. I think in a week we'll do that. What about Moscow? Are you going to miss Moskva Belokamennaya?

- What are you talking about? There is nothing here to miss.

Fima shortly told him the story about the palace and the sex symbol of the region.

The latter listened attentively and then laughed out loud sincerely:

- Did you expect something different, Fimochka? They are all complete generals there, and they appeared in this world as a result of oral sex. It is not only there. Here five years ago all the governors were constructing tennis courts and learned to play tennis when suffering from hangover. Now they construct mountain skiing routes and learn to ski.

- Right you are. Those symbols can be called complete bustards. It is still doesn't reflect the level of their mental capacity. But the term "complete general" does reflect the essence, as a "complete general" means the world champion in imbecility.

The next day Fima, walking along the boulevard with his Pin, saw a tourist group from Germany, with photo and video cameras in their hands, and he remembered that once, many years ago the Chancellor Helmut Kohl visited Odessa, and while walking along Deribasovskaya with the mayor of the city, he asked:

- Aren't we going to interfere in the traffic work?

They were lucky they didn't stop the traffic from Pushkin to Richelie Streets, otherwise the Germans would look at them like at real savages. Why "like"?

Fima looked at the Germans, who took photos of the half-destroyed palace, of the colonnade with the inscriptions and the garbage, a small car "Zaporozhets" nearby and a drunk bum sitting at the side. He frowned, turned back, took the dog to his hands and rushed home.

- Bosses! Metrs! Those who rule really have just a few meters, and . rather several millimeters long brains...

And Who are the Judges?

Vladimir Sergeevich had two weaknesses, which he couldn't resist. One of his weaknesses was regular one hundred and fifty grams of vodka with some substantial hors-d'oeuvre – just for the sake of health.

- Why don't you understand, - he used to say to those who protested, - this primarily is for the sake of health, secondly, it takes away stress, and, thirdly, it stimulates!

He did like to have a drink; he had liked it for several decades already. He didn't like just to have an ordinary drink, he liked to have a really nice drink, and a toast was a must. How eloquent he was, how rhetorical his toasts were! He was an irreplaceable toastmaster and the soul of any company, but before he had eight glasses. After the eighth glass he was not able to pronounce anything. His wife had already become humble, though during the parties she still tried to control him. He got used to all this, and on the sly he had his one hundred and fifty grams or more, if it was possible.

The other weakness of his was his great attraction to steam rooms. He had liked Russian baths since childhood, and he couldn't deprive himself of the pleasure of visiting a sauna once a week. Once, about fifteen years ago Vladimir Sergeevich was in the army. He had an important position there, as he liked to mention: he was the head of the political department of his division. And afterwards, after having a drink, he liked to tell about his past.

It was hard. You can't imagine, how hard the life of the head of the political department in Odessa was, especially in summer. Representatives of the upper levels wanted to have a rest at the seashore. They came all by themselves or sent their family members. Our task was to arrange meeting, accommodation and meals for them. And everything was supposed to be on the highest level. We arranged the same treatment for ourselves as well. We could afford that. We had a very good sauna, and every Thursday we did go there with our families. We relaxed, took steam baths and after that we, as a rule, had a one hundred grams drink. That' how it used to be! We were respectable persons!

Those, with whom he shared his delightful memories, agreed with him and gave him approving nods. But they did realize how hard it was the life of the Colonel in present, comparing to those golden times. He was much younger and had a different position in the society. Now he had to pay for his visits to sauna, while earlier he used to visit it for free. But this situation did not embarrass him at all. He made a long search and trial visits, and after all he did find a small but cozy sauna at Moldavanka. Former prosecutor officers ran that sauna.

It was comparatively cheap, and the customers were matching. Those were mainly persons of Vladimir Sergeevich's age, also ex-officers from the prosecutor's office, from the court and from the police. There were also former military men and former the communist party professional workers. Gradually Vladimir Sergeevich came to have a permanent company, which met in sauna every Saturday and eleven o'clock in the morning. They were: Ivan Matveevich, a retired deputy prosecutor of the region; Pavel Petrovich, who had fifteen years of experience as a judge in the regional court; Nikolai Ivanovich, ex-secretary of the regional communist party committee.

All of them were still working, in spite of their retirement payments and old age. Vladimir Sergeevich himself was an educator of military science and training in one of the municipal Lyceums, and he was rather good at it. Ivan Matveevich and Pavel Petrovich owned the private enterprise "Jurist", which provided legal services of different kind. Besides, they both worked as educators in the University of Business and Law. Nikolai Ivanovich was also an educator; he worked in the Academy of Management of the President of the Ukraine, in its Odessa department, to be precise. Vladimir Sergeevich also tried to get a job there, but his attempt was not a success. The reason was that the staff of the educators was almost the same, the cadre remained, and even the rectorial management was not changed. The staff had some new workers who were mainly former professional communist party workers from regional, municipal and district party committees. They needed new positions after the party was broken up in 1991. Vladimir Sergeevich and his friends laughed at Nikolai Ivanovich:

- Everything is as it used to be! You changed only the sign! And the pictures of Marks, Engels and Lenin were changed for portraits of Shevchenko, Grushevski and Kuchma.

Gradually the ordinary meetings in the sauna turned into real friendship, and it became a must for them to be every Saturday at eleven o'clock in their sauna, to which they had already got attached to a great extent. They had three hours at their disposal. They took their time taking a steam bath for about two hours. They switched from staying in the steam room to a shower or the pool, they had herbal tea, they talked easily on political and household topics, they spoke about their past times, which any of them considered to be interesting and nice.

After two hours of the steam bath treatment they spent one more hour together at a cozy table in a small bar, which was a part of the sauna complex. There they allowed themselves to have a one hundred and fifty grams drink of vodka and treat themselves to good cold beer. Every time one of them was a so-called "birthday guy". If during the previous week some event happened in the army, the birthday guy was Vladimir Sergeevich. If there was some news in political life, it was Nikolai Ivanovich. If something happened in criminal spheres, it was the turn of Pavel Petrovich and Ivan Matveevich. As nowadays every week there are many crucial events happening in any sphere of life, or even in several of them at one and the same time, there were no problems with the "birthday guys" nomination.

The "birthday guy" was supposed to make a report on the event and to share his own professional view with his friends.

During those discussions they even had hot arguments, but everything happened in the atmosphere of good attitude and humor, and this improved their moods, disregarding the topic they were discussing.

On one of Saturdays in August the "birthday guys" were the former officers of justice. At the end of July in a garage of a summer cottage at Karolino Bugaz a hanged up judge of the regional economic court was found. The man in the mature age – at forty, which is the age of creative activity, is dead.

Pavel Petrovich used to know the deceased man in person.

- What am I supposed to say? I will tell you about so to say creative career of the late. Being under the age of forty, he had fifteen years of experience in work as a policeman, as an officer in the district and municipal party committees, and he was a success. Later he was sent to Reni where he was the head of the customs department. After that he was directed to Kerchen customs department as the manager of the section dealing with smuggling problems. And all this career was achieved within almost ten years. At the same period of time he managed to work as a full-time deputy assistant of the Superior Rada, who "fought" for lawfulness...

- What the hell kind of lawfulness you can talk about? – Nikolai Ivanovich became angry. – During the Soviet rule it was impossible even the child prodigies couldn't dream of a career like that. Most likely, this person had successfully and obediently worked for somebody else.

Ivan Matveevich flapped Nikolai Ivanovich on the shoulder: - That's a good boy! You, a great party leader, think analytically. Look here, this young man got the position of a judge in the arbitration tribunal, he had a residency registration in Kerch, where he had not a bad house. And after four years' work as a judge in the arbitration tribunal in Odessa, having no residency registration in Odessa, he was elected as a deputy of the regional council. He acquired an apartment in Odessa and an expensive house at the seashore at Bugaz. Besides, he bought three Jeeps, is I am not mistaken. And all this was bought for the small salary of a judge.

Vladimir Sergeevich listened to the conversation attentively and during a short pause he contributed his own valid opinion: - His home was supposed to be a jail.

Ivan Matveevich laughed out loud: - My dear friend, his Jeeps even had plate numbers with the same serial number as the enforcement offices had. One of the cars had the same serial number as the police, and the other had the same as the prosecutor's office. What jail are you talking about?

Vladimir Sergeevich's answer was in the same manner: - In all the times all kinds of crooks worked in your offices, and that was not by chance, I presume.

Pavel Petrovich took the bottle of vodka, almost full, and made a drink for each glass:

- OK, guys, let's stop the discussion. The person is deceased. He, by the way, was also an educator, like us, in the University of Law. Bad or good he was, everything is in the past for him. Let's not talk either good or bad of him. Let's drink to his memory.

They drank in silence without touching glasses. In a while, after having a bite, Ivan Matveevich broke the long silence: - There are many unclear things in this death. He was a healthy bull, about two meters tall, cheerful. Everything was going smooth in his life, and see what happened. Was it a suicide? Or was it a murder? There many different guesses, but nobody can explain why the deceased appeared to be in the handcuffs. Nobody knows what was the reason of his refusal two weeks ago to accept the position of the Chairman of the economic court. Nobody knows why he, having good relations with the wife, filed for the divorce. There are many unclear moments, many fabricated facts, many very suspicious things. Actually, it is like this in any murder or death case of a well-known person in Odessa.

Vladimir Sergeevich expressed his own valid opinion once again: - It will be the same result this time: the investigation will not clear up anything, no suspects will be found. What is you term for that? One more investigation failure!

It looks like this, as there are no hints, no evidence so far.

Nikolai Ivanovich, idly sipping his beer from a large glass, said: - All this shows the corruption of the whole system of legislation. It doesn't matter if you want to admit this or not, but it is a fact. You will agree that we all live in one and the same country, in one and the same city, and, no doubt, a judge of any court, and especially the one from the economic court can be influenced by somebody mighty, who could be involved in the case. It could also be mighty firms, companies and other enterprises. And I am sure it is impossible to settle a case of the kind in court...

Pavel Petrovich interrupted him: - Sure, you are right, Nikolai Ivanovich, as in the economic court it is always only one part that is satisfied by the decision. Emotional judgments, remarks, even direct threats follow immediately. Sometimes the threats get real.

- Stop it, guys, be honest to yourselves. Look here, if a judge were fair during the court session, there would be no so to say emotions and threats. At least, they would occur quite seldom. In real life the judge comes to the courtroom after having received a thick roll of dollars, and not a small one, and often there is more that one roll. It is clear that his decision can't be fair. It is in this case when adequate reaction follows. – Nikolai Ivanovich continued the discussion. – "During my "golden age" I used to know a head of a criminal investigation department who detained and put in jail a great number of criminals, he was severe to any of them. But all of them understood his point and respected him, as he was a fair guy and fulfilled his duties honestly.

The friends agreed with him. They came to a conclusion that at the moment there were two main reasons for ordered murders, that is murders on political grounds, when a political rival is killed, or murders for great amounts of money, when somebody, who has been generously paid for some services, fails to fulfill his obligations. In the case with the judge it seemed to be the second variant. He seemed to have accepted some great amount of money from a big company and failed to make a decision, favorable for latter. As a result, the company could have suffered great losses.

- We can tell you a lot of stories based on the previous experience in the court. We also know a lot about the current cases. – Ivan Matveevich continued the conversation. – Do you have an idea what the lawyers of our company are busy with? They are just middlemen for giving bribes, they are middlemen acting between the defendant, his friends and family and the judge in criminal court. The judge determines the price in US dollars for reducing the detention term or for releasing for a bail, for arranging release with the written undertaking not to leave the place, for the verdict "not guilty" and for other services. The lawyer settles the question with the relatives of the defendant and includes his own interest into the final amount. There are certain secret price lists. And this practice takes place not only in criminal court, but in others as well.

Vladimir Sergeevich said with confidence and in a direct manner, which was common to him: - Right you are, my dear friend! I can easily give an example to you. One of our educators got in a car accident while driving his "Zhiguli". It was his fault. He damaged a little bit both his own car and the other car. It was a minor car accident, but see what happened! His driver's license was taken from him and the case was transferred to the district court. As you know, nowadays all cases public offence go to the court. He didn't waste his time and went to a lawyer whom he knew. He told him that there was a chance to be just fined, but there was also a chance of his driver's license to be suspended for several years. And this could be the punishment for a minor car accident. Really, it was just a small accident. The fenders were smashed, and that was all. To make the long story short, the lawyer told him that the usual price that the judge sets for that kind of cases was two hundred bucks and up, depending on the damage. He finally paid two hundred dollars to the judge and twenty dollars to the lawyer. As quickly as in two days he was called to the court. The judge lectured him on the importance of careful driving, told him about financial responsibility, fined him for twenty grivnas and returned his driver's license. And there are plenty of cases like that! As far as I know all the judges used to have an oath, like military men and medical practitioners. I wonder if they still have to take the oath, or not. Or if they still take the oath, but they have no shame?

Pavel Petrovich laughed out loud: - You are so naive, Vladimir Sergeevich. You think like a military man. A week ago I met a good acquaintance of mine. I won't tell you his name, as it doesn't matter. He is a well-known person, he used to be a General Prosecutor, a People's Deputy, a member of the Supreme Council of Justice. Now he is retired.

He told me that nowadays those apply to the position of a judge who doesn't have any other place to work, that is former cops, former tax officers and tax police department officers, former workers of Security Department of Ukraine. Actually, those are persons who are not able to make any further career in the enforcement departments due to their spoilt reputation.

They don't have sufficient knowledge. Eighty percent of the candidates to the position of a judge were not able to answer questions regarding the criminal court procedure. They are completely ignorant of financial legislation.

- But they do know how much is to be paid and how much they could get, - Vladimir Sergeevich added. – I have information that forty thousand dollars had to be paid to ensure being appointed for the position of the Chairman of the our district court. And the candidate did pay that amount! And now he is to do all his best to cover the expenses.

Oh, my dear Vladimir Sergeevich, this system works not only in the courts,

it is everywhere. The other day I had a conversation with the prosecutor. He had a watch on his hand that could be worth more than ten thousand bucks. Another example is a new judge, twenty-seven years old, who has experience as a tax inspection officer. He is driving a new Mercedes and he lives in a luxurious country house in Tzarskoe Selo. He is sure to have acquired all this not for the small salary of a tax officer.

At the end of their discussion they came to an opinion that at the moment it was relative and friendship connections, as well as financial situation, that played an important part in assigning to this or that position. It is very often when sons, daughters, brothers, sisters, by-laws, godparents of a local prosecutor, of the manager of a tax office and of some other representative of higher level officers, pick up the career of a judge.It is all done deliberately, as everywhere there is a necessity in a person who can be relied on.

What are we supposed to do? What is the way out? – Vladimir Sergeevich

asked his sauna companions at the end of the conversation.

- It is a common question for Russia and for our country as well. – Ivan Matveevich grinned. – You do understand that in order to become a judge, I mean a real judge, it is not enough to have knowledge and to obtain a diploma of a lawyer. Such characteristics as conscience, respectability and honesty are also necessary. Nobody should have even a shade of doubt in honesty of a judge. Everything is important to take into account: a judge's previous and current life experience, his way of earning money, his relations with the government and many other things.

That's it. And what is a judge supposed to do in the environment when the government officers shamelessly take bribes? And as for those traits of character that you have mentioned, they have always been lacking, so they are now...

An important thing is that a judge is elected for term of life, until he dies. It

means that he can do anything, and he won't be punished, unless he commits a crime. He could be put to shame. But what is shame? A judge has no idea of shame, neither have government officers. What should a judge have shame if the government officers don't? It is a question if the people still have shame. We could discuss the topic for a long time. The people are also of the same kind. We all take both kindness and shit from one and the same source. Well, guys, I think we need to be moving. – Nikolai Ivanovich said and picked up the bottle again. – Let's have one more last drink before we leave. Vladimir Sergeevich, what do you call the last drink? You are a great specialist in toasting. What do we drink to?

He distributed the remaining vodka over the glasses.

- Let's drink to our friendship, guys! To our life! - Vladimir Sergeevich proposed a toast.

His friends liked the toast and had their drink with pleasure, the drink was followed by a bite.

On his way home Vladimir Sergeevich remembered that not long ago there was a program on TV about a new faculty being opened in the Academy of Justice. The faculty was opened for training professional judges.

- That was good. They will graduate with some knowledge and a diploma, but what about such things as honor, conscience, decency?

He thought about a gird next door who is graduating next year from the same Academy, from the faculty, training prosecutors. Her father, also a retired Colonel, in a minute of openness, while having a glass of drink, once shared his thoughts with Vladimir Sergeevich.

- You know, Sergeyich, this puny girl is dreaming of only one thing: after graduating to get a position in a prosecutor's office in any district of Odessa, or even in the municipal office, or in the regional office, which is still better. The second thing she is dreaming of is to acquire one or two containers at the flea market "Seventh kilometer" and to lease them. She is already aware of prices for a prosecutor's services. I will just dispose her! I will dispose her as toilet paper! Can you imagine whom I have grown up...

But the time was passing by, the neighbor was getting sober, nobody was going to dispose anyone any more. Nothing extraordinary was happening in the courts of the City either. Somebody was giving bribes, somebody was accepting. The life was going on in its regular way.

Blasphemy

Gorbunov Matvey Vasilyevich, an old boatswain, retired fifteen years ago, liked to have a rest in the park at Soborka. Usually this promenade, as he called it, took him three to four hours. Usually he slowly went to along the alleys. He also dropped in the flower market, where he exchanged strong Odessa expressions about the weather, the authorities and the prices with the flower sellers whom he knew. After that Matvey Vasilyevich went to the chess players and attentively watched a game, Then he went to soccer fans who were real connoisseurs of the game and very devoted fans of the local team "Chernomorets", who usually gathered at Soborka and discussed the latest soccer news, as well as "Chernomorets" problems. They analysed the latest games and switched to discussion of the authorities and then back to soccer problems.

Matvey Valilyevich liked that park which had been called by everyone as Soborka for a long time. At that territory there used to be the Spaso-Preobrazhenskiy Cathedral, and the park took up its name because of that. In thirties of the last century the cathedral was blown up and on its place they made the park. Gorbunov remembers the time when among the high trees of the park there were constructed attractions for kids and other things necessary for recreation. Closer to Deribasovskaya Street in the park there was a gorgeous monument to the Duke Vorontsov, who was the General Governor in the South territory at the time of Ekaterina the Second's rule.

The fact that at that place there used to be a cathedral was almost erased from the memory of people, it was just the name of the park that reminded of that. But when the authorities changed it became fashionable to restore churches and to construct new ones. The wave did touch the Cathedral square as well. On a summer night part of Soborka was surrounded by a concrete fence. They demolished all the attractions and closed the fountain. The great construction started. The authorities called it restoration of the cathedral, and it was going on for more that a year. Odessa residents had different attitude to the fact. Some of them approved of the construction, some didn't. Most of Odessa residents were indifferent.

As far as Matvey Vasilyevich was concerned, he belonged to the third category. Everything seemed to be all right. But he was deeply indignant with the fact that they not just worshiped the restoration process, they were making a great show out of it. This fact made indignant not only him, but also many of constant visitors and lovers of Soborka.

On that very day he became a witness of a hot discussion of the construction in one of the alleys of the park. Two old women, two "blessed dandelions", sat on a bench having a hot dispute. Some more persons, who were walking with their dogs, joined them. One of the old women who took part in the discussion looked rather intelligent. She was skinny and had traces of faded beauty on her face. She was on the side of the Mayor who was restoring the cathedral.

- Our Mayor, God bless him, supervises the process of construction personally. He appointed his associate as the head of the fund raising board, so that the supervision was really effective.

The other old woman was a complete antipode to the first one. She was fat, with full cheeks, and her clothes and manners revealed the trading nature of the old woman.

- What is she talking about? Listen to her, guys! First of all, the construction was started on the initiative of the previous mayor and not the current one. The latter just stole the idea from him, but they started digging the foundation ditch at the time of the previous mayor.

Secondly, this current mayor of yours is a former Komsomol and Communist Party leader, he is a leader of the regional level, and he is an atheist. Had he ever given up his former ideas and viewpoints? He hadn't! Who had ever heard him renouncing his ideas?

- Could you please talk not so loudly, dear lady? You are not at the market right now to shout like this. – The skinny old woman tried to calm her down. A crowd of idle people was already surrounding them.

- Don't shut me up. It is the other situation in the country. – The market woman, as Matvey Vasilyevich called her, became more and more excited. – Your beloved mayor calls himself the master of the construction site. Could you please tell me who is financing all this construction? Donations? Who and where collect this money? In the grocery store there is a money box. Watch, how much money is put there in a day, even in a week. Go there right now and watch for a couple of hours and you'll see, that very seldom it happens that someone would drop a couple of coins into it.

- But you should take into account that beside those money boxes there are enterprises and different companies, as well as businessmen, who donate rather big amounts. – One of the women, who was walking with her dog, joined the discussion.

The market woman laughed out loud: - Look here, you, a lady with a dog! How much you personally donated for the cathedral? Or any of you, – She asked everyone in the crowd: - Have you donated any amount to the cathedral or not?

She looked at the crowd. No one answered.

- That's it! – The market woman said triumphantly. – And you say businessmen. You are supposed to know that the entrepreneurs are just pushed to pay to our municipal council. Those who don't donate to the cathedral, will not get their licence. Their companies can be just closed for that. The current authorities have so many restricting means, just lots of them! On the contrary, those, who share profits with the government officers get green light just like that. They even start getting government contracts. It is the flood of budget money to private pockets. Is it not just.

Suddenly there were found supporters from the crowd: - Right you are! They are just making a show of the reconstruction of the cathedral. It is not just a show, it is a show according to the communist style. It absolutely resembles a Komsomol construction, when money was collected by force, where there were held meetings. When there was the opening for the bell tower, every district got its own share for municipal maintenance services, for higher educational institutions and for hospitals.

- Do you know who is holding candles at all the church services and liturgies?

231

Alongside with the metropolitan or just behind him there stand mostly former municipal and regional party and komsomol leaders. Ten years ago they were secretaries of regional, municipal and district committees. Have they recently been baptised?" - The market woman was still arguing. – You also seem to be a member of the komsomol." – She asked the skinny old woman directly. – "Or are you from a party boss service department?"

The skinny old woman's face was blushing: - How dare you? You see only negative side in everything and also some underlying reason. Do you judge people according to your own level of thinking?

What kind of underlying reason you are talking about! Your mayor in recent three years had saved enough money to move to a luxurious apartment in European-style building at the seaside. And there he has security officers who are trained to chase people. What is the origin of the money? Is it just the mayor's salary, which is not at all great? The apartment costs about one hundred bucks. – Someone said from the crowd.

Pay attention to the roads. See, what kind of roads we have in the city. They say, they borrowed thirty million dollars from "Lukoil" for renovation of roads and municipal buildings, but in reality there is neither renovation, nor money.

Matvey Vasilyevich shook his head and went on in the direction of Deribasovskaya.

- It turned out to be a real meeting which could grow into a fight. – He thought and his moods became gloomy. He did understand deep in his heart that there was truth on both sides. Gorbunov was an old sea dog, and he was reasonable in his judgments when the situation around was concerned. At this very period of time most of the people, who were miserable, robbed and cheated, were no longer faithful to the country and to its flag. If there used to be something valuable in the present, some faith in the future, nowadays everything was destroyed and there was nothing more left but poverty, lawlessness, humiliation and a future without any hope. Is there a place a person could go for support with all his misfortune and hardships? Who can help him? He can go only to the church and there he can seek help only from the God.

He can't go to the mayor, he won't be admitted there. Only the celebrities can be let in there. Those admitted undergo strict selection. But those admitted would not get any help there either, they will get only promises. Matvey Vasilyevich himself applied to be admitted to the mayor's office. He protested against disorder that ruled when parking lots were constructed near his apartment building. There was no result achieved. Once he decided to go to the mayor at eight thirty in the morning. It was the very time when the mayor arrived at his office. But the problem was not settled. What happened was that one of the security officers of the mayor said to him: "If you come here once again I'll shoot you."

That's the time we experience. – Gorbunov sighed while thinking. – There is no doubt, cathedrals are supposed to exist. The reconstruction of the Spaso- Preobrazhenskiy Cathedral is also necessary, but not by the means and methods they use. That is the question. The relations with the God are very personal. A church should be in every city, village and district. But no one can make a show with great coverage in mass media, because it's a blasphemy and desecration of the faith. Those actions and church services, which are held in the constructed cathedral, in the sacred place for the Christians of Odessa, very vaguely resemble (by their contents and the way they are held) real church ceremonies. They resemble very much the communist party meetings with their speeches and praising of the leaders of the city. Those meetings are almost forgotten by the people. And the reconstruction of the cathedral itself looks very much like a construction site of the past, supervised by the central komsomol committee.

Matvey Vasilyevich spit angrily and hurried home. His moodswasspoiled.

- They demolished and reconstructed the cathedral in one and the same manner. Have they ever had shame? The authorities haven't for sure, but what about the metropolitan? He seems to have never had shame either!

Jewish Happiness

Odessa would be quite different if there were no Jews there. In all the possible publications about Odessa it is distinctly written that "Jews were one of the constituent part of the nation named Odessa, who contributes a lot to the creation and the development of Odessa slang. Jews are a means of transportation. In the past they were the main favorites of the Soviet people and the subject of constant concern of the Communist Party of the Soviet Union (it's enough to mention the fifth point of any application form, which would never exist without Jews). At last, Jews are the main consumers of the medicine produced in Odessa and used for any case, which has the name "Furain".

For dummies I just remind that "furain" is the main medicine of Odessa residents, which is consumed by everyone who are sick and tired of the low level of life, of dreams of bright future that during the communist rule lasted as long as a life, of stupidity of reforms during democrats' rule.

That is why by the beginning of the twenty first century, according to the opinion of many research workers, in Odessa "furain" became limited, and everything left of Jews was only their smell, Jewish street, Jewish hospital, Jewish cemetery. But there appeared something new – that was European style renovation, which in Russian sounded like "Jewish renovation".

It should be noted that the former KGB, not the Security Services Department of the Ukraine, as well as the Department of the Interior of the Ukraine in Odessa region were situated in the street which was proudly named Jewish – such a comic situation could exist only in

Odessa. It was especially honorable, as in that department there was no even smell of Jews. Have you ever heard of Izya – the security agent, or Abramovich – a General in the police?

And Jewish cemetery is situated at the place where the road leading to Kyiv starts. The place is called by Odessa residents "Have a good trip", because it is the regular route of "Odessa servants of the people", who go to the meetings at the Supreme Council. Lots on this cemetery are much more expensive than anywhere else in Odessa. They say, it is almost the same price as the cost of land in Miami.

In the city there used to be a joke: "why in Odessa there was a Jewish hospital and a Jewish cemetery, but there is no Jewish maternity home?"

The answer was simple and brilliant:

"They are not born as Jews in Odessa, they become Jews here".

Now the statement is very precise right now, as during the past dozen of years of the twentieth century there were so many persons who had nothing in common neither in the present, nor in the distant past, became Fimas, Izyas, Abrams, Sarahs and so on in a moment, having paid good money for that. They became Jews due to grandmother's, grandfather's or some other ancestors that appeared to be ever existing. In a while they left Odessa and as real Jews went to Israel, Germany, the States and to other overseas countries.

Old Isaac wondered:

- How come that so many people want to become Jews at once? And they go to Germany! And what if a new Adolph comes to the government? What happens then? What nationality those people would become? Or would they have time for that at all? Those, who took "furain", got well established in St. Petersburg and in Moscow and consider themselves to be residents of those cities, they even created a club of their own.

But Isaac was interested in another issue. For forty years he had been working as a surgeon in a Jewish hospital. During those years many changes had taken place in life and in Odessa. The flags, emblems had changed, from the happy future people had switched to electoral and advertising present. Though nothing changed in the way the residents of Odessa got their headache from the current "head", who is the same as former "the first". If, of course, that stuff could be called something else instead of "a head"...

In Odessa flora and fauna changed, as with the departure of numerous real residents of Odessa who escaped from Perestroika, shooting and other reforms in the city, everything changed in the city, and Odessa residents lost their immunity without "furain".

This fact could be noticed, of course, only by the real Odessa residents. But there was something that remained unchanged, that was the Jewish hospital! It had always been known for good doctors and very bad sanitary condition, starting with the porch and up to the attic.

In nineties during the years of shooting in business and in politics, when they shot politicians, businessmen and other strange persons who wanted to get something of the big and tasty pie, which actually was the state property and the government money, they divided everything, excluding the medical institutions. Even later the Jewish hospital didn't attract anyone's attention.

Isaac was well-to-do, he was not an outstanding surgeon, but he did good surgeries and he practically didn't have any lethal cases during the surgery and at the recovery period for many years. He was famous for that. At his age his hands were shaking, but before the surgery everything got fixed, there was no shaking in hands, the sight became sharp and his voice even became different, it became younger. At those moments he looked as a former young Isaac, who used to attract young female doctors on training, female students and, of course, nurses. He was a gallant and charming guy. In his young age he could handle any woman easily, and everyone was happy. Even at this age he was still able to seduce a nurse from time to time, or a female student on training, or a patient.

But the main thing about him was that since his independent work started in hospital, he had had two ambitious aims. The first was his desire to become the manager of the hospital and not of just any hospital, but of the Jewish hospital.

The second aim was connected to the first one. As soon as he became the manager, he wanted to ask all the Jews of Odessa to help to do the major renovation and reconstruction of the hospital. He wanted to make it a medical center with all the necessary departments: a walk-in clinic, a hospital itself, a drug mart, a rehabilitation department and so on.

The aims were linked to each other, and Isaac never forgot about them.

Decades passed, the Jewish hospital was gradually getting shabby, like the whole country, from the Kremlin to the smallest washroom. The heads of the state changed, the heads of the city changed, so did the managers of the hospital, but the situation in the hospital never changed. Like always, there were cracks in the walls, peeling drywall, dirt, gray linen coming from the laundry and so on. Patients were brought, some of them walked in themselves, they were checked, they had surgeries, they were treated.

In nineties the stereotypes changed. The leaders, that lead the region to poverty and lawlessness, quickly became the heads of the movement "Revival of the Region" and started to make something for nothing for themselves and their kids. For doctors nothing changed, it was just the salary that shrank and the number of patients with shot wounds increased. Isaac, who never had just salary as his only income, understood that he would never become the manager of the hospital.

But he decided to make his second aim a reality, that was to solve the problem with the renovation and the reconstruction of the hospital. Isaac operated so many different patients in those shooting nineties. In Odessa and the suburbs there were shootings almost every day, as well as machine guns shooting and explosions. In separate wards there were criminal bossed and representatives of force structures. According to the opinion of the old Jew all, who had security as strong as the president had, were criminals, as they were delivered expensive medicines, delicious food and other things, as if they were royalty, and of course, they were supplied with money for the surgery. Isaac was not a dummy and he took what they gave and never refused. When he spoke about the financing of the renovation of the hospital, the purchase of the equipment all patients and their company assured Isaac that everything would be done. The only priority for them was to recover.

The patients recovered, got discharged and went away on luxurious cars, and the hospital stayed with its problems awaiting for new patients who were brought after fights, elections and re-elections. New patients came in and everything was the same again.

Once Isaac visited the manager. He respected the latter as a specialist and a decent person.

- Stepan Stepanovich, let's talk to the point with those who is our patients right now. Let one ward be equipped as it should be and let them pay for this right now while they are still our in-patients. Then we will make others pay for the next ward, and in this way we'll put the whole hospital in order.

The manager agreed with him and they declared the ultimatum for the "respectable" patients, and the work did start at last. They renovated three wards and equipped one surgery room with modern equipment. There was no money for more work. At the end of nineties the rich people who became the patients of the hospital, said to Isaac:

- Dear doctor, five years ago we could waste the money easily, as they were not ours. Now we have learned to count and now we consider it to be ours. And we grudge it! So, you are to excuse us, my dear! I will pay you for your work for sure. But as far as the renovation is concerned, sorry, let your minister and the mayor think of that...

Isaac saw how the military hospital and other hospitals in the city were changing. His own Jewish hospital was declining more and more. The residents of Odessa considered it to be the dirtiest and the most neglected one.

But old Isaac didn't give up. He made an appointment to the mayor, but he was admitted to the office of the deputy mayor, who listened to him attentively, but he expressed his doubt regarding the help.

- You see, Isaac Efimovich, there is no money in the budget. And there is no money expected in the nearest five years for the renovation of the hospital. Now we have finished renovation of the oncological center, now we offer all the businessmen to take part in the construction of the municipal children's hospital. Everything is done with so much effort, you can't imagine that. It's so hard for us to work in this situation, I mean the whole municipal management. – Those were his words when they parted.

Isaac saw luxurious offices in the city council, Italian furniture, new luxurious cars of foreign make belonging to the officials, the suits that officials wore were made by the best couturier for more than a thousand of bucks. He went out to the entrance of the building and looked at the fat trimmed faces of the officials with hatred.

- You can't get even a penny from them. Village assholes, so many of them residing in Odessa nowadays...

He saw what villas the officials of district, municipal and other levels constructed for themselves near his home, at Fontan area.

- I am making money with my own hands. And they? – Isaac was indignant.

In a moment he conquered his feelings. – Stop! In Odessa it was not habitual to count somebody else's money. The mayor and his associates are real dummies, but the residents of the modern Odessa go along with them. Why should I care for all this?

Not long before Isaac met his old fellow-student Monya. They hadn't met for twenty years, and they went to a cozy bar. Drinking a glass of good cognac Monya told about his life in New Zealand.

You see, those dummies who are ruling now, you know them all personally, they were the same dummies in the past, but with the communist manners. They have only one thing to do – that is to erect monuments. Now and then they erect monuments to some Kazak soldier and his horse, to Bohdan Khmelnitsky, which is not far from our hospital. Do you know if those famous people and their four-legged friends are related to the history of Odessa? The modern type of a leader is a real dummy. You know, I went to the store "Knizhka" to buy a book for my grandson. There were all kinds of fairy tales there, Russian, Ukrainian, even the fairy tales of the peoples of the Far North, but there were no Jewish fairy tales there. It is discrimination. There are no monuments to Jews, no fairy tales, no life in this city.

Isaac told about his unreal dream to put the Jewish hospital to order. Monya laughed at him sincerely.

- My friend told me a short story yesterday, a new one about the life in modern Odessa:

Two managers are speaking:

- Do you have Jews in your stuff?
- Sure, the time has changed.
- I can't understand, where do you find them from?

Monya stopped laughing and said seriously: - I would like to ask you as well: how many Jews are left? Few of them. And those who are left don't usually turn for help to the Jewish hospital, do they? I don't think there are any at all. The Jewish hospital and everything Jewish in the city preserved only its name. No one is going to invest in the hospital, believe me. Neither local Jews, nor from abroad will. That's why you are not going to have either the European or just Soviet-style renovation. My advice to you is not to make a fuss for yourself and for everyone around you. Live and get pleasure, if you don't want to leave

Odessa. Get a lot at the Jewish cemetery for yourself, while there are some lots still available there and the prices are still reasonable. Don't spoil your nerves, don't waste money for the renovation of your hospital. Don't care for anything.

Isaac was returning home well drunk and thought:

- Why do we live so badly? In the States or in the Emirates, and in New Zealand they keep up due to oil, gas or high technologies, even due to tourism. We have always relied on dummies. That is what the Jewish happiness mean – it is the thing that other nations were happy to avoid.

Let Him Be Remembered for Ever

In the reception of the manager of the market "Privoz" it was very crowded. Everyone wanted to see the manager for at least a minute. The reception was small, with a tiny window which looked to the back yard of the market. In the middle there was the secretary's table, at the side of the table there were three chairs for visitors. The left door in the reception led to the office of the manager, the right one led to the deputy manager's office. The nice-looking Katyushka fulfilled her duties diligently, she calmed down the visitors, and she distributed the visitors politely between the manager and the deputy manager, depending to the problem they wanted to discuss. Some of them were not supposed to be accepted and a tall security officer in a uniform helped her.

Semen Semenovich, an experienced businessman, had already visited the manager, he was a long-term friend of his, and he settled the question of arranging several sales working places for selling cigarettes. At that moment he was casually sat on the chair near the secretary's table drinking coffee slowly. It was Katia who made coffee for him out of courtesy. He drank coffee in small sips, feeling its taste. Semen Semenovich was waiting for the deputy manager of the market, who had already received the order to vacant the working places, chosen by Semen Semenovich.

Semen Semenovich watched those entering the reception with interest. They were different in their clothes, expression of their faces, their manners. But all of them had one and the same purpose; they came there to ask for something. Some of them asked for working places, others to set a container, some wanted to rent a pavilion, some wanted to be hired to work, or they wanted their relatives to be employed by the market, some wanted to lower the rent payments. Everyone wanted something and all of them knew the unpublished rule in Odessa, no matter socialistic or capitalistic, but the manager could solve any problem. But he solved the problems depending on who paid and how much.

There also were those who wanted to get something for nothing on the market expenses. Semen Semenovich recognized those people at once. It was not the police, nor the taxation office, nor different inspections, which were so numerous in the authorities and which were considered to be permanent "milkers" who milked money for their own needs, and not for the government. Those people were from different public societies like "the society of blind persons, "the society of hearing impaired persons" and others. Semen Semenovich grinned to himself, thinking of those societies like "the society of pregnant participants of the was in Afghanistan". They were so numerous. Many people of Ostap Bender kind were organizing different societies in Odessa and using the name, they got benefits and support from the authorities. They also used the kindness of people; they actually collected money from all.

Suddenly Semen Semenovich saw a familiar face in the crowd.

- That's a surprise! What a meeting! How are you, Vasyl Semenovich? – He exclaimed, stretching his hand to a man of middle age in a dark grey suit, white shirt and an official looking grey tie. He was the manager of the department of stopping economic crimes at the railway Vasyl Semenovich Protsenko. As long as Semen Semenovich remembered him, he was in the rank of a major and his face had always been red with blue shades and swollen, that was the result of his strong addiction to alcohol.

- Hello, dear Semen Semenovich. – Protsenko pressed his hand firmly and smiled. – That's where we meet. At Privoz!

They started talking and went out to the corridor of the market, had a smoke. They got acquainted about fifteen years ago, when Semen Semenovich was reselling clothes brought by sailors from the Black Sea steam ship line. The process of buying and delivery was smooth. The process of wholesale and retail in the city was also smooth, due to the great activity of Semen Semenovich. Besides, Semen Semenovich organized the production of shirts, jeans, pants, ties in Odessa, and the same sailors brought labels to him. The saying which had always been mentioned in Odessa was true: all the smuggled goods were produced in Odessa, at Malaya Arnautskaya Street.

At that time Protsenko was a young officer of the department of stopping economic crimes, and they remembered those years with pleasure. They remembered the birthday of Semen Semenovich, where there were many guests, mostly entrepreneurs, who were called profiteers. Among the guests there were also many police officers.

- Do you remember your toast? Semen Semenovich, you said then that at one side of the table there were those who were being caught, and at the other side were those who were catching. You proposed a toast for our strong friendship and business cooperation. – Protsenko was telling with laughter.

Semen Semenovich was smiling because of the refreshed reminiscences. He answered:

- Yes, that was good time, there was order, respect to those superior, everyone knew to whom to pay and how much to pay. The department of stopping economic crimes! That was a firm! Now we have to pay to the police, starting with the district officer and up to chief of the district department, to the department of stopping economic crimes, to the department of stopping of organized crime, to the department fighting with illegal drugs distribution, to the special department of the police, to the tax police department. Those enumerated are wearing uniforms. There is also taxation inspection office, the department of protection of consumers' rights, firemen, administration and so on. No limit. Everyone wants to eat, and to eat good food. – Semen Semenovich said.

Protsenko burst out laughing: - Come on, Semen Semenovich, calm down. Do you think we are not paying bribes? Do you think I have come to the manager of the market to solve my own problem? We also have bosses, every month the head office orders a certain amount of money which we are to send to Kyiv. Just imagine that every month or even every week certain persons go to Kyiv from all directions. They carry brief cases with money to the minister, to the deputy minister, to the head of the department, to the president's office. Besides, do you know how many of them come to check the work as members of different commissions? It is good that the officials are not very picky, they are satisfied with food, drinks, restaurants, nightclubs and girls.

But the leaders are not like this. They demand cash, in green bills, in big amounts and rather often.

Semen Semenovich knew about it from his own experience, he and his partner constantly paid to an official in the government, and Protsenko's story didn't surprise him.

- There is one more example, from today's life. In Kyiv a deputy minister died, you must have heard about it. He didn't die while fulfilling his duties; it was an accident during the flight of the sport plane. Can you imagine that with a modest salary of a cop he could afford that? We are not supposed to speak badly about late people, anyway. We are supposed to keep silent or to say only good things. It's a pity, he was not a bad guy, and the death was so silly. We have always had a tradition to collect money for the family of the deceased person. Friends and associates collect some money, everyone paying as much as he can.

Semen Semenovich became interested when listening to Protsenko:
- OK, that is an old tradition, it is a rule.

Listen and don't interrupt me. – Protsenko objected. – Yesterday night the chief of the head office called and told us to deliver ten thousand from each department for the funeral. He stressed that it was not hryvnias, but US dollars he was speaking about. So, since morning I have been collecting the extra money.

Semen Semenovich understood that Protsenko was not a liar, and everything he was telling was true. Semen Semenovich imagined the amount that would be collected that day all over the Ukraine and whistled: - That's a really big amount of money to be collected, no less that seven digits amount.

Protsenko smiled: - You know me, I am not going to take more than I need. I can just have some spare money for a pub, to go there with my friends, to remember the late boss. Others, especially young people, collect ten thousand to Kyiv and ten to themselves, using the opportunity.

Semen Semenovich did know from his long experience that Protsenko would not take any extra money. He did take a little bit, just for drinking and girls. Vasyl Semenovich would go soon to the manager of the market, have a couple of shots of vodka and take the money. The manager had no choice; he would pay, and later would take money from those who sold at the market. That was the system all over the country, in all the cities there was the process of collecting extra money, and it was constant. There were so many officials in villages and up to Kyiv, and everyone wanted to be rich, to be able to afford anything they wanted, and they did it by contributing nothing to the budget, just filling their own pockets. Semen Semenovich remembered how at the beginning of the presidential election campaign every businessman at Privoz was supposed to contribute one hundred dollars.

Protsenko waved his hand as good-bye and disappeared behind the door of the manager. Semen Semenovich went to the market place together with the deputy manager, who was available. He thought about what he had heard.

They will collect all the money which is supposed to go to the family of the deceased man, it seems to be good. But they are not going to give the family everything they will collect.

Semen Semenovich understood that. And the family of the colonel-general did not need such big amount of money; they were far from being poor. Semen Semenovich's mood became blue. They will take the money from me too, no matter that I am a friend of the manager of the market. That's the reality. Let the late man be remembered for ever, but it would be better if he were alive. He was not on my way, and now I have extra expenses, I have to pay just for nothing. The thoughts drove him mad, he lost control over himself and said out loud:

- They collect money when they alive, they continue collecting money after they die!

If They Don't Take It – We Will Disconnect the Gas

Late on Saturday night Ivan Ivanovich returned back home from the beach. The summer turned out to be extremely hot, some days the temperature raised as high as forty and more. In Odessa it was impossible to stay during the daytime. The unusual heat came from the sun, from the heated pavement, even the air was hot. At night it didn't come any cooler, it was stuffy in apartments. The shade saved people, so did different fans. Those, who had more money, had air conditioners, which made many of them sick with cold. But the best of all was a cold shower; a person could feel happy for at least some time.

Beside a shower it was the sea that gave relief of the heat that made the brain melt, as Odessa residents said. Ivan Ivanovich didn't like the water at the city beaches, as the water there was dirty. It could be seen, as at some beaches there was even slime on the surface. It was understandable, as the sewage was disposed into the sea. That was why Ivan Ivanovich preferred to go to Karolino-Bugaz during the weekends. There the sea was clean, the water transparent and the sand not polluted. It was pleasant to lie in the sun there and to take a sea bath. It is a really great feeling to swim in clean transparent sea water.

Having parked the car at the parking lot in the yard, Ivan Ivanovich, in good moods after the sea, came up to the entrance with his wife. On the wall he saw an ad, saying in big letters on white sheet of paper:

Attention:

The amount of the debt for rent for the apartment building # 16 is 25,000 hryvnias. Due to this on 22 July, 2002 there will be complete disconnection of water in the building.

The Administration of the district.

Ivan Ivanovich was shocked and immediately turned mad.

- What does it mean? – He asked his wife. To the date we don't have any debt for rent. Are they mad? Is it the heat that has melted their brains? Don't they understand what the disconnection of water could lead to? There is sure to be an outbreak of dysentery, to say nothing of other diseases. Why should I suffer because somebody is not paying rent? I do pay my rent.

- Please calm down, they just wanted to make a warning, they are not going to disconnect the water. – His wife objected to him.

Ivan Ivanovich became still madder after her words.

- What do you mean – to make a warning? What if I post the following ad on the door of the district administration: "If you disconnect the water, I will kill you, clerks, for illegal actions." How do you think they will feel? I will just frighten them. Their advertisement is humiliating for me. Why should I be always afraid of something or of somebody? Why should I be afraid of the authorities? They always threaten to disconnect the heat, the power or the water. Is it going to finish? Everything can be settled in the court. You, guys, go to the court and sue the tenants or the owners you need to sue and act according to the court decision. In this case not the municipal department, but the court executor is to be acting. Besides, I or someone else can file for appeal to the supreme court.

And they act as bandits, illegally. It is the same situation as in the movie "The Diamond arm". The property manager there also declared that it the tenants would not buy lottery tickets, she would disconnect gas. This is the way today's administration behaves. On Monday I am going to the municipal council and I will find the way to manage those bandits.

The wife protested again:

- Why do you care more than all the rest? You don't need to go there, they won't disconnect the water, and they just frighten us. If they do disconnect, you won't get any results anyway, you will just make new enemies.

Ivan Ivanovich didn't start an argument with his wife. He knew that arguments on domestic and social topics, that concerned regular Odessa residents, would not lead anywhere, they will just cause spoilt atmosphere and worse health condition.

Ivan Ivanovich's spirit was low, he went up to his apartment and called to his friend, a famous actor, well known in Odessa and beyond its borders. Everyone knew him and respected him for his talent, kind heartedness. He was able to conduct easy talks and he was a speaker at all the parties and in all the companies. He lived next door, in the same building.

- Look here, Monya, do you know what is going on in our building?
- No, I don't. What is it?

Ivan Ivanovich briefly told him the contents of the ad and his attitude to it.

- What is it? Are they crazy? Maybe it is the heat that struck them? – Monya became mad.

- No, dear Monya. It is just the sign that the officials do not treat us as human beings any more. This ad, cynical in its form and contents, shoes once again, that we, common residents of Odessa are nobody, just like the cattle. To tell the truth, they are not very far from the reality. The pride of Odessa, the people the city was proud of, the people due to whose peculiarity, wit and good sense of humor the whole world new Odessa, left long ago. Those who stayed and the newcomers are not the best representatives of the society.

- Look here, Ivan, don't make general conclusions. Don't make it so bad. – Monya objected. Let's do the following: if they disconnect the water, we will call all the tenants outside and will block the traffic, we will call TV and newspapers men. I will organize that.

Ivan Ivanovich laughed out loud: - Monya, please tell me who of our building will go out to block the traffic? Five to seven persons, no more. All the rest will be watching from behind the curtains. Even if you pay to them they will think twice before they go out. To my mind, the authorities will not disconnect the water, they need to be completely stupid to do that. On Monday morning I will go to the district property manager and they I will go to the municipal council. I am not going to leave it as it is.

- Good. Let's wait till Monday and see.

Ivan Ivanovich hung up and took a calculator. There were thirty apartments in the building, it means that the average debt for rent for each apartment was about eight hundred hryvnias.

- No, it must be a mistake. – Ivan Ivanovich thought. – It turns out that they haven't been paying for a few years.

He knew that many tenants paid the rent in time and don't have any debts. It was mainly the elderly people who lived in the building. They had Soviet habits and they knew that the rent was to be paid in time. Those, who had debt, were sure to have it for one or two months, no more.

Ivan Ivanovich was indignant with such attitude of the officials to people. They could have made an ad of different contents, or it would be better if they went around and gathered the tenants together and explained to them that the situation with water supply was hard. They could ask to pay the debt, they could explain that they had to reduce water supply. They could explain the reason to people. The tenants are sure to understand and accept the decision. No, they did it in a rude way. They are authorities, and they can do whatever they wanted. People have hated the authorities for ages, and it is a mutual feeling. Mutual hatred.

The maintenance departments did almost nothing to keep the order in the buildings, in the yards and adjacent streets. Janitors swept the pavements but they never cleaned in the yards, except for some holidays. But janitors were supposed to keep the order in yards. They used not only to clean the yards, but they also managed the security in the yards. Now the buildings and especially roofs, attics, yards and entrances were in shabby condition. There had not been any renovation for decades. It there were any, it was on tenants' expenses. The illumination of the entrances and yards was also on the tenants' pockets.

At the same time, and Ivan Ivanovich knew that from his acquaintances, who worked in property management and maintenance department, the department paid regularly to cleaners of buildings and for janitors who never existed. They monthly accounted the burnt electric bulbs and wires for lightening of entrances and yards. They regularly made fake reports and invoices for renovation of entrances and yards. The construction material was sold and the money was distributed between the authorities. Sometimes some money was given to the managers, but neither foremen nor regular workers had anything. Janitors didn't quit for one reason: they were promised to be given some place to live, anywhere, at least in the basement. And they hoped to get that apartment some day. That was the reason they worked almost for free, and so their attitude to cleaning was indifferent. They swept only conspicuous spots where the administration passed and near the entrances to firms and stores, as the owners paid cash for that. Foremen in property management and maintenance departments, as well as other specialists, didn't stay long. There were many vacancies and those who were working were not specialists in maintenance. The managers of departments and their deputies had their own businesses. It could be a café, a bar, a store. Or they could be partners in several companies, and all of them lived on different donations, bribes, budget money, stolen for non-existing renovations and maintenance services.

Ivan Ivanovich lived in a building opposite the maintenance department. He, like many Odessa residents, witnessed how within three years the current manager of the department turned from a modest shy guy of medium size, who lived in one of the neglected areas, into a fat pink-cheeked, confident rude official. He knew everything, he could do anything, and he didn't stand remarks and prompts. He acquired a good apartment, renovated in European style, he bought a luxurious car of foreign make. He didn't neglect any way of getting money, they said he even took money from janitors. But in front of his manager he was an obedient clerk, serving and ready to please. He never refused any application, but he didn't do anything if he didn't see his own interest.

Ivan Ivanovich, in spite of all, decided firmly that he would talk on Monday to the manager of the property management and maintenance department. He wanted to know who was the initiator of that stupid notice, humiliating for the residents of the district. It was the district action, as similar notices with the threat to disconnect the water were in many yards.

Ivan Ivanovich spoke out loud to himself:

- They speak of democratization of the society, about civilized European way of development, they try to merge to Europe, but what do they have to offer? Their pig noses of fat officials, so numerous everywhere from Kyiv to the most remote village? It is easy to recognize one in the crowd, as he differs from the others in his clothes, manner of walking and mostly in his shameless bold expression of his face, wide with too much nutritious food and extremely large quantities of drinks at different parties and presentations.

It would be civilized, if the property management clerks went to the taxpayers and warned them in writing of their debts and of the possibility of litigation. According to the decision of the court the water could be disconnected just for some debtors.

He thought, walking nervously up and down the room.

- In our part of the building there are about three or four families consisting of retired people. How can they survive for one hundred or one hundred and fifty hryvnias, with the maintenance fee and utilities, including the telephone, paid, and there still should be some money for food and medicines, not to mention the clothes. Every debtor should have an individual attitude. – Ivan Ivanovich made the conclusion. He decided that after visiting the property manager he would go to the municipal council to discuss the problem.

On Monday morning Ivan Ivanovich wanted to take off the notice and take it to the municipal council. But it was not there. Some of the tenants peeled it out of the wall and left no traces. Ivan Ivanovich waved his hand in irritation.

- That is all they can do.

He meant the majority of the tenants in the apartment building where he lived. And in other buildings too.

- They are used to get everything for granted. – Ivan Ivanovich was indignant. It was not just him who was supposed to go to the property management, but hundreds of people, humiliated and insulted by the notice of water disconnection should be in the management too. No, he was to attend the office of the manager alone. How could that manager feel if early in the morning a crowd of insulted tenants would rush into his office. No, it was not like this. They should be busy storing water in pails, buckets, bathtub and thinking that they could still keep the water running. That was the mentality of an ordinary person. It was not the authorities that made the people look like a cattle, it was the people itself who mostly behaved like a cattle.

He was thinking of that when he entered the reception of the manager of the department. There was no one there. He knocked and entered the office. The manager sat reading some documents.

- Good morning, - Ivan Ivanovich greeted him. – I will take a couple of minutes of your time. Sorry about that. – He shook hands and sat down, not waiting for the invitation.

- Could you please explain what that notice about disconnection of water in our apartment building, starting with today mean?

The property management and maintenance department manager stopped looking at the documents in front of him.

- There is nothing to explain. Due to the lack of water in the city the water supply in the district will be restricted, that's it.

Ivan Ivanovich laughed out loud.

- Look here, my dear, in the notice they say clearly that on the twenty second the water will be disconnected. It is a great difference, as they say here in Odessa.

The manager frowned. – What is the difference? How can we make the tenants pay? We'll disconnect the water and they will pay at once.

- Sorry, but those who don't pay, they are not going to pay anyway. But it concerns me and many others who have no debts. This is the first issue. Secondly, if you want trouble, I will take people out into the street and will block the traffic. Who will benefit of that? Have we completely lost our skills to talk and act properly? Go to the apartments and talk to the tenants. Make everything clear. Most of the tenants don't have any debts. Maybe there are some among retired persons, but you are to understand that.

- Let them go and get welfare. – The manager was irritated and interrupted him.

Ivan Ivanovich went mad. – You accompany them and you will see yourself that before they go to every official and get the welfare they will pass away.

- I didn't create the procedure. Why do you lecture me? The talk is over. – The department manager said abruptly.

Ivan Ivanovich stood up and went to the exit. Before he left the office, he said in a low voice:

- Remember, you, scoundrel, if you post a notice like that again, or if you illegally disconnect water, heat, power of gas, I will break your arms myself, so that you were not able to sign such orders. If you don't make correct conclusions, I will cut off your stupid head, there is no brains and shame in it anyway. I will treat you the same way you, officials, treat us, like bandits.

Ivan Ivanovich slammed the door and walked out. He was mad, he was shivering all over. He came to talk in a decent way and they didn't want to listen to him. Near the building he met Monya who was outside with his cat. Ivan Ivanovich greeted him and told him the contents of the conversation with the department manager.

- I am going to the municipal council right now, Monya. I will figure out what is the degree if illegal behavior and rudeness there. Let's go together. Or you go to the chairman of the district administration, talk to him seriously.

- You see, Ivan, I can't scold with them, they give job for me. The district authorities gave me the opportunity to make small concerts in the district, the mayor of the city also gives me some job. I am in demand and I can't spoil relations with them. You go yourself.

Ivan Ivanovich was shocked to hear that. At that moment a female neighbor came up to them.

What's the news, guys? Are they going to disconnect the water? I haven't stored it yet.

Ivan Ivanovich looked at her at a loss and said to her indifferently:

- Yes, they are going to disconnect for about two weeks.

- Oh, my God! I need to go and store some water. - The woman clasped her hands and rushed to her home with her dogs.

Ivan Ivanovich spit angrily and went to the municipal council. On his way he analyzed the situation. Nobody in the yard and in the district, except him, seemed to be worried with the disconnection of the water.

- Why are they so indifferent to their life, to their situation, to their position? – Ivan Ivanovich was mad.

- Actually, people are like zombies, they have turned to be a crowd of nobody during the last ten to fifteen years. They take it for granted for not being paid, for not getting retirement money, for rising prices, illegally raised rates for utilities and other services. They take for granted the chain disconnection of power, starting with autumn till spring, it is disconnected for no less than for two hours a day, and as a rule it is done in the dark time of the day. They explain that with non-payments for the consumed power. At the same time in newspapers there were published figures showing that this year the debt for the Ukraine for the power was fifteen billion hryvnias, two of which was from the consumers. And who owes the rest of thirteen billions? It is different enterprises, which belong to the same officials, but registered on the names of relatives and other people. It is the common people who are suffering, who stay in dark apartments and houses, and the power at that moment is sold by the same officials to neighboring countries. The people buy in autumn candles and rechargeable flashes. The Odessa residents also got used to the complete disconnection of hot water from April till December. It is a regular thing that the steam central heating is just called so, as in many apartments the air in winter is no more than thirteen to fifteen degrees Celsius, and all the dwellings are usually heated with fireplaces and gas. In order not to pay more for the extra power, electricians for some payment render such kind of services as changing the figures at the meters. It is the country of total lies and deceit. The authorities cheat on people, the people cheat on the authorities, everyone is aware of everything and everyone pretend that everything is OK. It's like a game where everyone plays its part. And all this is happening at the beginning of the twenty first century! Even slaves in the Ancient Rome didn't live like that. They were given home, a job and food. Our people is silent, and the officials of all the levels become more and more beastly, they try to steal something from the budget and by cheating people. There is no end to that. The process is gaining strength. As they say, the appetite comes with eating.

Ivan Ivanovich hasn't been in the municipal council for about a year. It was eight forty five and the officials were driving to the municipal council in their cars after their weekend in their summer cottages and residences. They went out of the cars and went up to the entrance to the building of the municipal council with beautiful columns. Some of them entered the building immediately, others stayed at the entrance. The morning was fresh and it was nice to stay outside with the nice cool breeze from the sea. Ivan Ivanovich was surprised by so many new cars of foreign make, which brought the "servants of the people". But most of all he was surprised by the officials themselves. Many of them whom Ivan Ivanovich had known for a long time, had changed greatly. They were dressed spick and span, in expensive clothes, shoes, their faces were fresh, confident and they seemed to be rejecting everything, they seemed not available. But they changed immediately at the sight of the deputy mayors, on their faces there appeared a flattering smile, they tried to get into their view and to say their compliments. Ivan Ivanovich passed by the groups of talking officials. Some of them were shaking hands, some were nodding, but some of them pretended not to notice him. Ivan Ivanovich saw that and felt like a white sheep among the blind, deaf, indifferent to other people's misfortunes and problems. They were interested only in their own well-being, their private business, their bribes and donations, the situation at their country residences and their beloved children.

In the foyer Ivan Ivanovich was surprised because earlier one could freely enter the building of the municipal council. Now it was different. At the entrance there was a beautiful barrier of wood and to the right there was a narrow, one meter wide passage, with strict and strong guards.

- Stop! Where are you going?

- I have an appointment with the deputy mayor, he is waiting. – Ivan Ivanovich said.

- There is a phone at the entrance. Go and call from there.

Ivan Ivanovich was indignant with the behavior of the security officers. – You, young man, call and tell them. It is your duty.

But he didn't influence the security. They paid no attention to Ivan Ivanovich, he was nothing to them.

He didn't make a fuss, he went out to the entrance of the municipal council and saw the deputy mayor surrounded by the officials from the property management and maintenance department. Ivan Ivanovich came up and interrupted the talk of the officials. They didn't expect the persistent attitude and had to listen to him. Ivan Ivanovich explained everything briefly, but precisely and firmly.

The deputy mayor together with the manager of the department of the property management and maintenance assured Ivan Ivanovich, that they would investigate the case of illegal action and no one was going to disconnect the water.

- Tell the tenants of your apartment building and the others that the water would not be allowed to be disconnected. The water will be disconnected for those who had debts for a year or more. But it will be decided individually, others will not suffer, and the disconnection procedure will be legal. – The deputy mayor said at the end.

On his way back Ivan Ivanovich thought that the officials of the municipal council didn't care at all about his problems. But the deputy mayor couldn't help understanding that the commotion among the people would lead to nothing good. That was why he promised to Ivan Ivanovich to clear everything out and put everything to order. Anyway, the work was done, they were not going to disconnect the water.

At night, having returned from work, Ivan Ivanovich saw that the water was not disconnected. On the staircase he met one of his neighbors, a former sailor, who was drunk.

- You see, Ivan, Monya and I solved the problem with the water, and you appear to be just a talker. You said everything will be solved by the municipal council, and we solved all at the manager of the department.

Ivan Ivanovich was shocked.

- Look here, my dear, is it so important who solved the problem. Why are you like this – when the situation is bad, you are not on the scene, when it is good, you shout that you are so good to have solved the problem. What kind of folks are you?

He went up home and calmed down. There was no point of paying attention to the drunken person. He switched on TV and watched Odessa news. He was interested in the briefing of the deputy mayor in financial issues, the manager of the financial department of the municipal council.

- They use so many foreign words, such as briefing, manager, dealer, killer, presentation, mayor, consensus. And the essence of all this is cheating and they all steal and rob.

In the briefing he was just shocked when the manager of the financial department said that to the date the municipal council had budget money for the renovation of buildings in just one district of the city, and there were eight districts in Odessa.

- See that! Do the renovation in one of the districts, don't spend the money for a different purpose. Then you will renovate another one. No, it is easier for them to spend the money for something else, to cheat all, and to put the money to their pockets. It is a great amount of stolen money. They are silly enough to speak about it openly in mass media. Are they not afraid of anything? It is clear now why they want to change the district division of the city. The more official departments there are in the city, the easier for them to hide the evidence.

Ivan Ivanovich was indignant deep in his heart. In an hour they said in the news that in one of the apartment buildings a balcony collapsed and two children were seriously injured. And a piece of concrete window sill fell down from the height of the building of the philharmonic society and an eight-year old girl was killed. Ivan Ivanovich had a bad heart pain and he took medicine. He couldn't fall asleep for a long time.

The next day in the afternoon he met Monya at the entrance to the building. He was in his shorts and was trying to get connected with the chairman of the district administration over his cell phone.

- Look here, Ivan Ivanovich, right now the manager of our maintenance department said that in an hour a technical support vehicle would come and they would start disconnecting the water. It is about our building and two more. I am calling to the chairman, I will ask to solve the problem, but I am not going to spoil relations with them, you are to understand me. You scold with them, OK?

- Look here, Monya, now I will write a complain to the court, and you will sign it with me. We will start litigation against the district administration. As soon as they disconnect the water, we'll go to the court.

- No, I can't sign that. I am not to be involved. You are to understand me. – Monya asked Ivan Ivanovich.

Go to hell! – Ivan Ivanovich pushed Monya aside and went home. In a few minutes he was talking to the manager of the maintenance department of the city council.

- Don't worry, Ivan Ivanovich, mind your own business, I will fix everything. There would be no disconnection, I assure you.

In a while Monya called.

- Look here, Ivan, I spoke to the chairman, he is going to a meeting in the city council, he will discuss the question there. It is the water supply department, not the district administration who does it all.

- Monya, I have told you to go to hell. But you seem to be on the way. The district official of yours is a son of a bitch. He is lying, the notice was signed not by the water supply department, but by the district administration. The water will not be disconnected. And you go and serve them, entertain them, you, clown. – And Ivan Ivanovich hung up in anger.

- Jewish cheap guy. – He thought of Monya.

The water was not disconnected. Ivan Ivanovich was walking outside with his granddaughter and thought:

- Is it going to last long? Constant humiliation, every minute of instability. What else are the authorities going to present? No perspective, no future. Who is to blame? The people are to blame, as the officials grew up in the same areas, in the same yards, in the same streets. If one of the tenants is chosen to rule, it will be the same, if not worse. Decent, honest, kind and smart persons are so rare now. And there are so many evil, mean and wicked people. Everything is revealed in hard times, like with the help of litmus paper.

Are you a relative? You owe a rouble

Everyone remembers the popular comedy movie "Afonya" with such actors in the cast as L. Kuravlev, Ye. Leonov, S. Kramarov. There was a well-known dialogue in the movie:

- Who are you?
- A relative.
- If you are a relative, you are to give a rouble. Afonya owes a rouble.

The city came to the 21st century with a new Mayor. He is considered, to tell the truth, by many people to be an old inveterate "partycrat". Others speak about his Moldavian background and consider him a regular plutocrat, hypocrite and "ribbon-cutter". Still others say that the current Mayor has had access to a sinecure for more than a decade. He just switched from one party to another: CPSU, then "Region Revival", later in the party "Regions of Ukraine". That could be true, as during the long-term office wars, during his long journey this "sir-comrade-his honour" joined the parties, but he managed to avoid stepping onto shit.

That in itself spoke of his remarkable talent; the fact that he was not able to lead and manage, did not matter. He absorbed much useful information from the highest officers of the communist party. The fact that he had become the first officer was the main thing, which meant that he was in the upper classes forever, until his funeral or until a coup. Let him be strong and healthy, especially his hands, which he uses for taking bribes, sharing and cutting ribbons with scissors at different grand openings and presentations.

The Mayor could be accused of many sins, but there is also one thing that makes his serve as an example. That is the love for relatives and friends. He is a family man. He is really a good and wonderful family man. He behaves as a good boy, not like people from the last century, when the son was against the father, the brother was against his sibling and so on. Our "sir-comrade-his honour" is above that feud. His family means all to him. His family is his wife, his son and daughter, and his brothers, sisters, his children's godfathers and other close and remote relatives. All of them resided in his native country, in his own region. Thanks God, no one has emigrated so far. Was there any place to go? One cannot be too choosy. No bird would fly away from its feeding rack. He was to provide each relative with some occupation, some work, some kind of business, so that each could get some earnings.

Before people thought about the child's future education, about his joining the young communist league and the party, later – about the promotion of his career. Nowadays it was much easier. Those who think that to provide some kind of business, some work of some occupation means to find an employment at a production plant or at least to place someone as a salesperson at the market "7th kilometre", or at some other place and make him or her sell Turkish consumer goods alongside with vodka, guns and drugs, are mistaken. The slang of the government officers of the upper classes of the city defines the expression "to provide a business" means to enter all his relatives in the list of founders of a firm, so that the relative could do nothing and get monthly dividends from the firm in the reliable currency of USA, or at least, in Euro. For this, the firm would get benefits or some concessions in its business activity. The number of benefits depends on the amount of dividends.

A family! Moscow people consider a family to be a mafia element, a group of persons, united with similar political, economical and other values, who act according to their common purpose with some definite result. To put it short, they think they are to grab, steal or rob people to a bigger extend. Our definition is different. Our Mayor, with whom the city entered the next pile of shit, that is the 21st century, appeared to be wiser. He used the Moscow experience to his own benefit. There is also a kind of split, changes or something like this happening in a family. In out Mayor's family everything is decent. He is the head of the family. They are linked together by not only financial stuff, real estate and other assets. It is the blood, the genes that connect them.

The public should notice that. They should create an honourable title "The Head of the Family" and institute an Order with the corresponding benefits and regalias. The first person to be awarded in the independent Ukraine is our Mayor, as there is no one more eligible than he is. He would wait for this award for years. He would like to be immortalized in a monument. He would imagine a monument of himself with his family members, like the well-known monument to Potemkin's brothers-in arms in Odessa. The Odessa residents call the monument "a monument to hairsplitters". People laugh that one of the characters of the monument shouts: "Stop, brothers, I have found a rouble!" It is an old Odessa joke, which is known to everyone.

Someone could think that our "sir-comrade-his honour" would call managers of firms and companies to his office and would have a cup a coffee with them, and during the meeting, he would make the businesspersons accept his relatives to a business or to some affair. It is not like that.

As soon as the Mayor became a Mayor and not the chairman of the party, a line of managers and firm owners was formed immediately. They all offered him or his family members to take part in their business activity. When a firm is founded, the honourable founder is a member of the family. When a party is founded, the member of the bureau or of the executive committee, or even of the central committee is a member of the family. That is how it works.

With the people like that, it is time to conduct a competition. The winner will be the one who licked the Mayor's ass in a better way. Once one licks, there comes another lick, which can be followed with a municipal contract for the company. It is something more subtle, than playing with one's balls. The municipal contract means that the firm would spend the budget money and operate with it, and then it takes the profit for itself. Besides, there is a chance to sign a long-term beneficial rental agreement for a municipal property. To make the citizens be unaware of what was going on; the head of the city would not only play games with them, but would also play with their balls. Moreover, he makes a success!

During the last years of the 20th century, our "sir-comrade-his honour" provided the business for practically all of his family members, as well as the family members of his relatives. After all the perestroika and exchange of fire, those were hard years. Where was the money taken from? There was supposed to be no savings, as the family did not sell bear, did not work in a mine, did not work in a foundry, they were all modest officers, excepting the head of the family, they were all working or studying at Universities or schools, like younger ones. Therefore, with almost zero starting capital, they managed to become well-to-do persons within about two years, which meant that they were with money and with power. One of them is said to be able to compete with not only the manager of the market at the 7th kilometre, but also the manager of the special enterprise, that is of all the cemeteries, together with the manager of the garbage dump.

However, there was a trouble with one of the youngsters, his nephew, who fell out of the ranks, due to his own silliness or his own temper. Maybe there was some other reason. God knows... He was given the firm "The world of attraction". They bought him equipment for making drinks from overseas, having paid much money for that. He was given money to start the business. The question was where to start that business. It would be silly if he started it in Sanzheika. The family council decided that he would sign a forty-nine-years rental agreement for the Green theatre. The only problem left was to have the decision certified by the session of the municipal council, which was approaching soon. Moreover, all the deputies were in the line to the "sir-comrade-his honour" for taking part in the above-mentioned competition.

It was not the matter with the Mayor and his family. The Odessa residents should be grateful to the fate that it was not a Gypsy baron who one the election campaign, otherwise they would come to know what size family it could be. Anyway, there was a line. In Odessa, there have always been lots of ass-lickers. There would be lots of them in the 21st century and in the 30th century too. We are well known for that. We licked, are licking and will lick! We bore, are bearing and will bear! We stole, are stealing and will steal! We hung around, are hanging around and will hang around! He were f...ed, are f..ed and will be f..ed! We sat in shit, we shit and we live, to spite relatives, our friends, neighbours and ourselves.

As far as the Green theatre is concerned, for a decade there had been no one but drug addicts. Now, maybe, there is a chance that music will start playing; maybe young people and children will have a place to have fun. For sure, someone will make a profit on that. Let is be! We should be happy and not envy them.

Therefore, one should keep in mind that there is nothing eternal in this life. Today one is loved and licked; tomorrow he is blamed. There can come a moment, when someone approaches the relative, that is the nephew and would say:

- Relative, you are to pay. Afonya owes money.

Give some change, please!

Raisa Yakovlevna had worked as a teacher of the primary school. After graduation from a Pedagogical University she had been employed at school # 59 of Odessa for as long as thirty years. During the latest years of her employment they paid miserable salary. The payments were not made in time. A teacher had to teach up to forty or even forty-five students in class. He had to take heavy bags with notebooks home and spend long hours at night checking them. At last Raisa Yakovlevna was tired of all that. He husband, Semen Borisovich, used to be the principal of the same school. He was retired. His retirement money was hardly enough to pay for utilities and he had to work part-time as a security officer at a parking lot.

Raisa Yakovlevna was a short nice-looking woman with the mood of a strong woman. She tried to raise her co-workers at school to fight against the miserable position of the teachers. He went to the principal of the school, to the department of education; she even visited the municipal council. However, she concluded that teachers were not miners; they would not hit the pavement with their hard headpieces and empty bottles. Teachers would not march out for a demonstration of protest.

- We are considered intelligent people, but we wage the life of the cattle. It concerns not only the lifestyle, it also concerns the way of thinking. We are just the cattle. – She said to her husband once at night.

He listened to her without interrupting. Then he said quietly: -
Quit from school, Raya. You can make your two hundred hryvnias
somewhere else. Why should you be humiliated?

In a few days after the conversation she was called to the office of
the principal.

- If you go somewhere else and complain, if your keep talking about
those things with other teachers, I will just fire you. It is easy to find a
reason, you understand this.

Raisa Yakovlevna was looking at the principal who could be the
age of her daughter. She had graduated from the University with
difficulties. She had worked three years as a teacher and a year as a
deputy principal. Then her aunt, who was the head of the municipal
department of education, helped her to become a principal. Raisa
Yakovlevna was watching her and she could not understand, where
such monsters appeared from. Why medical doctors could not see that
during pregnancy and make abortions in time?

The principal was a walking miracle. She was twenty-seven and she
had already managed to create a system of bribes taken from parents.
She had already established prices for the gold and silver medals and
so on. She would also mention the fact that in the school canteen the
girlfriend of the principal was illegally selling cigarettes and alcohol to
students. Evil tongues also spoke about drugs being sold.

- I wish you health. I also want gonorrhoea or AIDS to attack
you. I want you could give birth to nothing but barbed wire. – Raisa
Yakovlevna became mad. She immediately wrote an application stating
that she was quitting.

Of course, no one supported her. No one even sympathized. She
and her friend had a bottle of vodka in the teachers' office late at night
on the day of her dismissal. Thus they celebrated the event. Her friend
was a teacher of the same kind, who was silently toiling in spite of all
the humiliation and she was practically not paid.

For two weeks after her dismissal Raisa Yakovlevna was resting.
However, she had to work; there was not way of surviving on bread
and water. The children, who had lived separately for a long time, did
not and would not help. They were looking for something to take from
the parents. She took up a job of a salesperson at the consumer goods
market "7th kilometre" in Odessa.

It should be mentioned that Odessa used to have lots of intellectual and honest people. Everyone disappeared in two directions, that is overseas and the 7th kilometre. That is why there is no wonder that in the government officers there are no smart and honest people. Where are they to be found from? The brains have gone in the mentioned directions. What is left cannot be called even ...

Raisa Yakovlevna worked as a salesperson in the container, which sold perfumes for a month and a half. She had to quit. She could not stand the requisitions on behalf of the tax officers, the police and other bribers, who daily made a tour around the market. She could not agree with the owner of the goods who made her conduct dual accounting and sell illegal goods as well.

- Nowadays I cannot find an occupation for myself. – She was sadly sharing her problems with her husband.

- What did you think? – He was mad. – According to you, the school is wrong, the market is wrong. The whole life is a hen house nowadays. The one who managed to climb the perch is the master. He shits from the top on those who are at the bottom. You and I are the ones who they shit on. That is why be silent, do not twitter, go and make your money. Or maybe you have any other opinion?

Raisa Yakovlevna did have a plan.

- I will become a beggar. I will work as a pauper. – She decided, but she said nothing to her husband.

The next day she examined all the old clothes in the closet. She remembered her young age, when she played in an amateur theatre in the Pedagogical University, and later at school. She put on her old shabby clothes and put on worn out shoes. She put on an old dirty kerchief on her head and pulled it on the face. When she looked at the mirror, she did not recognize herself. She decided to begin begging at the pedestrian subway at Deribasovskaya and Sadovaya. She stood there for about an hour and got just a hryvnia. Then two woman beggars like herself came up to her and told her to disappear peacefully.

- Look here, you lost-in-life-crook, you get out of here. Is it clear to you? All the spots have been paid for, and there is no subleasing here. Get away!

So, Raisa Yakovlevna had to go away. After that, she tried to beg near Gayevski drug store, near the central post office and at the New market. The same story was everywhere. Local homeless and beggars just made her go. At the New market a policeman took her outside the place.

- Go home, granny, he said. There are so many of your people here.

However, Raisa Yakovlevna would not get discouraged. She got acquainted with two district police officers with the help of the janitors she knew. The police officers allowed her to beg for a fee at the pedestrian subway and in the area of the books market at the Greek square, which people called "Knizhka".

She was to beg for a fee, which was a share of her earnings. Besides, she was to collect information for the police about all the suspicious persons in the area of the Greek square and Deribassovskaya. Raisa Yakovlevna felt OK about it. She could freely walk around in the area, which was rather important in this kind of business. She would stand at the entrance to the subway with a small icon of the Virgin Mary and cross herself with passion. She would also beg the passers-by in a miserable voice:

- Please, give some change for Christ's sake to the old sick woman.

When someone would drop some change into the plastic cup, which she held in her dirty hand, she crossed herself and said thanks:

- Let the God give you health and luck!

No one could recognize a primary school teacher with a strong character in that dirty messy old woman. In a week it was clear how much she could make. She was making fifty, even sixty hryvnias. If she worked five days a week, that would make about two hundred dollars per month.

In a month's period Raisa Yakovlevna had become the senior beggar among the woman beggars in the area, as she worked hard and helped the police officer. It was June, a tourist season. The city was accepting more and more people on vacation.

Her work at the subway was interfered with by begging musicians. They were poor by entrepreneur-thinking students. It was weird, but they were paid more than old and sick beggars. However, smart Raisa Yakovlevna found the way out. She charged the musicians ten hryvnias per day and kept the police away from them. It was good. They benefited, and as for her, ten extra hryvnias per day was good.

In three months Raisa Yakovlevna was training her husband the same skills. Semen Semenovich first was reluctant to do that. Then he agreed and in a while he was walking at Gayevski drug store area at Sadovaya Street in old shabby clothes, worn shoes, old sunshades with cracked glasses and with a cardboard table on his front, which ran: "I am sick with TB. Please donate for drugs and treatment."

He took the position at the entrance to the drug store, so that one could not enter or exit without encountering him. People would read the words on the table and would drop some change into an empty butter box, which he was holding. Then each person quickly went away, before he could catch TB. Neither doctors, nor the police and the government could remove him from that spot. The spot was very profitable; he collected from 150 up to 200 dollars per month.

Raisa Yakovlevna once said to her husband, grinning:

- You were mad when we started begging. You said we were humiliating ourselves, get to the level of the homeless, lower than the bottom. What about our government? They are also beggars. I am standing at Deribasovskaya, begging. Beside me there is a box where the government ask to drop donations for renovation of the Opera house. A little bit farther, there is the place where they ask for the revival of the cathedral. Later they start asking for something else. The process is constant, once it starts, it never ends.

In six months they were renovating their apartment according to European standards. At night they would work at their own computer, taking all kind of information from the Internet. On weekends they could afford going to the theatre, mostly to musicals. The Russian theatre named after Ivanov was closed for a long time either for renovation or for sale, or for changing it into a gay-club. People spoke different things, but Raisa Yakovlevna was sure that the Mayor's office was going to collect money from the people for revival of the spirit and culture, which means for renovation of theatres.

Once in TV news she saw the aunt of her ex-principal. She appeared to have changed her activity and had quit from the position of the manager of the municipal department of education. She had become the manager of the trade center.

- What kind of crook she is! – Raisa Yakovlevna was mad. Since some time she was using pure Odessa street slang, common for beggars and homeless. – She is a crook! How could he switch from the Mayor's office, from education to trade? I wonder, who is managing the department of education now? Maybe it is a butcher from "Privoz" or a salesperson from a store. Everything is clear. She had collected money in the municipal council and switched to trade. Where else should she go? Not to the prosecutor's office, that's for sure.

Semen Semenovich laughed and added:

- You can say whatever you want, Raya, but life in Odessa has become better.

Well-dressed persons seek for something in garbage bins. I wonder why it has never occurred to the Mayor and his team members that they could introduce a commission and start selling licenses for all, including us, beggars.

If people used to say that there was just one "architect" in Odessa, nowadays they were a team. What kind of talent must they have, so that they could make a decision and spoil the city to this extend from both the inside and the outside?

Damn it!

Anyone in Odessa and outside Odessa know the famous "Privoz", the market, which, as they say, has once became more popular than the well-known all over the world the market in Istanbul. There is an opinion that at Odessa's "Privoz" one could buy anything, from a piece, that is a bar of lard to guns and drugs. It is not so important, to which group of drugs Ukrainian lard and heroin belong; the things that matter are the price and the quality. The quality is of Odessa standard; the price is negotiable. This is the way at "Privoz" in Odessa. Nowadays, which is the most interesting time to live, there exist not only country presidents, but also presidents of some educational institutions, firms, government enterprises, even of some villages. The same is the situation with "Privoz": beside Odessa, there is "Privoz" in Ivanovka, Buyalyk, other settlements and villages of Odessa region and neighbouring Moldova. There is no way we do without Moldavians or they do without us. Furthermore, at the end of 2002 in Odessa there appeared outside advertising posts and mass media advertisements of the following contents: "Male and female citizens, visit "New Privoz" in Panteleymonovskaya Street. Quality and prices will be a pleasant surprise for you".

It is clear, what is "New market". However, what "New Privoz" could be? Many Odessa residents and people from neighbouring villages and neighbouring countries, who joined them, could not make it out on the spot.

The first persons who clarified the situation were the people from the Local Mills area. It was Senya with the nickname "Damn it!" went to so-called "New Privoz" with his old homemade vodka and cigarettes without excise-duty labels. "New Privoz" was located in new buildings, which had an adjusting parking lot in Panteleymonovskaya Street. Panteleymonovskaya was the street which fifty years ago had good pavement and which was Chizhikova Street at the time of the previous power. Gradually along the street new buildings began to surround Privoz. The buildings were constructed by a company, which was part of Odessa soccer team company "Chernomorets". Actually, the only thing that was reminding of the company was its name and the picture of a soccer ball on the emblem of the company. It was in fact working under the supervision of the head of the city. The company, we should say, was using the supervision and the emblem with the soccer ball for successful promotion in oil, construction, trade, exchange businesses, including changing, cheating and other kinds of activity. It uses its supervisors, protectors and other benefits skilfully. They manage to pay taxes in the amounts equal to the cost of a monthly license for a professor who was renting a garbage container.

The constructed buildings are nice looking and modern. God, help their owners to avoid pain in hands when they count the profits and expenses. Some day, maybe, "Privoz", which has turned into a garbage dump, stinking and smelling, will be surrounded with modern buildings. "Privoz" became like this due to its transfer under the supervision of a municipal maintenance enterprise a few years ago. As a result, government officers of all levels began sucking profits, like calves suck milk from a cow. They suck so intensely, that "Privoz" is working with losses. The situation would be different if they had a supervision of the head of the city with all the benefits.

All the residents of Odessa hope that after "Chernomorets and Company" surrounds "Privoz" with "New Privoz", they will take over the old "Privoz" without any fight, practically for free. Actually, there will be nothing to take over except the lot, which would require disinfection. Then, hopefully, "Privoz" will be revived under the new supervision and protection. The streets in "Privoz" area will enjoy new pavement. It will return honourable reputation of one of the best markets in the world. Hopefully, we will be able to come to make purchases at "Privoz" and well be able to negotiate the prices, to smile to nice-looking and polite salespersons, which would replace the current crooks with cheap bold-coloured lipstick on their lips and dirty hands, which probably did not experience the use of soap since their birth. We will learn once again what it meant to buy a quality item. As far as homemade and home bottled drinks are concerned, alongside with homemade cigarettes and drugs in syringes will move to another location, maybe to fruit mall, close to their protectors. Everyone will be content. However, it is all in the future… Now the situation was different. Sema "Damn it!" was just removed from the place by tall strong guys in uniforms with portable radio transmitters and other items which the court servants of district level usually have.

Sema "Damn it!" was born and grew up in the Local Mills area. The area existed long before the world was divided into overseas and neighboring countries areas. Its appearance is not connected to the change of political or economical courses and regimes. The Local Mills area has always lived its own life, independent on the color of the state flag. Anarchy has always ruled there, no matter there was monarchy, socialism or democracy around, democracy being the most favorable regime. Sema is a short strong guy with dark curly hair and cunning eyes, which would avoid direct look. He has spent all his conscious life at "Privoz". In childhood he would just run along the isles, stealing food or wallets where he could. He also did some random work, helping to carry, transfer or load goods. Anyway, he would spend the day from early morning till late at night at "Privoz". When he became older, he was working as a loader, he was even given a wheelbarrow to operate. However, being forty years old, he has never been employed and was not going to be. He went to school for four years. School caused disgusting feelings in him; he disliked any studies except course of life at "Privoz".

He acquired his nickname "Damn it!" because he would tell one and the same joke since childhood, no matter what the situation was:

"A famous female singer came to Odessa. She was in her late seventies. She came out to the stage, accompanied with applause and said: "I am going to sing to you the romance "I remember being a young girl". There came a voice from the audience: "Damn it! What memory she has!""

It was the only joke he knew and he was telling it every day, sometimes several times a day.

When time passed he would not be satisfied with temporary earnings and stealing from the counters. He began to sell homemade moonshine, especially during the period of the unforgettable struggle with drinking and alcohol addiction. In 90s he and his saucy neighbor Klava learnt how to mix low-quality alcohol with coffee and made cognac drinks, vodka and other kind of mash and had it sold by his people at the market.

Why was Sema so successful at "Privoz"? It was because Sema "Damn it!" since childhood had been an information agent of the police officers at the market police division. It happened after he was caught while pocket stealing.

By the millennium Sema was a well-known agent with experience. It meant that Sema was reporting to the police all the information, he told on everyone, he told everything, including sex affairs. Actually, he was a big rascal, who would report on his own mother for money.

Agents have always existed: during monarchy, socialism, democracy. They would not disappear in case of the next riot. There is an opinion that during the time of the USSR people became agents of the department of the interior or of KGB mostly due to their political opinion. Nowadays all the relations exist on commercial grounds. Market relations. This is nonsense, as in this territory there have always been lots of superglasses, who appeared and multiplied, like wild weeds in the vegetable garden. They, like Pavlik Morozov, were ready to betray and slander on anyone around, including his or her own mother. There is one political opinion for those people, that is to shit, to put shit and make shit. Moreover, they were paid for that! By the way, the superglasses have always been paid, during all the times and any regime; it was just the accounting forms in the police that were different. Police officers have always pocketed part of the money meant for paying to agents. They diligently signed the documents for existing and non-existing agents. It could not be called earnings, but it was a good addition to earnings in case one has a well-established net of agents, that is superglasses.

Today's superglasses are persons of different occupations and different level of well-being. Actually, almost every officer has managers and deputy managers, chief accountants of different commercial enterprises, government firms and companies, as well as loaders and homeless persons as their agents. They have no that they are reporting on each other. Sure, there are some volunteers. However, it is usually enforcement and non-enforcement offices, that recruit agents. They just catch them for some violation of the law and give them a choice: either go behind the bars or become a paid agent. In the whole history of security services and the police there practically no records of those who refused to become an agent.

Besides, the benefits the superglasses have are, according to Senya "Damn it!", like those of elected deputies. They have their monthly payments and they also get bonuses for cracked cases. It is only in movies that cops and KGB officers crack crimes using modern technologies, deductive and other scientific methods. It is all bullshit. In all the times the best method of cracking crimes or preventing crimes was spying and reporting, it is the same now and it will be for more than a century. Modern technologies such as lie detector, which is considered to be a great device, is just a toothpick or a rubber stick with metal balls, or it can be compared to a gas mask, a strait-jacket, handcuffs and other simple torture devices, which seem to have traveled to us from the Middle Ages.

Beside his salary and bonuses an agent benefits a free trip for him and his family for a vacation, which is paid in the amount of a monthly salary. Of course, these benefits should be deserves. All superglasses have a monthly schedule. He is supposed to crack at least one crime. Some of them like "Damn it!" manage to crack two or even three cases. So, if someone thinks that planning has gone together with the words ending with "ism", he is deeply mistaken. Everything is very serious in enforcement structures, including planning the activity of a department, of an officer and of an agent.

If it is required by the current situation, an agent can be placed behind the bars with some fake documents, as it is needed for the investigation. For the "business trip" to jail they are paid additionally, including money for clothes, travel expenses, bonuses and food expenses. That is how it works!

Sema "Damn it!" managed to avoid the district "monkey-house" for all his indecent life at "Privoz" and in the area. A "monkey-house" is a cell for temporarily imprisoned, which can be found in each police division. In old good times when he was a youngster, an officer caught him while selling stolen goods. They had a talk. The officer appeared to be smart and far-sighted, an experienced one. He managed to see in that plain-looking and messy guy a real crook, ready and able to fulfill many great deeds at such a populated and motley place, like "Privoz" in Odessa.

The cop drove Sema to the country to the Rowing Canal area (not to be mixed up with sewage farms) and they had a drink on the government expense, had a snack and spoke their minds. Sema did not have any choice. He would not accept the opportunity to spend several years in a jail for minors. However, he was ready to report as diligently as a woodpecker knocked his head against wood. Sema was a diligent worker. He immediately reported on everyone who sold drugs and vodka at the market. He was given tasks to spy on the management of the market and check if they took bribes, if they gave bribes, if they sold stolen goods, etc. The volume of work was big and "Privoz" gave many opportunities. During the years of his activity "Damn it!" sent many store managers, several chief accountants to jail, to say nothing of those who sold gun shells, homemade vodka, moonshine and drugs. Sure, Sema was not the only agent at "Privoz". Almost every second middleman, loader, every butcher were somebody's superglasses, they just reported to different "firms" and cops.

Sema had figured out long ago that if homemade vodka and drugs were sold, it meant that it was necessary. He was an agent, but the money that could be collected additionally, should be collected. All the profit which was big, was going to the offices and then to the bosses, but some of the profit still stayed in the offices. Each had his own interest. Now "Damn it!" had one task – that is to watch for competitors. As soon as he notices an alien with vodka or drugs, not to mention foreign currency, Sema would report to cops. A whole new case is started, with mass media involved, with loud investigation and a court hearing. It was really very serious if one found a shop where homemade alcohol, cigarettes of drugs were produced. Consequently, there come bonuses, awards, other benefits. It is very important that no one would accidentally report on his own salespersons. He did everything to prevent that, but shit happens.

Time is changing, manages at "Privoz" are replaced, cops and police managers are changed, as well as the forms of property. However, the order of things stays the same. It is a system, which can hardly be changed!

- Are you sick? Maybe you are a rogue to name matches a cheesecake and to name lard a drug? Maybe you want to chat with consequences for your health? Go and push your head into manure before I pulled my fists out of my pockets! – Sema would always say those words to anyone who dares to criticize the ways at "Privoz".

If one makes a survey of the history of Odessa, he would see that it was monarchists, anarchists, communists, democrats and even UNA-UNSO and RUH that joined them or on the contrary, separated them, declared themselves the head of the city. There were also different leaders from the criminal world, starting with Benya Krik and up to the latest modern "brigade leaders". Today we should take into consideration local oligarchs and serious guys from enforcement structures, who joined them, who had strong big boys who drove Mercedes. There were also different Diasporas of Armenians, Chechens and other non-Ukrainian nationalists, mixed up with red managers, repainted into yellow and blue. Blue was becoming to them, as they were mostly gays. They say, in Odessa there are businessmen and entrepreneurs from middle-size and small business levels who speak both in local Duma and Supreme Rada with trepidation and hope of the future of the mother Ukraine. The same persons later make decisions that drown the so-called middle class in shit of laws, which the very same persons accept.

The main owners both in "Privoz" and in Odessa, as well as in Ukraine have always been, are and will be ordinary government officers, plain-looking, somewhat flabby-looking, with cheeks, swollen with too much drinking or excessive eating, with a stout belly, cunning eyes, false speeches and exorbitant appetite.

It has always been like this. Nowadays the word government officer is written not with a capital letter, but in capital letters. We used to say "Party" and mean "Lenin", to say "Lenin" and mean "Party". Now a GOVERNMENT OFFICER is Lenin, party, leader, teacher, czar and God – all in one. One should pay attention that about ten years ago district committees, party committees, municipal committees, regional committees of CPSU and other SU organizations were eliminated. However, not a single office has become vacant, not a single square meter. On the contrary, the number of government officers per a citizen has multiplied by many times. In our native city the situation is like everywhere, including the well-known "Privoz", which serves as a machine for squeezing legal and illegal money with the help of well-adjusted official levers. The machine functions in any situation. They just shovel the money and would not choke with it. There is no escape from those lustful hands, sweating and sticking. Those hands pick up everything that smells like dollars. There is no escape. Therefore, one can become superglasses or, if lucky, become a government officer. It is actually very hard, as the latter have their own relatives, children and so on.

Sema "Damn it!" with his education, primary, secondary and even higher, received at "Privoz", all in one, at the job site, understood that very clearly. He could determine at the first site, using his narrow swollen little eyes, who was who. He could tell who was slowly walking along the isles, how many dollars he had in his wallet, as in spite of more than ten years of experience he extracted foreign currency and other banknotes out of wallets, purses and pockets of absent-minded fools. He would explain to his supervisors that he did not want to lose his professional skills. They would also like to check in others' wallets, but God did not gift them and they were too posh and too lazy to learn.

Sema watched the construction of the buildings of "New Privoz" and it did not upset him. He realized that the process of the construction and of sales of "Privoz" was supposed to be long not due to the complications of the process of change of the owner. The reason was that one of them wanted to acquire the market as a private property for a cheap price and the others wanted to make good money on the deal. God knows, when they come to an agreement, which would satisfy everyone, that is the parties of the process.

The other thing he understood was that at any social formation and any ruling type of property the superglasses Sema "Damn it!" would be employed. After the owner of the firm, that was constructing "New Privoz" finally acquired "Privoz", everything at the market and around it would become clean. Palm and other exotic trees will be planted everywhere, fountains will be functioning, nice-looking salesperson with nice-looking and affordable goods will appear. Furthermore, Sema will be given a civil suit, like a tuxedo with a bow-tie, as the market will become a civilized one. Let it be! Maybe then we will look like gentlemen, at least from the outside, as inside nothing is going to change. As for Sema "Damn it!", he still remembers the moment in his life when the chief cop of "Privoz" said to him: "Work according to your specialization, Senya. Do not be scared of anything. Good luck."

To tell the truth, Senya was not scared of anything, but it was nice to see a cop who was after all a nice guy.

Soldiers

Semen Semenovich Korotich after being retired from the work in the heroic cops ranks. He had served for twenty years in criminal department. He also worked in the security department of the bank "Aval". The job was far from being the best, but they paid money and the shifts were 24 for hours, followed with 72 hours of rest. During the days when he was free of his shifts, Semen Semenych made some money as an intermediary. He got his interest for transferring lumber from Prikarpatye.

He left the service in the police on his own will. He was not able to work in current circumstances. Professional skills did not matter. The main thing was hypocrisy, lies, bootlicking, bribery and meanness. Those phenomena have always been in the police, but not in such scale and not so obvious. He quit, but he still cared about the situation in the police, as it was his passion.

- I used to be an executive officer and now I have become a guard. – He would sadly make a joke of it, when having a glass of vodka with his friends.

His wife, Irina, was employed by the administrative department of the army, in the air-raid corps. The daughter was lucky to get married to a Jew and she had been living in far-away Australia for five years. His son, Igorek, was serving in the army in a telecommunication regiment in Odessa suburbs. He served as a driver of a passenger UAZ car; he was the driver of the battalion commander. Igorek was diligent, he did not speak too much and he was not a gossip teller. He was also a good driver, as his father had taught him driving since childhood. Those were the reasons for the battalion commander to hire Igor Korotich as a driver. Moreover, in a while he began to trust him more than his own deputies. Igorek would not tell anyone about his work and about what he saw and heard. Everyone knew about that and the management did not feel awkward in his presence, treating him as a deaf and dumb, blind, which meant he was one they could trust.

Therefore, he did share his thoughts and observations with his father, who had always been a model of honor and conscious for him. He respected him not only as a father, but also as a real military officer.

- You see, father, the army is not the same as it used to be in your time, like your beloved police. There are no skilled professionals in the army any more; even among officers and generals, there are very few on them. I mix with them and I communicate with their drivers.

Korotich, the senior, would listen to his son's reasoning. The son came home on a Saturday, his battalion commander allowed him to stay at his parents' place for the night on Saturdays.

- The soldiers in our army are divided into the suppressed, the suppressors and the ones who commit reckless things. The suppressed are young people who are confident that they were born to suffer. They joined the army with this thought in their minds. Every soldier who is one year older, a sergeant, an officer has right to torture him, to beat him up for he had courage to notice that the officer was stealing his belongings, for having louses on, for itching or for not itching. He was constantly beaten up and oppressed for everything, because he was a suppressed person. It was also because all the ex-suppressed persons had power over him, and those were the cruelest suppressors.

By the way, father, the suppressed do not get one-third part of what the government gives them. Many are aware of that, including the suppressed themselves. They know and they keep silent. How do you like it, father?

Semen Semenovich listened to his son silently, then he made a glass of vodka for himself, drank it in silence and then lit a cigarette.

- Right you are, my son. The picture is not encouraging. Nevertheless, you keep calm; tolerate it. If there is something wrong, tell me and I will take care of it. Do not wind up yourself, control yourself.

The son smiled. – I understand, father, do not worry about me. However, it is an offence to the country. Why are the things like that? There are no signs of improvement in the army.

As far as the second category of the soldiers is concerned, those are the suppressors. They are people who experienced hardships in life, but they did not get discouraged. Therefore, they became cruel in their heart. They consider it fare if they make other people suffer as mush as they did.

The third category is small in quantity. Those are people who suffered and the suffering made them think that there was nothing illegal for them, there could be nothing worse than their suffering experience. For a desperate soldier there is nothing impossible and nothing sacred. He can steal from his own friend, he can rob a church and desert the army, he can murder his commanding officer and his fellow soldiers, if he does not like them, and he would never repent of his crimes. A desperate soldier despises everything and enjoys the life.

Therefore, there are no soldiers who would like to serve in the army for the sake of the motherland, due to the given oath, and nothing is going to change in this respect. In the army, father, the soldiers are hungry, hardly properly dressed and poor.

Semen Semenovich would agree with his son. He knew that in Odessa they called soldiers "beggars", as they would beg for a cigarette in the streets in the areas of military units, terminals and the hospital. He saw that and he would grin. He thought that in the independent army they helped soldiers to quit smoking, as they gave them neither cigarettes nor money. However, the people and the army are together, as soldiers go around the city begging for cigarettes, and people go around begging for a couple of coins.

Semen Semenovich's neighbor was employed in a store near a military hospital. Once she met him and told the following:

- They recently used to beg only for cigarettes, Semen Semenovich. Nowadays they demand alcohol. They say that if they did not bring alcohol to the senior soldiers, they would be torn apart, like toilet paper. I feel pity for them and give them my own moonshine. I understand that I am undermining their defense ability, but I feel pity for the kids, as they would be beaten up otherwise. My own children will join the army soon.

Those words came to Semen Semenovich's mind and he asked his son:

- Igorek, what about the officers? Are they not struggling with the illegal relations in the army? Are they not fighting disorders

The son laughed aloud.

- Father, are you sick? Do you think they need it? All the officers are also divided into categories in our army.

The first category is the officers due to circumstances. Those feel that they would not find any other employment; they are unable to get means for their own existence. Those people are trash.

The second category is the unemployed officers, who despise the essence of military service. Most of them are far from being a military person, except for their uniform.

The third category, which is the most numerous, is the officers who are at the same time crooks. They serve in the army for one purpose that is to steal as much as they could by any means. Those are people deprived of the concept of duty and honour, they do not want to care for well-being of all, they are people who compose a corporation of robbers, they help each other to steal money, property, food, weapons, ammunition, etc. If they have a chance, they betray each other with great pleasure. People of this category consider honest to be silly, the sense of duty – to be madness. They are poisoning young officers who have just graduated from a military school with the system of open greed and meanness.

My commander of the battalion is a Tatarian by nationality and he does not care for Ukraine with its independence. He has a container at the market on the seventh kilometre. Besides, his wife sells hotdogs and serves alcohol at the same place. They make sandwiches, some other snacks. They use the food from the battalion. I deliver the food from the battalion warehouse. They use technical alcohol for making vodka, cognac and sell those illegal drinks with great success.

The commander of the battalion enjoys special attitude on behalf of the chief commander, when compared with other commanding officers. The reason of this attitude is that the commander of the battalion personally manages the construction of the chief commander, father, that is of the general. Generals in the army compose a caste. To tell the truth, they are crooks, who have experienced all kinds of humiliation to some extent. They buy their ranks and positions, paying mostly with real estate or some amount of cash in US dollars. Generals would say that the fact that the soldiers are not properly dressed, fed and professionally trained in the army, is the result of bad financing of the army. However, there are no generals who would be badly equipped. The chief commander and his deputies got apartments in elite buildings in Arkadia, where the cost of one square meter is from 400 to 500 US dollars. I took part in delivery of furniture to the chief commander's apartment. Dad, he has a kitchen, which is bigger than the whole of our apartment. The furniture is of foreign make, by the way, which is not cheap. It is not a second-hand store furniture. Besides, the chief commander is construction a country cottage in Sauvignon behind Chernomorka. Not every businessperson can afford that. My commander of the battalion manages the construction and he has received a lot on the territory of the battalion as a payment for that job. He is construction a residential house for himself at the same time. It is of course, much smaller than the one of the chief commander, but the source of means for construction is the same. The chief commander overlooks that. The main thing for him is that the country house is being constructed rapidly. It is a three-storied house, with a sauna, a billiards room, an indoor pool and an outdoor pool as well, with beautiful summerhouses, paths made of beautiful tiles. Exotic trees have already been planted. There is also a fountain and, of course, there are sculptures of different animals in the garden. In the fountain there is a sculpture of dolphins. Everything is made of modern materials according to modern design. All the work was performed by groups of specialists, except helpers. All the work was paid for, and the money, as I understand, is not in small amounts.

Do, you think, Dad, that is fits into the modest salary of a general, which does not exceed one hundred and fifty dollars? Just count the number of double glass window units for the three levels. How much can they cost? The same issue is about the expensive decorating stone for the outside, expensive finishing materials for the inside.

A general like him would never think of alertness, combatant value of his unit. He would never stay awake at night thinking of making the living of soldiers better, of their uniforms and footwear. Dad, he has only one kind of thoughts in his mind, that is about stealing, selling, cheating, taking a bribe. All his energy is applied for that. The rest of the generals are of the same kind. By the way, this general has recently acquired a prestigious car of foreign make for himself, that is a Mercedes. While such generals are in the army, there would be no order there, the financing would be scares. There will be lack of professional skills, the atmosphere of suppression, illegal internal relations, meanness and corruption. Today any general in the army is to some extend is a thief.

Semen Semenovich couldn't restrain himself and laughed aloud:

- You should also add, like the personage from the movie "The meeting place cannot be changed", Gleb Zheglov, would say, that "a thief should stay behind the bars". Sorry, son, it's a sad story, but it is also our life. Neither of us can change anything.

The senior Korotich was under the impression of that conversation for a few more days. The most offense for him was that officers and generals in the army had completely lost the sense of dignity and honor of an officer. He had always imagined an officer of the army as an educated and intelligent person, balanced and honest. He was supposed to observe the code of honor of an officer in any conditions.

- No, it is not like this. The time has changed, and real officers and generals left the army. The same picture is in the police, in the government security services. However, there used to be real officers and generals there too.

In two days, Semen Semenovich was taken to hospital with a severe heart attack. He stayed hospitalized for a month, before he was allowed short walks. The hospital was located in Shevchenko Park. His spouse came to visit him. Once a week his son came to him. However, the mother strictly forbade the son to talk to his father of his service, as that could upset the latter.

Semen Semenovich, having spent a month in the hospital, was wondering himself about the life in the country, to which he belonged. He remembered the words from "The Internationale" – "We'll change henceforth the conditions and spurn the dust to win the prize".

- In Odessa they call "The Internationale" a hymn of impotent men – because of the first line, starting with the word "arise". Besides, mostly aged people sing it. To put it seriously, the old traditions had been spurned to dust during the latest fifteen years, especially moral principles. When there are no moral principles, nothing can be created. Where can there appear officers and generals with understanding of moral principles, if they are absent in the society? Is it only in the army that there are the suppressed and the suppressors? Is it only in the army that they steal and take bribes? It is only the lazy that do not steal in the country. For the officers of all ranks and all levels stealing and taking bribes is a full-time job, the main occupation during the business hours.

Semen Semenovich remembered that he had recently heard lyrics of a song over the radio. The music and the lyrics were composed by persons who preserved the honour and the consciousness; maybe they had that since birth. Those things could not be bought. If one loses them, they cannot be restored. They are absorbed into the blood with the milk of the mother. In that song they said that we were living in a country where honour and consciousness were outlawed, as well as people, who had preserved those qualities, were outlawed. Lies, hypocrisy, taking brines and stealing were honoured and considered to be normal.

- Those hypocrites, fools, thieves and crooks did not come to us by UFO, they are not aliens, they are all from the people. They are us, most of us. – Semen Semenovich concluded. – In our environment an honest man, who is able to blush when he is caught on a small lie, looks like an alien. It is so hard for an honest and decent person to live in this country among those people. It is fatal.

On December 06, Semen Semenovich walked out to Shevchenko Park. He saw a march of military men accompanied by the first persons of the region and city administration, as well as people's deputies of Ukraine. They took part in the ceremony of laying garlands to the monument of the Unknown sailor on the eleventh anniversary of the Armed Forces of Ukraine. Generals and officers who took part in the ceremony did not look poor. Neither did they look like thinking of the situation in the army. They were perfectly dressed, well trimmed, their faces were well fed and they were drunk. The government officers and the folks called "elite" did not look much different. They all played the assigned parts, which they knew by heart, in that badly directed show, the director of which was deprived of any skills and talent.

Semen Semenovich could not understand how the Unknown sailor was related to the anniversary of the Ukrainian army. He died during the Great Patriotic War in combats for the liberty of the Soviet motherland. He was in the Soviet army. How the Soviet army soldiers who died in combats with fascists, alongside with whom Ukrainian nationalists were fighting with yellow-and-blue flags and a trident on the cockade were related to the event? The ceremony was blasphemous, to Semen Semenovich's mind.

- I can understand if it were Victory Day or the day of liberation of Odessa, but it is the event of the Ukrainian army, and to come to this sacred place is at least unethical.

At night Semen Semenovich heard the same regular speeches about consistent low level of financing of the army, which was worse every other year. The situation influenced the combat ability of the army, its discipline and support of soldiers.

- Yes, it is like this! However, why "the consistent low level of financing" allows generals to buy the best cars of foreign make, to buy the best elite apartments, to construct super castles on the seaside, to wage a lifestyle of a successful businessperson, and have their salary of one thousand hryvnias per month? No doubt, those are the most talented crooks, who can skim the cream from shit. If the army is called "school of courage", "school of men", I should say that the course of this school is better to be taken by correspondence. It is a better opportunity to teach a soldier near a church, I can arrange it with the police officer. That was the conclusion, to which the retired police major came regarding military service of soldiers at the eleventh anniversary of Ukrainian army.

No Pain, All Gain

The signs of autumn could be felt everywhere. The late dawn was one of the signs; the sun rose at around 7 a.m. Besides, the difference between night and daytime temperature was getting bigger. Of course, there were yellow leaves, falling from trees. As far as people's outfit was concerned, some was still walking around in their short sleeves; one could meet women in summer frocks, but others would put on some warmer clothing. Autumn could also be felt in people's mood.

Zhorka was going home after his eight hours' dayshift. Georgiy Ivanovich was in his late fifties, but he looked younger. He used to say that he was "well-preserved". Maybe that was the reason for everyone at work and in his neighborhood, for his friends and acquaintances to call him just Zhorka. He did not mind. He did not want to age and he hated when somebody called him officially – Georgiy Ivanovich. At old good time, when he could afford going once a year to a resort for a vacation, he would introduce himself as Zhora from Odessa.

Zhorka was Odessa born and bread, he even was not able to tell how many generations of his ancestors were Odessa born and bread. Zhorka was born neither in Moldavanka, nor in Peresyp. He was born in the very heart of Odessa, in Deribassovskaya Street. Moreover, Zhorka was proud of the fact that they lived at the address 1 Deribassovskaya Street. He spent his childhood in that neat-looking building. It was the residents who trimmed the neighborhood themselves. In the center of the front yard there was a beautiful chestnut tree. There were neat benches in its shade. Along the building there grew flowers in flowerbeds. Grapes were waving all over the walls. In the corner of the yard there was a playground for children. Most of the residents of the buildings were Odessa native people who were mostly employed or were somehow connected with the Black Sea Steamship Line, which had the main office in the area.

Zhorka spent all the summer time at his favorite beach Lonzheron. Later at night he would go to dancing in Shevchenko park together with his friends. The life was raging there. Zhorka had loved to go to the sea terminal since childhood. He would come there early in the morning, running quickly down Potemkinskaya Staircase. At the sea terminal he would walk slowly, looking at the sea, at the exit from the harbor, at the lighthouse. He liked to examine the ships at the berth. He especially liked snow-white cruise liners. They were of different kinds and did not look alike: Belorussiya, Shota Rustavelli, Ivan Franko, Admiral Nakhimov, Fedor Shalyapin and others.

Zhorka looked at the seamen, who were free to go up to the ships and come back to the shore. He felt his heart sinking. He would dream that some day he would become a member of the crew of one of those liners.

After all, his dream had become true. He graduated from one of Odessa sea schools and became a sailor. To be exact, he became a cook on one of passenger liners. First it was "Armenia". Then he was transferred to the motor ship "Lev Tolstoi" and stayed there for twenty years.

The years passed by. The situation in the city gradually changed. People were changing. Even the power underwent changes. The natural environment in Odessa also seemed to be changing. At the century line Odessa was not the same as Zhora used to know. Communists were no longer in power; the steamship line, once famous, no longer exited either. It stopped functioning gradually, without any loud scandals. "On the sly", as Zhora used to say, three hundred liners at practically no cost for the government were distributed to offshore zones. Their names were changed and they were functioning under different flags. Mass media used to talk about long-term litigation of one of Bulgarian companies. The item in question was a towboat. Zhora found the towboat story funny, as no one ever raised a question of the disappearance of three hundred first-class ships of the former Black Sea fleet.

As for Zhorka himself, he had been discharged from the ship for about a decade and was employed in one of the restaurants in the center of Odessa. He enjoyed respect for his professional skills and personal qualities. He did not live in Deribasovksaya Steet any more. His children grew up and he had to split his apartment. Zhorka and his wife were residing in a small one-bedroom apartment on the fourth floor of a Stalin-style apartment building in Petra Velikogo Street. To be precise, the new government renamed it to Dvoryanskaya Street.

Zhorka did not quite like the neighborhood and the residents of the neighborhood. The sidewalks leading to the entrance were broken, the trees were crooked and looked as if they were falling. One of the parts of the entrance gate went off; it was laid at the side. The yard pavement was broken, garbage was everywhere. The janitor cleaned up the yard only on the eve of big holidays. The entrance door was old, almost rotten and needed to be changed. The entrance area was dirty; the walls shabby and full of graffiti inscriptions; the window glass at the staircase was broken. The roof of the building was not renovated since the time it was initially installed; it was full of holes, like a sieve. The leaking roof kept the walls wet. There was practically no electrical light on the way to the building, at the entrance and at the stairs. It used to exist, but everything that could be stolen was gradually stolen. The electrical lamp sockets, switches and bulbs were torn out by the root.

But Zhorka was satisfied as the area was in the center of Odessa; it was a quiet street and it was not far from his favorite Deribasovskaya. With all his natural energy he began to put the area into order, as during decades of the service in the sea he got used to keep everything clean and in order. It hurt him to watch Odessa gradually turning into a garbage place. He gathered all the residents of the building at the front yard and made them feel ashamed for keeping the building in dirt. He called everyone to contribute to cleaning up the area.

- One cannot live like this! Let us raise some money and renovate the staircases areas, let us fix the pavement in the yard, let us plant some flowers, install benches and light up the area. There is much work to do. You will enjoy the changes and you will feel much better.

- Come on, - One of the residents became mad. Obviously, he was retired, he had service ribbons on his jacket. – Can you imagine how much it could cost? We have property management for that. Come on, you, activist. – He pronounced that, turned his back and went away.

Two old women said that there were many guys walking around and collecting money and left as well, contributing nothing. Therefore, a guy with a Jewish-style expression came up and said: - My name is Sasha.

- I am Zhora!

- You are wasting your time trying to persuade them. Can't you see what kind of people live here? The are all new. The people who used to live here are no better. It is my opinion that people should choose their residence according to their interests or financial situation. Then everything would be good. As for these devils, they are satisfied with their living in the shit. They are used to it; they think it normal. The guys like us are supposed to live with people like ourselves, where order, cleanness, respect to each other reign. But it is just an ideal project. In real life we have to share the same shit with this folk, as you can see. Therefore, I am going to support your initiative.

They decided to start with the renovation of the entrance gate. Then came electrical work and pavement in the yard.

In a while they managed to find skilled guys who did not charge much and renovated the gate. They also fixed electricity in front of the building, in the yard and at the stairs. In a month Zhorka and Sasha ordered new front door in the shops, which used to belong to the sea line management. Luckily, the manager of the shops used to work as a senior mechanic on board "Lev Tolsoti". In a couple of days they had new door at the front entrance. They also installed a code lock on it. After they had fixed the pavement in the yard with the help of the same skilled guys, Sasha decided to collect the money from the residents of the apartments.

- We are not on a mission; nor we are millionaires. Let them pay as much as they can afford. Let them pay at least ten hryvnias each.

But they failed to collect at least ten hryvnias from each apartment. In one part of the building it was just two apartments, which paid ten hryvnias each; in the other part there was none.

- You are to understand, - Sasha was telling Zhora, who was really mad. – Most of the people are people who like to live free of charge. You know, what it means. They are used to get everything for free. In their understanding, if there is no light at the stairs, if there is no water, if something else is missing, it is the property management that is supposed to fix it. If no one cleans up the stairs, if there is dirt and smell, they would rather pass by in silence, stepping on the dirt, but they would never clean it up. They would not even bother to call to the management.

Someone else is supposed to do this for them. They have lived like this for ages, giving birth and raising creatures like themselves. Why, do you think, during the war the Germans called us "rusish shvain", which means Russian swine? It was because they watched our lifestyle, which is, in fact, pig-like. There were the ages of cybernetics and technical progress, but in household life the relations have remained the same, pig-like.

Zhorka listened to Sasha attentively, without interrupting him. The latter became more and more excited.

- Look at me. I am half Jewish. As they say here in Odessa, almost Jewish. But we wage the same style of life. I visited some apartments from which Jewish people had just moved out. I was then looking for an apartment. They had moved out, but the smell remained. It is their specific disgusting stuffy smell, which is hard to get rid off, as it was there for years. Can you imagine the condition of the apartment? It is really awful and disgusting! And these people always presumptuous: we, the Jews, are the best! Damn them! They are the same piece of shit, sorry for my wording.

Zhorka couldn't help bursting out loud. – Sasha, you've gone too far. You see the world in dark colors. We have done a good thing and we feel satisfaction. This is a good thing too.

When returning home after his shift, Zhorka was thinking about the current life, about the relations in the neighborhood, about the situation in Odessa.

- Sasha was right, those people want everything for free. They trimmed and cleaned the yard and the staircases. Did anyone say thanks to them? No one did. It's OK; they did what they considered right. I have been changing the burnt bulbs at the staircase, in the yard, at the yard gate for a year. If I don't do that, no one would.

Once Zhorka just decided to check, if there is a singe conscious person among the residents of the building or in the property management. Maybe there was someone with ambitions, he thought. There were several burnt bulbs at a time. At night it was really very dark in the front yard, at the stair on the ground floor. It lasted for a week. It was dark and many were scared of the darkness. People stumbled in the dark, swore badly, using the nastiest wording. But there was no one who would change the burnt bulb. It was Zhorka's patience that was exhausted. He gave up his experiment and changed the bulbs. His neighbor met him and asked if he were a millionaire: - You will get bankrupt spending so much on the bulbs.

- I will not get bankrupt or rich because of that. But I would not live in a stinky pigsty with no light in it. I would not let anyone to foul where I live. – Zhorka answered him bluntly.

He felt tears in his eyes when he thought about his old neighborhood in Deribassovskaya Street, which had the real spirit of Odessa.

- Oh, my God! We did live a good life! We mixed with decent people. They were kind-hearted and caring; they also had good sense of humor! Those were real residents of Odessa! They moved away. The life spread them all over the world.

Sasha and himself had an appointment with on of Deputy Mayors, who was an old acquaintance of theirs. They managed to make a major renovation of the roof with his help. After they had renovated the roof, they raised the question of painting the ceiling and the walls at the staircase. Once again they encountered the strong wall of indifference on behalf of the majority of the building residents.

Zhorka grinned when he thought of his attempt to make a schedule of cleaning the staircase. He knocked to each door and said that he was going to place a schedule for cleaning on the wall. If it was your turn, you are supposed to clean the common area yourself or to hire a cleaner. It was up to you. Therefore, there was no one who would clean or hire a cleaner.

- It is the problem of the property management. There should be a position of a cleaner. Let them deal with it. The staircases were still dirty. Zhorka could not stand that. – I am not going to lose my crown. – He would say and would clean up all the four floors once a week. No one supported him and no one said thanks to him. People did not care. Moreover, in a few hours after cleaning the staircases had cigarette butts, candy covers; people also spit and blew their noses at the stairs. Zhorka saw that and got mad. He would shout so that everyone on all the floors would hear: "Bustards! I will catch you and do away with you!"

After having lived in the building for one winter, Zhorka and his wife understood, that the heat in the apartment could be maintained only with the help of an electrical heater. The water heating system was too ancient. The tubes were dirty from the inside. In the next buildings the central heating radiators were hot and one couldn't even touch them. In their building they were hardly warm. They made regular payments for the heating. Zhorka and Sasha wrote a letter to the central heating systems office and to the prosecutor's office on behalf of the residents, but most of the residents refused to sign it. But when they came to know that Zhorka and Sasha got a discount for heating as much as fifty percent, they began to ask them to give a tip how to get a discount for themselves.

Zhorka knew that most of the neighbors were using electrical heaters during the cold time of the year. To pay less, they adjusted their electrical meters manually.

There were many ways of adjustment of electrical meters, people invented them.

Zhorka would often think: "Is it possible that in the West, in developed countries the government would deceive people like this or people would deceive the government, in their turn? Or is this just our phenomenon?"

A recent event came to his mind. It was an event at Deribassovskaya Street not long ago. Several companies organized free treat for residents of Odessa. Some companies provided beer, others provided snacks. One should see the event with his own eyes! There were crowds of people of different ages, gender, political and religious denominations. They pushed each other in lines for free beer and snacks. They were extremely happy when they got a couple of bottles of beer for free or a couple of hot sausages.

Zhorka thought: - It has been the lifestyle of the majority of our population for ages. Government does not like individuals like Sasha and myself. We always demand something. As far as the rest are concerned, they do not disturb the authorities, they let them alone. They do steal here and there from time to time, and that's it. We steal from them, they steal from us. This is how the government treats people and people treat with the government.

Zhorka was deep in his sad thoughts when he was coming back home to Dvoryanskaya Street.

- There are no noble people in Dvoryanskaya (Nobleman) Street. Odessa has turned to be the city of slaves. – Zhorka came to a conclusion when he was entering the dark front yard. The bulbs were burnt, as usually...

So-Called Independence

On Friday, August 23, Petrov came to the municipal department of transport to meet his bosom friend Andrey Stoyanov. They had been good friends since childhood. Being little boys from Moldavanka, they would run across the gardens of Usatyi and Nerubayskiy. Their route also lay across Slobodka. They would hear an alarm: "They beat our guys!" and would rush to Deribasovskaya to defeat Malamskiy people as quickly as possible. Besides, they would look with envy at cadets and naval depot sailors, returned from the sea, and would chase about Peresyp after the local girls.

Many decades had passed since then. The fate separated them and they found themselves in different parts of the Union, which used to be a mighty state. After the country split, the friends met again in their native city. Aged, with grey hair, bold and experienced in life, they were still as energetic as they used to be in Odessa in their youth.

After the graduation from Odessa Police School, Petrov had served all his adult life in the ranks of Department of the Interior in the Far East. At the present time, he managed a law office and his business was prospering. Thank God, old friends, employed in Odessa police, helped to establish the business and were still helping with referrals, advice and practical assistance. To put it in a simple way, local cops were supervising and protecting Petrov.

As far as Andrey Stoyanov is concerned, he graduated from the "Higher", as Odessa Higher Engineering Sea School was called at that time. After the graduation, he had worked as a senior mechanic on a dry

293

cargo ship of the Black Sea fleet for two decades. At the present time, he was employed as a regular officer in the transportation department.

Petrov visited Stoyanov in order to invite the latter to his summer cottage for the weekend. His cottage was a Sukhoi Liman. He wanted them just to stay outside, to make barbeque and chat. It was a long weekend because of the Independence Day, and the coming Monday was a day off.

- What are they doing? Damn it. During the Soviet rule there were so numerous. Now they are still more numerous, including state, religious, political party holidays, devil knows what other holidays. People do not know those holidays and never celebrate them. However, they also do not work on those days.

Transportation department was located in an old 2-storeyed building on the first floor. The building was right behind the book market at Grecheskaya square, behind "Knizhka", as everyone called it. The market was like an eyesore for the municipal management department. It was quite close to the windows and the door and blocked the sunlight for the office windows. Besides, it blocked the access of fresh air. The folks walking at the market were far from being intelligent. "Knizhka" would have been moved to another location if it were just the books they were selling there. For more than ten years, "Knizhka" was dealing with currency exchange. Actually, it was an illegal market. The first thing one sees when approaching "Knizhka" is not the books, which are a lot there. It is the salespersons behind the counters, holding big packs of money in hryvnias, of different denominations, starting from 1 hryvnia and up to 200 hryvnias bills. There are enough banks and exchange booths in the city. However, the black market is located in the center of the city. Petrov was sure it would exist further, as it is protected by enforcement bosses from two administrative buildings at Evreiskaya.

- Stoyanov would rather work at "Knizhka" and not as an officer with his salary as small as three hundred hryvnias plus some miserable donations from the municipal transit routes owners. The latter could donate and could miss donations. However, as an officer he felt important. Damn, it has been our problem for ages. - Petrov thought entering a small office where his friend was working.

- Hi, Andrey. – He squeezed Stoyanov's hand. The latter did not have time to rise on his feet.

- Do not bother standing up, keep rubbing your pants against the chair. – Petrov was joking.

- Sasha, do not interfere with my work, - Stoyanov said tiredly. – Stick to the point, I have much work to be done today.

- What is going on? Is it a deadline coming?

- You see, tomorrow there will be a demonstration in the city due to the Independence Day. At 9 a.m. columns of marchers will move from the Opera house to Shevchenko Park, and there they will hold a meeting. The Mayor and his deputies will be in the front row. Every district is ordered to have its own column. They made it obligatory for the budget sector employees, such as medical doctors, teachers, maintenance workers and students to attend the demonstration. We are to provide their transportation from their districts to the center of the city by buses. This is what I am doing right now. I am making the owners of the routes to give the buses for free as nobody is going to pay them. The owners grudge, but provide the buses. They know they would not profit if they argue with the government.

Petrov was sincerely surprised. – Really? Forcing to march again? Demonstrations like before?

- Yes, my dear, but the conditions are different. If you don't show up, they will fire you. Students who miss the march can be excluded from the University.

Petrov grinned. – Our people are a crowd of cowards, just faint-hearted, sorry about that. OK, it's up to them. They get what they deserve, so to say. I, Andryusha, will pick you up tomorrow morning and we will go to my summer cottage. You'll relax at my place for a couple of days. We are going to chat, have some wine, make barbeque and cook fish soup. My garden is just gorgeous.

- No, Sashko, I cannot make it. Tomorrow I am working. I am responsible for the demonstration to go smoothly.

Petrov was surprised. – Are you kidding? Will they pay you for that? They won't!

Stoyanov agreed, nodding.

- What the hell?

- I have told you I cannot make it. This is it. Don't interfere with my work. – Andrey picked up the phone and began dialing the number of the next bus terminal.

Petrov looked at him attentively. He rose to his feet and asked him at the door: - Where can I find you tomorrow morning?

- Near the Opera House at 9 a.m. You can come. By the way, an alternative demonstration of communists is gathering at that location. They call them left parties.

In an hour Petrov was at home. He sat down in an armchair and thought. He was thinking about the Independence Day, which was the next day. He could not understand and no one could explain to him, what kind of holiday it was. On August 24, 1991, the Supreme Council declared the independence of Ukraine. Independence of what? Relief of Moscow dictatorship? However, there used to be as many Ukrainian officials in Moscow, as Russian ones. Relief from Russian influence? However, the Russian people suffered as much as Ukrainian did. Petrov watched their life during his service in the Far East. Petrov would understand in they declared self-dependence, but not independence. However, no matter what the name of the holiday is, it has the status of a government holiday. However, the people are not likely to celebrate it.

Again, there is pushing for the demonstration. No wonder, as the Mayor is a former communist leader. There is no way for a new kind of mentality to emerge, not to say anything about a new style of ruling.

Petrov wondered what was going to happen the next day, and he decided to go to the Opera House site and watch the events with his own eyes.

The next day he was at the site at 8.50 a.m. Petrov was not wearing his holiday outfit. He was in his jeans suit and snickers. He was strolling back and forth near the theatre. He watched the buses with the marchers arrive. Flags and posters were delivered.

- Yes, everything is as it used to be.

Petrov did notice that the moods of the folks who arrived for the march was far from being high. There was no spirit of fervor, joy, laughter and merriment.

At about 9 a.m. the municipal bosses walked up from the municipal council office building. They had a talk with those responsible for the demonstration. Then they took their place at the head of the marching columns. The demonstration started. The officials on duty were running along the columns and regulated the movement and the order. There was much fuss. Petrov noticed Andrey Stoyanov at the beginning of the column beside the leaders. Petrov approached him for just a few minutes. He greeted him and the Mayor with the holiday. The Mayor's expression was gorgeous and solemn.

- His place is on the stage. – Petrov thought. He almost laughed aloud, but restrained himself. He was eager to ask the Mayor about his attitude to the alternative demonstration of the left-handed parties. He wondered who would follow the Mayor in case there was not obligatory attendance for the budget officers. Petrov arranged with Andrey that he would call him as soon as he was available. Then he walked slowly back to Deribasovskaya. There he dropped in a café and ordered coffee. He was deep in thoughts.

What is a demonstration? It is an action of demonstrating something, like strength and talent, happiness and joy, pride for something, etc. He wondered if there was anything to be proud of or to be joyful with. People used to live from payday to payday. Now they live in the current day and did not think about the future. There are lies and hypocrisy on behalf of the ruling classed, likewise is the situation with the ordinary people. In the kitchen, behind the curtain they swear the authorities of all the levels. No one expresses the opinion openly. On the contrary, they try to please the officials and obey them silently in everyday life.

No doubt, the Mayor and all the government officers, including the lowest levels, are content with the life, as none of them has salary as the only income. They get several salaries from different companies. Besides, they have cash back payments and shameless bribes in other forms. The highest authorities of municipal and district levels have their own businesses, usually more than one. Most of them have their shares in other companies. They have accounts in banks. They do not keep their savings in glass jars, but they have cash in dollars in safe places in their country cottages. The amounts are just huge, as they say. They have something to be proud of, something that needs to be secured. However, they also have problems. In every day life they have to play the part of the caring "fathers" of the city. They have to look modest and nice. They have to conceal their assets. They actually do not care for people. They do not care for Odessa. For most of them Odessa is not their home city. It is just a part of their image; they have different lifestyle and different affection. For them Odessa is a place for enrichment and gaining power. Once they are deprived of the power, they are sure to move away from Odessa.

Petrov felt pity for his native city, which he loved so much. It was not the democrats, nor the current Mayor, nor the previous one who drove Odessa to the shabby condition as it currently was. Each of them contributed to that. It was being destroyed from the inside and the outside for a few decades. It came to Petrov's mind that at the end of the eighties his friends from Primorskiy region visited Odessa. He would have praised his home city before. After they came back to Vladivostok, they told him that they had an impression that Odessa had just been the front line. It was as if there was a devastating war there. Petrov did see that by himself, but was reluctant to admit that. He returned to Odessa in nineties, he found it had faded. He was shocked with the shabbiness of the buildings, parks, and the stadium of the Black Sea Port, the beaches, streets, and other places. He was shocked not just with the outside dirt. He was struck with the changes that occurred inside the people. Their humor became rude and unfriendly. Boorishness at the market places, at his favorite Privoz shocked him. Most of the natives had left; persons far from being good replaced them. They were seeking a better life; they were crooks and adventurers, bandits and robbers, differently disguised and baring different party membership cards. He was shocked that even those Odessa residents, who stayed in the city, got accustomed to the disgusting lifestyle, to the illegal rules, that had settled in the city.

To tell the truth, Petrov tried to be unbiased. Thirty years of police service developed his analytical skills. He did see some progress that had taken place in the latest ten years. It was developed market, full of both food and consumers goods of high quality. It was the open borders and the possibility to run one's own private business. There were some other positive things. There were numerous private restaurants, cafes, bars, casinos and other entertainment facilities in Odessa. The district of Arcadia looked like one of a fairy tale during summer months.

New modern stores appeared; there were exhibitions open all the year round. The city did gradually change, no matter one wanted to see the changes or not. However, those changes were so petty when compared with the regress of moral principles in relations between people. It influences the inside atmosphere of Odessa. It was hard to restore former decency. It would take a long period, if it could be restored at all.

Petrov would always ask himself: "Why after the fall of the soviet power the stream of Jews fleeing from Odessa considerable increased, in spite of the new opportunities to run a business, when one's party, gender and ethnic denomination did not matter any more?"

He answered his own question: "It is because they understood earlier than others that the ship had a crack and was going to sink! It was impossible to create anything positive in that country, in that city, with people like that. They failed to build socialism and communism. They are sure to fail building capitalism".

Petrov finished his coffee, paid for it and headed to the Opera House again. He was impatient to watch the situation and to hear what the opposing forces were speaking about. It was around 10 a.m. It was sunny and warm. He crossed the intersection of Deribasovskaya and Rishelyevskaya. Petrov saw a small column, stretching from the intersection to the theatre. There were multi-colored banners and posters.

A tall colonel in a camouflage uniform was standing at the head of the column. He was holding a red flag. He was in his early sixties.

- He must be retired. – Petrov thought. He noticed that there were many retired military men in the column. They had a special military bearing. Their faces were also typical, and Petrov could distinguish that. Those were mostly aged persons. Their slogans were short, fit for one transparent. Right behind the red banner there was the inscription: "6 years of Kuchma's constitution, which is a nationalistic grip-vice on the throat of the Ukrainian people!" The other slogan ran: "Whose holiday is this? This is a holiday of the bourgeoisie and the parasites."

Beside the column they were delivering the communist newspaper "The Truth of the Black Sea region" and different leaflets. Petrov came up to one of the distributors and took a package. Standing at the side, he opened the newspaper. He found nothing new there, and he came to a conclusion that Lenin's ancestors were zero. What could they be, if in a small four-page newspaper on page was taken by a TV listing. The leaflet was of the same value. The articles of the soviet constitution were compared to the constitution of independent Ukraine. It ran that the current constitution was providing expensive but primitive education, whereas earlier one could get any kind of education for free.

Petrov felt mad. – "I would like to talk to the author. Let him explain to me, how much one had to pay to get into medical University, of the University of people's economy, or in another popular University! Talented and diligent persons were not able to be enrolled and study free of charge; neither can they now. Lazy-bones and untalented student used to pay and are paying now. The difference is just the rate."

Petrov turned his back and headed for home. At the intersection, therefore, at the beginning of the column, an old man and a woman approached him. They were importunate. They were in their eighties. They stood at the corner delivering newspapers and leaflets. They looked like two dandelions.

- Take a newspaper and a leaflet, young man. – The old woman literally grabbed Petrov by the arm. He released himself abruptly.

- You don't have shame! Take one! – The old woman began to cry out loud. The passers-by paid attention to them. Petrov got mad. He was sick and tired of the morning comedy. It was a farce of one group of. comedians in power, which was replaced by another farce of other comedians, deprived of the power, but striving for it. He saw functioning officers of a new communist party, fussing around the column of old men and women. They had Versace suits on. Their faces were so familiar because they were the same as the faces of former Komsomol and Party secretaries. For sure, they were not coming from hungry and miserable strata.

- Look here, old woman, do not push me to take this waste paper. I do not need it. You'd better put it to a recycle bin; at least you will get a loaf of bread for that. There should be at least some use of this garbage, historical garbage. Are you being paid for this?

Petrov would no longer restrain himself; he was outraged.

- Look here, you blessed dandelions. Do you have children? You do, old woman. What about grandchildren? I think they are multiplying. Where are your ancestors now? Why aren't they here? They should be here instead of you. Your place is your home; your occupation is having a rest. Your children and grandchildren should support you. Where are the children and grandchildren of this old man with the newspapers? Where are the children of that retired colonel, the one standing under the banner? They either sell stuff at a black market or drink alcohol and party. Maybe, there are drug addicts, bad ones. What are they doing?

Petrov made a pause. No one argued with him. The passers-by stopped and watched the scene. They were wondering what would be the outcome.

- You failed to establish an order in your families. You failed to implant Leninism ideas in them. Now you get to the tribunes and try to get power. Are you able to have any gains, if you and people like you were given power? You are not. It would be a situation still worse than we have now, as you are not capable and lazy. You didn't even bother to read Lenin's books, you do not know them. Go and work with people. Do not go in for populism and cheap demonstrations. The first went out for the demonstration fearing the authorities. You went out for money. Did they pay you five hryvnias? Or maybe more?

The crowd was silent. Petrov spit madly and threw his newspaper and the leaflet to the garbage bin. He quickly walked away for home. His moods were completely spoilt.

Moral Principles and Manners

Tomorrow morning Georgiy Pavlovskiy is leaving to Moscow by air. He has been living there in Kutsevo District for four years. He has a beloved wife and children there. Even his mother-in-law is close to him. He loves his job; he has interesting projects, big plans and opportunities.

He seemed to have everything: money, position in the society, love. Therefore, he felt there was something that was missing. His heart would often ache. That something was Odessa. He began to understand this right there, in Odessa, during his short-term trip. He attended the celebration of the city anniversary day, he breathed in the air of his native city, he plunged into the rhythm of Odessa, he met his friends and his true love of the University years.

Those were unforgettable University years. He was Dasha's first man; she was his first woman. All the men of the University wanted to make love with her. She chose him. Dasha had already been married to a millionaire from an Arabic country. All of a sudden she and returned to Odessa.

Gosha loved Dasha for her beauty and passion. Besides, there was something else that united them. They were close to each other not only in a physical way, but also spiritually. They thought and spoke in the same way. He did not ask her about the reasons for her divorce. Neither had he asked about her current life. She did not ask about his life in Moscow. They spent those days mostly in bed. They made love and discussed life in Odessa. They met friends and walked around the city. They even managed to have a few hours' fishing trip to Dniestr.

Gosha liked Darya's country cottage. It was a beautiful detached house at the high-raised shore in Chernomorka. They called the place "Sauvignon". Rich people seemed to be residing in that area. There were no poor people there. The lot around the house was well taken care of. There was a nice small lawn and many flowers. Dasha lived alone, together with a cat, a dog, security officers and the housekeeper.

Dasha let her housekeepers go for a few days. Therefore, they were alone in the house. She was making coffee in the kitchen.

- Coffee is ready. Get up, you lazybones. – Dasha said, entering the bedroom. – Maybe you want coffee to be served in bed?

- No, my dear, I am getting up.

Gosha got up, freshened himself up and in a few minutes they were having coffee in a cosy living room.

Could you please tell me what business are you running now? What kind of life do intellectual people in Russia have? Is the situation the same as here? Have they become the servants of the authorities? I cannot believe it. Moscow has always been ahead. Even the weather forecast showed that if it became warmer in Moscow, we would be having the same warmth in three days. If it became colder there, it would become colder in Odessa in a few days as well.

Gosha laughed: - How can you see the connection here too. As for my business, I am working at an economic project "Ten years of privatization in Russia – pro and con". In a few months we'll have a TV show with the same name. As far as the intelligent people and the society in Russia are concerned, - Gosha stopped talking and became thoughtful.

- I will tell you a story. It happened about a month ago in Yasnaya Polyana. It depicts the state of the cultural inheritance in Russia very vividly. – He said to Dasha a minute later.

She smoked, waiting for his story. She was interested.

- This year is the year of 140th anniversary of the marriage between Lev Nikolayevich Tolstoy and Sofia Andreevna Bers. It is not a good round figure. Therefore, 80 ancestors of Lev Tolstoy gathered in Yasnaya Polyana. For a whole week they were celebrating the occasion. The youngest of them was three, I think, and the eldest woman was 87.

If we check the historical dates, Tolstoy had lived with his spouse for 48 years. They had as many as 13 children. Five of them died for different reasons in their early childhood.

What life did they have Many historical scientists and bibliographers tried to answer this question. Lev Nikolayevich himself would write in his memoirs that first his life looked like a fairy tale. I think that every couple feels the same, do you agree with me, Dasha? Most of the people say that the first month and years of their married life resemble paradise. Later... - Gosha stopped. – Let us go back to Tolstoy. During the last years of the writer's life they had deep conflicts. After she buried her husband Sofia Andreevna honestly admitted that she did not see any point in living without Lev Nikolayevich. The witnesses stated that she was a difficult person to live with.

A great-great granddaughter of the writer invited me to Yasnaya Polyana. I attended the event. You must know her. She is a TV show performer; she is one of the most famous TV show persons in Russian TV. To tell the truth, I would not want her to be a host in my show. However, I have another point. Her invitation interested me and the next day I wrote a draft variant of my script about the meeting of the ancestors of the great writer. A couple of days later I was in the family estate of the Count Tolstoy, accompanied by a shooting team.

I must confess to you, Dasha, that I have seen many beautiful and great things in my life. I also saw trash of different kinds. There is little left that could surprise me. The things I saw and heard there struck me in my heart.

It was a Russian village... It looked like a regular village with its almost destroyed and lop-sided houses and fences. Everything was messy; washrooms were old shabby constructions in the vegetable gardens, which demonstrated the ass of the visitor through big chinks. The picture could be seen at a long distance. Men were drunk and messy; women were gloomy. They wore dirty clothes. During the celebration, many of them put on their best clothes, as it was not every day that Tolstoy's relatives visited the place.

The celebration lasted for two days. The ancestors of the great writer were taking a complete relaxation program in Yasnaya Polyana. It was the Russian genes, which were working. There is no way one could stop the inheritance influencing the ancestors. Actually, almost none of Tolstoy's relatives who arrived from overseas, could not communicate in Russian, which was the language of their grandfather. It was a great language, which they considered to be a native one. I think it was just one grandnephew who spoke the language. Those people drank vodka in 40 degrees heat, no matter what gender and age they were, in quantities that were too big even for country peasants.

As early as by the lunch time everyone was not slightly drunk, but as they call it in Russia, Blind drunk. Most of them were soaking in the pond or sleeping in the bushes.

I found out that practically none of the Tolstoys who lived overseas had never read Lev Tolstoy's books, the books of their grandfather. When I asked him how it could be, they would answer: This is not the main thing in our life. What matters is that we are real Tolstoys in soul and blood.

As for the peasants from Yasnaya Polyana, they watched the heir of the writer having fun and enjoying themselves. They would share their sincere thoughts with me: "Our grandmothers were fools. They could have had sex with Tolstoy! In that case, we would be celebrating with them. We would have been served free vodka. We would have a life like theirs…"

On one of the celebration days the relatives were taken to Tula gallery "Yasnaya Polyana". They were attending the opening ceremony of the exhibition "Art traditions in Tolstoy's family". One should witness that. You can imagine persons who were driven in a hangover condition. On their way they became travelsick. They were two hours late for the ceremony. They got acquainted with the exposition as quickly as in half an hour. They were nervous while waiting for the party. Some of them were so impatient that they went out to the gallery backyard to drink a glass or two. The tables were being laid.

It was only one old lady, a "divine dandelion" from Sweden, aged 87, who got acquainted with all the exposition. She, unlike the others, listened to the greeting speeches, though she could not distinguish a single word, as she did not understand Russian at all.

The tables were being laid under the direct supervision of the organizer of the meeting of that crowd. It is hard to use another word. The main producer of the program was the manager of the museum "Yasnaya Polyana" Vladimir Ilyich Tolstoy. The moment the relatives were seated at table, their faces changed. They began to smile. Everyone began to express his gratitude to the organizer of the drinking party. The bottles of our vodka of Russian make were getting empty one after another.

One of the obligatory events of the celebration was a masquerade in the estate Yasnaya Polyana. If one watched the crowd from the distance, he could think that the participants were ran-away asylum patients.

Women were disguised in fancy animals' costumes. Men wore women's dresses. The main personage at the ball was the daughter of the manager of the museum. She made a speech in a perfect English language and she was the main entertainer and the queen of the ball. It was my understanding that his purpose was to seduce one of the relatives who had come from overseas. She had a good figure and she could be called a Russian beauty with some salt...

- You are sure to stick to her, you miserable Do Juan, - Dasha said, laughing. – I know you would not miss her. I just don't believe you would.

- To tell the truth, I really thought of it and even took some steps. The thing is that they all had something in mind; I mean the Russian half of the relatives. The others did not care; they just wanted to drink as mush as they needed, to play games and to sleep in the bushes... You should see how the "imported" Tolstoy family younger relatives learnt to drink in a hussar manner, from the countertop. They became drunk very quickly, especially women, then they were ready to suck each other's lips, to exchange French kisses. Then they hid in the bushes and one could hear just laughter and sweet moans from there. It went on till late at night.

It was different from reading books by Lev Tolstoy. I actually understood that the ancestors did not need reading the books. The local folks watched them and envied.

I would also like to fuck that one in a stack of hay. She would scream still louder. I could benefit from it, I could become a relative. – One of them would say. Others were mad and expressed their offence: - They are having fun on someone else's expense; they would not share with us. It is not a Christian-like behavior. They say, the count would treat for free all the people from the village on holidays. They would drink as mush as they wanted.

While expressing their offence, they did not waste the time. They searched in the bushes and picked empty bottles in great quantities.

The relatives also visited the family estate of the count in the village of Nikolskoye-Vyazemskoye. Local people dressed their girls in the best clothes, which revealed the most attractive parts of the women's bodies in a very conspicuous way. They wore high-heeled shoes and had to walk on nail-like heels on the sandy surface. The girls wanted to seduce men, it was obvious. They wanted to get at least acquainted with the male representatives of the family. I am not sure if it was a success, but I know for sure that some of the writer's ancestors had fun with the young girls from the village in fresh hay.

They had dancing, folk dancing, and the performance of the group "Litsedei". They even had demonstration hunting with Russian wolfhounds.

The event was a successful one, but I failed to make a film.

I know that much money was spent for the event, it was as much as a million rubles. Part of the expenses was paid by the Department of culture, part of them was paid by the museum. On the background of the poverty, ignorance and lack of cultural education the event looked like a feast during the plague epidemic. Their grandfather, should he had been alive, he would have torn them in parts for making feasts at the time when all Russia was moaning with hardships. Maybe, the minister had no other projects to spend the money for, I mean other that organizing drinking feasts… This is the answer about the Russian culture and intelligent people. There was no one to express any protest. No one stopped them as it was a common thing.

- I beg you pardon, Gosha, but the foreigners like to drink and eat for free. We usually say those things about ourselves. It all happened because the organizers were lacking intelligence and moral principles, so it is the Russian side to blame. Nowadays Tolstoy would write "War and Feast" instead of "War and Peace", as the civil war in Russia has been waged for more than ten years and would not stop. It is waged by all the enemies, using al the means and ways. At the same time, they make feasts. Is it only the Tolstoys who do this? All the officials and their surrounding have feasts. They have numerous presentations and receptions during the time when the Russian people are suffering. – Dasha sounded indignant. The story made her nervous. She came up to the bar and filled two glasses. She had on for herself and she gave the other one to Gosha. – "Have it, my dear, I have heard a sad story from you. Let's change the topic and talk of something funny".

- Is it funny? – Gosha drank the cognac at a draught and became thoughtful.

You see, Dashutka, there is not much fun in Russia nowadays. It does not mean that we are not supposed to see anything positive and discuss only negative things. No, we are not. We, including TV, must make funny shows as well. To my mind, they should be available for a big audience. No one expected the show "Field of Miracles" to become so popular among the public, not only in Russia. The show has been keeping its high rating for more than ten years. Lenya Yakubovich, though, is sick and tired of the show. However, there is no a good substitute for it, no new project. There also no good movies to replace the Latin American soap operas with our own. The ones we have now are of low quality, as far as their casting, scripts, and photography are concerned. They show trash, the movies demonstrate blood and violence, mixed with cheap sex. We do not have really good domestic erotic movies.

We do not have them and we have never had. I do not think we will ever have.

- I beg you pardon, Gosha, but our cinematography has always been famous for movies, which deeply depict the nature and fate of people. We lack this now. I know that the budget of "Siberian Barber" is 40 million dollars. What was the output? The idea was good, but what was the result? No result at all. – Dasha expressed her opinion, lighting a cigarette.

I must admit that in Ukraine the situation is the same. They shot the expensive movie about the Hetman Mazepa. The historic events were distorted. The result was the same. – Gosha answered. – You should understand that there is, to put it mild, something wrong in the movie industry, likewise in Russia and in the government. Everyone argues about the way of the development of the movies industry. Some of them talk about democracy, others about the monarchy; some speak about cathedrals and Orthodox religion. I think it is the talent that should rule in art. The art is supported by the talent and it should also support the talent.

- Ha-ha! Gosha, my dear, in this case the authorities are supposed to be talented. In Russia your people are constantly fighting for some shares in all the spheres and directions. It is high time you should contribute. There are so many awards presentations there nowadays.

There are lots of movie festivals. Most of them are of low quality and of high budgets.

Gosha looked at Dasha attentively. – You don't say so! Do you think it is different in Ukraine, in Odessa, where you live? We are all of the same breed. It is unacceptable to hurt as deeply as they do, but they did it and they are still doing it.

During my short stay, I have noticed that all the signs in Odessa, my native city, are in the Ukrainian language. Everyone admits the fact that Ukraine is a separate independent country. However, is it possible to declare the Ukrainian language as official if 70 per cent of the residents of Ukraine think and speak Russian, which is their native language? I know for sure that in everyday life the government offices, including the administration of the President and the municipal offices, as well as the rural offices use the Russian language or at least the mixture of the languages. It is a historically formed situation. Still, they impose the Ukrainian language using the force. It is impossible to force someone to love something.

Dasha smiled. – Right you are, Gosha. It is the same as declaring the language of Comanche tribe language an official language of the United States. Can you imagine that all the signs in New York are written in the Comanche language?

They both imagined the situation and laughed.

- Those moral principles… - Gosha sounded deep in thought. – It has been like this for ages. Drinking is in our genes, like in the family of Tolstoy. So is pettiness, envy, ignorance – they all have ancient history. Some of people do creative work. Others try to get some profit from this. If there is something wrong, they are ready to disgrace the ones who create. Talented persons experienced hardships in al the times. They have always been lonely. It was the same in all the ages, but now it is still worse. The example is show business. We actually have neither shows nor business. There are so many people in the industry. Once there appears a talented person, he is sure to be persecuted.

The situation is the same in other spheres, other than art. In show business it is more conspicuous. For example, a talented Ballet dancer appeared in Russia. She is nice looking, smart and talented. Immediately she finds herself in the atmosphere of gossips, feud and dirty situations. Another example is Kolya Baskov. He is a person pf a natural gift. He deserves to enjoy favorable conditions for creative work, for his projects and for sharing his talent with the public. However, he encounters a stream of lies, gossip and unprofessional criticism. The reason is envy and ignorance. If people are like this, so are the moral principles and matters.

Gosha decided to change the topic. – We are not to discuss sad topics, Dashutka. We have so little time left. – He came up to her and took her by the hands. She rose to her feel and leaned against him.

- You have beautiful eyes. They are green. Your profile resembles me that of Angelica. You are a beauty.

She pushed him back, smiling. – I am not Angelica, I am Dasha. However, there is no doubt – I am a beauty!

She came up to the bar and filled the glasses with Champaign. – Goshenka, let us drink to the beautiful, to the pure, which cannot be burned or destroyed. It is love. It is always gorgeous, no matter if communists or democrats rule, no matter if it is in Africa, in Ukraine or in Russia, no matter if it happens in palaces or in a stack of hay. It is sacred and eternal!

- To love!

They drank, embraced each other and went to the bedroom. They had something really very great in common. It was love that united them.

Something for nothing

Big tennis events were taking place in Odessa. At the beginning of May, a Davis Cup game between the teams of Ukraine and Bulgaria was planned to be held. The regional Federation of tennis made a great job adjusting the tennis courts of Chkalov resort to international standards. Businesspersons of Odessa rendered great help, which could hardly be estimated. They made big investments. The organizers of the event did believe that the money paid for advertising and the tournament admission payments would cover all the expenses.

Political leaders of Odessa were expected to attend the grand opening of the tournament between the teams of Ukraine and Bulgaria. Incidents did happen at the event. One of the newspaper editors from the capital city drove to the tournament in his new Audi. He dropped to Arcadia for a few minutes to have a cup of coffee in one of the cafes after the long drive. While he was enjoying Odessa coffee, the car was stolen. No clues for investigation were left. The editor did not feel like covering the tournament events.

Lev Nikolayevich Stas, known to his friends and acquaintances as Leva Stas, had been in grain-crop cultivation business for all his grown-up life. No matter the communists or the democrats were ruling, he, according to his own wording, was always in business and got his income. He had never gone in for tennis or ping-pong; he was never fond of sports. His daughters were tennis club members. Therefore, he had to sponsor them. When he came to pick up his daughters, he became acquainted with the managers of the club. They found out that they had mutual acquaintances. They also had some mutual interests.

311

Leva had especially friendly relations with the president of the club Sergey Ivanovich Podolyan. They became friends two years before. They often met on courts, in casinos, in nightclubs, where they had a good time. They also had common interests in construction business. They worked on the details in private and did not share those details with anyone. The friends were not greedy, but they tried to save every kopeck. They would not spend money without necessity. They did not miss a single opportunity of earning money.

Leva Stas was not planning to attend the Davis Cup tennis tournament. It was Podolyan who called to him and invited for the grand opening event.

- You see, Leva, the Mayor of the city will be attending the opening event. We will discuss out project with him in an unofficial environment. It is the best moment. Work is work. In an unofficial discussion, we could discuss the general opportunities. We could go into details later, in the Mayor's office.

Leva gave his consent and on a sunny Sunday, he drove to the parking lot of Chkalov resort. He parked his car at the side, though he was offered a parking space on the territory of the resort.

- No, there is no need. I am not going to stay long. – He was planning to talk to the Mayor before the ceremony and the games start. He did not feel like wasting his precious time idling on the stand and watching the game, thought it was super players who were expected on the court.

Having parked the car, Stas walked slowly along the alleys to the courts. The weather was nice; it was spring. It was sunny, but not hot. The resort was bright green with the plants growing all over the territory. Leva came fifteen minutes earlier. It was his habit to come to all appointments fifteen minutes earlier. Many of his friends and acquaintances wondered why he would do that. He would not explain; he just avoided direct answers, telling some jokes. It was his rule to make a tour of the appointment location, to examine everyone who happened to be in the area. That time he also watched the people arriving at the tournament. He walked slowly to the box office and bought a ticket, just in case he had to stay for the event, if he would not be able to have a talk with the Mayor before the event starts. The tickets were not cheap; they cost one hundred hryvnias.

At that moment, the manager of the district police department approached him. He had been acquainted with Sviderskiy, Vasiliy Ivanovich for a very long period.

- Hello, Leva Nikolayevich, - He greeting Stas. – I am glad to see you. I am really very glad. You look much better than you did three years ago. I can see the things are much better now.

- Sure they are. It is due to your help and the help of your colleagues. I know your life has also become better. – Stas knew about the restoration of Sviderskiy's previous position.

- Sure, the justice took the lead. I am in my shoes again. I am still a cop.

Leva laughed: - I remember your saying that one does not become a cop, one is

born a cop. It is correct. Any person should do the work he likes. If he does not like the work he does, he is supposed to quit.

Sviderskiy and himself walked along the central alley near the courts, talking quietly. Numerous small cafes, temporarily put-up along the alley, were opening. So were small shops selling souvenirs, sportswear and sports equipment.

- I do not recollect, dear Lev Nikolayevich, that you were a sport fan. – Sviderskiy said. – Something else should have brought you here.

- There is nothing you can conceal from this shrewd cop. – Leva smiled. – Sure, it is the business that brought me here. I need to meet the mighty of this world. This is it. We are not the kind of persons who go in for tennis or basketball because it is fashionable to and because there is an opportunity to meet the Mayor and to draw his attention to himself. Damn it. I hate those people. They are trash, not humans. Sorry about that.

Sviderskiy had the same opinion: - I do agree with you – he said passionately – Those people want to get everywhere for free. See your own example. You came here and you buy a ticket, though with your connections you could get a free pass.

- I will not become poorer if I buy a ticket.

- That is it. Others keep bothering me with their calls on my cell phone. Dear

Vasiliy Ivanovich, please let us pass through a VIP entrance, you can, as you are a person who provides security services there. Those who

call are not poor persons; they are mostly the government officers who
– He grinned – do not have salary as their only income.

They came up to a café and ordered coffee.

- By the way, speak of the devil and he will appear. On of the
callers is coming right now. – Sviderskiy pointed at a well-built man
with a sportsman-like body; he was wearing a light suit. He had left
his car and was walking towards them. – He is a Colonel General, a
Deputy Ministers of Defence. He has been retired for about half a year.
However, he is still very ambitious. Too ambitious.

The man whom the police department manager was talking about
came up to them.

- Good afternoon, Vasiliy Ivanovich. – He greeted him.

- Good afternoon, sir! Ivan Lukich, let me introduce you to one of
our respectable businesspersons. Please meet Lev Nilolayevich Stas.

Kutepov – the General introduced himself and stretched his hand
to Leva.

The discussed the weather, the coming tournament. Then Kutepov
asked to excuse him. He asked Sviderskiy to talk him in private. Leva
watched him persuading the police department manager to let him pass
through the VIP entrance. Then he called somebody over his cell phone.
In a few minutes, both of them came up to Stas.

Lev Nikolayevich, our police cannot help here. Maybe you could
get a free
pass for me. – Kutepov asked him.

Stas shrugged his shoulders: - I never ask for free passes and my
advice is that you should not too. Sviderskiy is a witness that I am not
telling lies. I bought my ticket with my own one hundred hryvnias.
How come that Generals, even Colonel Generals have become so poor
– He gave a piercing look at Kutepov. – Or have they become cheap?

Kutepov looked aside, asked to excuse him and went towards the
central entrance to the courts. At that moment, Podolyan came up to
them: - Hi! Why are you still here? Come on, they are already waiting
for us.

They went to the courts. Leva saw the Mayor talking to his Deputy
near the stands. The Deputy was the head of the tennis federation.
Beside him, there stood the chief medical officer of the resort and a few
more men, whom Leva did not know.

Together with Podolyan, they approached and greeted them. Then they had a brief talk with the Mayor.

Let us talk about it after the tournament starts. – He suggested.

Thus, Stas had to stay for the ceremony, though he did not wish to. His was in his low moods. He was not a person easy to impress; he was reasonable and balanced. General Kutepov just spoilt his moods. He actually did not want to know him at all. He just knew about him from mass media reports. That day he was introduced to him. He had an unpleasant feeling, which became stronger when he saw the General again sitting at VIP seats.

- Why are you so gloomy today? – Podolyan asked him.

- I don't know, Serezha. Do you know that person? – He pointed at Kutepov, so that no one could see his gesture.

Sergey Ivanovich laughed out loud. Why, I do know him. He is the Colonel General Kutepov in person. To tell the truth, he is no longer employed; he was dismissed. Now he is mixing in the upper circles somewhere in the capital city. He owns a luxurious apartment there. He also has an apartment here. Besides, there is also a cottage at the seaside. He says he is successfully employed and has an office with an air conditioner. So, he does nothing and earns seven thousands of hryvnias. He says his salary is just miserable.

So, he cannot afford a ticket which costs one hundred hryvnias, can he? He wants to get something for nothing. This is his life style. He is constantly bothering the neighboring club guys. He would call to them and come, saying that he wanted to play. One should buy a membership to have opportunity to play. It is not for him. He wants something for nothing.

Besides, when playing, he does not like to lose. He grits his teeth, he turns red with resentment and hatred. This is how he hates losing a game. Once I played a game with him. He is so stupid. He was boasting that he was given a diving suit as a gift, which cost five thousand bucks, that he had plans of going into diving. And he asked to find a trainer for him for free. Look here, - Podolyan suddenly said, - Don't we have some other topic to discuss?

Right you are. – Leva laughed. – He is not worth discussing.

They became silent and watched the performance. The opening ceremony was short but very spectacular. Everyone liked it. Even

Leva's moods became much higher. They still had time before the first game between the teams started, and the friends, accompanied by the managers, entered a cozy bar, close to the courts, and had a glass of Champaign to the successful start and to the good beginning of the tournament. It tool Leva tem minutes to tell the Mayor about their project. He Mayor was interested and he made an appointment for them in the Municipal Council for Monday, as he did not want to procrastinate.

Leva said good-bye in a warm manner to everyone and left in good spirits. While driving the physiognomy of the General Kutepov, however, came to his mind again, and Leva became thoughtful.

How many "something-for-nothing" seekers recently appeared? All of a sudden, he an article about a soccer game between the team of the USSR and the world team came to his mind. That game was organized by Oleg Blokhin on the eve of his 50th birthday. He organized the game together with his friends. They overcome many obstacles, as the officials would not understand what kind of team it was – "A collective team of the USSR". It was a political issue. They gave him the rental price twice as much as it usually was when events of the same kind were conducted there. Thanks God, his friends helped him. They sold tickets at low price, which was from 5 to 20 hryvnias, in order to give the opportunity for all the people to attend the game. Even then, Oleg Blokhin was bothered by his colleagues and deputies of the Supreme Rada. They asked for a free pass: "Is it so hard for you to get it?" Blokhin tried to explain to them that the prices were low and that anyone could buy a ticket, sending an assistant to the box office. He said that the money raised from the game would be transferred to homes for orphaned children. However, they would not understand him and would insist on getting a free pass. Most of the "something-for-nothing" seekers were Deputies from People's Supreme Council. More of them could be found among the officers from the President's cabinet, from the government and among the people surrounding them. The police, customs and tax officers as well as heads of administrations, including Governors, Mayors and others were also among them. Al the authority representatives are actually "something-for-nothing" seekers. Even if there is an event with free admission, with cheap tickets, with no line to get them, "something-for-nothing" seekers would not see that, they would create a crowd at the VIP entrance.

Stas felt very sad because the crowd of those spongers was big. Still more, he was upset when he realized that those people were not aliens, they were not of a foreign make, and they all originated from the people. If those "something-for-nothing" seekers are removed from their positions and the vacancies are occupied by other persons, originating from the people, from the remote areas, the new officials and their staff are sure to start demanding something for nothing as early as the next day. They would demand more than the previous ones. The ruling system does not matter. At the time of monarchy, the "something-for-nothing" seekers were numerous, at the time of communists they still multiplied. During the period of democracy, they became much more numerous. That had been the nation's disaster for many ages!

What is the reason for appearance of financial pyramids of different kinds? Why there is good environment for different kinds of cheaters, scoundrels and crooks to appear. It is because our people like to get something for nothing. It is like giving a hryvnia and getting a million. Everyone wants everything at once, without any effort. They can invent all kinds of benefits for themselves. They have big salaries for some vague job functioning, they have free annual tourist accommodation; they have free trips, retirement payments up to 150-200 dollars, etcetera. There are benefits, benefits and benefits for them.

Leva remembered his school friend Monya Averbakh. He rented and later bought a destroyed resort in Zatok at the seaside. He invested big amounts of money in that resort. He had modern renovation made. As a result, he had a resort with luxury rooms, with hot water running 24 hours, a separate beach and other conveniences. The first year was finished with losses. He even wanted to sell the resort. "Something-for nothing" seekers bothered him. Those were the regional and district authority officials, the police, the tax office, the border officers, the health department officers and ecological services officers. They were seeking recreation; he had to accept them all, to provide food, accommodation and entertainment for them. In a year he collected all his courage and refused the services to all the "something-for nothing" seekers, he just told them to get off. He equipped one room for them and told them to get in line. They were supposed to get a discount, but not to get all for free.

They had to get in line, no matter how funny and shameful it was. The room was booked up for the whole season as early as at the beginning of winter.

A conversation with the manager of the municipal steam and bathhouse came to his mind. In that facility, there were saunas with a pool and shower rooms. The admission was just 10 hryvnias. One could stay there enjoying sauna for two, even for three hours. Most of the people bought tickets not for 10 hryvnias, but for 5, using the discounts for war veterans or for Chernobyl participants.

The manager would say: - You see, Leva, I have an impression that today in Odessa have of the residents are Afghan war veterans or Chernobyl participants. Before 90s, just few people had such certificates. During the 90s they multiplied by many times!

Not long ago newspapers were full of publications about a new BMW stolen in St. Petersburg, which cost 120 thousand dollars and which was stolen from the wife of the Russian minister of the interior. A car belonging to the government and costing 120 thousand dollars was stolen. Why the wife of the minister appeared to be in St. Petersburg driving a government car, assigned to her husband? Why the price was 120 thousand?

Leva thought about his trip to Sweden as a member of the municipal delegation. It was three years before. The minister of transport of that country was meeting them. He was not using a separate car on his way from the airport; he was going in the same microbus as all the delegation was. When Leva asked if he had a car assigned for him at work, he smiled and answered that he did have one, but it was not worthwhile using several cars if they could use just one microbus. In a few days, they were flying to the south of Sweden, which was part of their schedule. They met the same minister on board the plane. It turned out that his family was still residing at the place of his previous employment. He was flying to visit his family. At the airport of the provincial town, to Stas' surprise, no one was meeting the minister. He took a taxi and left for home, promising the Odessa guests to visit them in the hotel.

Leva remembered that story and thought: - We are not to live this way. It is in our blood to get something for nothing. I would like to see the minister of transport of Ukraine coming to Odessa and taking a taxi at the airport.

While approaching to the office, Leva remembered that in 90s different trusts were blooming in Odessa, like "Solo", ""Elais" and others. People rushed to those insurance companies and they would not listen to anyone's advice. After those financial pyramids burst like a soap bubble, when the savings of the citizens invested in those companies evaporated, everyone rushed to the government, to the Mayor. He, as a father of all the people, was supposed to defend and help them. The Mayor was called a cynic and was hated by everyone after he said the truth to the people: "Nobody made you invest your money in those companies. You wanted to get something for nothing. It is your own fault. You are to cope with your problem yourselves."

That Mayor was replaced by another one. As far as the crooks are concerned, they still feel free to do anything they wanted. It was not the Mayor, not the city to blame; it was the people to blame.

- "Something for nothing" concept is permanent here. – Leva Stas made a conclusion for himself.